GW01019276

Secrets, Lies...
and Passion
LINDA CONRAD

Harlequin
Mills & Boon

Desire

First Published 2002
First Australian Paperback Edition 2005
ISBN 0 733 56223 X

Published by
Harlequin Mills & Boon
3 Gibbes Street
CHATSWOOD NSW 2067
AUSTRALIA

HARLEQUIN MILLS & BOON DESIRE and the Rose Device are trademarks
used under license and registered in Australia, New Zealand, Philippines,
United States Patent & Trademark Office and in other countries.

Printed and bound in Australia by
McPherson's Printing Group

LINDA CONRAD

was born in Brazil to a commercial pilot dad and a mother whose first gift was a passion for stories. She was raised in South Florida and has been a dreamer and a storyteller for as long as she can remember. Linda claims her earliest memories are of sitting in her mother's lap listening to a beloved storybook or searching through the picture books in the library to find that special one.

When Linda met and married her own dream-come-true hero, he fostered another of her other inherited vices—being a vagabond. They moved to seven different states in seven years, finally becoming enchanted with and settling down in the Rio Grande Valley of Texas.

Reality anchored Linda to their Texas home long enough to raise a daughter and become a stockbroker and certified financial planner. Her whole world suddenly changed when her widowed mother suffered a disabling stroke and Linda spent a year as her caretaker. Before her mother's second and fatal stroke, she begged Linda to go back to her dreams—to finally tell the stories buried within her heart.

Linda's hobbies are reading, growing roses and experiencing new things. However, her real passion is "passion"—reading about it, writing about it and living it. She believes that true passion and intensity for life and love are seductive—they consume the soul and make life's trials and tribulations worth all the effort.

"I am extremely grateful that today I can live my dreams by being able to share the passionate stories and lovable characters that have lived deep within me for so long," Linda declares.

To my very own real-life hero: the man who first taught me how to run aground, and then explained about getting out and pushing off once more. I love you.

Prologue

A soft, summer breeze whispered through the star-studded Texas night, soothing Reid Sorrels's senses and cooling his heated skin. Coming to such a blissful close, this was destined to be the magical eve for a perfect wedding.

Reid rolled to his side, running a finger down the naked hip of the woman he loved and would marry in the morning. He gazed into her crystal-blue eyes, finding such promise—such deep desire. At twenty years old, Jillette Bennett was everything he'd ever wanted. Everything the twenty-four-year-old Reid figured he would ever need.

She was the first thing he thought of when he awoke and the last thing on his mind before he slept. She'd become a part of him—the best part. When he looked at her, he saw his history and his future—their children and their children's children. A never-ending union of love and trust.

He glanced at the lighted alarm clock on her nightstand and pulled her close to him once more. "It's midnight...our wedding day, Jill. You sure you don't believe it's bad luck for the groom to see the bride before the ceremony?"

"No, silly. That old wives' tale has something to do with the dress, anyway. It certainly doesn't have anything to do with what we just did." She giggled and pressed a kiss to Reid's sweat-soaked neck.

Even though they'd made love only minutes before, his sex stirred once more. He simply couldn't get enough of this raven-haired pixie who'd captured his soul. Thank God graduation was over and they had three weeks to honeymoon before he began studying for the bar exam.

Then again, he hoped he could live through three weeks of nonstop lovemaking with Jill without his body giving out on him. They were so hot together. Hot enough to sizzle fajitas on a snowy, January day.

He reached his palm to cover her breast, massaging the quivering nipple, then smiled when it pebbled against his hand. She moaned into his shoulder and pressed herself closer to him.

"You amaze me," he said with a husky catch in his throat. "You're so responsive, so uninhibited. I can't stop wanting to touch you."

"Don't stop, my darling. You were my first lover and..." She leaned over and lightly kissed his chest. "You'll be my best and last. Everything I will ever know about love comes from being with you. I want this happiness to go on and on forever."

Her body shuddered when he lowered his mouth to her breast, wet the tip with his tongue, then blew softly on the sensitive skin. "All things happen in their own time, luv," he whispered against her breast. "I should go now. You need your sleep. We have a long day ahead of us."

"No. Not just yet. Stay a few minutes more. Please?"

She lowered her hand to his rigid sex and flicked her nail across the throbbing, slick tip. Instantly, he was lost.

He swung himself over her and entered her with one, swift penetration. She moaned and threw back her head, crying his name as her internal grip tightened around him.

The fever swamped them both. She climaxed deliciously against him again and again until, with huge ragged breaths, he shattered inside her.

A half hour later, Reid left his sated, sleeping bride-to-be and tiptoed down the wide staircase toward his future father-in-law's front door. He was surprised to see Jill's cousin, Travis, standing in the shadows at the bottom of the stairs. The rehearsal party had been over for hours, but it seemed as if Travis had been waiting there to speak to him for a while. Reid wondered what could be so important.

"Travis? What's up?"

Even though they competed at everything, Travis Bennett had been his best friend for forever. Eventually, the two of them would become partners in the firm of Bennett and Bennett. Of course, by then it would hopefully be called Bennett, Bennett and Sorrels.

"Hey, buddy. Great party, wasn't it?" Travis handed him a highball glass filled with Scotch. "Can you take a minute and see my uncle? He's got something he wants to talk to you about." Travis seemed jumpy and on edge.

Reid took a big slug of the smooth fire. "What's wrong, pal? Is your father in with him?"

Travis shook his head. "Nope. Dad left a little while ago. Your soon to be father-in-law, my illustrious Uncle

Andrew, is still working in his den. He's waiting for you. Go on in. I'm just on my way out.'' Trav nodded tightly, slipped past the front door and moved out into the night.

Brothers, Jill's and Travis's fathers were also partners in the medium-size law firm. Andrew Bennett, Jill's dad, had come to the little town of Rolling Point, twenty miles outside Austin, more than thirty years ago to set up a practice. A few years later Andrew's brother, Joseph, passed the Texas bar and joined the firm. With the encroachment of the suburbs, they soon had more business than they could handle. Within a few years, the two of them built the practice up to a more than decent level.

Reid had already come to think of Andrew as a substitute father. His own distant and unemotional father was a major rancher and oilman in the area, but the two had never seen things in the same way. Even now, they couldn't manage a truce long enough to celebrate the wedding. Reid's father would not be attending tomorrow. Or was that today by now?

No matter. The idea of Andrew wanting to talk to him made Reid smile. Jill's dad was all the things Reid wanted to be—ambitious, a superlative lawyer, and a kind and loving father and husband.

Reid found the door to Andrew's den ajar. He started to push it open and walk on in, but hesitated when he heard voices. Andrew obviously had company, and Reid wasn't going to disturb them. Whatever Andrew wanted with him could wait until tomorrow.

No, on second thought, tomorrow's schedule would be so tight there'd be no time for quiet discussions. Reid stood his ground, hoping whoever was in with Andrew would soon leave.

The two voices became increasingly louder. Andrew's booming bass tone could be easily distinguished, but the other man's voice was unrecognizable. His curiosity piqued, Reid leaned into the door trying to hear more of the words.

"Our deal is private. Just between us." The strange man's voice sounded belligerent. "It's imperative that no one else knows about it...or about me."

"But my brother...and, Sorrels, my daughter's fiancé. They could be useful to us."

With the mention of Reid's name, he inched his ear closer to the opening in the door. An ominous shiver suddenly made the night cold and deadly, but he tried to shake off the feeling.

"Look," the husky, unknown voice continued. "My employers insist this deal stays secret. They wouldn't take kindly to any sudden change of plans."

The whisper of a chair scraping across carpet let Reid know the end to the conversation must be near.

The angry voice lowered to a dangerous growl. "Don't fool with us, Bennett. If you do, you won't live to regret it."

Shock and fear for his father-in-law's safety threw Reid off-balance. Before he could catch himself, he fell through the open door and landed on his knees on the plush carpet.

Reid struggled to stand. In the background, he heard Andrew's cry of surprise and a sharp curse from the stranger. But he never got a chance to get up and check on Andrew's welfare. Without warning, a crack of pain zinged across his forehead and everything around him suddenly went black.

One

Jill Bennett glanced up at the gigantic gold and silver chandelier in the ballroom of the Hyatt hotel in Austin and silently prayed for patience. The big-haired, big-bosomed woman speaking to her droned on in a twanging, West Texas drawl. As one of the largest political contributors in the entire northern part of the state, the woman was too important for Jill to duck entirely.

"Now, sugar," the rhinestone-studded woman continued, while loading a cracker with a huge dollop of caviar. "You must let me throw you and Billy a Texas-size—" she crammed the cracker into her mouth but didn't stop talking "—wedding shower."

Jill couldn't understand much of what she was saying with her mouth stuffed the way it was.

LINDA CONRAD

Spewing cracker crumbs with every word, the woman went on. "I know all the best movers and shakers in the state. You do realize it's the wives who make most of the contribution decisions, don't you?"

Jill nodded but didn't manage to get in one word before the older woman was swept to the other side of the buffet table by a crowd of Stetson-hatted men. Jill took the opportunity to move away from the table and the boisterous crowd. She scooted around the twelve-foot ice sculpture of a long-horned bull and found a relatively quiet corner.

Looking down at the sparkling, two-karat diamond on her finger, she swallowed back the urge to scream. How dare Bill Baldwin place an engagement ring on her finger in front of a room full of contributors without the slightest hint to her in advance?

What had possessed him?

The man was the ultimate politician. She glanced over at him, across the crowded room, as he shook hands with the governor, accepting congratulations all around for his newly announced engagement—to her. With his blond hair slicked back from his forehead in the latest style, his tastefully understated designer suit and his outlandishly expensive tie, Bill was the very picture of the fair-haired boy in state government. As the Texas attorney general and darling of the media, he'd be next in line for the governor's mansion.

But why would the man, who had privately professed his love for her, pick an impersonal, crowded and noisy political fund-raiser to announce their engagement when she hadn't even said yes yet? Shaking her head, she tried to dismiss the thought that it had been just a political stunt. Could Bill really stoop so low?

"Congratulations, Jill." Her cousin Travis, now a state

er partner in Bennett and Bennett, arrived
leaned down and kissed her cheek. "I hope
ery happy."

She really didn't know what to say. Oh, she'd figured
Bill would pop the question sooner or later, but her heart
refused to deliver an answer. Bill had been a good friend,
and her son, Andy, seemed to like him well enough.
Still...when Jill kissed him, she felt—comfortable. Not
disgusted or repulsed certainly, but neither did she feel
anything like love or passion. It was more like—kissing
a brother—or maybe like kissing Travis.

Her cousin Travis, as youthful-looking as ever, despite
his many obligations, handed her a glass of champagne.
Close up, she saw, along with the freckles across the
bridge of his nose, a few wrinkles at the corners of his
eyes. He looked exhausted. Perhaps the stress of running
the family's law partnership and also being a state legislator was beginning to take its toll on him.

Smiling at how often in their lives she'd wished he'd
been her brother, Jill sighed against his pinstripe-suited
shoulder for a quick moment. "I still haven't given him
an answer, Trav. I'm just not sure what I..." With her
thoughts a jumble, she hesitated. Stepping back, she took
a sip from her glass, and gazed into her cousin's electric
blue eyes. She knew they matched her own, and the
thought gave her some comfort. Since her father's death
and her uncle's massive stroke, Travis had been the one
rock in her life.

"I've talked to you about this until I'm purple in the
face." Travis raised his eyebrow and started ticking off
reasons. "You need a husband. Andy needs a father. You
helped get Bill elected. He owes you. What more do you
need?"

"Those are hardly reasons enough to get married." Jill downed her glass and placed it on the tray of a passing waiter. "After all, I helped get you elected, too. If you weren't already married, would you expect me to marry you too, cuz?"

He rolled his eyes to the ceiling in frustration. "Very funny. You know I love you, Jill. I'm just trying to look out for your welfare." He drained his glass and set it aside. "Look. Why don't you take a few days and think it over?"

Respect for her cousin and confusion over what would be the right thing to do for everyone concerned left her momentarily silent. She nodded her head.

"All right, Trav. I won't make a decision about marrying him...not until I think about it, anyhow."

"That's my girl." Travis eased his arm around her shoulder and gave her a bear hug. "Uh, I have something else to tell you."

Jill's feet were suddenly throbbing and her head hurt. Judging by the troubled look on her cousin's face, whatever he had to say was going to mean more problems.

She stepped away to face him squarely. "This isn't about the business, is it? 'Cause if it is, can't it wait until tomorrow?"

"No. This isn't about business, cuz." Travis looked down at his spit-shined shoes. That really worried her. It wasn't like her cousin to be tentative in any way. What was going on?

Finally, Travis raised his gaze to look at her. "I've brought someone along with me tonight. I didn't think you'd mind, or maybe that you'd be too busy to even notice. But I also didn't know about Bill's surprise announcement." He turned to glance around the room. "The two things don't go together at all. I'm sorry, Jill."

"Travis, what on earth are you talkin…"

"Hello, Jill."

If Reid hadn't stepped into her view right then, she still would've known who he was just by his voice. She'd heard that deep, resonant bass tone in her dreams and nightmares nearly every night for the last ten years.

And then…there he was.

Before her stood a stranger with her former lover's eyes. She tried to take in every inch of the man without being too obvious.

He was about the same height as the man she remembered, but nothing else physically seemed familiar. His hair, always a warm brown and silkily soft, had tinges of silver sprinkled throughout, making him look much older than the thirty-four she knew he must be. He no longer had the slender, rail-thin frame of late adolescence. Instead, his shoulders were broad and muscular under the tobacco-colored cotton sweater he wore atop his casual khakis.

This was a real adult male standing here, glaring at her. She took one more second to study his face. The beautiful, patrician nose and jaw she could remember tenderly kissing had been replaced by rugged features and fractured lines. The boy that had captured her heart was gone. In his place, stood a man of considerable power and character.

She tried to steady her rapid heartbeat. "Reid." Her voice came out high-pitched and squeaky as she fought for calm.

"Yeah. Like the proverbial bad penny, I've turned up again just at the wrong time."

He took her hand in both of his, driving electrical charges through her arm and straight into her soul. "You look great, Jill. Time has been very kind to you."

Reid pinned her with a steady scrutiny, making her squirm internally. "Well, I suppose turning up at a bad time is better than disappearing at the absolute worst possible moment," she mumbled with a fake smile.

She involuntarily jerked on her hand, trying to free herself from his grip, but all the while she continued to meet his gaze. It cost her more than he'd ever know to stand there touching him with outward calm.

Despite her attempts to break free, he didn't let her go or acknowledge her dig. "Congratulations on your engagement. I apologize for putting a damper on your big night, but all Travis told me was we were going to a political fund-raiser for members of the state legislature and some of our old classmates. He didn't bother to tell me you'd be here, let alone what kind of shindig this was really going to be." He gave the other man a pointed look.

Jill was so engrossed in his eyes that she barely heard what he said. Those eyes were still as black and intense as she remembered—only even more so.

He finally released her and she dragged her hand away, waving it with a casual flair she didn't feel. "It's not Travis's fault. None of us knew what was going to happen…except Bill, of course. And he decided to keep it a secret."

"Uh. Excuse me, you two, but there are some constituents I have to speak to," Travis broke into the strained lull in the conversation. "I'll find you when I'm ready to leave, Reid. And I'll talk to you in the morning, cuz." Travis spun and went into his politician's mode, greeting people with a handshake and a colossal smile.

Reid was furious with his boyhood friend. *Damn that Travis anyway.* How could he not mention that Jill would be here? All Travis had talked about before the party were the good "contacts" Reid could make with his old law-school buddies at this fund-raiser.

As FBI special agent in charge of Operation Rock-A-Bye, Reid had reluctantly returned to his hometown on the outskirts of Austin, ostensibly to attend his ten-year, law-school reunion and to spend time with his mother and his old buddies. In reality, this trip was a cover.

He'd fervently wished for some other way to track down the head of the international baby-selling ring that they'd traced to the state legislature in Austin. But this reunion was too perfect.

For years he'd been after the bastard who'd ruined countless lives on both sides of the border. A few months ago, one of his undercover special agents had apprehended one of the middlemen in the ring. Under interrogation, the man had admitted he didn't know the main boss of the illegal operation but all his contacts had been through Austin, and those men were definitely on the outskirts of politics.

Reid hadn't been back to Rolling Point once in ten years. Not even when his father died. For the last few years, he'd managed to avoid the very thought of home and his lost opportunities and disappointments.

He certainly didn't want to be here now, but he was the best man for this job. A full three-quarters of his law school class was serving in some government capacity. All of them would remember his name. He could have access to things no other agent involved in Operation Rock-A-Bye would.

Using Travis to introduce him into the inner circles of the state legislature had, at first, seemed like the fastest way to ferret out the man he hunted. Now he wished for any other way. Travis had tricked him into coming face-to-face with the main reason he'd never returned before this—the main reason he ached when he thought of home.

"You look great, Jill." It killed Reid to get the words out, but they were the simple truth.

He mentally tried to steel himself against Jill's presence. His temples pounded with the hurt of seeing her again. The sweat beaded up and began to trickle down his chest under his shirt. He fought for some of his famous control. After all these years, the conflict he felt between wanting to hurt her and wanting to ravage her on the nearest table nearly finished him off.

She was supposed to be the impulsive and conflicted one. After that fateful night ten years ago, she'd been the one who had run off to Paris and got married before he could come back and explain what had happened.

To this day, Reid wasn't exactly positive himself about what happened on the eve of their wedding. Oh, he'd thought about it until his brain was weary. But some of the memories were gone forever. After he'd been hit in the head, he apparently was beaten bloody and left for dead two hundred miles away from home. Memories from the time he was unconscious refused to be captured.

It was a couple of months later before he was capable of speaking or piecing any of his shattered memories together. By then it was too late. The trail was cold. The only person that might have told him what happened, Jill's father, was already dead. And Jill had left the country.

From that disappointment, he'd learned the hard way how to detach and control. So why was he having so much trouble being close to her now? He should still hate her for not caring enough about him to go looking for him when he'd disappeared. But he didn't. Not by a long shot.

"Thanks," she said softly. "You look pretty good yourself. It's been a long time."

Within the space of a heartbeat, all the memories of her came flooding back. She looked much the same as she had at fifteen when he'd first met her and fell in love.

Still petite with those wide, flashing blue eyes, the only differences he could find in her were tiny little lines in the corners of her eyes and a figure that was more rounded than little-girlish. But those differences made her even more appealing than she'd been at twenty. Even in a navy business suit, she had a woman's sensuality about her that clawed at his gut and left him breathless and turned on.

He fisted his hands and tried a half-hearted grin. "My mother told me you'd been divorced a while back. I guess she didn't realize you were involved with someone again."

She looked confused at his words. "Involved?" Quickly, she appeared to recover as she glanced down at the oversized diamond ring on her finger. "Oh, you mean..."

"Involved. You know...like engaged?"

She looked up at him with that same vulnerable look she'd had at nineteen when he'd just asked her to marry him.

At that instant, he'd known she was the only woman for him. Eleven years and a lifetime of pain later, she was still the only woman for him. But it could never happen. Worlds apart, their lives now traveled far different paths. It would be impossible to breach the chasm.

But knowing that fact and being able to control his wayward body were drastically opposing ideas. He took a deep breath and was instantly sorry. The scent of her assailed his nostrils, filling him with the sweet smell of herbs that had always been her signature fragrance.

And nearly knocking him down with memories.

The memory of her standing naked at a closet door and turning to smile, blinded him with emotion. The ghostly remembrance of her hair's springy curls wrapped tightly around his fingers while they'd kissed, made his lips tingle with need and his fingers itch with desire.

He closed his eyes. He wasn't sure if he wanted to capture those memories and keep them, or if he'd rather shut himself off against them.

"Engaged. Uh. Yeah," she stammered. "Well, it took me by surprise as well."

The mention of an engagement had rocketed Jill back in time. To the sweetness of being in love and preparing to marry the man of her dreams. To the pain of being rejected and left before she could make it to the altar. To the desperation of later trying to find Reid when she'd learned she was pregnant.

It all came back with a horrifying rip at her heart. The spoiled child she'd always been grew up in a hurry that year. Even her dear, doting father had changed into a tyrant overnight. A few weeks after Reid disappeared on the morning of their wedding, she'd confessed her pregnancy to her father. She'd begged him to help find Reid. Instead, he ranted and claimed the man was no good anyway, then sent her out of town to face her mistakes alone.

She'd always had a feeling her father had known more about what happened to Reid than he'd let on, but before she could return and press him for answers, her father was killed in a car accident. Whatever he'd known died with him.

Later, after she'd returned home with her son and with a story her mother made up for appearances' sake, Jill learned that Reid had married someone else. She imagined that woman must have been why he'd left in the first place and her pride suffered greatly.

But life went on. There was someone else now who needed her and loved her. Her beautiful son, the light of her life and the reason the pain of losing Reid had faded to a dull ache.

At the moment, however, she was stunned to find that just looking at Reid brought the pain back so clearly. It was sharp enough after ten years to nearly double her over. Dear heavens. She had to get a grip on herself. But she also had to ask the big question—and right this minute.

"Why did you leave me before our wedding, Reid?" She straightened her shoulders and asked it all. "Was it because of that other woman Mother later told me you'd married?"

He suddenly looked stricken, like he'd swallowed something the wrong way. "God, no," he choked.

A second's hesitation and the look in his eyes softened to something resembling quilt. "I...I..."

Reid closed his eyes to avoid seeing the raw look in Jill's. He'd noted the quick flash of darkness in them before she'd recovered and composed herself. If he hadn't known her so well...if he hadn't dreamed about those expressive eyes almost every night for the last ten years, he might have missed it.

His first reaction was that the flash had been pain—or maybe anguish. But why? After all this time, why would thinking back to that time cause her anything more than a bit of regret? Hell, they'd both just been kids, and she obviously hadn't cared as much as he'd thought she had.

He reached out a hand to steady her shoulder and give himself a little balance as well. What he really wanted was to give her strength through his touch and make her life easier, but he didn't know why he felt that way.

Was he the cause of some of the pain so clearly written on her face? Even now, after all these years?

"Jill, I wanted to say I'm sorry about our wedding day. I didn't have a choice…" He could barely speak.

Everything inside him screamed to tell her the truth as he knew it. "I had to leave. It wasn't something I planned. But I can't…I don't want to talk about it."

Not telling her about being knocked unconscious and left for dead hundreds of miles away would be one of the toughest things he'd ever done. But Reid only knew one incomplete part of the story himself, and that part involved her father. It might be more than she could stand to hear now that he was dead. Anyway, Reid was sure it couldn't possibly matter *much* to her. Otherwise, why hadn't she come looking for him?

"Why? Why can't you talk about it?" she demanded. "Don't I deserve an explanation?"

"Jill, please. It over. Nothing we say can change the outcome. Let's just go on." He heard his own voice getting lower and rougher. "Was that day so terrible for you?" he asked in a hoarse whisper.

"No, not at all. My father took care of everything for me. He was wonderful. That morning, before I left for the church, he told me you'd changed your mind. He said you'd written me a note but that he'd ripped it up in anger. I understood exactly how he felt."

A look of pure steel entered her eyes as Reid saw the memories overtake her. "Poor Dad. He spent all day notifying guests and cancelling the arrangements. His whole staff pitched in to make sure presents were returned and apologies made. After I took off my wedding dress and

explained things to my bridesmaids, I had very little
to do.''

Right, good old Dad to the rescue. Why had her father,
the man Reid had idolized, betrayed him? Automatically,
the old questions welled up inside him. He pushed them
aside and reminded himself that he was a different man
now, and that his current FBI sting operation had to take
precedence over his past. Later. Later he would find answers to old questions.

''That's what your father told you? That I'd just
changed my mind about marrying you? And you believed
him?''

She jerked her shoulder out of his grasp. ''Of course,
why would my father lie to me? That's what your letter
said. Although, I always thought it was kind of obvious
by the fact that you weren't there for the wedding.''

''But didn't you think I owed you an explanation in
person? You didn't bother trying to find me. Why not?''

Reid noticed Jill's focus wavering and she glanced
around the room for the first time since they'd been
standing together in this corner. Why would that question
make her so nervous?

''I thought you said nothing could change the outcome
now. Why talk about this?'' she asked. ''Besides, Dad
said you'd left for good. I didn't know where to start
looking.

''Dad and Mom suggested I go off to finish under-
graduate school at the Sorbonne in Paris shortly after that
day, and by the time I returned the whole thing had blown
over.''

Despite her pride, he could feel her anguish. She'd
been so spoiled back then—Daddy's little girl. Reid truly
wasn't surprised she'd given up on him so quickly. It
didn't help his pride much, however. He didn't want to

feel sorry for her now. He'd spent enough time feeling sorry for himself.

"I suppose we were the talk of the town for a while, but neither of us was around to be bothered by the gossip," she concluded.

He wanted to blurt out the truth. To tell her everything he could remember. To force her to believe it wasn't his fault, even though his story might sound fantastic.

But he couldn't. He was petrified that by destroying her father's image he might be destroying her as well.

"I understand your father was killed in a car crash a few weeks later. Didn't you come back for his funeral?" he asked instead.

"No. I... I was very busy with school and midterms at the time. Mother and I had a quiet memorial together when I got home. It was really much easier on me to grieve for him in private."

His gut told him that was her second lie of the night. Something more was underlying her words, but he decided to let it pass...for now.

"Is your wife with you on this trip?" she asked.

"We've been divorced for many years now, Jill."

"Oh?" She hesitated, once again glancing away for a second. "So why are you back here after all this time?"

Reid opened his eyes to the thirty-year-old woman she'd become and studied a wayward tendril of hair that had escaped her attempts at a twist at the back of her head. Instead of scholarly and professional, which was the look he figured she'd been going for, the effect was electrifying in its innocent sensuality.

Her question brought him back to reality with a thump. "I'm back for my ten-year, law-school reunion."

"Are you staying with Travis then?" Jill blinked and straightened.

Reid shook his head to answer her, but decided to watch her carefully for any flashes of emotions he didn't want to miss. "I'm out on the ranch with Mom. I've decided to take a little time off. Use this opportunity to revisit some of my old friends. Get reacquainted with Mom."

"Time off from what, Reid? Where are you working?"

For an answer, he went right into his undercover mode with no trouble. "I work for the federal government. I head up a compliance agency for the Treasury Department."

Her surprised look was clearer than the last fleeting emotion in her eyes had been. "You're a bureaucrat? What happened to the law? You were always so sure of what you wanted to do with your life. What changed?"

He shrugged a shoulder. "I guess I was just young and full of some misguided sense of justice. Reality intruded."

She was different from most civilians. He felt he had to say something more to her than he might say to anyone else. Even though the whole cover story was basically a lie, he let a little bit of the truth sneak out.

"After a few hard hits in life," he began softly. "We all make our way the best we can, Jill. Enough pain, and eventually you end up taking the easiest, least stressful route to get what you want."

She nodded once. "Yes. Enough pain will change your entire outlook. That's a fact." Looking uncomfortable, she quickly changed the subject. "I'd better find my *fiancé.*"

Her words knifed through him, stopping him cold for a second. But he was a big, bad special agent in charge for the FBI. He couldn't let anything so personal throw him off track. Especially not something that he had no control over—nor any right to dispute.

Grimacing inwardly, he squared his shoulders and tried for equanimity. "Sure thing. How about introducing me to him? I'm really anxious to meet this young, rising star I've been hearing so much about."

Two

On the way home in the car with Bill a couple hours later, Jill couldn't stop thinking about the look in Reid's eyes. *Damn him.* He'd been the one to leave her standing at the altar. What right did he have to be hurt at the mention of her new engagement?

None. Zip. Nada. He'd given up those rights when he disappeared and quickly married someone else.

And why in the world had he questioned her so intensely about her trying to find him back then? The truth was that the morning sickness had stopped her. That and her pride. But she sure as heck wasn't going to mention either of those things to him.

Jill hadn't been so sure that introducing her former fiancé to the man who fancied himself to be her current one was the smartest thing. But since Bill had walked up to them just at the moment Reid had asked to meet him, she'd been stuck. She'd plastered on her best fund-raising smile and gotten through it.

The thing was—she'd been horrified to find that she couldn't take her eyes off of Reid. Bill's reactions or lack of them hadn't mattered one bit. Her biggest concern had been Reid's feelings. She'd seen the fleeting look of pain in his eyes when she'd mentioned Bill, and it had chipped away a piece of her soul.

Jill shook her head to disengage the unwanted thoughts and realized Bill had been asking her a question. Fortunately, he hadn't taken his eyes off the road long enough to catch her inattention. Maybe she could cover.

"Excuse me, Bill. Could you repeat that? I was just thinking back to how surprised I was when you pulled out that ring tonight."

He stole a quick glance at her out of the corner of his eye. "What's wrong with you this evening, sweetheart? You're so distracted you don't even listen when I'm trying to cajole you into going away for a weekend with me."

Now he had her full attention. "We've talked about this many times, Bill. You know my feelings about sex before marriage. I'm trying to set a good example for my son. I don't want him to grow up to be irresponsible or to ruin his future by getting some stranger pregnant."

She found herself squirming in her seat. Her words had a particularly hollow sound this evening and she wondered if Bill noticed.

"Yes, but now that we're engaged I thought perhaps you could relax your rules a bit. You wouldn't even have to tell Andy we're together. You could just call it a business trip or something."

"Hmm. More like monkey business." She folded her

arms over her chest. "No. That wouldn't be the honorable thing to do."

Something about this conversation was nagging at her, but Jill just couldn't get a grasp on what it was.

"Besides, I still haven't said yes to your proposal," she insisted.

"But you accepted my ring. You let me announce our engagement in front of all those contributors. Of course you're going to marry me."

"I didn't 'let' you do anything, Bill. You were the one who decided to turn the fund-raiser into a surprise engagement party." She turned to stare out the window. "By the way, I don't appreciate you springing such a personal thing on me in such a public way."

"Oh, come on. You know a politician's life is in the public eye. You'd better get used to being in the spotlight. After we're married, nearly everything we do will have public relations overtones. The governor's wife doesn't have a life of her own."

"Yes, but we're not married, and you're not the governor...yet. This is a big step for me. I have a lot of things to consider. Not the least of which is whether I want my son to have his whole life exposed to the public's view."

"Well, think fast. Late summer will be a perfect time for our wedding and you'll need to get busy with the details. We'll time it to coincide with the announcement of my candidacy. It'll be great PR to kick off the campaign."

Jill sighed inwardly. What was wrong with her, anyway? Marrying Bill made perfect sense. He was a man destined for great things and she loved working behind the scenes of politics. He seemed genuinely fond of her and Andy, and her son certainly needed a man's influence in his life right now.

If her father had been alive, he would have been pleased at their union. Her father loved politics and having a son-in-law in the governor's mansion would have made up for some of the disappointments Jill had given him.

But this was going way too fast for her. She simply refused to be pushed into agreeing to something so monumental without giving it time to sink in.

"Please slow things down a little, Bill. Andy has to be my first consideration. In fact…" She slid the ring off her finger and slipped it into his coat pocket. "I want to talk to him about this before I even start wearing your ring. Try to have some patience with me. I'll come to the right decision for all of us in the end."

"Oh, I wouldn't even let you out of my sight if I doubted for one minute that this time next year you'll be my campaign manager and wife. So I'll wait for a while, but not very patiently, I'm afraid."

He turned his head to flash his dentist-enhanced, white teeth. "Please don't make me wait too long. Remember, we have a great future ahead of us, Jill."

If that were true, how come she felt so bleak and empty at just the thought of what lay ahead of her? Yes, this decision would take a lot of soul searching and introspection. Something she hadn't attempted since the only man she'd ever loved had walked out of her life on the day of their marriage and never returned.

Now she would be forced to take a look inside herself just when that same man had stepped back into her conscious mind—and, unbidden, was slowly seeping back into her heart.

*   *   *

A few days after having to face Jill at that fateful political fund-raiser, Reid shoved the old, straw work hat back off his forehead and ran a sweaty palm across his eyes. It had been so long since he'd done any ranch work that he'd forgotten how hot and dry it could be.

And it didn't help things one bit that he couldn't concentrate on settling his mother's bull into his temporary new home due to thinking about Jill Bennett and the way she'd looked the other night at the fund-raiser. If he had to be thinking about things besides manhandling a two-ton Brangus, he should've been trying to sort out some of the potential suspects for Operation Rock-A-Bye that he'd run into over the last few days—not lollygagging about a woman lost to him long ago.

"That should just about do 'er, Mr. Sorrels." The young ranch hand closed the bull pen gate and grinned at Reid. "Ol' Pete will begin his 'donations' work tomorrow. Don't you worry about him none. We'll have him back to you by end of next week—just as good as he is today. The vet'll see to it."

"That's just fine, Bobby Ray. I'm sure Pete will enjoy his stay." Reid slanted the kid his own version of a grin. "Now, can you fetch Sonny for me to sign the papers? The insurance company insists the Double B has to take formal delivery of Pete or their policy won't cover the temporary move."

"Sorry, Mr. Sorrels." Bobby Ray squinted up at Reid and covered his eyes, blocking the shaft of sun that hit him square in the face. "Sonny had to go over to San Angelo today for the quarter horse auction. He won't be back till late. He said for you to go on up to the house and have Miz Bennett sign whatever you need."

Damn. Now what?

The only reason Reid had agreed to run this errand

was because he was sure he wouldn't need to deal with Jill's mother. His own mother had insisted that he could just deliver the bull to the Double B, have the foreman sign the insurance forms and leave. He wasn't supposed to have to face the woman who probably hated him more than dirt for leaving her daughter standing at the altar.

Well, shoot.

Reid's mother had made a kind of peace with the Bennetts over the years. Once both the mothers had become widows, they'd even begun to do business together. Between them, they now ran two of the most profitable ranches in ten counties. Reid was proud of his mother, but right now, he could just strangle her.

Finally, he shrugged with resignation, grabbed the papers from the truck and headed toward the main house. When the front door opened to admit him, it was not Mrs. Bennett who'd answered the bell.

Before him stood a good-looking young boy. The nearly five-foot-high, dark-eyed and rather sullen child stared silently up at him. Reid couldn't have been more surprised if someone took a shot at him.

"Well hey, partner. And…just who might you be?" Reid sputtered.

"Whatta you want?" the kid bounced back at him.

Reid removed his hat and studied the boy. "Yeah, okay. I guess that's a fair question. My name is Reid Sorrels and I need to see Mrs. Bennett about some papers for the bull I just delivered."

"Sorrels? You related to Miz Sorrels over to the Sorrels' ranch?"

"I'm her son. May I come in?"

The boy stood his ground for a second then backed up a step to admit Reid to the house. Reid slowly stepped over the threshold, using the time to speculate about just who this child might be. He was a good-looking, rail-thin preteen, with black, curly hair and eyes that made Reid think of shadows in the dead of night.

The young boy was dressed in jeans and a work shirt, with his oversized feet stuffed into cowboy boots that looked well scuffed and worn. With those feet, this kid was bound to grow into a pro basketball player.

Just who was he anyway? He didn't look like he belonged to the Bennetts, who were all blue-eyed and petite. Even Jill's father had been of relatively short stature for a man. Maybe this kid belonged to the foreman, or perhaps to some of the household help?

"You wait in there," the child said, pointing toward the huge great room that took up the entire front half of the house. "I'll go get Nana."

With that remark, the boy took off toward the far reaches of the ranch house. Did he say 'Nana'? Good Lord. Could this be Jill's boy? But that was impossible. This child looked to be ten or eleven, and it was only ten years ago next week that Reid and Jill's wedding would have taken place. She certainly hadn't had a kid back then.

In fact, Reid remembered his mother telling him that Jill married a Frenchman, had his son and was divorced a few years after she'd left town. That should make this kid more like seven or eight. Maybe the boy was already a giant for his age?

But then, what Reid knew about kids could fit into the point end of a hollow-nosed bullet.

He was still working on the incongruent appearance of the child when he heard a noise behind him.

"What do you want here, Reid?" The sound of Jill's voice startled him out of his reverie.

He turned to face her. "Oh, hi. I...I brought over Ol'

Pete as a favor for Mom. The foreman's out of town, so I need to get your mother's signature on these insurance papers." He held them out as if to prove he wasn't telling a lie.

Staring down at his outstretched hand, she focused on the papers like they were contaminated. Jill looked absolutely fantastic today. With no makeup and in her stocking feet, the too-tight jeans and scarlet cropped-top she wore made her look ten years younger. The coal-black hair she'd tried desperately to tame the other night flew free in a cloud of curls around her face and down her back.

She stood frozen to the spot. What had he said that was so hard to understand?

Reid cleared his throat. "Uh. Didn't expect to see you here, Jill. Travis told me you had a house in Rolling Point near your office."

He pulled the papers back to his side and waited for her gaze to find his. When she finally glanced up at him, he was dumbfounded to find a look of pure panic in her eyes.

She finally seemed to find her voice, but didn't answer his questions. "Give me the papers. I'll take them to Mother. You wait here."

"But…"

"Mom! Mo…ooom!" The sound of boots clacking on wooden floorboards filled the entry way. Within a second, the young boy who'd greeted him at the door came barreling around a corner. "Oh. There you are. Nana says to bring the guy back to her office."

"Andy!" Jill grabbed up her son and pulled him to her. Reid watched as a dozen different expressions ran across her face.

He tried to sort through what he saw in her eyes, but

the overwhelming impression she gave was that she was scared to death. Reid narrowed his eyes to watch her more closely. What was going on in that beautiful and super-smart head of hers anyway?

He looked down on her as she gently pushed back a lock of shiny hair from the boy's forehead and Reid noted her tremendous struggle for calm.

"Andy," she whispered. "Say hello to Reid Sorrels. He's an old friend and neighbor."

The boy turned to Reid while his mother stood stiffly behind him with one hand on his shoulder.

"Reid, this is my son Andy Bennett. We're staying out here with Mom for his summer vacation."

So this boy was really her son. Named Andy after his dead grandfather and going by the name of Bennett? Reid's split second of hesitation caused Jill to draw in a breath. What was the problem with her?

Reid promptly stuck out his hand. "Pleased to meet you, son. How're ya doing?"

The child's wary eyes relaxed slightly as he quickly moved to shake hands. "How do you do, sir?" The kid had an impressive grip.

Reid's gaze moved from the boy to his mother, but her face had become a mask. Suddenly, the woman he'd always thought of as an open book became a mystery.

"Are you a cowboy?" Andy's question jerked Reid's attention back to the youngster.

"I want to be a cowboy when I grow up. I already know how to ride, and I practice my roping every day. You ever been to a rodeo? I'm going to be a big star there someday."

Reid couldn't help but grin at the boy. "Yes, I've been to the rodeo. In fact, I rode the broncs there sometimes, but it's been many years ago."

"Mr. Sorrels is being modest," Jill said with a smile aimed at the back of her son's head. "He won several titles on the circuit as a teenager, Andy. He was quite the rodeo star."

"Really? Cool!" The kid's whole face lit up. "But I wanna be a calf-roper when I grow up."

"Maybe I could give you a few pointers some day," Reid said to the earnest youngster. "I used to have a fairly steady hand with the calves."

"Would you? Wow. That would be so cool, wouldn't it, Mom?"

Jill shook her head at Reid with a grimace, but she softened the look as the boy turned to her with wide, pleading eyes. "I don't think Mr. Sorrels really has the time to work with you," she murmured. "Besides you're too young to practice on the real thing. We've talked about this before."

"But, he said…" Andy whined.

"Andy, let me talk to your mother about this a bit, son. Maybe we can work out a compromise." Reid was surprised how his own voice gentled. "For right now, though, why don't you show me where your Nana's office is? I need to get on back to my mother's ranch with these papers."

"Yes, sir." The boy straightened and looked so deadly serious Reid almost pulled him to his chest for a hug. "I hope you and Mom can work out a com-proo-mise. I'll be real good. I promise." Andy turned and took off toward the rear of the ranch house.

Jill laid her hand on Reid's arm to stop him as he began following Andy's path. "It was very kind of you to offer to help him," she whispered. "But I know how busy you must be. Don't think that you have to live up to some offer you made in haste. He'll be okay."

She'd left her hand on his forearm. Instead of answering her right away, Reid looked down at the spot where she touched him. Urgent sensations of smoldering heat and flaming desire spread out along his skin and raced directly to his gut.

When he could finally raise his gaze, her eyes widened in surprise. Something distinctly sexual and enormously intense passed between them. Jill jerked her hand back and dragged it through her hair in a nervous and self-conscious move. Suddenly, Reid's brain felt scrambled and for the life of him he couldn't remember what she'd just said.

"Don't worry. I'll explain things to Andy," she mumbled, pulling her hand back to her side. "For now, do you want me to get Mother to sign those papers for you?"

Andy? Oh, yeah...the boy. There was still something drastically wrong here. Maybe it had to do with the kid's father.

"Jill, I want to help him with his roping. It would make me happy. He seems like a good kid. A little too serious and sincere maybe, but he reminds me of me at that age."

Another series of varying emotions ran across her face, and Reid wanted badly to get to the bottom of the trouble—whatever it was. "How often does his father get to see him?" he asked. "Can he teach the boy anything about ranching or roping?"

"His father doesn't... His father doesn't ever see him. He's cut him out of his life for good."

"I'm sorry. Boys need a father...to learn how to become men." Reid watched as Jill's demeanor became tense and nervous once again. "How about your fiancé? Can he teach him the things he needs to know?"

"No. Bill is a very busy man. He and Andy get along okay, but he can't spend much time with him."

"Too bad. Boys need…"

She waved off his words. "He has plenty of men around the ranch to emulate, and Travis tries to spend time with him. The reality is he has me to be both his mother and his father. He'll do just fine." Her hands fluttered in front of her with distressingly jerky movements.

"Do you have any boys of your own?" she asked.

He sadly shook his head. "The marriage was a mistake from the beginning. Fortunately, we didn't compound the error by having children."

"I'm sorry. I know how much you wanted…"

"Um, yeah," he said hastily. "But getting back to Andy, unless you can give me a real good reason why you don't want him to learn anything about rodeoing, I'd like to spend a little time with him. Show him a few tricks. I have the time and I can't think of a better way to kill a little of it."

The pain of Jill's betrayal had faded over the years, at least enough to make him care if she was in trouble. A deep curiosity, born from years of being an undercover agent, fueled his concern.

There was more than one mystery for him to solve around his old stomping grounds. He was determined to give both the mother and the child enough time to find out what was behind Jill's strange behavior. He would know the truth. It was only a matter of time.

After the papers were duly signed and Reid had left the ranch, Jill stood facing her mother's inquisition.

"Why didn't you tell me Reid was back in town?" Caroline Bennett demanded.

Jill sighed and plopped down on the leather sofa in her mother's office. "I didn't think it was important. He's just here for his law-school reunion. He'll be gone soon."

"Not important? The man caused this family undefinable pain and disgrace. Now he shows up on our doorstep and you don't think that's important?"

"Mother, please." Jill knew dramatics were her mother's stock in trade, but she'd hoped her newfound confidence at becoming a good rancher would have tempered them somewhat. No such luck.

At nearly sixty, Caroline was still what could be called a "raving" beauty. She always was a bit disappointed that Jill had been born short with unruly hair and startling blue eyes instead of being sleek, sophisticated and gorgeous like herself.

Jill's attitude only made the disappointment worse. Today, for instance, Jill was in old jeans and battered tank top, while Caroline wore a leather skirt and vest, tailored denim blouse and stylish high-heeled boots.

"Please, what? Is it too much for me to be concerned about my only daughter and my only grandson's welfare?"

"No, Mom. Concern is good. Overreacting is bad. Reid's only going to be here for a while. Besides, you and his mother have made peace enough to do business together, why shouldn't Reid and I make peace as well?"

"You know perfectly well why. He's the one person on earth who could cause you more pain. You can make 'peace' with him all you want, but if he ever finds out the truth... Well, I'm afraid even your hard-earned, University of Texas law degree wouldn't keep him from making your life miserable...and just when you're about to snag the most eligible bachelor in the whole state of Texas."

Jill took a deep breath. It wasn't as if she herself hadn't thought of these things, but to hear her mother speak them aloud, made the whole deal with Bill sound sordid.

"I'm not about to *snag* anyone. Bill asked me to marry him. I haven't decided whether I want to be his wife yet."

At her mother's stricken look, she hurried to get out the rest of the bad news.

"Reid wants to spend some time with Andy."

Caroline looked horrified so Jill quickly continued. "Oh no, he doesn't have any idea about the truth." At least, she prayed he didn't. "Andy asked him to help with his roping and Reid told him he would. That's all there is to it."

"You're not going to permit it, are you?" Her mother found her voice again.

"I really have no choice. If I made a big fuss, Reid would want to know why."

Jill knew disaster with Reid was potentially only a few misspoken words away. She would never lie to Reid about his son, though she wasn't quite ready to admit the whole truth either. But she had an even bigger concern.

"I really don't want Andy to start asking the wrong questions. I don't want to tell my son any more lies."

"He's a baby, Jill. He's too young to understand. You told him the same story we told everyone else. Why change things now?"

"Oh, Mother." Jill stood, heading for the door and fresh air. "Andy is not a baby anymore. I don't want him to figure it out before I get a chance to explain things."

"Then for heaven's sake keep them separated."

"They have a right to get to know each other. It'll be fine. What could happen?"

Three

"**W**hy are you so interested in Jill? I thought you made it clear ten years ago that you couldn't care less about her." Travis rested his elbows on the solid wood of the old neighborhood bar. He raised a longneck beer to his lips and took a swig while studying Reid over the bottom of the amber-colored bottle.

Reid took a careful and calculated sip from his own bottle. Although he and Travis had been best buddies once, they hadn't contacted one another in ten years. At first, in the hospital, it had been impossible for Reid to contact anyone. Then, as time went on, he didn't want any reminders of that earlier period in his life—those kind of thoughts only brought depression and frustration. So Reid deliberately stayed away, letting people think whatever they wanted about him and his reasons for leaving.

But now he needed Travis. Oh, he wouldn't be letting

Trav in on the truth of who he was or his real reason for coming back. But Reid could make up something to satisfy his old buddy. Travis was his ticket to the legislature.

So far, Reid met or had been reintroduced to a couple dozen of the lawmakers. He felt comfortable enough with them to share a few beers and surreptitiously ask most of the questions he wanted. But that wasn't all he needed. His job demanded he ask intricate questions about political procedures and the internal processes that go into a legislator's life.

Operation Rock-A-Bye's main suspect had to be an attorney as well as a politician. A man that would also have access to politicians from across the border. He would have been in his position for at least five years. Reid's FBI tech support managed to narrow down the list of possible suspects to less than fifty of the lawmakers in Austin, but that wasn't much help.

And that left Reid with one hope—Travis. But although Trav had made introductions and taken him to political gatherings, he seemed hesitant to answer Reid's questions without an adequate explanation. Maybe the real trouble between the two old friends stemmed less from ten years of noncontact than it did from something pertaining to that night so long ago. After all, didn't Reid remember that Trav had been nervous and jumpy before he'd left the house?

Or perhaps it came more from Reid's supposed treatment of Jill back then. Maybe Travis had bought his uncle's lies too. The same as Jill had so easily done.

Right now, Trav was still waiting for an answer. Reid had only asked about Jill as a way to warm her cousin up. Obviously, the ploy had backfired.

"I congratulated her on her engagement the other night," Reid managed at last. "And then yesterday when

I ran into her, she wasn't wearing the diamond ring. I didn't want to seem too nosy. Do you know what happened?''

''What's it to you, old buddy? Maybe she's having the ring sized. You lost the right to ask anything about Jill when you jilted her the day of your wedding.'' Travis's words were rough, but his eyes held an old echo of sympathy.

Reid knew he had to be careful. Although he couldn't really believe his old friend could be involved, Travis's name *was* on the list of fifty suspects. But his need for Travis's help far outweighed any other consideration.

''Look, Trav. It's a long story and it happened a long time ago. I'm not terribly comfortable going into the details but, believe me, I didn't leave voluntarily. Be a friend and don't ask me to explain more.''

Reid watched his old pal with the practiced eye of a trained investigator. Travis hadn't flinched at Reid's partial explanation. Perhaps Jill's father, Andrew, had told Travis what had happened after Reid was knocked out. That idea didn't exactly sit well with Reid. Surely Travis would have said something more if he'd known the whole story.

Reid couldn't take the time to inquire about personal matters right this minute. His own puzzling past wasn't the mystery he was currently working to solve. Later, when he'd located his quarry, he vowed to come back and question Travis further.

But that was later. Right now, Reid needed to make peace with Travis. Whatever it took.

''You'll never know how sorry I am that I hurt Jill. I'd have moved heaven and earth to keep that from happening. I still care enough not to want to see her hurt again.'' Reid sighed and set his beer down on the counter.

"I was just curious to know if this jerk fiancé of hers took his ring back for some reason. And, if so, should I take the guy's head off, or what?"

Travis's grip tightened around his bottle. "Look, *you* weren't the one who spent hours, days...damn it...weeks having her cry on your shoulder. *You* weren't the one who watched over her for the last ten years, making sure nothing else bad touched her. She sure as hell doesn't need *you* now." He drained the bottle and hung his head.

"Aw, never mind. Just leave her alone, Sorrels. Bill Baldwin is the best thing to happen to her in her whole life. In eighteen months, he'll be governor of this great state, and if I have any influence over her, she'll be the first lady."

"Travis, I didn't mean..." Reid knew by the look in his friend's eyes that it was time to shut up and take his losses. Apparently, talking about Jill was not going to win him any points tonight.

"Yeah, okay," Reid mumbled. "Let me buy you another beer."

He hailed the bartender and indicated they'd have one more round. "Why don't you tell me about this Baldwin guy? What's he done that's so stellar?"

"For one thing, Bill Baldwin would never leave Jill...for any reason." Travis gave his friend a cutting look, then shook his head. "Sorry. That wasn't fair. I do believe you didn't want to hurt her, even though I'd like a better explanation of what really happened."

Travis hesitated, but when Reid didn't interrupt him, he went on. "Okay, forget it. Back to Baldwin. He's by far the best politician I've ever run across in my eight years in state government. Not only will he make a great governor, he'll be one of this century's greatest presidents. You mark my words."

Reid nodded but kept a questioning look in his eyes. Travis took the bait and continued his recitation of Bill's virtues.

"When he served in the legislature with me a few years ago, he formed one of the first committees to conduct talks with our neighbors to the south." Travis ran his hand down the wet, slick longneck and began picking at the paper label. "Now that Baldwin is attorney general, he holds regular discussions with the governors of our bordering states, including the states within Mexico. His contacts alone have saved us from many an international incident."

Travis went on for another half hour extolling the attributes of Bill Baldwin. Reid let him ramble, but something kept nagging at him. By the time Trav wound down and went home, Reid had a gut suspicion that Baldwin would make a good suspect. The man seemed to meet all the criteria even though he hadn't appeared on Operation Rock-A-Bye's "top fifty" list. Reid placed a call to his office for more intelligence about Baldwin while he thought more about Jill's current engagement.

Later, he headed back to his mother's ranch. Regardless of the consequences, and regardless of what it might cost him in self-respect, Reid figured he had to spend more time with Jill. She was the fastest way and best bet for getting close to his new suspect.

Not to mention the fact that he would delight in seeing to it that Jill Bennett didn't end up marrying the guy. Reid hadn't cared for Baldwin from the first minute they'd been introduced, standing there with his arm around Jill in all his slick glory. Baldwin obviously would do whatever it took to win politically. Maybe he'd found a way to add to his own political coffers—illegally—on the backs of stolen babies and heartbroken parents.

Reid refused to think that his own motives weren't totally pure…that he might be trying to deliberately cause Jill trouble and pain. After all, he was a better man than to hold that kind of grudge for all these years. He would never hurt her or her innocent son in any way. No, he vowed to try to keep both of them from being devastated.

But he had a job to do. He needed to bring down his suspect. Besides, it was her fiancé Baldwin that turned his gut inside out with all his phony macho bravado, not Jill. And it was Baldwin he was now determined to go after.

And damn it all, but the best way to spend time with Jill was to spend time with her son. He would really feel like a slimeball using Andy to get to Jill—to get to Baldwin. But if that's what it took to bring down the master criminal of an international baby-selling ring…so be it.

A few days later, Jill stood in the cool depths of the foaling barn and watched as Reid set up a small barrel and bale of hay in the middle of one of the pens. Andy followed close behind him, dancing in and out of his shadows and babbling endlessly about the rodeo.

In the whole ten days since Reid first showed up at the fund-raiser, she hadn't been able to think of much else but him. Well, that wasn't strictly true. She'd also thought a lot about her son.

She reflected about all the years she'd grieved over the fact that Andy had no father. Jill clearly remembered a time when she'd imagined what a wonderful father Reid would've made. But that was before he just up and disappeared, leaving her to raise their son alone.

Regardless of what she'd told her meddling mother,

Jill knew she would eventually have to tell both Reid and Andy the truth. It was the right thing to do. And in the long run, she'd really have no choice. One way or the other, they'd find out anyway—then *she'd* be the bad guy. Goodness knows, she never wanted to experience Andy's disdain—if she could possibly avoid it.

Right this minute, she could only hope time was on her side. Maybe, given a little time, they'd learn to respect one another, and she could find an easy way to tell them both the truth.

All she had to do was pray that Reid didn't question Andy too closely about how old he was in the meantime. Her son's age might be her biggest pitfall. She felt confident that Andy had no reason to mention his age. At least not until it was closer to his birthday, which was over eight months away. But her grace period was perilous at best.

Soon. She needed to find a way to tell them—soon.

It didn't matter if Reid would be furious that she'd never told him about his son. She'd been plenty furious at him for leaving her almost at the altar. But it did matter what Andy thought. She didn't want her baby's life to be ruined by hate for a father who'd never been around—or hate for a mother who'd never told him the truth.

She looked out into the sunshine as Reid bent on one knee in the dust, explaining the finer points of knot tying to Andy. Their two heads leaned together in serious discussion. Jill mused about the differences between the man and his son.

Of course, their similarities were clearly visible. The dark, smoky eyes. The lean, wide-shouldered build. The big feet that always managed to be where they shouldn't be.

But it was the differences that captured Jill's attention.

Reid's work hat was pulled low on his forehead, covering his chestnut-colored hair. Andy wore no hat in the bright sunshine and his black curls shone with radiant highlights. As her child concentrated on the lesson, the tip of his tongue snuck out from the corner of his mouth, exactly the way hers always did when she was deep in thought.

Andy was definitely an eclectic combination of both his mother's and father's genes. That fact had given her some comfort when she'd thought about Andy spending time with his father. She'd figured Reid wouldn't be able to see his own eyes reflected in his son's because her family's features, so strong in her child, would shroud their true relationship.

But deep down, Jill knew the day of reckoning was coming. Somehow, one of the two of them would learn the facts. She wanted to find a way to ease them both into the truth first. They needed to learn to like each other, maybe to become friends before they had to face down their reality.

That was the real reason she'd agreed to letting them spend this time together. It definitely was *not* because she wanted to spend more time with Reid.

No way was she interested in the man anymore. Just because her body jolted every time he stood within three feet of her. Just because the sheer pleasure of looking at him made her relive the savage, raw passions they'd shared with glittering intensity. None of that meant anything today.

The things she'd been experiencing were strictly lustful memories. But she knew she could conquer those baser emotions if she put her mind to it. At this moment, her son was the most important consideration.

"Hi, Mom." Andy had spotted her and was waving. "Come on over here."

Too late to duck, Jill stepped out into the sunshine and strode over to them. "How's the lesson going?"

Reid stood, placed his hands on his narrow hips and eyed her with a purposeful gleam. His biceps and chest muscles rippled under his navy blue T-shirt as he fisted his hands. He smiled at her with the same charmingly crooked smile she always remembered, while she swallowed hard and tried to concentrate on her son.

Andy moved toward her, then bounced back to pick up the lasso he'd dropped.

"Great, Mom." Andy's body fairly shimmered with enthusiasm as he pulled the rope through his fingers. "Mr. Sorrels is teaching me all his secrets."

"That's wonderful, sweetheart." Jill placed a hand on her son's shoulder in a futile effort to keep him still.

Her hand slipped over his rough, denim shirt as Andy spun to talk to Reid. "Tell her what you just told me." He ran to Reid's side and tugged on his shirtsleeve. "Tell Mom, Mr. Sorrels."

"Andy, for goodness' sake, calm down." Jill moved closer to the man and boy in order to get a firm grip on her son—then wished she hadn't.

Up this close, she got a whiff of Reid's aftershave. Citrusy and musky all at the same time, the smell of him threatened to open forbidden doors in her heart. Doors she'd closed off years ago in order to protect herself. Her knees started to shake and she made a quick grab for Andy's shoulders to help her keep her balance.

Reid grinned down at Andy. "Take it easy, kid. We'll get everything said that needs to be said. All things happen in their own time."

His gaze traveled up past Andy's forehead and centered about the middle of Jill's chest, making her wish she'd worn a bulky sweatshirt instead of this thin T-shirt. The look on Reid's face darkened as he took the time to dwell on her body before he finally settled on her reddening face.

"Jill." He took off his hat while his eyes never left hers. "I didn't think you were coming out to the ranch today. Weren't you supposed to be in court?"

Heat flared inside her as she clung to her son and at the same time kept her shoulders back and her spine straight. She wouldn't let Reid see that he could get to her. She refused to be so...so... Well, she just refused, period.

"The case settled at the last minute." Her voice sounded reedy and too high to her ears.

She gladly turned her attention to Andy. "Son, have you been good for Mr. Sorrels like we talked about?"

Andy nodded so hard she worried that he might break something. "Yes'um. But wait'll you hear what he said." Andy pulled a shoulder free from his mother's grip.

Reid chuckled softly and fingered the hat in his hand. "I was just telling Andy here that he has a natural way with a rope. It also seems like he might've been born to the saddle. He'll make a rodeo star someday, for sure."

Jill took a deep breath. She had no intention of talking about what her son had been born to do. Not yet.

Reid must've caught her hesitation. His expression hardened and he furrowed his brow as he studied her.

"You're not going to make a fuss about him trying his hand at an event are you? He won't go until he's ready. I promise you that." Reid's dark look threatened to strip bare every one of her secrets.

She dropped her hands to her side. "Oh no. It's not that at all."

Great. She'd just denied a reasonable explanation that might've covered for her real problem—at least for a little while. Now she was left with no excuse. No defense.

Luckily for her, right then Andy's stomach growled loudly enough to be heard in two counties. Saved.

She gathered all her motherly instincts and turned to her son. "It's lunchtime, Andy. Better head on up to the house and see what Nana has cooking."

"Aw, Mom."

She watched her son battle between his hunger and the desire to continue with his favorite pastime. Hunger won. Andy grabbed Reid's huge hand with his small one, and Jill had to stifle a sigh, wishing for things that couldn't be.

"Come on, Mr. Sorrels. Let's go get something to eat."

When he looked up at Reid, Jill's heart thudded in her chest. Her son's gaze held such trust, such worship and longing that she wondered if allowing the two time together might become one of the worst mistakes of her life.

What if Andy grew to love the man? What if after he knew the truth, Reid didn't want to be tied down with a son? Would he disappear from Andy's life, leaving their son with only broken dreams—the same way he'd left her?

Suddenly everything she'd done so far seemed all wrong.

"I'm sure Mr. Sorrels is too busy to spend any more time with you today, son. You go on up to the house. I need to talk to Reid for a few minutes, then I'll be up to join you."

"But…" Andy whined.

"You do as your mother says, boy," Reid urged. "We

can work on your roping another day. The rodeo isn't going to shut down. It'll still be there when you get ready for it.''

Reid had been fascinated by the mix of emotions he'd observed on Jill's face. The last time he'd seen her, he'd wondered if she had something to hide. Now he was sure she did.

Only now, Reid feared she was not only hiding something from him but hiding something from her son as well. Perhaps she was afraid to tell Andy about her engagement. Maybe Baldwin didn't really care much for the boy.

That would be one more reason to see to it that Jill broke off the relationship. Reid decided to make sure that happened. He decided to use whatever means necessary to keep them apart permanently. After all, having to tell one more lie to her or anyone else wouldn't be the end of the world.

''Go to the house, Andy,'' Jill demanded in that motherly tone that made every young boy cringe.

''Yes'um.'' He swung around and shuffled off reluctantly.

Restless, Reid worked his jaw. He ached inside every time he thought back to ten years ago. Every time he got close to what he'd lost.

He hadn't wanted to put that much of an emotional investment into this mission for Operation Rock-A-Bye, but it was already too late to stop. Much too late.

Jill turned to look at him. In the sunshine, her eyes were the color of a clear West Texas sky at midday. How often had he dreamed of seeing her gazing up at him in just this way? How often had he longed for the comfort of her lithe body nestled in his arms, the sweet agony of her kiss against his lips?

He shook off the images. This was undercover work. Nothing more. Putting on his hat and taking her by the arm, he ambled in the direction of his truck, wondering what she had to say. Wondering if he could keep his hands to himself and wondering if he could keep the memories locked inside his professional outer shell long enough to complete his mission.

Jill silently walked beside him. They made it through the foaling barn without saying a word.

"Reid, I..." she began.

"Jill, I..." he said at the same time.

Together, they laughed at their own nervousness. How strange to be so self-conscious with her. There was a time when the two of them had melded into one being. They'd been as close as two separate entities could be without losing their own identities.

Now... Now he wasn't sure he'd ever really known her. But he was determined not to let old memories stop him.

"You go first," she chuckled.

At the barn's far door, he hesitated before they stepped back out into the sun. "Jill, I need a friend." He took her hand in his, felt the electricity but held on. "My life is so messed up. I really appreciate you letting me help Andy. It's mending my spirits. But I also want to spend a little time with you. I want to be your friend as well as Andy's. I need someone to talk to."

She stared at him as if he were a perfect stranger.

"We used to be able to talk." He let a pleading tone seep into his voice, knowing she'd never resist an injured soul—just like she'd never been able to resist taking in sick strays as a girl.

"A lot of things have changed, Reid."

Steel words, but the softness he remembered was there

in her eyes and in the tone of her voice. "Yes they have. But some things will never…"

"Miz Bennett!" One of the ranch hands flew around the corner of the barn, his face contorted and his breath ragged.

"Miz Bennett, come quick!" The man gulped in air and grabbed Jill's arm.

"What is it? What's wrong?" she cried. "Has something happened to Mother?"

He shook his head violently. "It's your boy. He…" The man fought for his voice. "He's fallen into the pen. Oh God, ma'am. He's in with Ol' Pete."

Four
_____

If Jill had been capable of rational thought, she'd have wondered how a person could manage to go the two hundred feet or so from the foaling barn to the breeding pens without remembering having taken even one step. But suddenly she was facing chaos and horror as she stumbled into the heat and brilliant sunshine of the open yard.

When she'd stumbled, Reid grabbed her around the waist, steadying her for a second with his quiet, reassuring presence. But not for long. He stepped away and beat her to the wooden fencing separating them from her precious son—and from the huge, black-hided animal pawing the ground and snorting in the wind a few yards away.

She fought for breath as she reached the fence and tried to take in everything. Her brain was going in slow motion, while the world seemed brighter and more surreal somehow. She desperately tried to assimilate the scene before her. This wasn't a nightmare. This wasn't a movie.

That was Andy lying there so still and quiet just a few feet inside the fence rails in the dust. *Oh my God!*

Without missing a beat she climbed up the rails and prepared herself to jump over. He was hurt—in danger—and she had to get to her son.

Several strange arms reached for her, hauling her back to the ground with a shattering thud.

"You can't go in there, ma'am." One of her mother's ranch hands was screaming as he held her back.

"Let go of me," she wailed in frustration.

From the rear of the pen, a couple more of the men were making a racket, yelling, screaming and waving their arms at the confused and increasingly agitated beast. They were trying to take the bull's attention from the boy who lay silently a couple of feet away in a heap of rumpled clothes and a cloud of dust.

"Get him out of there!" Jill cried.

"We have to get the bull backed into the chute first, ma'am." The ranch hand with a tight grip on her arms screamed over the riotous noise. "If anyone goes in there now, we'll just end up with two dead people on our hands."

What had he said? Two…*dead*…people.

"Noooooo." Impossible. Not her son. Not Andy.

Her eyes teared over, blearing her vision and infuriating her. She needed all her strength and a clear head to get her boy out of this disaster.

Through the wet haze of anger and fear, Jill saw a movement from the far corner of the pen. Reid? Yes. He'd thrown a large bale of hay into the corner of the bull's pen and jumped in after it.

A cry of protest arose from the various men who

ringed the pen and the man holding her let her go to join them.

"Get out of there. You're aggravating him," someone hollered.

"Quiet!" Reid spoke in the most commanding voice Jill had ever heard.

If he'd been a general and all the men his soldiers, he couldn't have made more of an impression on everyone concerned. Including the bull.

Nothing moved. For one instant, silence filled the air.

Reid was the first to make a move. He stepped around the hay and stood there, quietly appraising the bull.

"Hey, Pete," he finally said. "You upset with us?"

The bull stared at the man in his pen, but the soothing words seemed to temporarily paralyze him.

"Now I know this isn't home, and these old boys aren't your regular friends. But they don't mean you any harm."

From behind his back, Reid pulled a length of rope. He dangled it through his hands while the bull watched in a fascinated stupor.

Reid took a couple of steps toward the bull, putting himself between the mighty animal and the boy. "It's time to calm down now, Pete. Are you hungry?"

He picked up a handful of the hay and waved it at the bull's face. "This isn't your usual gourmet feed, but maybe you'd like to try a bite?"

The bull lowered his head and snorted a couple of times. The animal actually seemed to know the sound of Reid's voice.

Reid used his booted toe to push the broken bale of hay in the direction of the chute, used mainly to move the bull into his private enclosure. "Come on, Pete," he murmured.

Jill was stunned to see the gigantic beast move slowly toward Reid and the hay—and away from Andy's body. At the thought, she turned to inspect her son. He was so still. She couldn't even be sure that he was breathing.

Things were going way too slow. She needed to get her son out of the pen and away from the danger—immediately.

All of the ranch hands were silently staring at Reid and the bull at the far end of the pen. Jill figured with everyone's attention elsewhere, she'd have a perfect opportunity to go for Andy.

Silently, stealthily, she crawled under the bottom rail of the wooden fence nearest her son. No one seemed to notice or pay her any attention. Including, thank God, the bull.

Reid's actions were so mesmerizing, she was on her hands and knees at Andy's side before anyone saw her.

She had only a split second to discover that Andy was, indeed, still breathing, before a ranch hand cried out in shock at her position.

"Hey, you shouldn't be in there!" he shouted.

Suddenly everyone's attention became focused on her and the lifeless body lying beside her. The bull made a strangled noise in his throat and then roared his disapproval, pawing the ground and bucking his back.

Instantaneously, Jill pulled Andy into her arms and jumped to her feet. Her child was a heavy load, but she knew she could get him to the fence by herself. She took the four or five steps, her feet barely touching the ground.

At the fence she had time to blink once, wondering how on earth she would get herself and her son over or under in a hurry. Instead, they were both whisked up by a pair of muscular arms and thrown unceremoniously over the top. Jill landed, her body covering Andy on the other side. Shifting to her hands and knees in a desperate effort to move off of him, she tried, at the same time, to find out how close the bull might be by now.

She could hear the sound of heavy, thundering hooves that seemed to be right above her head. Looking up through a haze of dust and a mass of her own curls that had flopped into her face, Jill saw Reid vault over the fence—just in time to miss Ol' Pete's furious charge.

Almost.

Pete caught Reid's right leg at the ankle, smashing it into one of the posts and nearly coming through the fence on top of them all. Fortunately, the fence held and Reid, dragging his leg up and over the highest rail, tumbled to the ground, landing next to Jill with a thud.

Reid winched as the emergency room doctor gingerly tightened the bandage around his right foot. The woman doctor was smiling at him while she gave him a lecture on how to care for a sprained ankle. He didn't need any lecture on his health. He'd spent so many months in the hospital after being left for dead ten years ago that he knew the name of every muscle and bone in the human body, along with the required treatment for every injury known to affect them. After all, he wasn't called the "master of wheelchair racing" for nothing.

The doctor smiled at him again as she wrote on a prescription pad. At this late hour, he didn't feel much like smiling. Not since this afternoon when he'd been forced to relinquish his hold on Jill as one of the ranch hands helped her into the back of the Suburban to ride to the hospital with her son. Until then, he'd kept up a steady, calm front.

Reid knew his own injury was minor—a slight hindrance for a couple of weeks, nothing more. But he wasn't so positive about Andy. After he'd thrown the mother and child over the fence and hoisted himself away from the bull, he'd whisked the two of them into the ranch house as fast as he could manage with his injured ankle.

Andy had moaned low in his throat as he'd placed the boy down on the living room couch to await a ride to the hospital. So he knew the child still lived, but obviously he had a head injury, and there was no way of telling how bad that might be without the equipment and expertise at the regional hospital.

Frustration gnawed at him. Since arriving at the emergency room, he couldn't get anyone to tell him anything about Andy's condition. He couldn't even manage to get out of emergency long enough to push someone in administration for the information he desired. He had a few contacts here that he could manipulate, but before trying that route he'd been forced into letting them treat his own injury.

So far, he'd been x-rayed, prodded, packed in ice and now wrapped. His patience disappeared with the pain.

"You Reid Sorrels?" A burly man in a white uniform stuck his head inside the closed curtain surrounding Reid and the lady doctor.

"What?" Reid was startled out of his personal fog. "Yeah, I'm Sorrels.... Why?"

"There's a woman upstairs that's concerned about you. She asked me to check up."

Only one woman could be in this hospital that might have reason to ask about his welfare. Jill.

"Where is she?" Reid eased off the table and tested the strength of the tightly wrapped bandage.

"Hold your horses," the doctor snapped. "Let me at

least get you a wheelchair before you go gallivanting off around the hospital corridors.''

''No, thanks.'' Reid reached for his socks. ''Can you hand me my one remaining boot, please?''

The doctor turned to the closet as the man at the curtain shifted impatiently. ''So whatta you want me to tell her, bud? I gotta be getting back,'' he grumbled.

''I don't want you to tell her anything. I'll tell her. You just show me where she is,'' Reid demanded as he slipped on his socks.

The doctor handed him a rather dusty but perfectly intact lizard-skin boot. One. For the left foot.

''Sorry we had to cut the other one off you,'' she said. ''I don't suppose you'll be able to replace one boot.''

He shook his head as an answer. It didn't matter. The boots weren't new. They'd been new ten years ago. For all this time they'd sat in his mother's house, waiting for him to need them again. It'd been difficult to put them on without facing his memories. A new pair would be easier to live with, anyhow.

Reid reluctantly accepted the crutches the doctor insisted he use. Awkwardly, he followed the man, who'd turned out to be an X-ray technician, into the elevator and up the three flights to pediatrics.

Following the technician's instructions, he rounded a corner heading for Andy's room. Because he was so focused on relearning how to use crutches, he nearly rammed into Jill's back as she stood leaning against a wall talking quietly on a pay phone. She was engrossed in her conversation and missed his clumsy intrusion.

He stopped, but didn't have the wherewithal or the desire to back up and give her the privacy he knew she deserved. Shamelessly, he quieted his breathing in an attempt to overhear her side of the call.

"Yes, I know how important this trip is," she said in a hushed tone. "But I thought maybe Andy was important, too."

The hallways were deserted this time of night, the lights lowered to a twilight hue. Jill's shoulders were slumped with fatigue, her hair a mass of tangled curls. Reid's fingers itched to smooth the wayward strands back off her face. But he stood still and let her finish.

"Of course I realize you need to make the meeting in order to ensure our future." She listened silently, then spoke through clenched teeth. "Right Bill, I know that means Andy's future too. But..."

She straightened her spine and stepped away from the wall, still not aware of Reid's presence. "It's just that you meet with the Mexican governors of Neuvo Leon and Coahuila nearly every month. I thought this one time you could assign someone else to take your place."

In the dim light, Reid saw her silently shake her head in an apparent response to what was being said to her. "Never mind. I understand," she said soberly. "I'll talk to you in a couple of days."

Jill lowered the phone to its cradle, heaved a heavy sigh and rolled her shoulders. He felt an unexpected surge of tenderness toward her, as if he had every right to pull her into his arms and comfort her.

He reached out to touch her arm. "Jill," he whispered.

She whirled around, surprised by the sound of his voice. "Oh, Reid. There you are. Are you all right?"

She stared down at the crutches and his one stocking-clad foot and shook her head. "Oh, dear."

Stepping quickly to his side, she studied his face as if doing so would reassure her that everything was going to be okay. Tears welled in her eyes, making them darken to a deep, blue-velvet color.

"I'm really fine, Jill. It's just a little sprain. How's Andy?"

He'd deliberately spoken in a hushed but commanding tone. He sensed she needed a quiet, steady hand right now, and that was one thing he could provide.

In the shadows of the hall, he saw her bite her lip as if unsure of her answer or unsure of what to say to him. The hesitant gesture was so unlike the new, confident Jill that he flashed back to the vulnerable, innocent girl she'd been when they'd first found love. He'd never stopped thinking about her that way. Not really.

In his mind, he pictured that bottom lip the way it was back then. Swollen and moist from his kisses or quivering with anticipation as his hands moved across her body's curves. He remembered the taste of those lips—hot, sweet and silky. Instantly, he needed to taste them again. To feel her smooth, honeyed mouth underneath his own once more.

As if she'd read his desires, she took a step back. "I'm not sure... How Andy is doing, I mean." She took another step back, putting distance between them and between him and his memories. "The doctors say he has a concussion. A mild one. But they're concerned because he seems so groggy still."

"What are they doing for him?" He swung his crutch, taking a hesitant step in a direction he thought sure would lead to Andy's room.

"Nothing. They say we just have to wait. The nurses have been rousing him every hour, looking in his eyes, that sort of thing. I guess they plan on doing that all night."

He could see the purple smudges under her eyes now. The deep fatigue that this day had caused was clearly visible even in the dim light. Confused by the ache inside him at the reminder of her pain, he turned away from the sight and fumbled with the crutches as she moved ahead of him into Andy's room.

As his eyes adjusted to the dim lighting in the room, Reid was stunned at the sight of the boy lying asleep in the hospital bed. Andy looked so small. Reid had thought of him as a big, strapping kid—healthy and so alive. Now he looked like the little boy of six or seven that he really was. The child in front of him was sunken into the huge bed, quiet and…still. Too still.

A skyrocketing feeling of protective guardianship coursed through him for the second time in the last five minutes. He'd never felt anything like this before. This deep, irrational possessiveness toward both the woman and child. It was almost like they were his to take care of and worry about.

Of course, that was nonsense. Perhaps this urge came from his years as a special agent in charge, totally in control of his agents' welfare. But it really didn't feel quite the same, he decided.

A nurse walked into Andy's room, slowing when she realized Reid and Jill were hovering over his bed.

"Ms. Bennett? I'm taking over your son's care for the third shift. I have orders to sit with him for a few hours."

The nurse scrutinized Jill's face, then added. "Why don't you go on home and get some rest? I'll be here, and if anything changes, I'll call you back immediately."

Jill shook her head. "You're as bad as my mother. She's been calling all night, wanting me to come home. I'm not leaving. I'm fine."

"Ma'am, the hospital is full, we don't have any extra beds. You look like you're about ready to fall down right here. Please go home." The nurse turned to Reid as if he could help convince the stubborn mother.

Jill sighed deeply. She knew she was exhausted, but she feared if she tried to sleep now, all the emotions of the last twelve hours would come pouring out to swamp her.

"Is there a couch somewhere where she can lie down?" Reid's look was compassionate—and something more. But Jill was too tired to ferret out what was going on with him.

The nurse looked thoughtful for a second. "Well, yes. Since this is the pediatrics wing, we have a playroom and waiting room combination that should be empty at this hour. I can't recommend it for any quality sleep, but if you refuse to go home, it's down at the far end of the hall to your left."

Jill was stuck between needing to sit down and not wanting to leave her son's side for one instant. Reid made the decision for her. He took her arm and urged her to move out the door while he followed behind with his crutches.

"Come on," he said. "I'll sit with you so you won't be alone."

She was grateful to Reid for being there when she needed a friend. At the stray thought, she suddenly remembered what he'd been talking about right before Andy fell into the bull's pen and knocked himself out. He'd said he needed a friend to talk to.

She decided maybe whatever he'd wanted to say would take her mind off Andy for a little while. Slowly strolling toward the darkened and peaceful waiting room, she stayed close to Reid as he inched his way down the slick hall.

"Jill, quit pacing and come sit down." Reid patted the space on the plastic covered couch next to him.

She'd had every intention of resting when they'd first entered the waiting room. But after settling Reid down and storing his crutches, she'd decided he was probably hungry since he hadn't eaten all day. She found an alcove nearby with food and drink machines and brought him a couple packages of cheese crackers and a hot coffee.

Not much of a supper she knew, but better than nothing at this point. Guilt for getting him hurt in the first place was beginning to nag at her conscience. So far, she and Andy had caused him nothing but trouble.

Nervous energy and pent up anxiety kept her standing as Reid choked down a few of the crackers and gulped a bit of the steaming coffee. He raised one eyebrow.

"I thought we came in here so you could rest." His voice suddenly took on that same commanding quality it had in Pete's pen this afternoon. "Sit."

She plopped down next to him and squeezed her eyes shut. Visions of Andy lying facedown in the dust filled her mind.

Reid put a warm hand on her arm and immediately blood rushed not only to that spot but also to other parts of her that didn't need awakening at the moment. She was too vulnerable right now.

He must have felt it too, because he removed his hand, leaving her cold and filled once more with the caution and fear that had been her prison for the last ten years. She shivered involuntarily.

"You're cold." Reid shifted, putting an arm around her shoulders and pulling her close.

Warm and inviting, the smell of real male and hot coffee was too comfortable—too inviting. She couldn't deal with this—with Reid—tonight.

She started to shake, waves of nervous tension crashing in around her. The defenses she'd placed around her heart all day to stay strong for Andy began to crumble. Here in Reid's arms was a safe haven.

No, safe was not the word for Reid's arms. She'd thought she'd been safe there once, a long time ago. Now they were inviting, strong, and...sexy as all get out, but she would be far from safe in his embrace.

She would never be completely safe again. Not like she'd dreamed about as a girl, anyway.

Older and much wiser, she knew that she must stand on her own two feet and be the solid foundation for herself and her child. But, oh, the way he was looking at her was so compelling—so sweet and understanding.

Assailed by needs and rocked by the fears and horrors of the long day looming back to devil her, Jill tried to stem the tears suddenly building up behind her eyes. She bit down hard on her bottom lip and sniffed with the losing battle.

"Don't," Reid warned quietly. His soft words and stirring presence made the tears flow even stronger.

"Ah, hell." He reached out, pulling her tighter to his chest and locking his arms around her back. "It'll be all right, sweetheart. I'm here. Everything will be all right."

Five

Jill melted into Reid's body like warm butter. The feel of her delicious curves pressed against him and her obvious struggle to stem the tears made him lose control. He forgot the years and the pain that separated them. Forgot that he had to use her and Andy to get his suspect. Forgot they were in a public place.

"Damn, Jill. Don't cry." He pressed a kiss into her hair, wanting to sooth her with tenderness and strength.

She cried all the harder at his caress.

"Please don't," he begged, as he moved his lips to her delicate earlobe.

She sobbed openly, and he skimmed his mouth over her jawline, wet with salty tears. His heart contracted at the taste of those tears.

Without thinking, he lightly cruised his mouth over hers, silencing her sobs in the only way he could. He wanted her to know he was sorry for her pain, that he'd never let anything hurt her or Andy again. When he brushed those inviting lips with his own, he felt her settle against him, quieting as she began to accept the comfort he gave.

The emergence of desire took him by surprise. The soft brushing of lips became hungry and desperately needy. He slanted his mouth over hers and deepened the kiss. Putting all the pent-up wants and dreams of ten years into his burning caress, he tried to give her all his strength.

Jill slid her arms around his neck and clung to him. Her sobs turned into mewing little moans. She opened for him, and he feasted on her wet warmth and inviting tongue.

Ten years disappeared. He was home. Where he belonged.

Fisting his hands in her hair, he let the silky strands float against his palms, losing himself in the sensuous sensations. Like the first food after a long fast, he consumed her.

He inhaled her womanly scent, moved his hands to her arms and rubbed lightly over the velvety skin there. He wanted her essence to surround him, wanted to lose himself ever deeper into her being.

Reid pulled her into his lap, eager to let her feel what she'd done to him. Jill was way ahead of him. She ground her bottom into his arousal, making it thicken and lengthen even more. She groaned as he slid his hands around her ribcage and softly skimmed them over her breasts.

Perfect. He dipped his tongue into her sweetness once again and fell into his memories. Like an echo off a steep canyon wall, she tasted like the promises of forever and

trust—in the same ways she always had. She was everything he remembered, and more.

He swallowed a tortured groan, forgetting all the heartache of the past. Forgetting everything but the here and
now—the fire racing through his veins. Lightly, he ran
his tongue over her moist lips in slow, tender passes,
feeding the flames between them. The realities of who
they were and where they were slipped away, leaving raw
passion and a shameless, wanton need to possess.

Reid sucked her deep into his mouth, desperate to satisfy her every desire—assailed by the sudden wildfire
spreading across his body with abandon. His soul remembered this place as a shelter of positive energy, a haven
for the body and a sacred closet for the spirit.

Somehow, out of his haze of desire and over their
heavy breathing, Reid heard footsteps clicking against the
linoleum down the hallway. He jerked his head away
from the honey of her lips and looked over her shoulder
to find the source of the noise.

Jill buried her face in his shoulder and moaned.

Two nurses, apparently on break, whispered to each
other as they passed the waiting room and headed for the
alcove containing the food and drink machines. When
Reid finally managed to think and breathe again, he
gently pushed Jill back from his chest so he could talk
to her.

The bruised look of her swollen lips assaulted his
senses. Wordlessly berating himself for the loss of control, he swore he should've kept his damn hands to himself.

Slowly, Jill opened her midnight eyes and gazed at him
with heavy-lidded, undisguised desire. Oh, man.

Reid had done a lot of underhanded things in the name
of justice over the last ten years, but he'd never moved

in on a woman that belonged to someone else. And Jill was apparently still engaged. For now.

"That shouldn't have happened," he managed with an unsteady rasp.

He let his fingers smooth away a dark curl that had matted itself to her cheek—because he really had no choice. Also without permission, his wayward thumbs rubbed lightly under her eyes, drying leftover tears. But he quickly decided he couldn't look at the creamy-white skin on her cheeks, touch that silkiness, or gaze into the depths of those dreamy eyes for one more second.

He wrapped his arms around her tightly and used his palm to press her head back against his shoulder. "Sleep, Jill. We'll talk later."

The next two days went by in a whirl for Jill. Andy was released from the hospital when, by the afternoon following the incident with the bull, he'd been as alert and clear-eyed as normal.

His doctor shook his head with a chuckle and said, "I wish we could all bounce back as fast as kids do."

Her mom came in the SUV, complete with her normal histrionics, and drove them back to the ranch.

Jill was amazed that although Reid hadn't left her side in over twenty-four hours, they'd never had an opportunity for the conversation that was, by now, well overdue. He was concerned and giving, exactly like the husband and father she'd imagined he could've been. And not at all like the low-down scum that had left her for another woman the day of their wedding—the way she'd thought of him ever since.

She'd been so concerned about Andy's welfare that she'd practically forgotten Reid's request for her friendship. But she hadn't forgotten the late-night kiss. Probably she never would.

Jill insisted that Reid recuperate from his sprained ankle at her mother's ranch rather than trying to go back to his own mother's house. They had plenty of room and her mother kept a ton of household help on the payroll, unlike Reid's mother, who managed to get by alone.

Jill felt she owed him something for helping to save Andy. Secretly, she was also curious to find out what he might have to say about the surprise kiss they'd shared. With no idea at all what to think about the seductive desire and deep need that kiss had stirred, she was hoping maybe Reid could make some sense out of it.

Perhaps if they talked civilly, the mystery and the urgent wanting would be cleared away. She had to continue with her life and stop walking around in a fog of confusion.

Andy needed her.

She stood in the late afternoon shadows on her mother's flagstone patio and gave a quick backward glance to her childhood home. It was such an odd mixture of all things Texan—and—the snobbish, Old South. Stucco and brick in varying shades of sand and cedar spoke to a heritage of the Old West. Huge arches with stately cactus standing over beds of wildflowers in a profusion of yellow and orange hues seemed somehow to be a mixture of both east and west. While this patio with its manicured grass and magnolia trees felt like a typical Louisiana plantation.

Jill felt she was also a curious mixture of two heritages. Her father's family, Texans for four generations, had sent their two boys to law school in Houston. Her mother's family, Shreveport gentry who'd lost their land, sent their only daughter to school in Houston to find a rich oilman to marry.

Love brought the two sides together.

If Jill hadn't come along when she did, her mother's family might've disowned their daughter forever. As it was, Jill's maternal grandparents only managed to tolerate her father—until he began making money and contributing to their retirement. In the last few years of his life, Jill's father had come into his own, making his in-laws proud—and rich.

Jill turned to face the setting sun and gazed down the little incline to the many out-barns and cattle pens in the distance. She knew beyond them, past acres of grazing pastures, lay the thickets of cedar and pines surrounding Long Lake, one of the many sapphire-colored lakes that blessed the Austin vicinity.

As suffocating and boring as she'd always found the ranch, she loved this land. The look and the feel of it soothed her soul. Perhaps Andy would one day want to make the place his home.

That would've pleased her father no end, Jill silently smiled to herself. He'd bought this place when she was a child because it had been his dream to own a Texas-size ranch.

When he died, Andrew Bennett left his share of the legal firm entirely to his brother, whose son, her cousin Trav, now ran it. A few years later, Travis took Jill into the firm when she'd passed the bar, giving her a job and a new lease on life.

But it was her mother that had turned their rural homestead into a real working cattle ranch. As pampered and prone to overreacting as she was, Caroline Bennett turned out to be a terrific businesswoman. When her husband left her with only a small amount of insurance, she turned a few head of cattle and ten thousand acres of land into a showplace.

Both of her parents had wanted the place to become a family heritage. The Double B Ranch—the Bennett Place.

Reid and Andy appeared from the shadowed depths of the nearest barn. At the mere sight of the man, her pulse started hammering and she ran a hand through her unruly hair.

Father and son moved closer, at a tortuously slow gait, Reid leaning on Andy's shoulder for added support. With his other arm, Reid worked a cane like an old master. Meanwhile, Andy gazed up at him in a rapt, hero-worshiping, way.

Jill knew just how he felt. With Reid's shirtsleeves rolled halfway up—displaying arms corded with muscles—and his jeans riding low on his washboard-flat belly, the man was too good to be true.

She flashed back to the other night when, for a few minutes, those tanned, sinewy arms felt strong and solid and safe—the way she dreamed about for her whole life. Today, he wore a black stretchy shirt and black Stetson that shadowed his eyes. Walking beside Andy, he looked big and tough and just a little bit dangerous—and a whole lot more like a cowboy than the desk-bound bureaucrat he claimed to be.

"Hey, Mom!" Andy yelled, when he looked up and saw her standing there. "Look how good Reid can walk on his hurt ankle now."

Jill smiled at her son's grammar, but knew mothers everywhere would disown her if she didn't correct him when he made a mistake. "It's 'how *well*'…"

Whoa. Had he said *Reid?* "Andy, I don't think you

should address Mr. Sorrels as 'Reid.' It sounds disrespectful.'' *And perhaps dangerous for keeping secrets.*

''Oh, that's okay. He said I could. He said since we've become friends, that it's what friends do.''

Jill bit down on her lip. That they should be friends was what she wanted, wasn't it? So why, when they'd done just that, did she wonder if the whole idea was a mistake? Between her growing guilt for not telling them the truth immediately and her worry over Reid asking Andy his age, her nerves were frayed.

She looked up at Reid and found her answers at once. The way he was looking at her made her feel like a coward. When he and Andy discovered the truth about each other, it would be better if they were friends. But when Reid did find out, it would be the end of any friendship chances she might've had with him. He would be furious with her, and perhaps rightly so.

On second thought, how selfish could she be, for heaven's sake?

The two of them deserved to know about each other. Besides, Jill wasn't sure exactly what kind of relationship she really wanted with Reid, anyway. She'd told herself when he'd mentioned a friendship, that maybe they could put the past behind them and become something close to that.

The thought now seemed ridiculous. Every time they were within two feet of one another, the intoxicating pull of sexual lust between them left very little room to build a platonic relationship. Like right now, for instance.

His gaze burned inside, making her feel beads of sweat forming in all her hidden, dark places. A tug deep in her belly drew her attention to the fact that she was already wet at the juncture of her thighs and squirming internally at his nearness. When just a glance from the man could do that to her, Jill knew they could never be just friends.

There was too much between them. Too much hurt. Too much guilt. Sex would only compound the problems.

"Jill?" Reid's gaze suddenly changed to confusion and his shoulders tensed with concern. "Where'd you go there, sweetheart?" he probed.

She glanced around, wondering what had happened while she was so lost in thought.

Reid finally chortled at her dazed look. "Andy was asking you a question."

She looked down at her son's earnest expression and her heart sank. What would he think when he learned the truth?

"Mo...ooom." When he saw he finally had her attention, Andy repeated his question. "If Reid's ankle is good enough, he wants us all to go to the rodeo this weekend. Can we, puleeeease?"

"Sure, honey." Jill answered with her heart's desire before she had a chance to consider the ramifications...or her other obligations.

"Yippee! I'm going to the rodeo." Andy was jumping and pumping his fist in the air.

"Uh. Wait a minute, son." Oh, how Jill hated to back-track and disappoint her son. "I forgot that I promised Mr. Baldwin we'd go with him to the regatta this weekend. You remember. We talked about it a few days ago."

She could barely believe that she'd totally forgotten about Bill. She hadn't given him even a blink of a thought since they'd returned to the ranch from the hospital.

As if this whole situation wasn't complicated enough, Jill wondered what Bill would think when he found out that Reid was Andy's father. Not to mention what he'd say when he realized she hadn't been married when Andy was born. Appearances were paramount in any political campaign.

"Aw, Mom," Andy whined. "Do we have to?"

He turned to Reid for support, clearly hoping for divine intervention. "You talk to her, sir. You can make her say yes. She really likes you. I can tell."

"Is it really so important, Jill?" Reid asked, turning his dark, intense eyes to her. "I hate to see the boy disappointed. Can't you put Baldwin off this time?"

Despite suddenly wanting—no needing—to do whatever it took to make Reid happy, she forced herself to shake her head. "It's politics. The governor and many of the legislators will be there. The regatta's a fundraiser...and in memoriam to one of Bill's biggest contributors."

A series of strange looks spun through Reid's eyes. He appeared to be a man warring within himself. After a brief period of silence, he clenched his jaw and the darkest of those expressions moved over his face, setting his features into a hard cast.

"Perhaps we could arrange both." Reid's words were caring, compromising and clever, and not at all scary.

"We could all go to the regatta in the afternoon, then I'd drive us to the rodeo straight from there. Do you think Baldwin would mind if I tagged along to this fundraiser?"

After agreeing to talk to Bill, Jill took Andy into the house to clean up for supper. Alone, Reid limped his way down to one of the paddocks and, with the aide of one of the hands, saddled a horse. Kicking himself twelve ways from Sunday for having to put both Jill and Andy in the middle of an Operation Rock-A-Bye investigation, he rode out of the barn area and onto the open plain.

He was angry. Mad at the situation. Furious that he wanted her. Livid that he cared too much.

If he didn't know better, he'd be convinced he had a bad case of Austin's famous cedar fever, making him crazy.

Riding out across one of the Double B's pastures, Reid watched the sun glinting off one of the many coves long the shores of Long Lake in the distance. The last ten years dissolved as he was transported back to the impassioned days of his youth. That time, so many years ago, when he'd been so sure of himself, his goals and his darling Jill.

The two of them had spent hours riding in the hills around Rolling Point, planning their future. As soon as he'd passed the bar, he would've taken a job as assistant D.A. in Austin. Jill would've eventually gotten her law degree.

A few years of hard work later and they both would've joined his father-in-law's firm, right behind his best friend, Travis. The three of them would be the next bright generation of lawyers in the family.

His plan had been to eventually go into politics. He'd wanted to change the world for the better, with Jill by his side.

Hell. He'd been so naive. So gullible.

He spurred his mount to a gallop as the last ten years of his life dragged into his mind, reminding him of the pain and the heartache of growing up and finding out that all his solid foundations were mere figments of his imagination. Politicians couldn't change the world. There was a ruthless underbelly to life that would find a way around any law—or any man wanting to cure the evil.

The only way to make a dent in the darkness of crime was to be a lawman. Capture the criminals—the ones who broke the laws that politicians made. Put a finger in the dike of corruption. Slow the tide of evil in this world.

He also thought about how his own father had assumed the worst of him when he'd disappeared. His dad had always figured Reid for a no-good loser, because he hadn't wanted to be a rancher. When Reid disappeared on his wedding day, the man never gave another thought to his only son.

Jill's father, who Reid had always thought personified everything right on earth, also betrayed him on that last night for some reason. Reid was convinced it must've had to do with greed. His daughter, Jill, was just as bad, betraying him by hurrying into another marriage and having a child. She'd been spoiled, impressionable and weak.

At least, that was the way he'd always thought things had gone. Now he wasn't so sure.

Without thinking, he urged his horse to an all-out run when he began to contemplate about the way Jill had raised a son alone. And done a damn good job of it too. She'd gotten her law degree without Reid or her father's help and had continued with their old dream of changing the way things worked through politics.

Reid was impressed, though still stung by her past casual disregard. She hadn't come looking for him ten years ago. She'd pitched Reid's memory in the back seat of her mind and sped on with her life without him.

He wanted to hate her.

So many times during the last ten years he'd been sure he did hate her. Wanting to see her die a torturous death.

Reid came out of his daydream and found himself racing over the countryside with no consideration for his poor mount. He slowed the horse and pulled up under a stand of live oak. Both man and gelding were breathing hard.

He didn't hate Jill. Far from it. But his feelings for her were still a jumble. Every time he looked at her, tenderness, protectiveness and lust warred inside him.

No, he certainly didn't hate her.

So many things in his life were in a state of complete confusion. But his first loyalty had to be to Operation Rock-A-Bye. Find the bad guy. Finish the job.

Once that was done, he'd take a real leave of absence and spend the time here, investigating what his father-in-law had been involved with ten years ago. All his inquires back then had come to dead ends with Andrew's sudden death. But today he had training and contacts he never could have imagined possible.

Perhaps he'd also spend a little time figuring out how he really felt about Jill.

He'd already decided that he had to spend more time with her son. Andy was a too serious little boy who so obviously needed a father.

Reid dismounted and let his horse graze on the surrounding grass. Removing his satellite phone from its metal loop on his belt, he placed a call to a former special agent. A man who'd up until recently been part of his team.

As he listened to the phone ring he smiled, realizing he would be glad to hear the other man's voice. Reid needed someone with a clear head to help him evaluate the situation and the people involved. He knew he'd lost some of his objectivity here, and there was no one on the face of the planet whose good sense he trusted more than Deputy Manny Sanchez.

Six

The next morning, Reid leaned his backside against a stucco column adjoining the ranch house patio, tipped his Stetson lower, and squinted through the blazing colors of the rising Texas sun. Pinks, deep blues and brilliant lavenders streamed around the early morning's patchy clouds, competing with the strains of softly bellowing cows and late crowing roosters for his attention.

He raised a steaming coffee mug to his lips and swallowed the black gold. Lord, it felt good to be back to his homeland. He'd never given Rolling Point a second thought when he decided not to return after being released from the hospital all those years ago.

Not that he hadn't thought plenty about some of the people here. All those months of lying there immobile and with his jaw wired shut, he'd dreamed of Jill. Of her, fighting to find him, torn and devastated with worry.

Ha! That was a joke. By the time his mother finally

located him with the help of a private detective, she told him that Jill had left for Paris and the rumor was that she'd married another man.

After he'd survived that blow to his ego, he built up enough walls to shield himself from the emotional pain. He figured he'd never return to this part of the country again.

Rachel, the kindhearted, physical therapist that Reid had hastily married before being released from the hospital, always swore he'd never be whole again until he faced his demons. For ten years he'd managed to dodge those perils.

If in all this time he hadn't really been whole, he'd sure done all right. Of course, he'd never felt the same kind of contentment anywhere else that he did standing here, looking out on this familiar countryside.

He should've tried coming home years ago.

Shaking his head at his own foolishness, he realized that his pride would never have let him confront Jill about her betrayal before now. To this day, he wondered if they would ever be able to discuss it openly.

A couple of times over the last weeks, Reid figured maybe they could have a relationship without ever delving into their past. Just build a new friendship and leave the old hurts buried. He wanted it badly. But since that spectacular kiss, he doubted if such a thing was possible.

Setting aside his coffee and wandering out past the white rails bordering the show ring, Reid's eye caught sight of a little paint in the working ring behind the foaling barn. She danced and pranced in the dusty, early morning, sunlight.

He rambled over and draped his arms over the fence to watch her cavorting.

"Mornin', Mr. Sorrels. Looks like that ankle of yourn's about healed up."

The Double B ranch hand, Bobby Ray, stepped to his side by the fence. Leaning against it, he lazily folded his arms across his chest, studying Reid while he watched the horse.

"Pretty little filly, ain't she?" Bobby Ray asked idly.

Reid nodded. "Why is she so full of life this morning?"

"I reckon it's cause that young Bennett boy's been working with her. He's the one who saddled her."

For the first time, Reid noticed the young paint was saddled and not looking the least bit happy about it.

"*Andy?* Where does he think he's going to ride her? She's too young to go very far."

In fact, the filly was too young and inexperienced for a child to ride—period.

Without waiting for an answer, Reid headed toward the barn behind the show ring. Approaching one of the stalls toward the rear of the barn, Reid was surprised to hear Andy softly talking. But he couldn't hear anyone else's voice. Was the kid talking to himself?

Quietly, he peered down over the stall door to find the boy standing with his back to the door, rope in hand and swinging it back and forth in front of a two- or three-month-old calf who cowered in the corner.

"Aw, come on, Essymae. Please stand still a minute. I won't hurt you. I just want to put this rope round your neck. I gotta practice, don't I?" Andy pleaded.

Reid knew Jill had forbidden the child to practice his roping or anything else without adult supervision. He also remembered distinctly explaining to Andy about the proper age and weight of the calves used for roping. This baby wasn't even weaned.

Judging by the early hour and the boy's secretive demeanor, the kid knew what he was up to would qualify as trouble—with a capital T.

"Mornin', son," Reid began, in his best "law officer" voice. "Do you have permission to be here today?"

Andy jerked around like he'd been stung. When he spotted Reid, he dropped the rope, jumped to attention and froze.

Reid didn't much care for the serious and frightened look on the child's face. He hadn't meant to scare him this badly. The poor kid was literally shaking in his boots.

Suddenly, Reid's protective reflexes kicked in. What Andy had done was misguided and childish, but not really bad enough for this much fear. Besides, the last thing he wanted was for the boy to be afraid of *him*.

Reid decided he'd better be cautious and careful of what he said and did next. He pushed his hat back off his forehead and softened his mouth into a grin.

"Just look at that poor baby. She's scared to death of you. I don't believe your mama raised you to be a bully, did she, boy?"

Andy fisted his hands and hesitatingly turned to the calf in the corner. Essymae provided a great sound effect at the exact right moment and issued a plaintive bleat. It did the trick.

Andy forgot about his own fear and went to the calf's side. "Oh, I'm so sorry, Essy. I didn't mean it." He knelt down and wrapped his arms around her neck. "I won't let anyone hurt you."

Reid watched the child with a soft swell of something that felt like pride. The boy had good instincts. Reid wasn't totally sure why that should make him proud, but he figured it had something to do with the fact that Jill was raising a basically good son, who would become a caring and fair man.

He'd been right about her all those years ago. She'd become a fantastic mother.

Reid bent on one knee beside Andy and put an arm around his shoulder. "You know you're not supposed to practice roping by yourself, don't you?"

The child lowered his head. "Yes, sir, but..." he said quietly.

"And you remember what I told you about how old a calf should be for roping?"

Andy nodded but didn't look up.

"Well, can you tell me what you were thinking?"

A pair of ebony-colored eyes hazarded a glance at him. Reid could see the fight between wanting to do the right thing and wanting to do the fun thing going on behind those eyes. His heart went out to the boy.

"I was wr-wrong, sir. I should be punished," Andy admitted.

Reid felt a clutch around his heart. Watching this child own up to his wrongdoing and be sincerely sorry was giving Reid a sympathetic ache. He wanted to wrap his arms around him and protect the boy from all the bad things that would happen in the rest of his life. But he knew that Andy would never allow anyone to baby him.

"Knowing you've made a mistake is the first step to being a man." Reid watched the guilt begin to turn into hope. "If you were the grown-up here, what punishment would be appropriate?"

"I..."

Reid knew how hard that question would be for a child to answer. It wouldn't be a snap for an adult. He held his breath and waited.

"I shouldn't be allowed to go to the rodeo this week-

end, sir.'' The bleak look in Andy's eyes clearly told
Reid exactly how difficult that answer had been.

Reid nearly broke down and hugged him. He truly was
a remarkable child.

''Hmm. And what do you think your mother will say
when she finds out?''

Andy straightened and, this time, the serious look was
not frightened but remorseful. ''She'll be hurt that I disobeyed.''

''Hurt, but not mad? She won't yell and send you to
your room?''

''Oh no. She never yells. She loves me.'' The beginnings of a tear formed in the corner of Andy's eye for
the first time since being caught.

At this moment, Reid knew he would always love this
sensitive child, too. ''Maybe we'd be better off not telling
her?''

''No, sir,'' the boy said softly. ''That wouldn't be the
honest thing to do.''

Reid heard a soft groan behind him. He'd thought he'd
felt someone's presence nearby earlier, but he'd been so
wrapped up in Andy he ignored it.

He stood and moved to the side so both he and Andy
could face the intruder. It was Jill. Reid wondered how
long she'd been standing there and how much she'd
heard.

''There you two are.'' She breezed into the stall and
smiled. ''I wondered where you'd gotten off to at such
an early hour. Aren't you ready for breakfast yet?''

Reid took in everything about her in an instant. He
missed nothing. Not the crystal-blue eyes about to brim
over with tears. Not the pencil-slim jeans, hugging her
rounded hips. Nor the rise and fall of her cropped top
under the hand she'd placed against her breast.

The cornflower-blue top she wore was the same color as her eyes, but it couldn't compete with the milky whiteness of the skin showing both above and below it. And nothing could compete with her soft and compelling gaze. It was hesitant, but anxious. Concerned, but loving.

All of a sudden, Reid's heart went out to the mother as well as the son. He wanted desperately to help her. But he had no business butting in. He didn't really belong here.

Andy finally broke the silence. "I did a bad thing, Mom."

The boy eased his hand into Reid's and squeezed, asking for strength through his touch. "I came out here to practice my roping alone. I'm sorry."

Jill rushed to her son's side, but slowed before she got there and knelt in the dust in front of him. "Can we talk about this for a minute?"

Andy nodded, watching her carefully.

"What exactly are you sorry for?"

"I'm...I'm sorry I disobeyed you." A gleam in his eyes told her that's what he figured she wanted to hear.

"I see. Well, that's a good thing. Are you sorry about anything else?"

Andy considered that for minute. Finally, his head came up and he looked at Reid. "I'm sorry I didn't listen to Reid and did everything wrong. I'm sorry I'm going to be punished." He took a breath and blurted out his final apology. "And I'm really, really sorry I scared Essymae. I'll never do it again. I promise."

Reid studied Jill's face. She had a couple of hard decisions to make here. Ones that might affect her child and their relationship forever. Again he wished he could do something to ease her way.

She reached out and gingerly touched her baby's

cheek. Reid figured she'd fold Andy into her embrace and soothe away his emotional turmoil. That's sure what he'd been wanting to do since he'd first found the boy here.

Instead, Jill brought her hand back to her side and stood. "Have you really learned something?" she probed.

"Yes, ma'am." The guilt was back in Andy's whole demeanor. He looked scared and defeated and he sniffed back a sob.

"A good man takes care of all the people and things that are weaker than he is. He never takes advantage of them. I love you, son, with my whole heart. I want you to grow up to be a good and caring man." The tip of her tongue slipped out of the corner of her mouth as she considered her options.

"I'm proud of you for being honest," she finally said. "Can you tell me what you're going to do about this?"

Andy slowly nodded his head. "Next time I'm going to think real hard about who's going to be hurt if I do something."

The corners of Jill's mouth creased into a near smile, but she held off. "That's good." She bent her head and lowered her voice. "And what should *I* do about this now, Andy?"

"You should punish me, Mom." His shoulders began to sag as he added, "I shouldn't be allowed to go to the rodeo this weekend."

Jill sighed deeply. "I'm not sure yet if we're even going to rodeo this weekend. But if that's a possibility, not letting you go would be as much of a punishment for Reid and me as it would be for you."

Andy couldn't stand still. He ran to his mother and threw his arms around her waist.

"I'm so sorry I hurt you, Mom," he sobbed.

Reid's knees were weak with wanting to go to them both. Wanting to soothe and somehow make things right. But he stood rooted and watched.

Jill put her arms around Andy and hugged him to her. "I know you are. I love you all the more for it."

She eased him back and put her hand under his chin, raising his face so he could see her eyes. "You're a good person, son." She put her other hand over his heart. "In here, where it counts the most."

Jill took one step back and straightened her shoulders. "I think the best thing for you to do is to take some time and really listen to what's in your heart. You need to think through what you've learned."

Andy mimicked her stance and prepared himself for the worst.

"For the rest of the week, you will not ride or practice your roping. Instead, you'll spend the time currying the horses, bringing feed to the pens and mucking out stalls." She grinned down at the top of his head. "Learn what the animals need. Listen to them. Befriend them. If you want to use them for fun, you should be able to see it from their point of view as well as your own."

The boy's eyes grew wide and he nodded quickly.

"If it's possible for us to go to both the regatta and the rodeo, we'll all go together. It won't hurt you to see that real cowboys respect their animals and treat them with kindness if you're going to be there someday."

Relief and happiness spread across Andy's features. He hugged Jill again. "I love you, Mom."

Reid came to a rather startling conclusion right then. He loved her too. He'd never stopped loving her. With every fiber of his being and every beat of his heart.

He knew she loved him too. She didn't really care for

that Baldwin guy. Reid had known it by the way she'd kissed him at the hospital. Known it also by the way she looked at him and lowered her voice when she spoke. He just hadn't opened his heart and soul up to listen to hers.

No more. Reid wasn't afraid of being hurt anymore. The pain and the doubting were behind them. He suddenly knew the past meant nothing. It could stay buried for all he cared. The future was all that mattered. His future with Jill and her son.

He would find a way to be with her and her good-hearted child forever. No more what-ifs and should'ves. The girl he'd loved so long ago was gone, but the woman she'd been inside was what had drawn him then, and that was what would keep him by her side throughout eternity now.

They belonged together. Irrevocably joined by their love.

He would make sure that happened. He was no longer the boy he'd been back then, either. Today he was a man of conviction and determination—not easily dissuaded or discouraged. Nothing would stop him from convincing her that they belonged together. Not a job, not a fiancé—nothing and no one.

When Jill stepped into her mother's kitchen, the smell of sizzling bacon and steaming coffee nearly knocked her over, reminding her that none of them had eaten yet. She sent Andy to wash up and change his shirt while she told the cook what they'd like for breakfast.

Reid poured them both mugs of dark, rich coffee, set them down on the huge kitchen table, then went to wash up himself.

The ambiance in the ranch's gigantic kitchen seemed cozy and warm. Even though it was the middle of June,

the early mornings in the hill country still carried a bit
of a chill. But here, in her mother's idea of an industrial
but homespun kitchen, a fire had been laid in the hearth,
gleaming brass-bottom pans hung from above the cook-
top and two dozen tiny pots full of herbs sat in the green-
house window still glistening from their morning misting.

Sitting down at the rough-sawn, wooden table that
could seat twelve, Jill blew on the hot liquid in one of
the mugs and tried to sort through the swirling impulses
assailing her.

Had she done the best she could with her son this
morning? She didn't know for sure what the best thing
was. Andy was her first experience at being a parent and
she had no one to talk to about it. Many times in the past
she'd wished that Andy had a father, not only for his
sake, but for her own peace of mind as well.

A man's opinion would've been invaluable. After all,
what did she really know about being a man?

The fact that Andy's real father had been only a few
feet away during their conversation this morning made
taking the whole responsibility alone that much more difficult. She'd overheard the concern and caring in Reid's
voice when he'd spoken to Andy. It was lucky for her
that Andy's need had been so great and so immediate.
Otherwise, she might have broken down and told them
both the truth on the spot.

And that would not have been a very intelligent thing
to do. They both deserved to know, but she needed to
find a way to break it to them gently. She knew that
simply blurting it out could cause no end of problems—
for them as well as for her.

Her thoughts shifted to the one main reason she wanted
desperately to tell the truth. Reid. She was beginning to
ease back into old her familiar feelings about the man.

The exquisitely sensual longing. The building, pulsating craving that seemed to slowly occupy more and more of her mind.

For a long time, it had been as if a piece was missing from the jigsaw puzzle of her life—the king of hearts lost from her deck. Silly, but when Reid was nearby, she knew all the missing pieces had been found. Perhaps still not in proper order or perspective, but close at hand.

Jill took a swallow of coffee, burnt her tongue and once again blew lightly on the steaming liquid. She found herself arguing both sides of the dilemma. She and Reid had too many problems to ever go back to where they'd been.

He was still the sexiest man alive, and even today he could make her feel like he could right any wrong or capture any star from the sky. But she was afraid that she'd never really be able to forgive the callous way he'd used her. When she thought back to how hurt and embarrassed she'd been when he'd left her before their wedding, she knew she'd never fully trust him with her heart again.

To make matters infinitely worse, her guilt about not finding a way to tell him about his son long before now was building to unbearable proportions. Her pride might be standing in their way now, but his anger over not getting to know his son would be an irrevocable source of division.

The trouble was, she'd sell her soul to have one more hour in his arms, one more night to forget herself in the roaring rampage of his kisses.

What would their relationship be as they both worked together to raise their son? She was positive now that he would want to play a role in Andy's upbringing. He had that right. But what part, if any, would she and Reid play in each other's lives?

All of those things raced through her mind, then lodged in her throat when Reid sauntered through the doorway. He'd changed into a saddle-colored, muscle enhancing T-shirt and had raked his fingers through his wet hair in an effort to remove the hat marks. She blew out a breath and blinked. The man simply reeked of potent masculinity.

From across the room, his dark, compelling eyes lingered on her like a red-hot caress. Turning, he retrieved two plates of food from the cook at the other end of the kitchen and set one down in front of her and one at another place.

"Did I guess right on which one is yours and which is Andy's?" he asked, pulling out a chair at a third place and straddling it.

"Yes, thank you." His simple gesture caused a fluttering sensation in her stomach that had nothing whatever to do with food. "Aren't you going to eat, too?"

He picked up his mug and took a gulp of the black brew. "Not this morning, thanks." He took a second sip and moaned his appreciation. "Mmm. I'm sure going to miss the great coffee around here. Nobody makes it quite this way."

"Mother uses a variety of imported beans and..." The truth hit her squarely between the eyes. "You're leaving soon?"

His heavy-lidded gaze stayed locked with hers. "Will you miss me when I'm gone?"

The smirk of masculine ego in his expression strengthened the delicious throbbing between her legs she'd failed to notice before. She squeezed her knees together in order to stem the insistent pulsing and cleared her throat to cover her hoarse voice.

"Where are you going? Is your ankle that much better?" she rasped.

"It's time I went back to Mom's, Jill. I really appreciate your hospitality, but the ankle's good enough for me to drive, and I have some things I should be doing."

By the time she'd recovered her voice, he'd gotten up, swung his chair around and downed the last of his coffee.

"You sure you'll be all right?" she murmured.

"No sweat. I'll be fine." He sat the mug on the counter and then stood, towering over her. "I wanted to tell you what a great job I thought you did with Andy this morning. You were spectacular."

Depthless, dark eyes hinted at the undercurrents of something vibrant and cosmic between them. He reached out and gently tucked one of her wayward curls behind an ear.

Letting his fingers linger on her earlobe for the longest time, he finally sighed, then spoke. "You're a terrific mother, sweetheart."

Jill stopped breathing and closed her eyes. Need, guilt and just plain old lust battled inside her.

"I recall a night long ago when I told you that you'd make the best mother ever. Remember?"

How could she ever forget that night? The sound of their favorite music suddenly filled her ears, and the tingling remnants of remembered passion leaped through her blood.

Forget that night? Impossible.

The memory of the erotic and narcotic friction of his steeled muscles against her yielding flesh, her crisp sheets sliding under their steamy bodies, the heady taste of champagne on his tongue as he kissed her lips—all came back in a flash, giving her flushed warmth and shivers of longing.

Forget the night that Andy was conceived? Never.

"We were rather young and impetuous back then, Reid. If we'd only known…"

"Known what the future would bring? That's never possible, Jill. All we can do is live in the now and take each new dawn as it comes. The past is over. The future may never be."

The connection Jill felt to him at that moment was so acute that she believed every word he hadn't spoken.

Everything would work out—somehow.

"Will you call me when you know for sure about Saturday?" he asked.

She nodded, wondering how to get to see him before then. She wanted him. Wanted him back in her bed. She could swear that he wanted her, too.

Their day of reckoning was still in a future that might never be. Meanwhile, one more taste of the paradise of his kiss couldn't be wrong. They'd just shared intimate memories. Surely they could share one more moment of magic.

"But… But I thought we were going to talk. We haven't had a chance. And what about Andy?"

He moved toward the door, turning back to search her eyes. "I need to see a friend this morning, and I might be a little busy for a few days. But if you… or Andy…needs anything, just call."

He walked out the door, leaving her sitting at the table alone. She tried to get herself under control. Had she gone nuts for a moment?

She had no business wanting him. There couldn't be any magic moments in their future. When he learned the truth, an unbridgeable distance would probably come between them. If she seduced him before that, he'd likely never speak to her again. And what would that mean for Andy?

Seven

Reid flexed his ankle and pressed down on the accelerator. Damn, but it felt good to be back behind the wheel of a truck.

While on the Double B, he'd been glad for the opportunity to ride something besides a desk or an FBI issued vehicle.

But horses could only take you so far. To meet Manny Sanchez in San Antonio, he needed motorized transportation.

Watching the dusty miles tick by, Reid enjoyed the freedom of independence, the feeling of being master of his own fate once more. He knew the exhilaration wouldn't last. After all, he was back to the investigation in earnest. But as he drove toward the city, he let the warm feelings he'd had all morning wash over him again.

It had been nearly impossible for him to walk away from Jill at the kitchen table. But it was the proper thing to do. The timing wasn't right for them yet. First, he needed answers to his questions about Baldwin.

Reid hoped to find reasons enough for Jill to be free to accept that she still loved him. Just putting Baldwin on the suspect list was one thing, proving he'd had anything to do with the baby-selling scheme was entirely another.

Reid had seen the way Jill's eyes glazed over at the table this morning. They'd both been surrounded by sweet memories of shared passions. She'd been so sensitive to his desires.

They'd always been so hot together. He'd suspected that she'd never forgotten that. He knew he certainly hadn't.

In that moment, when she'd closed her eyes for a second, Reid guessed she'd been trembling with need. Lost in the desire that raged between them to this day.

He'd fed the flames, almost without thinking it through. He'd wanted her to need him again, with the same intensity as he needed her. But it was just a little too soon to complete this reawakening.

First he must find the proof that would implicate Baldwin and get him out of her life. He knew it must be there. All he had to do was turn over the right rock.

Jill crossed her legs under the cloth-covered table and took a sip of wine. Having lunch with Bill in this fancy restaurant near the capital was not the way she'd have chosen to spend her time today. But there were a few things that needed to be settled.

"I'm sorry I was going out of town the other night when you called me," Bill began. "Is Andy all right?"

"Yes, he's fine. But, uh…" Jill set her glass down and firmed her resolve to say what had to be said. "I must tell you something, Bill. Coming so close to losing him has made me reexamine my life.''

Bill narrowed his eyes and took a sip from his own glass. ''And what conclusions have you reached?''

She took a deep breath and rushed ahead. ''I'm sorry, but the truth is, I don't love you. Not the way a wife should feel about her husband.''

He visibly relaxed his shoulders and smiled at her. ''Don't worry about that. You'll learn. Most great marriages are built on mutual respect and trust. It takes time to grow into a loving relationship. My parents never loved one another, but they had a long and fruitful marriage.''

''That's not the way I want to live. I've decided that I'd rather live alone for the rest of my life than to marry someone I don't really love.'' She held out her hand, palm up, in a pleading gesture. ''Please understand.''

Bill's cheeks flushed and his jaw ticked as he studied her with an intense perusal. ''Is there someone else?''

''No. Not...really.'' She jerked her hand back and placed both hands in her lap. ''This is a decision I've been considering for quite a while. I believe it will be in everybody's best interest. I'm truly sorry.''

He didn't miss a beat. ''Will you still be my campaign manager?''

Jill was a little taken aback by how quickly he'd recovered his composure. ''Of course I will. I wouldn't leave you stranded at the last minute.''

''And you'll still be a hostess for the Lake Austin regatta this Saturday?'' he demanded.

''Uh. I wanted to talk to you about that, too.''

''You can't renege on this, Jill. Your cousin Travis already backed out on me this morning. He'd promised to carry the governor on his yacht in the parade of sails.

Now Travis says we can use his schooner but he's too busy to be there himself. You'll have to take over as skipper and sail his yacht in the parade.''

"What? But I don't know how to sail. I can't be a skipper.''

"You must know how. You grew up around here. Everyone knows how to sail.''

"Well, I don't.''

"Then you'd better learn in a hurry.'' Bill set down his wineglass and motioned to the waiter that he was prepared to order.

He lifted his chin, turning back to her. ''This is one of the most important events we've scheduled for our precampaign activities. You were the main organizer, remember?

"It's the least you can do after backing out of our engagement. I refuse to be further embarrassed by having to move the governor and his wife when they already expect to be on Travis's boat.'' The waiter arrived and Bill picked up his menu. ''Learn to sail or find someone else to do it. Either way, you and the governor's party will be aboard that boat on Saturday. It's your responsibility.''

A couple of hours after leaving Rolling Point, Reid pulled the truck into the parking lot of the FBI's regional office in San Antonio, and checked his watch. A few minutes early. Manny wouldn't have been able to drive here from his new home in Willow Springs in such a short time.

Until last fall, Manny Sanchez had been Reid's right-hand man in the field. They'd worked on Operation Rock-A-Bye together for over six years. Then last December, as they were wrapping up a sting near Del Rio,

Manny had fallen hard for a young woman he'd been forced to use as part of the assignment.

The lure of love, family, and the home life Manny had never known proved to be stronger than anything the FBI had to offer. Reid was secretly glad his friend found what he'd always seemed to have needed.

Manny left the Bureau and had taken a job as the local deputy sheriff. But not before he'd captured one of the midlevel cogs they'd been seeking in the international crime syndicate—that gang of creeps, specializing in stealing babies from all over the world and selling them to rich U.S. couples desperate enough to pay outrageous sums. The man Manny arrested had pointed them to Austin and directly to the state lawmakers.

Reid parked and, after passing through security, found the cafeteria. He'd promised to meet Manny there, before the two of them entered the secured conference room Reid had ordered for their think tank session.

Twenty minutes and another cup of coffee later, Reid spied Manny as he appeared in the doorway to the cafeteria. He looked good. Dressed casually in jeans and long-sleeved shirt, he seemed a few pounds heavier than the last time Reid had seen him, but on Manny the added weight appeared healthy. His hair was considerably shorter than the last time, too. He looked exactly like a happily married man who worked in public law enforcement—and loved it.

A prick of jealousy pierced Reid's inner shell, but he stuffed the emotion back into the corners of his heart where it belonged. He was truly happy for Manny, and he was very glad that his old friend had agreed to spend a couple of days advising Reid on his current suspect.

"*Qué paso*, boss," Manny said as he swung past Reid's table and headed for the coffeepot.

When he'd poured himself a cup, he returned to sit across from Reid. "How's the investigation going?"

"I'm not your boss, Sanchez. You know the name's Reid...and the investigation stinks." He took a final swallow of coffee. "Thanks for coming. I figure it must be tough to leave your family."

Right after they'd married six months ago, Manny and his new wife adopted a baby that had been directly involved in their meeting. Reid helped with the paperwork.

Manny's eyes glinted in the fluorescent light. "Tougher than you know. Randi just told me last night that our family is about to grow."

"A child? You and Randi are expecting?" That same stab of jealousy came back to bite Reid in the heart.

He shook off the alien weakness and related what he'd found in Austin so far. Manny still had full security clearance, and Reid's former underling could think circles around the department's criminal analysts. His years in the field meant he could get into the head of the bad guys and ferret out what their next moves might be.

Reid wanted the two of them to find the key that would narrow the field of suspects down to Baldwin. It was the best way he knew to get the man out of his path to Jill. He hoped if he gave Manny enough information, they'd figure out a plan of action together.

After a cursory explanation, the two agents moved into a specially designed conference room. Reid had ordered computers, satellite phones, decent chairs and a sofa. Printouts of all the previous six years' worth of investigations for Operation Rock-A-Bye lay scattered across the broad slick surface of one of the mahogany conference tables.

Reid also had obtained all the necessary approvals to use the Bureau's computer research files and secured Internet access. With the option of ordering food in and a refrigerator already stocked with drinks, Reid prepared to hunker down for as long as it took to get his answers.

Their move to the conference room gave Manny time to think over the facts as Reid related them. "Okay. Let's say for the moment, the Bureau's intelligence was flawed and Baldwin should have been put on the list of possible suspects," Manny began as he settled down. "What do we know about his background?"

Reid handed him the dossier they'd gathered on the Texas attorney general. "This is only a partially complete file. Intelligence didn't have much time to compile all the facts."

"Hmm." Manny noted the file number on the folder in his hand and turned around to punch a few strokes into the computer behind him. "Are they still adding info?"

"As we speak."

A couple of minutes later, Manny rested his hands on the keyboard. "There's a few glaring holes in this file so far. Go away for an couple hours and give me some time to do a little research on my own."

"You going to go through regular channels? Won't that take forever? Just give Intelligence a little more time."

Manny grinned at his old boss, rolling his eyes in mock exasperation. "Takes too long. I have my own channels, thanks." He looked back at the blinking screen and began to type. "Go away," he muttered over his shoulder.

Reid spent the time checking with his INS and border patrol contacts. He wanted to know if there were any new rumors about baby-selling activity around the Texas border. Since Operation Rock-A-Bye pulled in that last middleman, the crime syndicate boss had either backed down on his activities or he'd buried the illegal operation so far underground that the FBI would never be able to dig them out. Reid fervently prayed they'd forced their man to the edge.

In exactly two hours, Reid was back in the conference room and seated next to Manny and his computer. "Well?"

"Odds are, Baldwin is not our man," Manny said quietly but with assurance.

"What? How can you be so sure?"

"Do you have some old grudge against this guy from your college days?"

"No, of course not."

Manny shrugged. "Then I can't imagine why you'd consider jumping him onto the suspect list. He doesn't fit the profile at all." Manny narrowed his eyes to study Reid. "And I know you'd have already figured that out if there wasn't some kind of trouble between you two."

Reid swallowed hard and fought the urge to argue with his friend. But he trusted Manny's judgment implicitly.

"Maybe I've been a little hasty. Convince me I'm wrong," he urged.

Manny turned back to the blinking screen and pointed to a list of numbers. "For one thing, not enough money."

"Huh?"

"You know as well as I do that there are big bucks in baby-selling. *Mega* bucks. One kid with the right coloring can bring in as much as a quarter of a million dollars."

He tapped a finger on the keyboard and another list appeared. "But Baldwin's finances don't add up to anything like that. To run for governor, he's had to file disclosure statements with the state's elections board. His campaign committee does have millions, but they can account for every penny."

Manny smiled at the screen and continued. "I also

have a buddy who works as an investigative reporter for the Fort Worth *Star-Telegram.* He's been digging for years into Baldwin's financial dealings, trying to find the dirt. But there are no hidden bank accounts. No phony corporations to launder the money. No nothing. The guy's clean.''

Reid sank into his chair. He couldn't believe he'd stepped out of character so far as to allow himself to be blindsided by his desire for Jill. He needed to get back on track.

''What else?'' he probed.

''The man we're looking for must have contacts and private offices to work from. But he doesn't necessarily have to have connections to any government officials in Mexico.'' Manny clicked a couple of keys and the screen blinked on a new page. ''In this millennium, all you need is a computer hacker or two on your payroll. They break into any government system they want, alter a few records, and poof, they have whatever documents they need.''

''Like what kind of documents?''

''Birth certificates. Immigration records. Marriage certificates. You name it.''

Reid gave the computer a suspicious glance. ''Does that help us narrow it down to who's in charge?''

Manny turned to him. ''Maybe. All we need to do is track down the hackers.''

''Is that all?'' Reid grumbled. ''That could take months.''

''You've been buried in your own mission too long, old buddy. The Bureau has ten different operations going right now that involve the use of the cyber-technology section. The nation's security depends on the integrity of the Internet and our government's computerized systems.''

''And?''

''Let me contact an old friend or two in the Bureau,'' Manny added. ''Maybe we can get a quick approval from the Justice Department for the use of one of their track and trace devices for a few days. We'll be able to backtrack our man through the system. We'll hack into *his* operation and have him cold.''

Reid needed to move. Needed to begin hunting for the right man. Needed to find the right way to get back to Jill.

''Can you handle this alone?'' he asked.

''No problem. Let me take one of the Bureau's satellite computers with me, and I can run the whole thing from home.''

''Do it,'' Reid urged fiercely. ''Oh, and Manny...'' As he picked up a portable phone to issue the orders, Reid stopped for a second, the phone suspended in midair. ''Thanks for making me face reality. You saved my hide. I owe you.''

The day after her lunch with Bill, Jill took the afternoon off. She squinted up into the glare of the noonday sun and pulled a pair of sunglasses out of her floppy bag. It had been years since she'd even placed a big toe in Long Lake. Slipping on her shorts this morning, she'd been dismayed at how pale her skin looked.

The lake hadn't changed much, she thought as she stepped out onto the quiet dock. Since the property surrounding the lake was mostly owned by ranchers in the area, very little development marred the landscape. This marina with its tiny gas dock, even smaller café, and a few scattered homes on the hillsides were the only signs of civilization.

As teens, she and her friends had literally lived on the lake every summer. They'd taken motorboat rides, water-skied, even did personal watercraft racing—before the county outlawed it.

Most of the year, kids in the area had ranch chores to do before school, riding lessons to take or give and, over all, just be busy young Texans. But during the summer months, everyone found some time to spend on or in the water.

In college, the main weekend activity had been tubing down one of the rivers near Austin, with beer kegs tied to one of the inner tubes, floating beside them. But in high school, it had been the many lake activities that held the young people's attention.

All that was long ago and far away from the person she was today. Mother, attorney, campaign manager.

"Jill," Reid called to her, breaking into her thoughts as he walked toward the dock where she stood. "What's this all about?"

The man looked positively wicked today in his khaki shorts and a pale yellow T-shirt, loosely covering his broad chest. Her heart thumped wildly in her own chest and she fought her lustful impulses so she could tell him why she'd called for help.

"You said you knew how to sail. That you can skipper any boat with a mast. Well, I need to learn how."

"Now? Today?" He stepped onto the dock and grinned. "Can't this wait for a better time?"

She shook her head. "I wish it could wait forever. But I guess I have no choice."

He picked up the cooler she'd set down by her feet and studied her face. "I vaguely remember that you were never very interested in sailing. You always said you wanted the security of a motor-powered craft...that you didn't like being at the mercy of the wind. What's happened?''

"It's a long story. But it's imperative I learn how.'' She waved her hand toward the small sloop she'd borrowed, indicating that they should climb aboard while she still had the nerve. "This is a girlfriend's boat. She said we could borrow it for a few hours. Do you think it'll take that long to teach me to sail?''

He chuckled and swung himself and the cooler onto the deck. "Things take however long they take. Learning to sail in one afternoon seems like pushing it, though.''

He set the cooler down and reached a suntanned arm up to give her a steadying hand. "Will you explain why it's so important to rush this?''

"Later.'' She placed a soft-soled, canvas shoe onto the edge of the gently shifting boat and jumped, landing with a thunk against Reid's body and nearly knocking him down.

He threw his arms around her in an instinctual move to keep them both upright. The gut level reaction she'd had when jammed against his muscled chest annoyed her. She simply didn't have time today for her body to be aroused by an accident of proximity.

She pulled back, intending to move away from him and the temptation he represented. Reid tightened his grip on her and searched her eyes behind the sunglasses for the connection he knew they both had felt.

The blazing sun heated her skin while the sultry gaze he gave her heated places you couldn't see. He'd aroused her with merely a touch, a glance, a muffled groan.

Not now, please. She begged her body to behave. There wasn't time. This wasn't the place.

''What'll I do first?'' Gathering her wits and her determination, she shoved gently at his waist and he let go.

Reid quickly stowed the cooler inside the little cabin and came back toward her, donning a baseball cap he'd found there. ''Do you remember back to our motorboat days when I taught you how to cast off?''

''Sort of.'' Mostly what she remembered from that time was being young and in love. The memories became stronger with every ragged breath.

''Just hang on to the dock for a second,'' he scoffed.

She did as he asked and within a few minutes they were drifting away from land. Reid checked the wind direction and frowned up at the gathering dark clouds on the horizon.

Usually, the winds were brisk on Long Lake. But with a storm threatening to move in later tonight, the breeze had died and the sticky, stale air barely stirred. The water softly lapped against the sides of the sloop.

''We've got a small problem,'' he admitted. ''It's going to take two of us to get out of this tight harbor with so little wind. And you won't be much help, I'm afraid.''

She grinned up at him. ''I can follow instructions perfectly well. Show me what you want me to do.''

Eight

"**Y**ou man the tiller," Reid grumbled. "I'll raise the mainsail."

When Jill mentioned being capable of following instructions, from somewhere out of the misty past, he remembered everything he'd ever taught her. He'd fought off the bombarding images of her naked, rising over him with the same seductive smile on her face that she now wore. His mind refused to let go of their hot, sensual lessons.

Reid needed to get a grip. He wasn't a horny young kid anymore. Adult enough to put his pulsating desires on hold, he vowed to wait, at least, until he found a way to make sure she didn't love Baldwin.

"What's the tiller?" she asked, turning toward the sloop's stern in the direction he'd indicated.

He showed her where to sit and lightly placed her hands on the smooth, wooden bar. "As I recall, you used to be fairly proficient at driving a ski-boat. The tiller is the steering wheel. It's attached to the rudder.''

She let her palms slide lazily up and down the long, glossy handle.

In those thigh-topping white shorts and white eyelet, short-sleeved blouse that tied at the waist, she was exactly the picture of perfection he remembered. She'd pulled back her thick mane of ebony curls into a loose ponytail, making those blue-ice eyes stand out starkly against the creamy background of her cheeks. That is, they did when she took off the sunglasses long enough to see them.

The woman was very nearly too beautiful to bear.

He hissed out a pent-up breath and stepped away from her, determined to continue the cursory instructions from a distance. ''Just remember that when I tell you to go left, you push the tiller to the right—and vice versa.''

Reid unfisted his hands long enough to take off his shoes and moved up the starboard passenger seat to the bulkhead and rigging. As he unfurled the sails and put the boom behind him, he caught a glimpse of Jill as she screwed up her mouth and worked at keeping the bow where she thought it should go while they glided gingerly away from the marina.

With little makeup and those impossible Hollywood sunglasses, she looked fifteen again. The same fresh-faced dynamo he'd wooed and won. He noticed her tongue peeking out between her lips while she was lost in concentration and his heart was totally lost in return.

Keeping both the jib sheet and the mainsheet in his hand, he moved back to sit across from her. ''You doing okay?''

She nodded but didn't take her eyes off the horizon.

He gave her a couple of general sailing instructions and watched her smile as the sloop responded to her touch.

The muggy weather and still back bay began to take its toll on them both. While he gazed at her, sweat broke out on her forehead, trickled down her cheeks and long slender neck. At last, it dripped shamelessly to her breasts and slowly disappeared into the valley between. With such a sight, his own overheated skin broke into a million tiny jets of itchy, tingling sweat that he tried his damnedest to ignore.

"Sure hope the wind picks up when we hit open water," he gurgled past the sudden lump in his throat. "Otherwise, this might turn into a very short and sweltering lesson."

"I'm sure the wind will cooperate." She hazarded a glance in his direction. "And maybe the rain will show up early to cool us off."

"Maybe." He studied her profile and eased off the sails, giving them plenty of leeway. "But if that storm closes in before dark, it'll be an old-fashioned gully washer."

"Mmm." Another smile bubbled across her face.

"You worried, or hopeful?" he asked casually.

"Hopeful." She beamed at him and pushed gently on the tiller. "It's been years since I've been outdoors in a rainstorm without running for cover. When I was little, I remember loving the cool feel of the rain on my skin on a hot day and of all the fun Travis and I used to have trying to catch raindrops with our tongues."

It was Reid's turn to smile at the thought of her as a mischievous pixie dancing through the rain. He leaned back and watched the bald cypress and stately pecan trees pass by on the shore as the sloop slowly made its way out of the harbor. He took a deep breath and thought he smelled the pungent odor of ozone that permeates the air right before the rain begins.

But then, maybe he just wished for it to be so for Jill's sake.

When they reached the open water of Long Lake's main bay, Jill relaxed enough to kick off her deck shoes and put her feet up on the shelf where he sat. Putting one foot on either side of his hips, she leaned back and raised her chin to the sun.

"I'd forgotten how much I love it out here," she said with a sigh.

He wanted her to remember how she'd loved other things as well. But he had a big problem to dispense with first. They needed to have a long discussion.

"Jill, tell me what was so important that you had to take a day off to learn to sail?" He wanted to get her talking.

"I had lunch with Bill yesterday."

Reid caught the frown, pinching the bridge of her nose before she continued. "I wanted to ask him about you going along to the regatta so you could take us to the rodeo afterward, but I didn't get the chance. He informed me that I had to skipper Travis's sailboat in the sail parade on Saturday." She sighed. "I guess my cousin found something he'd rather do than play host to the governor."

"And you are forced to do as Bill demands because…?"

She slanted a dark look at Reid, but quickly looked back to the bow.

"I was the one who thought up this fund-raiser months ago. I've done everything I could think of to publicize it and Bill's campaign. The governor holds the big key to

Bill's getting the party's nomination. I don't want anything to jeopardize that or to make the governor angry.''

Reid's mission for Operation Rock-A-Bye meant he needed to go to that fund-raiser. But he decided all this talk about Baldwin was a good opportunity to get a couple of things out in the sunshine first.

''Sweetheart, why haven't you been wearing Bill's ring lately? Is there something wrong between you two?''

Jill bit down on her lip and threw a quick, furtive glance in his direction before answering. ''I know it looked like I accepted his proposal the night of the ballroom fund-raiser, but I never did.'' She took a deep breath. ''For your information, I wouldn't go around kissing other men if I were truly engaged.''

She threw him a pointed look and pushed the sunglasses higher on the bridge of her nose. ''I insisted he take back the ring that same night. Yesterday I told him to stop hoping...that we'll never be married.''

''Did you decide you didn't want the loss of privacy that being married to the next governor would mean?'' he asked warily.

''Nope. I decided I didn't want to be married to someone I don't love. I've never really loved Bill, and now I know that I never could.''

Reid stifled a sigh. His shoulders felt lighter, and the whole day seemed brighter somehow.

Almost as soon as that thought came, another stronger sensation hit him. Where the heat of the afternoon had been sticky and uncomfortable before, his body now felt on fire. Unbearable needles of electricity burned through his veins.

The lonely, gray desolation that had been his life for so long, cleared away enough for him to see the patchy turquoise skies beyond.

But the time still wasn't right for them. Jill might not want Baldwin, but she also hadn't made it clear she wanted Reid. He couldn't look at her, so he glanced down at his hands and found them shaking uncontrollably.

Any other discussions they needed to have, would have to wait. He couldn't manage to be coherent now if his life depended on it.

"I think I'd better check the…uh…water depth," he sputtered. "There's a couple of shallow spots out here. I don't want us to get into trouble." He stood, swung himself over her outstretched legs and moved to the bow in record time.

Jill watched him stand on the bow with his back to her, checking the sails and gazing out over the clear, blue water. Just how the heck was she supposed to concentrate on sailing when her view of the horizon was blocked by the most amazing specimen of manhood she could ever remember seeing?

The yellow T-shirt he wore, that earlier fit him loosely and now was soaked with sweat, clung to his sculpted contours. That spectacular vision forced a curling warmth to race along her arteries, moving to her center core. She tried harder to think about the direction the boat was headed, but found herself, instead, considering what the muscles of his chest would look like with no shirt at all.

This was definitely not the same male body she'd known so well as a girl.

That thought made her become ever more aware she didn't really know this new Reid. He didn't look quite the same, his voice was deeper now, and he'd apparently given up his old dreams of getting justice and right through the law and politics. Who was he now?

Yesterday at the breakfast table, she'd been kidding herself when she thought that having sex with him would be the same as it had been so long ago. Perhaps there might be a kernel of her old lover buried deep inside him, but the outside was foreign—and just a touch scary.

Jill vowed to keep their relationship on a friendly basis. She'd thought she wanted to talk to him about the kiss they'd shared at the hospital. Now she'd rather they both just forgot it. It simply couldn't happen again.

Soon, she'd ease her guilt and find a way to tell him about Andy. After that, together they could discover new ways to deal with each other as their son's parents. Period.

Today, she *would* keep a steady head. She *would* learn to sail.

That's all there was to that.

A half hour later, Jill's head swam with all the instructions about tacking, which buoy to keep on which side of the boat, and who has the right of way when you encounter a powerboat. Her thoughts seemed scattered, not at all like her usual self. She couldn't concentrate anymore. Perhaps it was the sun, beating down on her head and frying her brain.

Reid must have noticed her sudden quiet, because he lifted an eyebrow and scrutinized her. "You doing all right?"

She wasn't positive how she was doing.

"You're getting too much sun. Even though it's a cloudy day, you'll burn." He quickly moved inside the cabin.

It was cloudy today? She pulled off her sunglasses to glance up at the sky overhead and found only tiny patches of blue, mingling with the multicolors of gray and the threatening black.

Reid returned, took the tiller from her hands and handed her a bottle of SPF-30 suntan lotion.

He sat down opposite her again. "What's happened to you? When we were kids, you always had a tan. Your skin got so dark back then that it lasted all winter."

She shrugged. "There's not too much sun in a courtroom or buried in a law book."

After managing to unscrew the cap, Jill fumbled with the bottle and dripped more lotion on the boat than she did on herself.

"Here let me," he offered. "The wind's died down a bit. Just hang on to the tiller, but don't worry too much about our heading." Reid grabbed the bottle and pushed the wooden bar her way.

He poured lotion into his palm. "Stick your foot up on my knee."

She propped her foot and waited… And waited. Static electricity charged the air, and her nerves went on edge.

Finally, she lifted her head to look at him. His hand was frozen about two inches above her shin and his gaze was locked on her thigh.

"Reid?"

"Wha…what?" He had to clear his throat to speak, making Jill wonder if he felt the same tension that she did.

"The suntan lotion?"

He grinned sheepishly, but the smile didn't put the calm back into his eyes, now ebony colored and flowing with molten fury. Moving with deliberate care, he eased his hand onto her calf and began rubbing the liquid into her skin with circular motions.

Without warning, the humid, steamy heat turned erotic. Jill flushed with the fever of need and shivered with the chills of desire. She demanded that her body behave and attempted to cram the sudden ache of arousal down into a hidden corner where it had resided ever since Reid kissed her.

She gave her body a shake and tried to remember all her good intentions. *Sailing.* She must learn to sail. *Andy.* She had to tell Reid about his son.

But, oh, how this man oozed raw sensuality. His coarse fingertips skimmed over her tender skin and the sensations they caused called to something primal and elemental within her. Her only thoughts were of having those fingertips on other parts of her body, the ones now tightening and sensitive beyond bearing.

Reid moved to the other leg and glanced up at her, his dark eyes burnished with raw desire. She gasped, sucking in air and shaking her head. This had to stop.

"Aren't you finished yet?" she whispered. "Don't you think I'm covered well enough?"

"No," he answered with a rasping voice. "But I don't think I can stand much more."

The smack of the sails against an unexpected gust of wind caught both their attention. She jerked her leg to the deck with a thud. Reid stood to watch the horizon, turning his broad shoulder back to her.

"I suspect we'll be getting that rain you wanted," he warned, as he capped the suntan lotion and pitched it into the cabin.

Jill scrutinized the horizon and coughed to clear her throat. "Is that rain over there already?" She pointed to the far western edge of the lake.

Reid nodded, pulling down hard on the brim of his cap and placing his hands on his narrow hips. "Want to run toward the storm? It'll be good practice in tacking."

She silently acknowledged that both concentrating on her lessons and flying across the water with the wind in her hair might be just what was needed to clear her head. Somehow she had to calm her shattered nerves.

He drew the lines attached to the two sails through a cleat to tighten them and handed her the ends. "There you go. Let's see what you've learned."

Bracing her legs, she held the lines in one hand and grabbed the tiller with the other. Following the wind turned out to be a real challenge, as well as a lot of fun.

The sleek sailboat skated long the tops of the waves when the billowing sails tightened with the rush of air currents. At times, the wind proved to be stronger than she was. Jill had to wrap the lines from the sails around her wrist so that she could hang on to the tiller with both hands.

She found herself exhilarated and laughing—shrieking into the gusts as she moved the boom from port to starboard while Reid scrambled to stay out of the way. She hadn't had this much fun in years.

In a bit, Reid waved at her to slow the boat down. Disappointed the ride had to end, she let the lines loose and the sail luffed in the changing breeze.

"We're a little too close to the shoreline," Reid called to her.

He'd moved up onto the bow once again and gazed down into the darkening waters. "I sort of remember where the channels are, but it's been a long time. I'm sure you'd rather not run aground, skipper."

Jill didn't think that sounded like much fun. Being stuck out here would be embarrassing. She swiveled in her seat to look for other boats that might be available to help if necessary, and was surprised to find that the few others she'd noticed earlier had all disappeared.

The shore didn't look particularly inviting either. They were drifting past a part of the lake where limestone bluffs rose twenty feet straight up from the shallow waters.

"Drop the jib sheet altogether, and turn hard to port…go left. We're about to miss the channel," Reid yelled.

She jerked on the rudder and let go of both lines, feeling the sloop's forward motion slow.

"Not *that* way. The other left." Reid turned to her, at the same time reaching to brace himself against the mast.

"The *other* left? What…" Jill started to question his directions when the sailboat came to an abrupt halt with a sickening thump.

Deathly silence filled the air. The only noise was the soft lapping of still waters against the sides of the now inert boat. In the shallows and lying dead in the water, the smells of rotting fish and freshwater debris filled the air and closed in on Jill's senses.

"You forgot that 'left' means 'turn the rudder to the right.'" Reid broke the quiet with a grin aimed at her.

"Are we stuck here?" she asked.

"We'll see." Reid slowly moved back to the bow, unfurling the smaller, jib sail as he went.

When he finished, he came back to the stern where Jill sat watching him work.

"What can I do to help?"

He chuckled low in his chest. "Nothing at the moment. I'll let you know what to do when I need it."

Reid tore the cap from his head and threw it toward the cabin hatch. Reaching down to pull his T-shirt's hem from the waistband of his shorts, he yanked the garment up and over his head. Then with one swift movement, he vaulted over the transom and splashed into the water next to the boat.

Jill jumped to her feet, shocked at the sudden move

and the fleeting sight she'd caught of the man's muscular chest, covered by a patch of thick dark hair. He'd actually gone into the water still wearing his khaki shorts.

The splash of cold water against his overheated skin caused Reid to utter a single, sharp and descriptive oath. But as he stood, waist deep in the crystal clear shallows, he realized the drastic change in temperature wasn't having the desired affect on his ferocious and growing need.

"What are you going to do?" Jill leaned over the side of the boat to check on him.

Ah. What he wanted to do and what he was going to do were miles apart. This was a fairly public place and she hadn't made it clear that she wanted him to make a move yet.

As Jill bent over the side to peer into the water, his eyes were drawn to her blouse's open V neck. The top button had come undone and Reid's resolve slipped a notch as well.

Two rounded mounds of pink-toned flesh swelled delicately above the lace edge of her blouse. A sharp, sudden pull ran swiftly to his hard arousal. He opened and closed his fists and breathed deeply.

With an immense effort at internal control, he waded around the sloop to find the deepest spot. "We're going to rock this boat back into the channel."

She moved to port, shadowing his movement within the boat. When she was no more than a few inches from his new position, she stopped, holding his gaze with those stunning eyes, the very same color as the lake on a bright day. He found he couldn't take the painful intimacy of the moment and glanced toward the shoreline to get his bearings.

Breaking their connection made him feel like a downright coward so he quickly looked back, only to catch her appraising him with an approving, wry smile on her lips. Seems Jill was having some of the same distracting thoughts he was having. Good.

Reid stood still and did a little more appraising himself. The breeze tousled her curls and a stray strand of hair blew across her lips. His hand gripped the boat's edge as he fought the urgent demand to reach up, gently brush the unruly curls from her mouth and replace the silky stray strands with his lips.

He groaned with the effort of not letting his body move as it demanded and decided the immense pleasure of just looking at her would temporarily have to do. Wondering if he could tap the staggering volcano of burning hot sexual energy and adrenaline building inside him, he shoved hard on the side of the sloop and watched Jill's eyes grow wide as the boat rocked against its natural anchor.

After a couple more violent rocking movements, and with Jill's help on the tiller, the sloop slid back into the channel. Reid clamored back over the side and landed with an undignified thump on the deck.

"Wow! That was terrific. But…" she looked both impressed and wary.

He stood, steadied his breathing and moved aft. "But what?"

"Do all sailboats get stuck in the shallows like that?"

Smiling at her, he decided to tease. "Only if their skippers are inexperienced…or are distracted by a beautiful woman."

She blushed the most exquisite shade of rose, competing with the sun for color in her cheeks.

"But Travis's yacht would be too big for me to push off. What should I do then?"

"Yacht?" Reid was suddenly very interested. "Just how big is Trav's boat?"

"Well, I think I heard him say that it's nearly fifty feet long. I know it's the biggest schooner on all of Lake Austin. That's why the governor expects to be aboard on Saturday."

"Jill, you can't skipper a fifty-foot yacht. At least, not with only a couple hours of lessons on a twenty-foot sloop. Besides, you'll need a crew to man the sails on her. And a schooner that size will have auxiliary engines. In fact, you won't even be under sail for the parade."

"Oh." She looked a little taken aback, but he could see the wheels turning under those soft, dark curls. "Then *you* be the skipper and I'll be the hostess. I'm sure Travis has a decent crew all lined up that we can use."

Reid considered the implications. That would be one way for him to do a little undercover work at the regatta and fund-raiser.

"Okay. I'll do it. But in that case, you really don't need anymore lessons, do you?"

She shook her head slowly, looking a little forlorn and disappointed.

"I'll bring us in," he murmured, hating to see that look in her eyes, but needing to leave her heady, sensual temptation and go back to work. "Maybe we'll get a chance to sail together another day."

He raised the sails, took control of the tiller and began slowly negotiating the shallows. He wanted them back on the main part of the lake and headed toward the shore before he stopped thinking altogether, gave in to his instincts and took her in his arms right here.

"Look," Jill shouted.

Reid's gaze followed her pointing finger, just in time to catch the line of opaque rain moving across the tops of the waves and coming like an onslaught of rotary blades directly towards them.

By the time he moved the tiller again, the driving rain hit their sloop and swung the aft section around violently. The sails were less than useful, and Reid had the fleeting sensation of impending disaster.

Nine

Jill never would forget the way Reid's eyes turned deadly serious as he'd spotted the purple and black threat of an approaching storm front.

"Uh-oh." He left the tiller and dashed up to the mast, unfurling the mainsail as he went. "It's coming too fast for us to outrun. We'll have to sit it out." He'd hollered at her to be heard over the roar of the sheets of rain, pounding against the churning lake water and steamrolling in their direction.

"Wonderful!" She felt the excitement race up her spine at the same instant she noticed the first drops of rain hitting her arms. "I can't wait."

"This is serious." He threw her a frustrated look, finished tying up the folded sails and reached into a storage compartment, dragging out a heavy metal anchor.

At that moment, a flash of lightning split the sky. Two

seconds later, the rumble of thunder crashed frighteningly around them.

They were alone on the bay. No other boaters were stupid enough to stay out in such a terrifying storm. Together, on their small boat, they faced the elements of nature by themselves.

The rain began for real. Jill leaned her head back, closed her eyes and stuck out her tongue.

''Ahh,'' she moaned. The cold prickles of rain against her sensitive tongue were as thrilling as when she'd been a child.

Another crash of thunder and the heavens opened, spilling out the life-giving liquid and returning needed moisture to the earth.

''Let's hope the anchor holds.'' Reid grabbed her arm. ''Come on. We're going below. It doesn't offer much protection from the lightning, but at least we won't drown in the rain.''

He dragged her in the direction of the stairs heading down to the cabin. The boat lurched with a slight roll and the wind swung the stern back around hard, daring the anchor to give way.

She lost her footing and fell into him, realizing for the first time that he was still minus his T-shirt. He never slowed down but slid his strong arm around her waist, steadying her as they headed for the shelter of the tiny cabin.

Reid moved through the hatch first, jumped the three narrow stairs into the cabin below and turned to help her down. She'd just placed her foot on the top rung when the boat pitched once again, throwing her off-balance. Jill tumbled down the short staircase, closing her eyes to await the crunch of knees on the hull bottom when she landed.

Only the crunch never came. Instead, her hands hit a solid, warm wall of pure muscle. At the same time, sturdy arms molded around her, steadying and unnerving her.

Jill's eyes snapped open. Mere inches separated them. And that was suddenly too much space to suit her. She splayed her hands across the searing flesh of his chest and drove her fingers through the coarse, dark hair.

"Uh. It's too tight in here for us to stand, you'd better sit down, honey." He tried to back away, watching her carefully. "I'll find us some towels to dry off." Reid's voice was barely audible.

"No. I want you to be right here."

"Jill." He sighed her name and covered her hands with his. "I've wanted you for such a long time. Seems like forever. Don't say things like that unless you're sure about what you want."

Even with panic and excitement fighting inside her, she stepped closer, anxious to feel the warmth of him.

"Please don't ask me to be reasonable and sure, Reid. I don't want to think right now. I want you to make me stop thinking." On a moan, she breathed a prayer that he wouldn't ask for explanations or demand promises she simply couldn't make.

"Another few seconds and I can't guarantee I'll be able to stop anything," he murmured.

"I don't want you to."

He folded his arms around her and drew her into his embrace. He held her like a fragile doll, yet as he breathed into her hair, she felt his powerful male presence, giving her intensely feminine and decidedly sexual sensations deep inside.

The two of them could never again have a committed relationship. There was too much in their past—too much

between them in the future. They'd been separated far
too long, become different people, with different needs.

Jill knew all her reasons meant she should back away
before he wanted something more from her than she
could give. Whatever else he'd done or not done in his
life, she knew he was honorable enough to let her go if
that's what she demanded. But she wanted this moment.
Needed it like she needed the rain.

Ferocious cracks of thunder noisily exploded through
the sky. The wind thrashed against the boat, rocking it
wildly. Jill sucked in a breath at the thrill of the wild,
savage elements of nature. Reid crushed her closer to
him, keeping her enclosed within the safety of his arms.

Wet bodies and dripping clothes melded together with
a steamy kind of heat. The tingling feel of his hard thighs
against her own softening body, drove her into a sensual
haze. Her bones liquified. Her knees refused to hold her.

Reid's heart leaped into his throat. He backed her up
a step and gently guided her down on the narrow bunk.
She was unsteady on her feet, but he was afraid his
wouldn't hold the two of them either.

He stood beside her, reached for her face and drew
aside a soggy curl that had matted itself to her cheek. He
tucked it behind her ear, but he couldn't force his hand
away from the satin of her jawline. She leaned her face
into his open palm and breathed a sigh.

His eyes devoured her, taking in every detail. His gaze
came to rest on her eyes and searched them, needing
answers, but not wanting to wait for them.

"Make love to me, Reid," she whispered between
breaths.

That same old tingling sensation took over his body
and he relaxed into it, easing down beside her. The first
thing he'd dreamed of doing was tangling his fingers in

her hair. He watched her eyes grow wider while his fingers stroked and sifted through the luxurious black curls.

Taking a steadying breath, he let the scents of rain, musky sweat, and the hint of herb perfume, still lingering in the air, wash over him. No, he couldn't wait for the right words from her, maybe it was still to soon for her to know how much she loved him. But he knew it. Knew it like he knew every crevice and secret, sensual spot on her body.

He'd dreamed of this for far too long. They didn't need words for such a momentous occasion. What he needed was a strength of body and spirit to show her what was in his heart. To take the time necessary to prove that he worshiped her.

The low, dull ache in Jill's belly intensified as Reid's brilliant eyes took on a typical male gleam of appreciation. That look became all the promise Jill needed.

She gave way to the driving impulse that had consumed her ever since the first riveting glimpse of golden brown skin now quivering under her fingers. She let her palms roam over his wet shoulders and down his chest, kneading the hard muscles and reveling in the slick sensuous flesh.

He closed his eyes and groaned—a deep rumbling from within his chest that competed with the thunder for her attention. The sound stirred her senses to new heights. She loved the feel of him, and let her hands move over every inch.

Her fingers unexpectedly encountered an indentation that felt like an old wound. He hadn't had any scars marring his body years ago, and she wondered what had happened to give him such a slash.

Within moments, she found several more old scars, jagged and angry. She started to ask him to explain, but remembered in the nick of time that there were some things she wasn't ready to confess to him. Deciding this was not the right time for *anyone's* questions, she leaned in and placed a light kiss against one of the ragged marks instead.

"You need to get out of these wet clothes," Reid said with a wink.

Never letting his eyes leave hers, he reached for the buttons on the front of her soaking blouse. His big hands fumbled with the tiny buttons as she felt both his trembling need and his frustration with the time consuming task.

"Let me," she said shakily.

She began undoing the blouse from the bottom up, savoring his frustration and the anticipation of the sensual promise of skin on skin. Her breasts began to swell, tightening into aching prominence.

And still, his dark eyes held hers with a steady-as-a-rock gaze. His lean, hard-boned features intensified the devastatingly masculine awareness with which he scrutinized her.

The back of his knuckle grazed her breast as he continued to tug on the buttons. She licked her lips in response, making him groan again. He gave up his struggle, dropped one hand to her waist and used the other to tenderly brush away a trickle of rainwater from her cheek with his thumb's raspy pad.

"Please...take it off," he said hoarsely.

She ripped at the rest of the buttons and shrugged out of the shirt in record time. A cool whisper of humid air wafted across her bare, wet shoulders and she shuddered.

He reached for her again, pressing his lips to the column of her throat. At first, he placed gentle, light kisses on her neck and shoulders, occasionally licking at the rivulets of water cascading down from her soaking hair. But soon his mouth began to claim, devouring her in hungry, arousing kisses.

His mouth commanded. Her gooseflesh rippled in response.

Placing a searing, soulful kiss on her lips, his hands moved to span her rib cage. The sight of her lace-covered breast, full and crested with pouty, rose peaks jutting toward him, made his breath quicken. He should have known his Jill would wear lace under lace.

Everything about her and about their relationship was complicated. But Reid was determined to show her how simple and basic the passion between them could be.

He wanted her to lose control. That way she'd be free of her misgivings and become vulnerable to his spirit. His love surely must've been imprinted upon her soul long ago. He knew her love had resided in every cell of his being from the time he'd been nineteen years old.

He bent his head to lathe her nipple through skimpy material. She sucked in a breath and reached for him with a frenetic movement.

He pulled back and gazed at his darling love. "Easy, honey. All things happen in their own time. I've carried your memory around for ten years. Give me a chance to experience you for real."

Slowly, barely touching her, he skimmed his fingers over the edge of the lace bra, lightly tracing the curve of her breasts. Watching her eyes light with desire, he fingered her nipples through the flimsy, see-through covering, softly pulling and rolling them between his thumb and forefinger.

When she fisted her hands at her sides and closed her eyes, he slid the thin bra straps down her shoulders, unclasped the back fastener and removed the last obstacle to the sinful, satiny sensations he'd been craving. Her eyes opened when the humid air bathed her naked skin in cool sensitivity. She jerked her arms across her chest to cover herself, but he gently tugged them back down.

"No, luv. Please just let me look at you. It's been so long. You're so beautiful."

Helpless, Jill could hardly bear to sit still while his gaze swept over her. But she managed to remain motionless as he held her arms to her side and perused every inch. The erotic caress of his loving look made the blood rush under her skin, tantalizing and sensitizing every inch.

Finally, when she thought she might not be able to stand the assault of his gaze for one more minute, he reached out to reverently touch her breasts. Sliding his palms under the curves, he held their full weight gently and with exquisite care. She felt delicate and adored.

When he began again to explore her skin with lazy, patient hands, her head fell back on a moan. Then his tongue replaced his hands and she jerked as the sensations moved directly to her gut, setting up a throb between her legs.

He exhaled hard and swore under his breath while he licked and nipped her swollen tips. She was so responsive, so sexy. The smoldering desire had darkened her eyes to a midnight blue and began to drug him with need. He cautioned himself to give her more time for relearning their love—their passion. His own needs be damned.

Her hips bucked as he sucked a heated nipple deep into his mouth. Impatience flared and he grabbed the waistband of her shorts and panties, ripping them down her legs, tossing them behind him. It wasn't so much the outside covering he wanted to remove, but his inner being demanded that he strip her to the very essence of her soul.

Finally, she was there before him as he remembered her. And he did recognize every inch of his lover. Patience, he warned himself. There was a time for everything.

This was the time to explore the edge of ecstasy. To bring her to an age-old place of pleasure and massage away all her doubts. Slowly.

He stroked the tender skin on her upper thigh, watching as her whole being rippled with relaxed joy the same way it always had. Placing one hot palm flat on her stomach, he could feel the shudders moving along the deep recesses of her body. Reid was transformed into a conductor, playing a symphony along the plains of his darling's passion.

"Please," she begged. "I need..."

"Yes, my love," he whispered, blowing on the silken flesh below him. "I know what you need. I need, too. But I'm only just getting a good start on telling you how much."

With infinite patience and experienced care, he touched her in places she'd forgotten she possessed. His hands sculpted her muscles, lingered on tender spots. With gentle urging, he brought her to the edge, only to soothe and smooth until she floated back down again.

She was greedy to share this slow burn with him, to take pleasure from watching him writhe under her hands and lips. But Reid wouldn't allow it. Every time she reached for him or began to place a fiery kiss across his skin, he lightly pushed her hands away.

He licked the dripping water from her body, beginning with her toes and moving up her shins to the responsive flesh of her inner thighs. Soon, along with the pulse beat of desire thrumming at her very core, she began to feel cared for, watched over—and loved. Her body responded to his ministrations exactly the way it always did in her dreams. And her heart urged her to remember their soulful unions of the past.

Reid had to tap the immense reserve of control he'd built up over his life alone to refrain from becoming too greedy. Whenever he was tempted to rush, to release his own building fire, he tasted her downy skin once more. Spun honey and fine cognac.

Filling himself with her unique flavors was enough for the moment.

Anxious to sample all of her tastes, he encircled her thighs with his huge hands and spread them wide enough so he could slide between. He slipped a hand under her hips, kneading the silkily tight flesh and lifting them toward him. Blowing lightly over her feminine mound, he smiled as Jill jolted in response.

No longer able to contain himself, he tenderly opened her intimate folds the same way he would peel back the petals on a delicate rose. Finally, he took pleasure in drawing his tongue across the engorged and sensitive bud he found waiting for him. Jill squealed and shook with heated delight.

Letting himself have the treat he'd craved for what seemed like forever, his tongue stroked and his lips sucked the velvet at Jill's core.

She screamed into the howling wind and pleaded with him for the release of the fire consuming her bit by bit. A lightning bolt illuminated their little nest through the tiny portholes, electrifying the air and contrasting its violent onslaught with Reid's slow ministrations.

With a murmuring sigh, he shoved his shorts down and onto the floor then slid up her body, leveraging himself on his elbows until her flushed face was directly below his. "Jill," he reverently whispered her name.

Her legs came around his waist and the look in her half-opened eyes was glazed, tantalizing and erotic. But he wasn't done teasing, preparing her for the love he wanted her to know throughout her entire being.

He allowed his throbbing arousal to nudge her slick opening. Then slowly, carefully, he entered her. By now he was desperate to feel the tight glove of her body surround him. Still, he vowed not to rush.

Half an inch inside—and he withdrew. Jill's breath caught and he watched her try to focus on his face.

Bending his head, he brushed a light kiss over her lips to still her protests. Then with more control than he thought he possessed, he gradually entered her cavern once again. Only to withdraw—just as unhurriedly as before.

Using the shallow-deep thrusting method of the ancient Taoist erotic masters, he continued to bring them both to the very edge of oblivion time and time again. She tried to buck her hips against him, begging him with her movements, but he reached below her once more and, with one hand, held her rounded bottom tightly in his grip.

At last, Reid could stand it no more. Sliding fully into her waiting warmth, he stilled—rejoicing within the blessed tightness and nearly crying out at the pleasure of being joined with the woman of his dreams.

Jill's whole body was afire with little pinpoints of sparks. Never. Never had she thought that being with a man could be so consuming. Her dreams of Reid had recalled a passion and a fire of desire, but this...

This was unspeakable pleasure, an unknowable drive to fulfill a wild and savage command.

He linked his fingers with hers and they began to move

together in a building tempo that suited their intense rapture. Before, Jill imagined that she might spontaneously combust with the flames he'd kindled. Now, her vision blurred with passion and she held on to the cosmic fireworks, riding the explosion to the top of crest. Finally, she detonated in a shower of burning light, calling his name over and over as he swept them both cascading past the pinnacle.

Jill's limp, sated body lay entwined with Reid's and she placed a soft kiss against his throat. The howling storm outside began to subside while the two of them tried to steady their own rapid breathing.

Vaguely, from the back of her conscious mind somewhere, she remembered the jarring thunderbolts of lightning illuminating the cabin as they'd made love. The wind and waves had rocked their boat wildly, but neither of them paid much attention.

The scattered, crashing blasts of nature matched what was happening inside them. The thrill of being at the mercy of the elements couldn't compete with the spine-tingling intoxication of his hands and mouth on her skin.

He stirred, eased back from her and leaned up on an elbow. The loss of his warmth distressed her.

"Don't go." She slid her arms around his neck and pulled him down to her.

Reid chuckled. "I won't go very far away, sweetheart. We're not finished here. But right this minute, I think I'd better check on the boat before we make love again."

"Again?" She swallowed a gasp. "You're kidding."

Leaning his forehead against hers, he whispered lightly over her still heated skin. "No, ma'am. One afternoon certainly won't be enough of you to fill me up...a lifetime might not do it either. But quitting now would only leave us both wanting.''

He pushed up, picked up his shorts and pulled them over his hips. ''And we've both spent far too many years in that state already, thank you.''

Gazing down on the dazed eyes and swollen lips of the woman he loved, Reid wasn't sure he could manage to make a cursory inspection of the boat before his body clamored for him to rejoin their two souls. But for safety's sake, he figured he had to try.

He reached past an interior bulkhead and pulled a towel from a secured compartment. With tender care, he covered her head and rubbed lightly over her hair, drying the excess moisture and warming himself with the friction against his palms.

''Dry off a little, honey. I'll be right back.'' He handed her the towel and ducked under the cabin's hatch for his quick trip to the deck.

Reid scanned the horizon through the softly falling rain. Not another sign of humanity was visible. He worked his way through the rigging, checking on the sails and lines. All seemed to be in order aboard their floating love bed.

He returned to the stern and tugged against the anchor rope, hoping it would continue to hold them for a while longer. It seemed secure, so he swung back to the cabin, not willing to be separated from Jill's warmth for one more second.

''Is everything all right?'' She stood, half in and half out of the hatch, looking up at him.

He nodded and reached for her, but before he could grab her up in his embrace, she scooted out onto the deck. And that's when he noticed she hadn't put on any of her clothes.

Staring down at her naked body, he felt his own stir beneath his shorts. She waltzed around the deck, holding her arms out to encompass the gentle wind and rain. Throwing her head back to blink up at the drizzle, she drank in the delicious mist.

Reid smiled. What a little imp she was. His body hardened as he watched her prancing around, her dark curly hair hanging loosely down her back and a decidedly feminine swing in her gait.

In a few moments, she lay flat down on the passenger bench and closed her eyes against the heavier droplets of water. "Hmm," she purred.

He went still for a long second, then sat down on the opposite bench almost afraid to breath. "Just had to feel the prickle of raindrops all over you, didn't you?"

She nodded, but when she opened her eyes, the heavy-lidded passion he found there tripped him up and ran past all good reason.

As he dropped his shorts on the deck, he watched the water run down her breasts and move into the same crevices he wanted to revisit. She opened her eyes to peruse his body, moaned and raised her arms, beckoning to him.

When he didn't move to her fast enough, she touched him, stroking and rubbing with unbearably erotic stimulation.

"Wonderful," she murmured, just before she arched her back like a cat and lazily spread her legs apart.

That was the all the invitation Reid needed. Gathering her in his embrace, he let the undulating movement of the boat under her hips drive them both to a slow, second burn. The snap of static electricity, left behind by the lightning, hummed down the mast and contributed to the sizzle he felt running through his veins.

At the zenith of their lovemaking, as she gripped him

deep inside and cried his name, he realized Jill was as essential to him as life itself. Too soon, she lay whimpering while he cradled her in his arms, both of them totally spent with shattering release.

Reid pressed a kiss to her temple and wondered why he'd suddenly been struck by a flickering sensation of guilt. He loved her with everything he had to give, and even though she had yet to admit it, he knew she loved him with the same glittering intensity.

So the guilt was a surprise. It certainly wasn't about anything they'd done together.

All right, so maybe he'd neglected to use protection, but frankly, if she became pregnant from their coupling this afternoon, he'd be glad. Grateful, even. He'd give the whole world to have a little brother or sister for Andy, and to watch his darling Jill grow round with a child— their child.

After giving it some more thought, Reid knew the problem. He'd been lying to her. Even if it was for his job at Operation Rock-A-Bye, he simply couldn't let a lie continue to come between them.

Before he told her that he loved her and that their futures were destined to be entwined together forever, the truth of who he was and why he'd really come home would have to be revealed.

A hollow sense of foreboding rose in his chest and he had to close his eyes against the sensation. Fighting the cold, dark intuition, he tightened his arms around the only person that had ever really mattered in his life, shutting out the entire world and along with it, a haunting portend of loss.

Ten

Sunlight glinted off the rippling waters of Lake Austin and bounced against stark-white, billowing sails as Jill watched Reid and Andy help the crew of *Bennett's Pride* secure the yacht to its moorings. Her heart had twisted like the red and black flags atop the many masts when she'd spied father and son working together.

It had been two days since the most spectacular sailing lesson of all time and the guilt was slowly, and without mercy, killing her. She still loved Reid with her whole being. No question about it. Though, she realized making love to him before he knew about his son had been a very foolish thing to do.

The guilt that had held her back before now threatened to destroy her. Never in her life had she let so much time go by before doing what needed to be done.

She turned back to the lake, gazing out at the spectacular sight of a hundred sails moving like multicolored ballerinas over the choppy waters on this perfect late June day. The air fairly reeked of politics and the lingering scents of power and money.

The parade was done—the regatta underway. The governor and Bill would be delivered to the reviewing stands and in a few minutes, she and the two most important men in her life would be able to slip away to the rodeo.

All things should be in perfect order. But of course, they were far from it.

Why hadn't she had the courage to tell Reid about his son in all these years? The night after that magnificent sailing lesson, she'd vowed to tell him the truth the very next day. Unfortunately, Reid had left town first thing in the morning, saying he'd had a problem at work to see to, but that he'd be back by parade time.

So she'd spent the last two days mulling over the best way—and the best time—to tell him about Andy. During those long hours without him, she'd also figured out some of her motivations for not seeking him out during the last ten years to tell him the truth.

Mostly, it was her stupid pride. And, if she really wanted to be truthful with herself, a touch of revenge came into the equation as well. She'd been dumb enough to want Reid to pay for the pain he'd caused her by withholding the joy of watching their beautiful child become a young man.

She sighed aloud, but the breeze scattered the sound in much the same way that her thoughts were jumbled and disjointed. Pain from his youthful rejection still stung, despite her overriding love for the man he'd become. And despite her well-deserved guilt.

The feelings were all tied up with her father's rejection and dismissal when he'd sent her away to Paris. If it hadn't been for her cousin Travis's kindness after her return, she probably would've sworn off of men forever. Maybe she still should.

"Hey, Mom." Andy, skipped over to stand beside her. "Reid says we're all set to change for the rodeo."

Jill placed a palm against her child's cheek, remembering that there would always be at least one man in her life—one young man to whom she also owed a lot of explanations.

But Reid had to be first. She only hoped that both of them would eventually forgive her.

"What's Travis doing here, Jill?" Reid kept one hand firmly holding onto Andy's shoulder while he directed his gaze to the box seats right above them.

Andy twisted and jiggled up and down, trying to break free long enough to run to the railing of the calf-roping ring.

Jill took hold of her son's other shoulder to get his attention. "Stand still. Reid will take you over to meet his friend in just a second."

She looked up at Reid's dark eyes, nearly invisible under the brim of the black Stetson he'd pulled low on his forehead. "I don't know." She threw a glance over her shoulder to Travis and a couple of other men seated in the best seats in the stands. "I mentioned to him that the three of us would be coming after the sail parade today. Maybe he thought it sounded like fun."

"If he'd wanted fun, why didn't he skipper his own yacht this afternoon?" Reid shook his head absently. "Trav never cared much for the rodeo back in school. Why the interest now?"

She shrugged her shoulders. "He said he had to work with one of his legislative committees this afternoon and that's why he couldn't make the parade. And as to why the interest in rodeo now... I have no idea. But I can ask him while you take Andy to meet your old friend.''

"Legislative committee?'' Reid's eyebrows went up. ''I thought the lawmakers were on summer hiatus.''

"They are,'' she admitted. "But he's chairman of a permanent committee with oversight responsibility for the state's Department of Child Protective and Regulatory Services. Seems like Travis spends more time with them than on anything else he does for the legislature.''

Reid shot one more thoughtful look toward Travis, then smiled at Andy while he addressed them both. "We won't be gone long. The rodeo can't come to a complete halt just because two cowpokes want to talk to one of its calf-roping stars.''

Andy twisted out of his mother's grip. "Yeah, Mom. We need to go *now*.''

Jill laughed at her son's excitement, even though she knew her carefree times with both of them were quickly coming to an end. After they took Andy back to the ranch this evening, she had plans to tell Reid the truth. Andy's turn would come tomorrow.

"Don't worry about Andy and don't go very far, sweetheart. Stay near Travis.'' Reid bent to place a blazing kiss across her lips. "When we get back, I believe it'll be about time for Andy to call it a night.''

He winked at her and the gleam in his eyes made them turn that shiny, ebony color they got when he was aroused. "You and I have some things to talk about later.''

Yes, my love, she thought, as she swallowed back a sob of panic and regret. We most certainly do.

Reid had always loved the sights and sounds of the rodeo. The roar of the crowds in the stands. The whirring colors of the buckskins and roans as they kicked up dust, obscuring the fans' view. The giant screen, broadcasting their antics to every corner of the arena.

He breathed in the sweet fragrances of sawdust, leather and sweat, both man's and animal's, while he guided Andy past a retaining wall and into the area behind the chutes. Normally, the strains of country music playing louder than necessary and the crackling energy of the waiting competitors' nervous tension combined to rush adrenaline through every part of his body.

Tonight he had too much on his mind for any such luxury. As he and Andy searched through the mingling cowboys, all waiting their turns to compete, he tried to sort through the various thoughts and emotions all clamoring for attention in his brain.

He should have told Jill who he was long before they ever made love. Failing that, he should have told her immediately afterward.

He frowned at the thought. Too damn much misplaced sense of duty, he derided himself. This overriding need to do everything by the book, to make sure the path was right and the way was clear, might be the death of him yet.

Spending the last two days informing his FBI superiors that he would be breaking cover long enough to tell Jill the truth about himself, then rushing Intelligence to do a speedy minimum security check on her, kept him from doing what his heart knew was the right thing. Simply telling her that he needed her and wanted her to marry him.

Tonight, no such compulsions would stop him. After ten long years, the time was finally right again.

"It kinda stinks back here, don't it?" Andy dragged Reid by the hand as they passed the roughstock pens.

"No worse than the foaling barns when they're all closed up for winter," Reid answered with a smile.

But he knew what the boy meant. A few seconds ago, they'd walked by the concession stands with their mouth-watering smells of Italian sausage, fried onions and cotton candy, and the contrast with the animal smells could knock you down.

Fortunately, at that moment, his old buddy Clayton McCloud came into sight.

"There he is. Hurry up!" Andy jumped with excitement at meeting one of his idols.

Reid greeted his old friend and introduced Andy. Clay sure looked a lot older than the last time he'd seen him.

The thought reminded Reid of the many wasted years without Jill. So much unnecessary heartache. All about to finally be put behind him.

"You on track in the circuit standings again this year?" Reid asked his champion friend.

"I expect I have enough points for the Buckle, if that's what you mean." Clayton pulled a pair of leather gloves from the back pocket of his slightly too-tight jeans. "But this'll be my last year for competition. I'm retiring."

Andy's eyes were round with wonder and admiration. Reid suppressed a chuckle and breathed a silent prayer that someday the boy would gaze up at him with that very same wide-eyed admiration.

For most of his life, Reid had been secretly hesitant to become a father, determined not to rush into making the same mistakes as his own father. But this child made the whole idea seem easy. And definitely worth all the effort.

"You're giving up the spotlight?" Reid poked the cowboy in the ribs and threw him a broad grin.

Clayton chuckled and drew on a glove. "My body won't hold out much longer, old buddy. Besides, it's time

I gave back some to the sport that's done so much for me.''

"Really? What're your plans?''

Reid watched Andy hanging on every word.

"Well, you ever heard of the Little Britches Rodeo?'' Clayton asked.

"Sure,'' Reid answered. "They've been doing good work with kids for years.''

It was Clayton's turn to beam. "Right. They've asked me to come on board. Work with the youngest children, help develop new programs.''

Reid slapped his old friend's back. "Wonderful! I'm impressed. You'll be doing a great public service.''

A buzzer sounded over the distant applause of the crowd.

"That's my cue. I'm up.'' Clayton smacked the glove he'd been holding against his chaps, turning quickly to Andy. "Sorry, we didn't get much time to visit, kid. Maybe I'll see you at one of the Little Britches training camps.''

Andy bobbed his head up and down with gusto. "Yes, sir. I sure hope so.''

On the long walk back to the stands and Jill, Andy was subdued. Probably dreaming of his future and of winning a silver buckle of his own some day.

Reid was grateful for the few minutes of relative quiet. A couple of things pertaining to Operation Rock-A-Bye had been niggling at the back of his mind, and he wanted a chance to sort through them before he totally gave up on thinking altogether when he and Jill had their long-overdue talk.

Being on board that hugely expensive yacht today had made him curious about how his old friend Travis had become so filthy rich in the last few years. Then seeing

Trav tonight with a couple of men who looked more like they belonged on America's Most Wanted list rather than at a rodeo, only served to stimulate his curiosity.

And what was it Jill said about her cousin spending much of his time on the Department of Child Protective and Regulatory Services committee? Just over a year ago, a couple of his Operation Rock-A-Bye agents captured a woman on the Texas-Mexico border who ran one cog in the international baby-selling racket.

That woman had been using her position as an area director for the department to bring non-U.S. babies across and give them legitimacy by placing them temporarily in nearby foster homes. When apprehended, the woman tried to strike a deal with federal prosecutors, but she hadn't known enough about her superiors in the organization to lighten her sentence.

She'd always claimed the big boss was someone high up in the Texas department that protected children. But Reid could never find any evidence of wrongdoing by any one of those hardworking bureaucrats, men and women who selflessly gave of their time to make sure neglected and abused children in the state were nurtured and adopted out to deserving parents.

So... Wealthy, powerful Travis Bennett was chairman of the department's legislative oversight committee? Now wasn't that interesting.

Reid needed to make a couple of phone calls. Which he promised himself he would do, just as soon as he gathered Jill and Andy up and ushered them away from these crowds and out into his truck.

As they rounded the path past the last taco stand, Andy tugged on his hand. "Reid, I've been thinking."

Reid slowed and waited for whatever the boy had to say.

"You know just about everything and everybody that's worth knowing in this whole world," Andy said.

"Well, maybe not everything," Reid amended, grinning at the boy's serious demeanor.

Andy ignored him and continued with what seemed to be a little speech. "I think you'd make the very best dad a kid could ever have. Do you think that might happen someday?"

"What...might happen?"

Andy puffed up his chest and squared his shoulders. "That you'd be my dad."

Reid's heart flipped and he ached to hug this special, little boy. He remembered just in time that at Andy's tender age, hugs were only allowed by moms—not between men.

Needing to clear his throat to say what was in his heart, Reid eventually answered one of the most important questions he'd ever been asked. "I can't think of anything I'd be more proud to do in my life than be your father, Andy." He stuck out his hand to shake. "Let me work on your mom a little bit. I'll see if it can't be arranged."

From her seat in the stands, Jill watched Reid and Andy make their way back to where they'd left her. God, she loved them both so much. Seeing the light in their eyes go dark as she told them the truth, would be the hardest thing she'd ever have to do in her life.

Being deserted before her wedding, finishing law school part time, and raising a child alone were a snap compared to watching the pain in her loved ones faces when they realized she'd been lying to them for all these years.

She forced her wobbly legs to propel her down the

stands' creaky stairs, then waited in the wide aisle with as close to a smile on her face as she could manage. In less time that she cared to think about, all her smiles might be gone for good.

She deserved everything she got—and more. What kind of a horrible person would keep the truth from the men she loved? If they would let her, she'd work every day for the rest of her life to make it up to them.

Andy tugged on Reid's hand and danced his way over to her. "Mom! It was great. Mr. McCloud even talked to me."

"That's wonderful, son. Did you thank Reid for introducing you?"

Andy nodded and grabbed her hand with his free one. "Wait'll I tell you what Mr. McCloud said."

Jill knew, if she let him ramble, they'd be standing there for the next hour while Andy told her every detail. "You can tell me all about it later. Right now, I think we probably need to be going. It's almost your bedtime."

She glanced up at Reid, who stood patiently holding on to the hand of her gyrating son. But he wasn't looking at either of them. His attention seemed riveted to the stands behind her.

"Reid?"

He jerked his chin around to ask his own question. "Where's Travis, Jill?"

"He left as soon as I reached my seat near him. His cell phone and pager went nuts...apparently there was some kind of computer foul-up back at the office and he had to go see about it."

"Computer glitch...on a Saturday night?"

She shrugged a shoulder. "I guess so. Travis has an extra shift of people who work odd hours on special computer projects for him."

"Law projects?" Reid probed. "Or legislative projects?"

"I really don't know." She shook her head and tried hard not to look as foolish as she felt. "Computers aren't exactly my thing. I manage to use them for law research, but anything harder than that sort of loses me. Travis handles the computer department."

Reid looked up in the stands again, absently rubbing his jaw with his free hand. "Did the men that were with him leave as well?"

"Yes." She shuddered remembering the creepy appearance of the two characters Travis never managed to introduce before they all left. Day-old beards, greasy hair and Armani suits all seemed way out of place at a rodeo.

"Do you know who they were? Friends of Trav's, maybe?" Reid's voice got stronger, his words slightly clipped and harsh. "Were they clients, Jill?"

"I really don't know." She shook her head and raised her shoulder blades. "I'm pretty sure they weren't friends."

"Mother!" Andy impatiently pulled his hand from hers and swung that arm in a circle. "I have to tell you about the kids' rodeo."

"Don't interrupt, dear. Later, you can..."

"But, Mom, Mr. McCloud said there's special camps for kids, and junior rodeos...and that maybe he'd see me there...and everything!"

Jill glanced up at Reid. "What...?"

"Clayton is retiring after the last event on this year's circuit." Reid's eyes softened and he chuckled lightly. "He was telling Andy and me about joining up with the Little Britches Rodeo. And..."

Andy jumped up and down, pulling his hand from

Reid's and clapping wildly. "He said he'd see me there. Didn't he, Reid? I can go, can't I Mom?"

Reid squatted down, looking the bouncing boy right in the eyes and lowering his voice to calm him down. "I'm sure that when you turn eight, your mom will consider letting you take one of their training camps."

"Eight?" Andy drew himself up in huff. "I'm no baby. I'll be ten on my next birthday in January and grown-up."

"Well, then," Reid began with a smirk. "Give your mom and me a chance to find out more about..."

Every noise and every movement in the whole arena seemed to still as Reid stopped speaking and stared at the young boy's face in front of him. Even Andy apparently sensed the need for quiet. He glanced up at his mother with apprehension. Jill forgot to breath while she watched Reid making the connections and counting back the years.

Silently he glanced down at his clasped hands, elbows resting on his bent knees. She could see that his knuckles were whitening as he gripped his fingers together.

At last, he looked up at her, the pain and confusion visible on his whole body. "Jill? Why didn't you tell me?"

Uncomfortable and confused himself, Andy moved out of earshot over to the arena's fence and soon became engrossed in the girls' barrel riding. Jill let him go.

"I'm so sorry, Reid." She managed to say on a half sob. "I swear I didn't realize I was pregnant before you disappeared. And I should have told you sometime during the last ten years, but...I...I..." Her voice was raw with emotion, and the words died with her despair.

"Then he *is* mine." Reid bolted upright, fisting his hands, his words a statement more than a question.

But those hard words and betrayed glare widened the hole that was burning through her heart. "Of course," she choked through the haze of pain. "There's never been anyone else."

Jill's brain was a jumble of emotions. Guilt at having kept the two of them apart for all these years was the overriding one. Everything was all her fault. She'd wanted so badly to find a way to save her relationship with both father and son. And now everything was ruined. Both might hate her forever.

Was there some way for her to make amends—even at this point? She had to try. The two of them needed each other, and she needed them. Desperately.

"Reid." The words would be difficult. "Forgive me for not telling you all these years. I was angry. My pride got the better of me."

He stood in silence, rod straight with his hands still fisted at his side. He wasn't going to make this any easier. He'd probably never forgive her.

Deep in her heart, she knew that she'd probably never be able to trust him with her heart again either. But she would trust him with her life—and her son's. That would have to be enough.

"I want you to be his father. I want the two of you to get to know each other now. Don't punish him for my wrongs."

Finally, he managed to speak through gritted teeth. "Just what would you suggest at this late date?"

"Why don't you take him to your mother's ranch for a few days? Get to know each other better. The only thing I ask is that you wait to tell him the truth until I can be there."

"Neither one of us needs your lies anymore, Jill. I'll tell him when I think the time is right."

Without another word to her, he strode over to Andy. "How would you like to spend a few days with me on my mother's ranch...son?" Gentling his words, he turned his back on Jill.

Wary hope lit Andy's eyes and he glanced around Reid's body to the woman holding her breath. "Can I, Mom?"

Building tears blurred the sight of her sweet son while the guilt of not telling him the truth nearly overwhelmed Jill. "Yes, Andy. I think that would be fun for you. But I need another minute to talk to Reid right now."

Keeping his broad back to her, Reid bent on one knee to talk to his son. "Andy, why don't you go get us a couple of corn dogs?" He pulled a few bills from his shirt pocket and handed them over. "Give me a chance to talk to your mom."

"Go ahead, sweetheart," she said, with as much calm in her voice as she could manage. "But just don't forget what I've told you about strangers. Be careful."

"Yes, ma'am." Andy took off, unmindful of the currents of pain and anguish circling the two grown-ups.

The man she'd loved for most of her life stood stock-still in the middle of the wide aisle and stared at her with a mixture of disbelief, hurt and disgust on his face.

"You stole ten years of my son's life from me," he roared at last. "And we made love, but you never once..."

His whole body shook with frustration, and he pulled off the Stetson to wipe his shirtsleeve across his eyes. "I thought you cared. How could you keep my son from me? From his grandmother?" Reid's eyes glinted hard and cold. "And to lie to your own son, for God's sake?"

"Listen to me, please," she cried in earnest. "I fought with everyone in my family, trying to find you. When you left, I was devastated, my pride destroyed. But I swear to God, Reid, I did everything I could to find you…to tell you…until Dad and Mom forced me to leave for Paris.''

He narrowed his eyes at her. ''There never was another man in Paris?''

She shook her head vehemently. ''Never. That was a story Mother told around town to save my reputation. You've got to understand. When I came home, everyone believed it…. And you were living somewhere else, married to another woman.''

Grabbing his arm, her knees buckled. She let her gaze plead with him for some kernel of compassion.

Reid shook her off like he was shooing away some annoying bug.

''I'm taking my son home to get to know his other grandmother. I'll tell him the truth his mother never thought important.'' At her gasp, he spat out one more hurtful statement. ''I think maybe you'd better get yourself a good child-custody lawyer. I certainly intend to do so.''

''Hold on, Reid. Remember I'm an attorney…and his mother. You wouldn't stand a chance in court.''

He turned his back on her and searched for Andy in the crowd. ''We'll see, Jill.''

''Don't do this, please.'' She reached to touch his arm, but once again he jerked away. ''I don't want to fight you. No one would win. I want what's best for Andy.''

Without another word, Reid walked toward his returning son. She couldn't possibly bear to face him in a court.

Jill dropped her hands to her sides and slumped. She deserved every bit of this. But, oh dear Lord, the pain was excruciating.

Eleven

"I understand that your pride is hurt, son." Reid's mother slammed a cookie sheet onto the worn-out butcher block counter in her kitchen and reached for a spatula. "And, of course, you have every reason to be indignant."

Taking a deep breath, Reid figured he was in for a lecture. In the two days since dropping Jill off at her mother's ranch and driving away with his son, he'd given himself enough lectures to last anyone a lifetime. He'd sort of hoped that his mother would take his side and go easy on him. But sympathy was apparently not on her agenda this afternoon.

Holding one edge of the sheet with her favorite "antique" kitchen rag and shoving the burnt-edged, wooden spatula around with the other, June Sorrels spoke her piece. "I mean, you being so *honest* and all." A little biting sarcasm served with chocolate chip cookies was exactly his mother's style. "To me…it seems like a man who's never told a lie should have the right to expect everyone else to treat him with the same respect."

"Very funny, Mother. You know that my job is the reason I have to make up stories. I'm undercover in order to bring criminals to justice. It's not the same thing at all." Reid reached over to snag a chocolate chip cookie before she could shovel it onto the waiting platter, only to burn his fingers in the process. "Ow."

"Hmm." She set the spatula down and drew him to the sink and placed his hand under the cold water faucet. "I'll bet my grandson knows the difference between a lie and the real truth. And I'm positive he has more intelligence than to get his fingers burned stealing cookies."

She shook her head, leaving his hand under the running water as she picked up the scraper once again. "Now, just *how* did I go so wrong with you?"

Her eyes crinkled at the corners, twinkling with obvious delight, even though a frown turned down the edges of her mouth.

Standing here in the old kitchen where he'd been raised, smelling the delicious aroma of baking cookies and hot apple crisp, Reid fervently wished that his life had turned out the way he'd always hoped. He'd give anything not to have become this jaded, fatigued captor of bad guys—one who'd not only learned to lie easily, but who'd also been forced to make his mother learn to lie for him.

She'd never complained about telling friends and neighbors made-up stories about what he was doing for a living and why he hadn't come home in over ten years. But it had always hurt to ask her to lie for him. Hurt deep inside where he'd buried all the distasteful things from his past life.

A mere two days ago, he'd made the decision to begin living his life by the truth again. And he'd been planning on starting with Jill.

Now, he couldn't even face the prospect of telling Andy that he was his father. Some truths seemed harder to tell than others.

"Cookies!" Andy burst through the back door, his boots still caked with cow manure. Streaks of sweat and hard-earned dirt colored his face and neck.

Reid's heart nearly popped right out of his chest with love for this child who was all boy, yet sweet and considerate enough to capture anyone's heart.

Except—when there were chocolate chip cookies involved.

Taking after his father, Andy reached for the still too-hot platter only to be swatted away with an old kitchen rag. "Ouch, Grammy." He looked emotionally stung by the woman who'd asked him to call her Grammy even before he knew the reason why. "Can't I have a cookie, please?"

Her face dimpled into a broad smile. "You *may* have lots of cookies..."

He started to reach again and she grabbed his hands in both of hers. "*Just* as soon as you wash these hands and take off the hat and those filthy boots."

Andy frowned for a second then grinned up at her. "*How* many cookies?"

She tsked at him and pursed her lips to keep from laughing out loud. "Lots. And I have a special treat, too."

His eyes widened.

"Some good boy, who comes back into this kitchen

with boots off and hands scrubbed clean, will get to lick the mixing bowl if I haven't already washed it by then. You have any idea who that'll be?''

''Me!'' He took off, clopping across the linoleum at a gallop. ''I'll be back in a minute.''

Reid watched his mother smiling at the disappearing back of his extraordinary son, and found himself wishing they'd had so much more time together. *All* of them.

He'd finally gotten hold of his pride enough to realize Jill had only done what anybody would have done under the same circumstances. She'd been young and in trouble, and the person she'd thought she could count on to be there for her had disappeared.

It nearly undid him to remember her wounded look, standing there in the middle of a crowded arena aisle pleading with him to see the past through her eyes. Her pale face and the haunted cast in those crystal blues seared him with an ache that he'd been wallowing in ever since.

Part of his pain had come from guilt. From allowing his pride to stop him from going to her in Paris when he'd been released from the hospital all those years ago.

Reid didn't doubt for one minute that *she'd* tried to find him at first. The real question in his mind now was why her father had been so adamant that she stop looking. Had he known what his daughter would've found?

''You going to tell Andy today that you're his father?''

His mother's rather chastising tone of voice broke into his thoughts. ''I'm not sure I have the words, Mom.''

''Oh, for goodness' sake.'' She went back to the oven, opened the door and checked another batch of cookies. ''The words will come from your heart. You think too much.''

Before he could argue his point and explain how he

couldn't bear to see the hurt in his child's eyes when he found out his mother had been lying to him for his whole life, Andy appeared in the doorway. Hair combed, feet clad in socks only, and hands held out palms up for inspection, he smiled shyly at his irascible grandmother.

"Was that fast enough? Do I get to lick the bowl?"

"Sure you do. You win. You're the fastest and cleanest kid in all of Texas." She went to him, wrapped an arm around his shoulders and guided him to the kitchen table. "You start on this bowl while I get you a glass of milk."

She set the mixing bowl in front of him and turned around to Reid. "Would you like some cookies and milk now, too?"

He chuckled at his mother's tendency to use food to soothe away any problems. But he sat down opposite his son and dug into the platter of cookies with gusto, just the same.

"Yes, ma'am. I sure would," he mumbled past a cookie.

She busied herself getting glasses and milk, all the while talking over her shoulder to her grandson. Both Reid and his son would've had trouble answering any questions with their mouths stuffed with cookies and dough, but she never asked them any. She simply babbled on about baking for people who appreciated her efforts.

When Andy was done with the bowl, he moved on to the enormous mixing spoon. His grandmother poured him another glass of milk.

"You ever thought much about your real, true father, boy?" she asked as she put away the milk carton.

Reid nearly choked on a chocolate chip. Andy just nodded and took a sip of milk.

"Yeah, I figured you had," she said, and threw Reid

a keep-your-mouth shut look. "What do you think he'd be like?"

"I know what he'd be like. He'd be 'xactly like Reid is."

"Oh? How do you know that?"

"Mom told me," Andy mumbled through cookie dough. "She said he was big and strong and knew about everything."

"Did she say anything else?" Reid couldn't help but ask one little question of his own, even if his mother did smack him along side the head with the rag.

Andy thought about it for a second. "She said he wanted to help people and that he'd never lie to anybody on purpose...and that she'd loved him very much."

Reid's mother rested a hand on her grandson's shoulder and spoke gently. "You know, Andy, sometimes things don't work out the way we want them. Sometimes people accidentally hurt themselves and others when they don't really mean to."

Andy nodded and reached for another cookie. "Oh sure. Like when I fell in the bull's pen. I didn't mean to get hurt or to scare Mom, but it just happened."

"Right. Like that." She sat down next to him and waited until he looked at her face. "What would you say if I told you that Reid *was* your really, true father, and that he didn't mean to stay away from you so long, but things accidentally turned out that way?"

Andy shot a glance at Reid, hope coming alive in his eyes. Then he turned back to his grandmother, looking decidedly thoughtful and too grown-up for his own good.

"Mom knows you're telling me this, right?"

Reid held his breath. His own mother had started this, and he prayed she had a good way to finish.

She smiled at Andy and put a hand on his arm. "Yes,

son, she does. But she hasn't known how to explain it to you. Parts of the story are complicated and you need to be a little more grown-up to understand.''

A very long and suspenseful couple of seconds later, Andy jumped up and ran to Reid. ''You're really my dad?''

Reid chanced a hug and whispered in his son's ear. ''Yes, son. I'm your father and I love you very much. I'm sorry I haven't been a part of your life in the past. But now that I've found you, I promise we'll never be apart for long again.''

Andy drew back and studied his father's face. Reid wondered what truths or lies he saw there.

''Should I call you 'Dad'?''

''Certainly, you may.'' Reid's heart turned real flips. ''Or maybe you'd prefer 'Papa'…or 'Daddy?' Call me whatever feels best to you.''

The truths of a child's life came simple and unhampered by old guilt or remembered slights.

''Way cool!'' Andy moved back to his grandmother's side. ''Can I have a cookie now, Grammy?''

Jill lowered her cheek to the cool, shiny surface of her mahogany desk. Coming in to work today had obviously been a mistake. But being at the ranch with her mother's I-told-you so's and her own conscience nagging at her had been more than unbearable.

Talking to Andy on the phone hadn't helped much either. He'd babbled on about Reid being his ''really-truly'' dad, and she never could hear any blame in his voice. She needed to talk to him in person, but she didn't want to spoil his time with his father. Mrs. Sorrels had invited her to the ranch several times. Jill couldn't bear the sight of Reid's disdain, so she'd declined.

She closed her eyes and fought the images she'd imagined of Andy's face as he learned of his mother's mistakes. How long would it take before he stopped hating her deep down inside, she wondered?

The phone on her desk buzzed loudly next to her head. She dragged herself upright and forced her hand to pick up the receiver.

"Jill?" Her caller was Bill. "You sound terrible."

Shaking her head, she wondered what else life could do to aggravate her today?

"Yes, Bill, it's me. Thanks for reminding me of how bad I feel."

"I hope you're not sick," he mumbled politely, but then never gave her a chance to deny or confirm it.

"I heard a terrible rumor this morning, Jill. And I want you to tell me that it's not true."

"You know better than to believe everything you hear," she cautioned him.

"Well, this came from a particularly reliable source." Barely taking a breath, Bill started in with his interrogation. "I want to know if Reid Sorrels is your son's father. I've heard the stories about you two coming close to a marriage some years ago. But I thought the deal fell through at the last moment."

Jill cringed. There was only one "reliable source" who could have told Bill. Her loving cousin Travis.

"Is it true that you weren't married to Andy's father? And if so, was the story about the husband in Paris also a fabrication?"

"Yes, Bill," she sighed. "All of that is true."

"I see." He followed that pronouncement with a couple beats of dead silence. "Look. I don't want to appear to be a rat deserting a sinking ship, but you must know that a political campaign can ill afford to have any scandal lurking around the corner.''

"Yes, Bill," she managed. "I understand."

"Good. Because then you can understand why I'm forced to fire you as my campaign manager. I've already contacted a party professional to take over in your place. I'm sorry, Jill, but I have to watch my backside. You know that."

"Yes, Bill," she said through clenched teeth. "I know that your backside is the most important thing in the world to you. And I sincerely hope you two will have a long and fruitful life together."

She slammed down the phone and hung her head in her hands. *Men.*

The first one to betray her was Reid when he left with no word. Next came her father when he turned a cold heart to her pleas for help in finding her lost fiancé. Then Reid showed up, only to break her heart all over again. Now, foolish Bill Baldwin was cutting off an easy path to the governor's mansion with her as his chairman just because of his injured pride.

And then there was Travis. Her cousin had been acting so strangely lately. What was with him, anyway? Normally easygoing and competent, lately Trav seemed scattered and distant.

This morning she'd tried to talk to him about her heartbreak and fear over what Reid would say to Andy. But Travis had cut her off, claiming he was swamped with troubles in his computer department. For the life of her, Jill couldn't understand why he didn't just hire someone to solve his problems. Or what the heck was so important that they couldn't get along without the computers for a few days?

And then for Trav to betray her by telling Bill about

Reid... Well, all men were jerks. She vowed to be done with them forever.

All of them except Andy, of course. She just had to pray that he wouldn't decide to be done with *her* forever.

Like a miracle of faith, at that exact moment, Andy burst into her office with his usual youthful exuberance.

"Hiya, Mom. Guess what?"

Her throat threatened to close with the emotion of seeing her only son standing within inches and smiling as if he hadn't a care in the world. She could do nothing but shake her head in amazement.

"Grammy Sorrels says we can all come live on her ranch if we want. She bakes the very best cookies in the world, you know. Dad says she can cook all kinds of good stuff...and she knows how to rope steers, too. Not just calves, but big giants...and she puts brands on them and everything!"

Andy finally had to take a breath and Jill quickly reached for him, tugging him close. "I take it you had a good time, son," she said, smiling into his hair.

Without releasing her grip on Andy, she glanced up and found Reid leaning against the door frame and grinning with the silliest expression on his face. With no hat, his silver-tipped hair hung casually on his forehead. Dressed in jeans and a long-sleeved western shirt, he looked as young as the first day she'd met him—over half a lifetime ago.

She gently placed her hands on her son's shoulders and set him back far enough so that she could see his face.

"Isn't it great about Reid being my dad?" Andy wiggled out of her grasp. "Now we can all live together forever. You were right when you said God will answer your prayers if you're good and ask real nice."

She touched her son's warm hand to satisfy herself that

he was truly there—and seemingly not angry at her at all. But welling tears kept her silent and biting on her lip once more. There wasn't much chance of them all living together. Not with Reid hating her forever.

Reid stepped closer. "Sorry to just barge into your office like this, but…" He placed a hand on Andy's bare head and rolled his eyes with phony exasperation.

He gazed down on his own soul in the form of the beautiful woman who'd stolen his spirit so many years ago. He wasn't sure exactly what to say to her to let her know she was his whole life. How to tell her what was in his heart? He only knew that lies would have to stop coming between them. There was too much at stake now.

"Uh. Can you take the rest of the afternoon off, by any chance?" he asked over Andy's bobbing head.

She stared up at him with a mixture of stunned confusion, lingering hurt and perhaps a little bit of love. That last feeling was the one Reid wanted to explore—and maybe to build a life upon.

"Ye…yes," she stuttered. "I guess I can. Why?"

"I think you and I should have a long conversation. There's something important that you need to know about me."

Her eyebrows narrowed, but she kept her gaze focused.

"But right now, can you close the office down for the day and drive Andy back to your mom's ranch? I have a small chore to do here first, then you and I can ride out to that little creek where we used to talk. Remember?"

"Of course, I remember." The look in her eyes softened but was still confused and wary. "But why can't you drive back with us?"

Without answering her directly, he slipped into his professional shell and got ready to face his nemesis. "Is Travis in his office?"

"I think he's back in his computer room," she said warily. "But I haven't seen him since this morning. Why?"

"This has nothing to do with you, Jill. Take Andy home," he urged. "I'll join you in a little while."

Twelve

Reid found Travis alone in a back room, shredding papers and packing up boxes of computer diskettes and CDs.

"You won't get very far, Trav," he muttered as he stepped into the room. "We've got men surrounding the place, and everyone else has been evacuated from the building. Why don't you take your chances making a deal with the federal prosecutor? Maybe you'll get lucky?"

"You?" Travis plopped down in a nearby secretary's chair and stared up at Reid. "I should have known. Ever since you came back to town, things have gone to hell. And then Saturday when we noticed our security had definitely been breached, I figured the Feds would show up soon. That's why we destroyed all the hard drives this morning."

Travis waved his arm at a nearby easy chair, indicating Reid should help himself to a seat. "Any deal is likely not in my future, buddy. My…uh…'backers' from up north wouldn't let me live long enough to collect my end.'' He rubbed a hand roughly across his forehead. ''What agency are you with, Sorrels?''

''FBI. Though it doesn't really matter.'' Reid wondered if Bennett was armed and decided to remain standing for this little chat. The man looked haggard and nearing exhaustion.

''So, how'd you all of a sudden get so smart?'' Trav asked wearily. ''Or have you been trying to trap me into something for the last ten years and only just now got a clue?''

If he'd been the true professional he'd always imagined himself to be, Reid would have frisked his old friend, placed him under arrest and read him his rights. Instead, at the mention of old times, he felt compelled to probe Travis for some answers as to what happened on that fateful wedding eve so long ago.

''I guess I'm still not smart *enough*. What part did you play in what happened to me back then?''

Travis scrutinized him with a raised eyebrow, a frown and, at last, a heavy sigh. ''I suppose it doesn't matter anymore whether you know the truth or not. It's all over.'' He slumped farther down in his chair and crossed his arms over his chest. ''I knew you'd end up causing me trouble…ever since I first learned that those idiot goons I hired hadn't managed to actually kill you ten years ago.''

''*You* hired?''

Travis shook his head with an absent motion. ''Jeez. I guess I'll have to spell it out for you. I set you up, old buddy. You were *such* a goody-goody, and I had *such* a lucrative deal about to take shape with that character from Philadelphia.'' Trav smiled, shaking his head again.

"Well, I couldn't let you ruin things, now could I? Besides, your days were already numbered. There was no way in hell I would've let you become a partner in Bennett and Bennett. You weren't born to be one of us. You didn't deserve it."

Reid was flabbergasted. He'd reconciled himself to the fact that his old friend was now a crime boss, deeply involved in international baby-selling and murder, without scruples or remorse. But it never occurred to him that Travis had been this cunning and devoid of principles ever since they'd been kids.

"You hated me enough to kill me?" he asked somberly.

Travis waved the question off. "Hate has nothing to do with it. I certainly didn't hate Uncle Andrew, but I had no trouble at all ordering him killed when he got in my way. It's all a question of money, pal."

"Jill's father was murdered?" The revelations kept coming fast and furious and Reid had trouble keeping up with the evil spewing from the man he'd once considered a friend.

The look in Travis's eyes turned absolutely fiendish, and Reid felt his own hate and anger boiling up from some dark place within him that he hadn't known existed.

"One can order anything done...with enough money." Travis snapped his fingers. "Easy. Besides, the old jerk managed to piece together what was really going on with me and the firm."

Travis's smile became malevolent. "Dear Uncle Andrew belatedly realized I'd lied to him. For months I'd been trying to talk him into making what he'd thought would be a legitimate deal with that syndicate guy from Philly. But then that idiot knocked you out in front of Uncle Andrew instead of waiting until you'd left the house. So I had to tell Andrew that you two had been in cahoots and had lied to us both.

"A few weeks after that, my uncle figured out the truth." Travis's eyes glazed over with the memories. "With his daughter safely sent away, Andrew spent a couple of months checking the company's records. He was just about to turn me over to the authorities and begin searching for you.

"He had to go."

A red haze of fury rioted through Reid's veins. The man before him was the devil personified. He needed to be dead.

Fisting his hands, Reid shoved them in his pockets to keep from putting them around Bennett's neck and squeezing until the life ebbed away, taking along with it all the man's heinous acts against mankind—and saving the government a lot of trouble and expense.

Instead, Reid backed up a step, clenched his jaw, and slowly withdrew the weapon he carried in his waistband holster. He'd always sworn to defend and uphold justice. He would not take revenge.

Despite this almost incredible coincidence of Travis being the man Operation Rock-A-Bye had hunted for so long, Reid was relived that two mysteries had been answered with one capture. Travis was not the same man as the one he'd thought he'd known as a boy.

He narrowed his eyes, trying to judge if Travis would reach for a weapon, but the pitiful blob of humanity before him was obviously defeated. Reid was almost grateful to Travis for telling him the truth of what happened long ago. But not enough to offer him any significant advantage.

"You know it's all over, Trav. On your feet. I need to

read you your rights. Then you can call an attorney before we head off to find you a cell.''

The long shadows of approaching nightfall streamed
across the wide Texas hillside, bathing Reid and his horse
in dappled sunlight as he rode silently next to Jill, sitting
atop her old favorite, roan mare. She breathed in the scent
of cedars, hay and Fourth-of-July wildflowers.

Curiosity nagged at her from every side. Instead of
showing up at her mother's ranch in ''a little while'' like
he'd said he would, it'd been almost three hours later
when Reid finally arrived and they'd saddled the horses.
He'd looked like death warmed over, tired, haggard and
beat down further than she'd ever seen him.

What had happened to him after she'd left was only
one of the many questions she needed to ask. But he'd
soberly asked her to wait until they were alone before he
answered anything. Jill suspected he needed time to get
his head together and figure out what he wanted to say.
She'd remained quiet, but her mind raced ahead in full
orchestration.

Had he gone to Travis seeking legal advice on how
best to take their son from her? Did he want to share
parenting responsibilities, or did he hate her enough to
try stopping her from ever having any say-so in Andy's
upbringing?

Her mind raced. She didn't want a court fight, *please
God*. There had to be a way of working this out so that
Andy wasn't hurt any more than he'd been already.

Stunned when Andy acted so casual after learning the
truth, she figured you could trust kids to cut to the real
meaning behind all the fuss. He didn't care one whit
about the past. All her child wanted was a bright future

that included both a mother and father—now that he actually had one of each.

Just when she thought she might explode with curiosity, their old meeting place next to the stream came into view. The willows by the side of its bank brought back memories of steamy kisses and passionate make-out sessions under its boughs. Light breezes rippled the tops of the tall, summer grasses in fields beside the stream, reminding her of their long walks and soul-revealing talks.

As they dismounted, she remembered that long ago they'd fallen in love at this place.

Turning to watch Reid's tall, broad figure while he tied the horses and pulled a couple of blankets from the saddlebags, Jill realized she loved him more than ever. As a girl, she'd been self-centered and controlling. She hadn't really been prepared for the kind of love she'd found in Reid.

Now, even with the fear that he might try to take her son, she knew that his was the only love that would ever matter to her in life. There could never be anyone else who touched her soul like he did.

But this time—she was strong enough and prepared enough to go on without him. Just as long as he didn't take try to take Andy with him when he left. She'd be forced to fight him, and that might destroy her relationship with her son.

He handed her a thermos of coffee and spread the blankets. She made herself comfortable as he poured each of them a cup of the hot liquid he'd begged from her mother's cook.

Longing for his deep-set, ebony eyes and practically drooling over the way his full lips moved over the edge of the coffee cup made Jill squirm in her jeans. This would not be the same as the old times they'd had in this place. Her dearest love was about to give her some very bad news, she could just feel it coming.

She straightened her spine and promised herself she wouldn't break down. If he was going to ask for her son, the least she could do would be to face it with a little pride.

"There's so much to tell you, Jill. I barely know where to begin." He glanced over to the stream and looked like he was about to say something they'd both regret forever.

She steeled herself a little more. "Did you see Travis?" she whispered and bit down on her lip.

"Yes, and telling you about that will be difficult, but first... I have something else I must get off my chest."

He watched her eyes grow round and her tongue peek out from the corner of her mouth as she tried to concentrate on his words. The little speech he'd practiced would be the absolutely hardest thing he'd ever had to do. Things like hiding in a dismal swamp for thirty-six hours while waiting for a suspect to cut and run or having to shoot a man you'd befriended in an undercover sting... None of that compared to the pain he was about to cause the woman who'd become his every reason to live.

"Jill, I've been lying for so long...and to so many people...that I'm not sure I can..." The confusion began to overtake the wariness in her eyes, and he forced himself to get on with it. "Look. I don't work as a bureaucrat for the Treasury Department like I told you. I'm really a special agent in charge for the FBI...head of one of their major undercover operations."

"The...FBI? You mean you're in federal law enforcement?" she stuttered.

"Yes, sweetheart. You want to see my ID?"

She shook her head. "I believe you, Reid. You never used to be a liar."

That small hurt couldn't possibly compete with the pain of telling her the whole truth. "I did stay with the law like I always said I wanted, Jill. Just not in the way we'd planned."

"But how...why?"

He found himself gazing down into the depths of the black coffee in his hand. If he had to look at her through this, he'd either break down and cry or end up smothering her in his arms before he finished. He had to tell her about her family. The rest could wait. But revealing family secrets could easily put a wedge between them forever.

"It's a long story. Just hang on long enough to hear me out. For the last six years, I've headed up an FBI undercover operation that was created to hunt down a very clever gang of kidnappers. Men who've been stealing babies from both sides of the Texas-Mexico border and selling them for top dollar to desperate and wealthy Americans unable to have their own children."

He took a hard breath and hurried to finish so he could take her in his arms—if she'd let him. "Following a promising lead, I came back to Austin in the guise of a bureaucrat on vacation, headed for his law school reunion. We figured the main boss of this syndicate had to be in the state legislature, and that maybe I could find him through my old friends."

Her confused and anxious look nearly stopped him cold. Somehow he wasn't telling this right. Unfortunately, he had no choice but to barge ahead the only way he knew how.

"I came back intending to use Travis...and *you*...if need be, to get our man." He rubbed at his aching jaw.

"I didn't have any idea what surprises were waiting for me here."

"You mean about Andy?" Jill's voice suddenly felt raspy, cracked and raw.

He blinked a couple of times, then softened his gaze. "Well, that. The identity of the man we'd been seeking...and a couple of other things, too."

Jill could barely sit still. She couldn't be angry with him for lying to her. She hadn't been the most truthful person on earth herself. At least his lies had been for the job.

The questions and confusion about why he chose now to tell his story were burning her from the inside out. How did Andy figure into this?

"So you found your suspect?" she ventured.

He nodded, and she wondered if that meant he'd been trying to tell her he was now free to leave—taking their son with him.

Reid glanced down at the ground and when he looked up again, his eyes were full of pain. "Jill, I can hardly believe this myself, but our suspect was Travis."

She could feel her head shaking uncontrollably. "My cousin Travis? No way."

As Reid patiently explained about Travis's kidnapping scam, Jill began to see the truth of how her cousin could've been exactly what Reid claimed he was. She didn't like it. After all, Travis had been the one she could count on for all these years. But the more she thought about his odd behaviors the more she believed.

When she was totally convinced, she began to worry. "Am I in trouble too? I mean, because I was his partner?"

Reid smiled. "No. It's clear he kept you and his legitimate business and political dealings separated from his illegal pursuits.''

She breathed in a long, cleansing breath. But her real concerns had not been addressed. All the men in her life were deserters or just plain bad. All but one. And she just refused to lose Andy. Not now, when everyone else was gone.

She couldn't stand the suspense any longer. ''Reid, are you planning on taking Andy away from me? It would be terrible for him if we go to court.'' She hesitated, needing to clear her throat and get ready to beg. ''I swear, if you'll give me a break, I'll find a way for us to share custody. I'll move wherever you want to live so we can be partners in his upbringing. I'll do everything the way you want it. Just please don't fight to take away our son.''

''Take him?'' Reid's dark eyes searched hers with something akin to a confused glare.

She ventured one more plea. ''Just talk to me about it first, please?''

He grinned and reached for her, but she shrunk back. ''I have no intention of taking Andy away from you, sweetheart.''

The look of tenderness on his face made everything a thousand times more confusing and potentially more painful.

''I love you,'' he began. ''I've never stopped loving you. I just had to clear away the guilt and the pride long enough to recognize it. I have no intention of going any-where without you...and Andy. I want you and I to be married. To be together the way we were always meant to be.''

She looked so shocked, so stunned, that he needed to reach out to her. He wanted her to feel the love and the need in his heart through the warmth of his body. To give her the truth of his feelings with his kiss.

She remained outside his touch.

"Nnn...no," she stammered at last. "We...can't. I...can't."

"Can't?" Was it because he'd arrested Travis? Or had she decided she couldn't love him because he hadn't come looking for her all those years ago?

"We can be friends, Reid. Partners in caring for our son. But I won't marry you."

Fear and panic seized him. There was no way she could really mean this. Gruffly, he dragged her into his arms.

"But...you love me. I know it as sure as I'm breathing air. I can see it in your eyes when you look at me. I felt it within your body when we made love." He held her close, breathing in the sweet, seductive smell of shampoo and the old scent of herbs he'd craved for so long. "Why won't you marry the man who loves you—the father of your child?"

A very real desperation was beginning to creep into his voice and he fought to remain calm. "Don't let old problems stand between us forever, my darling. We have a son who needs us both...together."

She trembled within his embrace and shoved against his chest until he had to let her push back. Her eyes were bruised, tear-streaked and red from her constant brushing them with the back of her hands. He couldn't stand the icy determined look he spied behind the deep pain.

"I do love you, Reid. More than even I imagined possible. But..." She sniffed and set her chin. "It isn't guilt that will keep us apart... It's fear. I'm petrified that you will leave me again like you did before. I can't need any

LINDA CONRAD 179

man the way I'm beginning to need you. The last time just about killed me.''

"Wait a minute. Let me finish explaining." Reid tried to keep the panic out of his voice. "I didn't leave you ten years ago. The night before our wedding Travis contrived to kill me. He muffed the job, but I was knocked unconscious and nearly every bone in my body was broken. I awoke weeks later two hundred miles away in a hospital bed with my jaw wired shut.''

He rushed to finish what he never thought he'd tell her. "It was Travis who was the liar. He...he even ordered your father's murder. He's an evil man, Jill.''

"My father's accident was planned? No...no! Please stop. I can't hear anymore.''

She looked stunned and like she might be about to go into shock, but he knew his Jill was strong enough to take it. He had to finish. Had to make her understand.

"Mom finally found me in the hospital and told me your father was killed...that you'd gone to Paris and married someone else.

"Jill...darling Jill... My pride was crushed along with my body. I thought you didn't care enough to come looking for me. Once or twice, I even imagined that you'd been in on whatever happened to me. I was hurt... devastated.''

"And the woman you married?'' Her voice was cracked, rough but still strong.

"My physical therapist. I turned to her for comfort. She was kind and I desperately needed to believe I was still lovable. It was totally unfair to her. I can't believe I managed to end that marriage in friendship, but thank God she was as wise as she was kind.''

Jill pushed the back of her hand against her mouth, trying to stifle a sob. This was the truth finally? It was

too much to take in all at once. Her father. Her cousin.
The guilt of not being there for Reid when he needed her
so badly. She began sinking into a pit of depression that
was far worse than the guilt of not telling him about
Andy.

He reached for her, but she moved away again. Too
soon. Too much. She could forgive him, but could she
ever really forgive herself?

"I can't," she moaned.

"Can't what?" Reid narrowed his eyes. "Can't forgive me? Can't trust me?"

"I'm sorry. I...just can't."

Battling back the urge to curl up in a ball and disappear
into her own despair, she ran toward her horse and back
to a life full of emptiness. She deserved far worse.

The next day, Jill had a visitor. Deputy Manny Sanchez stopped by on his way to give a deposition in
Travis's case.

"This is none of my business, ma'am, but I hate to
see my old friend hurting so badly," Manny said, as she
offered him a chair.

Oh God. She'd hurt Reid yet again. He would be so
much better off without her.

"Reid loves you and your son more than life. I can't
stand to see needless pain."

Manny scrutinized her from behind big chocolate-
colored eyelashes. "Yes. As I suspected. You're in about
as much pain as he is."

He sighed deeply. "You two belong together. Perhaps
you always have. And you have the boy to think about,
too."

"I'm no good for Reid. I've caused him too much
heartache. He'll never really forgive me," she sobbed.

"Love is a strange thing, ma'am. With two separate people it can be hurtful and miserable. But put those two together and it can make all the pain disappear."

Manny rose to leave, but added one more thing. "Maybe it all boils down to trust. Sometimes you have to decide if love is worth the risk."

A few hours later, Jill once again found herself under the willows facing the man she'd loved for more than half her life. Yes, she did love him. More with every passing minute. But could they learn to trust each other again? Could she risk letting herself need and be needed in that all absorbing way she knew it would be with him?

"Don't let Travis's betrayal spoil the rest of our lives, my love," Reid finally said as a single tear leaked from the corner of his eye. Jill's heart tore into little pieces.

"I know you've become strong and independent," he said over a cracking voice. "But you're my every reason for living…you've always been my soul…the better part of me."

He reached for her and the warmth she found waiting in his embrace had her collapsing against his strong chest, encircled in his comforting arms. Her soul recognized his, her body ached to become one with him once more.

They'd both been hurt by others' actions, and their own. It was past time for all the hurting to end. And way past time to give in to the physical desires she knew they both had suppressed for far too long.

"Just let me stay near you while you figure it out." He kissed her ear and whispered softly, "Let me prove my love…I beg you. Don't set me aside due to fear. I could never hurt you. It would be like ripping my own heart out."

She pulled back and, for the first time in his entire life, Reid felt a real pang of fear. "Jill, don't…"

"When?" She tilted her head to gaze at him with those shimmering crystal-blue eyes, while the corners of her mouth curled slightly upward in a half smile.

"Excuse me? When...what?" Cautious hope began to replace his fears.

She reached to grasp his shoulders then, dragging him back with her to the blanket under the trees. "When are you going to shut up and begin proving it by making love to me? We've wasted ten years of desire-filled caresses and passionate kisses. I don't need to rethink those."

He gazed down at her and saw the smirk in her eyes, so wickedly sexy he had to blink to believe it.

"All things happen in their own time, honey," he teased with a breathless sigh of relief.

Grabbing her up and placing a feverish kiss on her waiting lips, he told her in the best way he knew how, that he'd always be ready to make love to her...

Now and forever more.

Epilogue

A soft, late summer breeze whispered through the star-studded Texas night, cooling Jill's heated skin and soothing her senses. Coming to such a blissful close, this had to have been the most magical of all wedding days.

She lay, steadying her breath against Reid's naked chest and wondering at how fast the years had fallen away—leaving only the same two souls who'd found everything they'd ever wanted in each other's love. He rolled them to their sides and twisted, spooning himself behind her. She could feel his heart pounding through her back, and the rhythm brought with it a life-affirming beating in her veins.

"Happy, my love?" he whispered against her hair.

"Mmm-hmm," she murmured, sated and smug in her love.

"You're sure you're okay about not having a huge shindig like you'd wanted the first time around?" His question wasn't terribly serious. She knew because they'd talked this over more than once.

"I'm positive. I really didn't want a big deal the first time either. That was Mom and Dad's idea." She turned her head to plant a kiss on his muscular bicep, and breathed in a heady scent of the aftermath of lovemaking.

She had everything she ever wanted—her dearest love and her precious son together forever.

In the last month, she'd gone with Reid to his Houston office to wrap up the paperwork for Operation Rock-A-Bye—and he'd come with her to the law offices of Bennett and Bennett to close the files and sell off the assets.

His bosses fought to keep him with the Bureau. Her clients had pleaded with her to keep her office open. But at no time did either of them consider anything but a completely new start to their lives together.

Jill giggled as he blew a heated breath over her sweat-soaked skin. Squirming, she ground her bottom into his groin. Immediately hard and desperately ready again, he just couldn't get enough of this raven-haired pixie who'd stolen his heart so many years ago. But he wanted time for a few more words before he followed his body's urging.

"Sweetheart. Are you really sure about all these changes in your life?" Ridiculous how much more he could want and love her with each passing second.

She flipped over and pressed herself into him, nuzzling under his chin and whispering against his shoulder. "With you running for Justice of the Court of Criminal Appeals next year...and both of us working to combine our mother's ranching operations, I'll have almost everything just the way I want."

"Jill," he breathed on a ragged groan.

She quivered in his arms, reaching out for the length

of him. He grew thicker in her hands and moaned with
the delicious torture of her touch.

"There's one more big change coming to our lives,
my love," she said with a sigh. "Uh...I hope you don't
mind another little calf-roper begging you to teach them
all your rodeo tricks. I only hope this time...it's a girl."

"Another child? Oh, my God, Jill. You are the most
wonderful...the most beautiful..." The words stuck in
his throat.

He swung himself over and entered her with one swift
penetration, needing some way to show her what was in
his heart. Taking them both to savage release with a fren-
zied coupling that demanded everything, he gave all there
was to give and ended with the familiar exchange of
souls.

In the aftermath, full of joy and the glow of truly being
one with the woman he loved, Reid held his precious
wife in his arms and realized that what he'd always said
had been truer than he'd ever known.

All things happen in their own time.

*   *   *   *   *

Baby & the Beast
LAURA WRIGHT

First Published 2002
First Australian Paperback Edition 2005
ISBN 0 733 56223 X

Published by
Harlequin Mills & Boon
3 Gibbes Street
CHATSWOOD NSW 2067
AUSTRALIA

Printed and bound in Australia by
McPherson's Printing Group

LAURA WRIGHT

has spent most of her life immersed in the world of acting, singing and competitive ballroom dancing. But when she started writing romance, she knew she'd found the true desire of her heart! Although born and raised in Minneapolis, Laura has also lived in New York City, Milwaukee and Columbus, Ohio. Currently, she is happy to have set down her bags and made Los Angeles her home. And a blissful home it is—one that she shares with her theatrical production manager husband, Daniel, and three spoiled dogs. During those few hours of downtime from her beloved writing, Laura enjoys going to art galleries and movies, cooking for her hubby, walking in the woods, lazing around lakes, puttering in the kitchen and frolicking with her animals. Laura would love to hear from you. You can write to her at P.O. Box 5811 Sherman Oaks, CA 91413 or e-mail her at laurawright@laurawright.com.

To my wonderful editor, Stephanie Maurer—
here's to our beloved "Beasts!"

One

Snow fell relentlessly from a gunmetal-gray sky, coating the naked trees with an icy frosting.

Isabella Spencer pulled her wool hat down over her ears, trying to ignore the wintry glaze forming on the scarf that covered her neck and mouth. Pushing back a mounting sense of worry, she closed the door on the remaining warmth inside her lifeless car and stepped out onto the deserted road. She was two hours outside Minneapolis—and thirty miles from the small town she wanted so desperately to return to.

But fate seemed to have other ideas.

It was barely November, yet the frigid morning wind whipped at her face like tiny knives, batting her from side to side as though she were nothing more than a crumpled ball of newspaper.

Flares. Go get the flares. Someone will be by soon.

Her center of gravity newly broadened by several inches, she trudged carefully through a foot of snow to the trunk of her car, cursing the imbeciles at the weather station for their false predictions, cursing her cell phone with its short-lived battery. And as she rooted out several orange flares, lit them and laid them in the snow, she cursed the car that her husband had assured her was in fine working order.

Of course, that had been more than seven months ago. Before Rick had left her for the freedom divorce provided, before he'd gotten drunk, plowed into a telephone pole and died just a few hours later.

The shiver that ran through her had nothing to do with the cold this time. Her husband was gone. He hadn't wanted her and he hadn't wanted the child growing inside her, and the sooner she put that stinging piece of knowledge behind her the better. She was going home, back to Fielding, to start a new life with the new year. And she'd be damned if she was going to let a snowstorm and ghosts from the past stop her.

As the now familiar jabs of pain invaded her hips, then shot downward, Isabella slipped back inside her car, being careful of her protruding belly. The car's interior was only slightly warmer than outside, but at least she was free of the raw wind. Whatever had caused her car to break down had nothing to do with the battery, thank God. She turned the key and switched the heat to high. The delicious warmth that shot from the vents could only last for a few minutes, she reminded herself. Then she'd have to turn it off, conserve as much as she could for as long as she could.

"It's okay, sweetie," Isabella cooed, laying a hand on her belly. "I won't let anything happen to you."

Her child gave a healthy kick, urging its mother to ignore the chill in her chest and legs and the scratch of what felt like icicles in her throat. She would fight for warmth. She would fight for her child.

Her gaze lifted. First to heaven, asking her late father for help, then lower to the windshield. Snow pelted the glass, shutting her off from the outside world one perfect snowflake at a time.

Michael Wulf glanced out the tinted rearside window of the town car whisking him home from the airport. Beyond the car's warm borders, the wind roared, causing the car to pitch slightly.

Just yesterday he'd been in Los Angeles, chuckling at the paltry first offer he'd received from Micronics to purchase a prototype of his vocal-command software. The heads of corporations never fully understood whom they were dealing with when they first met with him. They'd heard rumors that he was a mystery, a hermit, a genius, but they were never certain how to play the game.

Michael taught them quickly enough.

He'd finally left the warm sunshine with a very profitable deal closed, returning home to freezing temperatures. But the early-season snowstorm that met his plane wasn't an unwelcome sight. He appreciated Minnesota and its climate, valued the hiber-

nation, the solitude, the solace. Although he did miss
the long daylight hours now that the beginnings of
winter were here.

It was only early afternoon and yet the gray sky
and unrelenting snowfall had turned the surrounding
landscape dim. It was hard to see fifty feet in front
of the car. But even with the hazardous conditions
and his position in the back seat, Michael's gaze
caught sight of a faint orange light glowing against
the snow in the distance. And near it, on the side of
the road, something resembling an igloo with side
mirrors and an Illinois license plate sat in ice-coated
silence.

"What the hell is that?" he muttered.

The driver slowed, glancing to his right. "Looks
like an abandoned car, sir."

Abandoned. That word fisted around Michael's gut,
warning him that things weren't always as they
seemed. It would take all of five seconds to see if the
car truly was abandoned. Five seconds he was willing
to risk even in such a blizzard. "Stop."

The driver did as he was instructed, pulling over in
front of the car. In a flash, Michael was out the door,
his bad leg stiffening in the cold as he trekked the
few feet to the car. But he hardly noticed the dull
ache. He was alert as he swept several inches of snow
from the window, intent to see for himself that no one
remained inside.

Suddenly his breath came out in a rush of fog. A
woman sat in the driver's seat. She was bundled from

head to foot in down and wool, asleep—or at least he hoped she was asleep.

"Miss? Miss? Can you hear me?" He yanked open the door and ripped off his glove, then bent down and dipped a hand inside her scarf. A strong, steady pulse beat against his fingers.

She stirred then, her eyes fluttering open. She stared up at him with large, deep-blue orbs that, though shrouded with uncertainty, spoke directly to his soul.

Deep-blue windows he'd seen somewhere before.

Her lips parted. "You found me."

And that voice. It was scratchy and raw, but he knew that voice.

The snow swirled around him like an ominous cyclone. Michael quickly shoved aside the questions forming in his mind. He needed to get her out of the car and to safety. But where? The hospital was forty-five minutes away. Too far.

"The heater stopped working…maybe half hour ago," she said softly, slowly. "I must've fallen asleep."

"You're damn lucky," he said, easing her out of the car then helping her to stand. "Another half hour and…" *And that car would've become an arctic tomb.* He didn't say it.

The wind burned his face and neck as he stripped off his coat and covered her. "You're going to be fine. Hang on."

"All right," she whispered.

He picked her up and started toward the town car just as the driver rushed up beside him to help.

"Sir, would you like me to carry—"

Michael ignored the offer. "Turn the heat on high and get us home as quickly as you can."

The man nodded. "Yes, sir."

Once tucked safely inside the car, Michael stripped off the woman's boots and rubbed her cold toes.

"Feels good," she said. "Itchy, but good."

After her feet were warm, he slid off her gloves and rubbed her small hands between his large ones. Then he gathered her in his arms and held her close.

"How long were you out there?" he asked.

The woman let her head fall against his shoulder as she answered with a sigh, "Since ten. This morning."

Five hours.

He cursed softly. "Just try to relax. You're safe now." Although a trace disoriented, she was going to be okay, he knew it somehow. But still, deep worry pricked at him. Her padded down coat couldn't hide what he could feel against his side.

"When's your baby due?" he asked.

She looked at him. "About a month."

His jaw tightened. What idiot would let his wife travel alone through a snowstorm at this stage of her pregnancy? Well, he was sure going to find out.

With gentle precision, he drew off her scarf. He'd been so intent on getting her to shelter, he hadn't been able to take a good look at her until now—except for her incredible and very familiar eyes. And what he could see made his chest tighten. Long waves of pale blond hair, heart-shaped face and a soft mouth. Again familiarity rapped at his mind. How the devil did he know her? He rarely went to social events, never went into town.

"Thank you," she mumbled, letting her head fall back onto his shoulder again. "Thank you for coming to get me, Michael."

At that, he froze like the icicles hanging off the stand of trees they passed. His mind worked, sharp and quiet, feeding information piece by piece until an answer formed.

And what an answer it was.

Falling asleep beside him sat the girl—no, the woman. A very pregnant woman. And the one person on earth to whom he owed a debt. One he'd vowed to pay back a long time ago.

He grabbed his cell phone, pushed a button and uttered, "Dr. Pinta," into the receiver.

The old doctor who had treated three generations of Fielding residents and was as close to a friend as Michael allowed himself to have picked up on the second ring.

"I need you, Thomas."

Visions of hot chocolate and electric blankets danced in Isabella's fuzzy head. Along with a grainy movie of her childhood crush dressed in shining armor, rescuing her from a white dragon who breathed hail, instead of fire. It was lovely, but the closer she got to the chocolate and blankets and handsome knight, the more her toes itched and her throat hurt.

"Isabella?"

The voice came from far away, through a snow-covered haze.

"Isabella, I need you to wake up."

The tone was parental and she forced her eyes to open and focus. She could feel that she was fully dressed, see that she was covered by several blankets and in a room that was not her own.

As she glanced around, her heart thumped madly in her chest. The room was large and furnished in dark wood. Drawn curtains made up the wall in front of her, a fire roared and crackled to her left, and a man sat beside her. A man she recognized instantly. His balding head, scholarly gray beard and hook nose gave him away.

Dr. Pinta's kind eyes settled on her. "Well, we're very glad to see you, my dear. How are you feeling?"

Her mind whirled with thoughts and questions, but none more important than one. "My baby?"

"Your baby's just fine. And so are you." He smiled. "You were very smart to set out those flares."

Her hands went to her belly, felt the warmth, the life there, and she sighed with relief.

"It was a close call, but thank the good Lord some-one came along in time," the doctor added.

The doctor glanced over his shoulder and Isabella followed his gaze. Sitting in a thronelike chair up-holstered in emerald-green velvet, facing the fire, was a man. Something inside her, perhaps inside her heart, knew instantly that the knight in her dream had been no vision, after all.

As images flashed through her mind—snow glazing her car, the door opening to reveal her rescuer, lying against the solid wall of his chest—her knight met her gaze, firelight illuminating his steel-gray eyes, rumpled black hair and granitelike features.

''Hello, Bella.''

Only two men had ever called her that. One was her father, Emmett, who had passed away almost fifteen years ago. And the other was the sixteen-year-old runaway from a boys' home in Minneapolis her father had taken in.

Even at the age of thirteen, Isabella had known that she loved that boy, with his quick mind and brusque nature—even with the limp that had roused teasing and taunting from other kids in town.

But she'd lost him after her father's death. The boy had left Fielding after her great-aunt had taken her in, but couldn't take him, too.

Michael Wulf.

The picked-on outcast who'd turned into the misunderstood genius. A celebrity. She'd kept track of his progress and had even thought of getting in touch with him when she'd read that he'd moved back to Fielding three years ago. But she'd been married by then and living in Chicago. She'd had to put every ounce of energy into saving her marriage, into trying to find out why her husband had changed from charming to disinterested the moment they'd said, ''I do.''

A curious smile found its way to her mouth. "Michael. Thank you."

He gave her a quick nod. "It was nothing."

"You saved my life. And my baby's. That's something."

"I'm just glad I was there."

He never *had* taken a compliment well. "So am I. I thought I was dreaming when I woke up and saw you. It's been such a long time."

His shadowed gaze moved over her, pausing at her belly. "A long time."

His voice was low and deep, but tender, and she was instantly taken back in time. The gruff kid who had never been gruff with her.

A smile curled through her. Michael Wulf had been the boy she'd wanted to give her first kiss to, her heart to. Lord, how time flew. Certainly enough for her to see—and sense—the difference in him. He'd grown handsomer in fifteen years, but those gray eyes that had once been angry and troubled were as hard as steel now.

She knew some of his past hurts, but whatever had happened after he'd disappeared from Fielding had left him far more scarred. And she wondered about it.

Dr. Pinta put a hand over hers. "Is there someone I can call for you, my dear?"

She shook her head. "No."

"Your husband?" Michael offered, the hard lines of his mouth deepening.

Isabella looked away, suddenly feeling very tired. "He died seven months ago."

"Oh, I *am* sorry," Doc said softly. "What about someone in Fielding? Anyone expecting you?"

When she'd married Rick four years ago, he'd urged her to cut the lines of communication with anyone in Fielding. It had practically broken her heart, but in an effort to save her marriage, she'd done as he'd asked. She had no idea what to expect when she returned home, no idea if her old friends would embrace her.

"I'm going to stay at the hotel for a week or so until I can get my father's store back in working order," she said. "I've decided to turn it into a pastry shop." She looked at Dr. Pinta, sensing she had to explain further. "I'm planning on living in the apartment above it. It'll be a perfect home for me and the baby—once it's cleaned up of course."

"We'll all be glad to have you back, my dear. And a pastry shop," Doc said with a slow grin. "Good, good. Are you going to be selling those cinnamon rolls of yours?"

She nodded, returning his friendly smile. "When do you think I can go—"

"I think you should stay right where you are," Michael said firmly.

Doc nodded. "I agree. You and the baby should rest." From his coat pocket came a loud beeping sound. He reached in, took out his beeper and stared at the message. "Good Lord, it's certainly a day for emergencies. Mrs. Dalton has had an accident, something about her hip.''

''I hope she'll be all right,'' Isabella offered, her mind scattered with the events of the day.

Doc looked up. ''Sorry, my dear, I need to go. I have to stop in town and get some supplies. The Dalton place is at least twenty miles out. I don't think I'll be able to come back until morning.''

Michael nodded. ''I'll take care of her, Thomas.''

An unfamiliar tug of awareness spread through Isabella at that simple promise. She grabbed for the doctor's hand. ''I don't want to put anyone out. I could go with you. The hotel is right on the—''

Doc Pinta stood up. ''No, no. The snow has let up quite a bit, but it's getting colder. I don't want you picking up another chill. Not in your condition.''

''She'll stay here,'' Michael stated firmly. ''I'll move my things into the guest room.''

Isabella felt her cheeks warm as she once again looked around the room. This time she noted several personal items: the silver watch that her father had given Michael for his sixteenth birthday on the nightstand, a book about solar-powered homes on a bench, aboriginal paintings on the walls and framed photographs on the mantel, each depicting what she imagined were Michael's ''children''—the high-tech interiors of cars, boats and houses.

This was *his* room, *his* bed.

Her pulse stumbled and the room suddenly compressed into a sort of tunnel with Michael Wulf at the end. Lord, she must have caught more than a chill.

Only a fever could make her childish crush seem in danger of turning into a full-fledged, grown-up one. She was in Fielding to start a new life, create a future for herself and her child, not return to teenage dreams from the past.

"I really can't stay here," Isabella said, hearing the ring of panic in her voice. How could she sleep in his bed, against his pillows, surrounded by the scent of him? "I need to be at my place. I have a cleaning crew coming from St. Cloud to help me get everything—"

"They won't make it out in weather like this, Isabella." Doc Pinta reached down and gave her hand a squeeze. "What you need to do is calm down. You're in no shape tonight to brave the elements. It's not good for the baby." He turned to Michael. "If anything changes, please call me."

Michael nodded. "Of course."

"You and that baby get some rest, young lady." Doc Pinta left the room, calling over his shoulder, "I'll see you first thing in the morning."

An unwelcome cloud of anxiety floated in the air just above Isabella's heart as she watched the doctor go—leaving her alone with the subject of her teenage dreams.

Dressed in simple but expensive black, Michael crossed to the bed, his limp more pronounced than she remembered. But that minor limitation hardly diminished his striking appearance and the commanding manner that burned around him like a living, breathing thing.

Up close he was even more fiercely handsome than she remembered. Dark, hooded eyes, sensual mouth, olive skin—he nearly took her breath away. He'd grown, well over six feet now with the body of a gladiator. Obviously his impediment hadn't stopped him from staying fit, she mused as a twinge of pain erupted in her lower back.

But though Michael had grown in stature and appearance, Isabella could feel the oppressive heat of the anger and the resentment he still carried. A weighty burden he looked unlikely to discard anytime soon.

"I want you to know that I really appreciate your putting me up," she told him. "I won't be a bother, I promise."

Michael's features tightened. "Fifteen years ago you and your father took me in, Bella, treated me like family. It's a debt I've never forgotten. And one I intend to repay." He graced her with a slash of a smile—something she imagined he didn't do very often. "I'm glad you're here, and you're welcome to stay as long as you want."

Her heart began to soften like clay in a warm palm, but she fought it. His voice was thoughtful, but the meaning was clear. He was offering her his home and his protection because he felt he owed her and her father.

"Thanks," she said with a calm she didn't feel. "That's a very generous thing to say. But you don't owe me anything. One night's stay is all I'll be—"

"We'll see about that," he interrupted, plowing a

hand through his hair. "We'll see what the doctor says tomorrow."

Just then, an arrow of pain shot into her lower back, making her wince. These little jolts were coming all too frequently the past few weeks. Her little one obviously wanted to see the world. *And Mommy can't wait to see you, my sweetie. Just give me a little longer.*

"All right, Michael," she said, too tired to argue something that sounded so reasonable no matter what his motivations were. "But I don't want to take your room from you. I can easily move into a guest room or—"

"That's not necessary." His smoky gaze briefly scanned hers. "You look very comfortable right here in my bed."

Her eyes widened and her breasts tightened. *One night. Just one night.*

"I won't have you moving," he said. "I'm going downstairs to make sure that Thomas is on his way. I'll bring you up some dinner. Soup sound all right?"

She nodded, grateful that he was going to leave for a while so she could breathe normally again. "Sounds perfect."

"My housekeeper only comes during the week, so we'll both have to suffer my cooking until tomorrow. Anything else you need?"

"A little sunshine would be great," she joked lamely.

He turned then and uttered the word "drapes," and

the wall of chestnut fabric in front of her parted to reveal floor-to-ceiling windows.

Isabella gasped, both at what seemed to be his magic and at the view. The dim bluish light of a late afternoon in early winter seeped into the room. Outside, she could see gnarled, leafless trees, a pond frozen over and acres and acres of white under a gray sky. To any true Midwesterner, it was a beautiful scene.

And Michael's amazing technology had brought it to her in one simple command. She'd certainly read about his inventions, just never seen one.

"Very impressive, Michael."

He shrugged. "It's actually a pretty simple process."

"Not to the technologically impaired. My VCR has been blinking 12:00 for a good decade."

"Well, I can't make a cinnamon roll. To me, that's impressive." He regarded her for moment, the cogs of his mind working behind his eyes, then he turned to leave.

"It's good to see you again," she called after him.

He paused at the door, but didn't look back. "It's good to see you, too, Bella."

Then he was gone, and the room felt cooler. Which was odd because his attitude and manner were not particularly warm.

She turned toward the fire. Why in the world did she feel so safe here, in his lair, his hideout from the world, as the media called it?

"The millionaire recluse who lives in an enormous

house of glass on thirty acres of woodland high above a sleepy town,'' she'd read. ''Driven to levels of success that most mortals wouldn't dare strive for.''

He was an enigma, they said. At thirty-one, Michael Wulf made the world wonder—about his personal history, as well as his extraordinarily profitable high-tech developments.

Though he seemed to have no past, he was truly a man of the future. He created houses with brains and cars that responded to vocal commands. But unlike others in his field, he had no taste for celebrity.

They also wrote that he had no wife, no family, few friends and a giant chip on his shoulder. They said that he walked with a limp. And they speculated that perhaps the lone wolf had once been caught in a trap.

But Isabella knew a truth that all those journalists who wrote about him would never know. How he'd been tossed away by his parents for a handicap he couldn't control and shoved into a boys' home. How he'd been treated by his peers for being different. How determined he'd been to rise above them all.

And it seemed that he'd succeeded. He did indeed live high above a sleepy little town, a town that had once rejected him. But in her opinion, living in hiding was no way to live.

She exhaled heavily, her hands moving to her belly. Perhaps it was this new nurturing side of her, but she wanted to help him, lift him out of that black hole that held him hostage. But somehow she knew that if she did, if she got close to him again, the odds of reviving that adolescent crush were great.

Not that her potential desires mattered. The boy from years ago had looked on her as a little girl, while the man today apparently looked on her as an unpaid debt.

Not to mention that you're eight months pregnant and resemble a beach ball.

She rubbed her stomach and said softly, "But I wouldn't have it any other way."

What she needed to do was concentrate on this new life she was carving out for herself: opening her pastry shop, creating a home, raising her child and putting the past to rest.

But rest appeared unlikely as long as she was under the same roof as that past: the very handsome and disturbing Michael Wulf.

Two

Michael leaned back in his armchair and took in the view.

Several feet away, Bella lay asleep in his massive bed, wrapped in the royal-blue robe he'd loaned her. She'd grown into a beautiful woman over the past decade, and her pregnancy only accentuated that beauty.

She hugged the down pillow like a lover, her face content, her tawny lashes brushing the tops of her cheekbones. And as the last flicker of red from the fire illuminated her long blond hair, he couldn't help but wonder if this angel from his past had been sent from heaven to torture him.

Tonight, however, he hadn't let himself spend enough time with her to find out. After Thomas had left, he'd gone down to the kitchen and opened a can of chicken soup, made some toast to go with it, then brought it up to her on a tray. She'd wanted him to stay and have dinner with her, but he'd declined.

He never ate with anyone. As a child, the chaos of living and eating with sixty hungry boys, of having to fight for every scrap of food, had made him yearn for solitude and peace. And he'd found them both out on the road when he'd finally escaped from Youngstown School.

Even when he'd come to Fielding, stayed with Bella and her father, his newfound independence had continued. Emmett would say something like ''A man has to have a little space,'' then hand Michael a plate of food and a glass of milk.

Emmett Spencer had been one in a million. Michael knew he would never forget how the man had taken him in, no questions asked, and acted as a father figure, a mentor, even taught him all about electronics. Then there was Bella, who had taught him about kindness and given him her friendship.

But tonight, Michael thought as he watched her, tonight, as he'd laid that dinner tray before her, he hadn't looked on her as a friend. He'd even contemplated making an exception to his dining rule. For her. And both of those realizations unnerved him. Unnerved him enough to cry ''work'' as an excuse and get the hell out of there.

Just then, Bella sighed in her sleep. Rubbing his jaw, Michael cursed softly. He'd never been a voyeur.

And he didn't have time to think about the past. There was work to be done and deals to be made.

But today, when he'd opened that car door, seen those eyes—held a very grown-up Bella against him in that car—an addictive warmth had seeped into his icy blood, making him want to stay put, hold on to her this time. And that sense of longing hadn't subsided one ounce in the hours since. Instead, it had seemed to grow.

Obviously she was potent acid to his ironwill, eating away at his resolve, and he knew that he'd better remember why she was here. Remember the only thing he wanted from her.

Acknowledgment of a debt paid in full.

So although his mind warned him to get out of this room, what was left of his sense of duty would not allow it. If she needed him for anything, he would be here.

On another soft, sleepy sigh, Isabella kicked the covers off her legs. The robe she wore lay open from toes to midthigh, and Michael couldn't help but catch a glimpse of those long, toned legs before he forced his gaze back to the dying fire.

He slid his heel along the rug and stretched out his leg. The damn thing hurt tonight. More than usual. But he fought the pain head-on, always had. At three when he'd taken a tumble down the basement steps and broken his leg, he'd been as brave as a three-year-old could be. When the simple break had damaged a nerve and turned into a not-so-simple life-long affliction, he'd held his own. And even when his parents couldn't handle raising a crippled child and had abandoned him to the state's foster-care system, he'd done his best to take care of himself and get on with it.

Flinching slightly, he stood up and walked over to the window, gritting his teeth as he shoved the ache away. The break in the snow this afternoon had been fleeting. Outside a storm of white raged against the night sky, glazing the trees, blanketing the earth as far as he could see. And it showed no signs of stopping.

It would be a miracle if Thomas made it out to the house tomorrow. What Michael had imagined to be a couple of days caring for Bella to pay back an old debt was beginning to look as if it could stretch into a week.

His gut tightened. Why did that worry him so much? He didn't have to see her except to bring her meals, watch over her at night.

Pushing away from the window, he went to stand beside the bed. Damn, she was beautiful. And harmless and pregnant and... *And what, Wulf? What is it? What's she doing to you?*

The devil's response hung in the air as he covered her with the blanket she'd kicked off, then returned to his chair by the fire.

Bella made him feel...alive.

By five o'clock the following afternoon, Isabella had one bad case of cabin fever.

All hopes of being released from Michael Wulf's

hideout and the heat of Michael Wulf's gaze had disappeared the moment she'd woken up that morning
and seen God's endless shower of snow. The cleaning
crew had been canceled, Doc Pinta hadn't been able
to come, and neither had the housekeeper. Isabella
and Michael were alone, trapped by a blizzard that
showed no signs of ending.

Ever the gentleman, Michael had brought her some
magazines that his housekeeper had left behind and,
of course, two square meals. But he never stayed, and
she was growing increasingly weary of reading about
secret celebrity hideaways and the world's largest pan
of lasagna.

What she needed was a respite from rest.

She wrapped the terry-cloth robe tighter around
her—the robe that held the faint scent of spicy male
to it—and headed for the door.

Fortunately, when Doc Pinta had phoned that
morning, he'd told her that if she felt strong enough,
she could get out of bed for a bit. And that was just
what she intended to do.

Snug in a pair of Michael's large wool socks, she
stepped out into the hallway—a glass hallway suspended ten feet above the ground to be exact. Isabella
glanced around, feeling a little off balance, not unusual considering her center of gravity had shifted
considerably over the past few months.

Twilight came early at this time of year and even
earlier in a storm, so the passage was dim. It appeared
unlit, but that quickly changed the moment she took
a wary step into it. Apparently the floor was pressure

sensitive, because for each step she took, another section of hallway lit up.

Isabella just stared, openmouthed. How could she help it? It wasn't just the glowing floor that impressed her, it was the view the hallway presented. On either side of her lay acres of snowy woodland, and over her head, a blanket of thick white covered the glass ceiling.

Extraordinary.

It was with great regret that she left the hallway at its end and entered a large room with a marble floor, a grand piano and a jungle of plants surrounding an elevator.

An elevator that stood open, waiting.

She took a deep breath and looked around her. Okay, Michael probably wouldn't love her poking around his house unaccompanied. But he was obviously too busy with his work to entertain guests. If she looked at it that way, she was helping him out by entertaining herself, right?

With that bit of warped logic to fuel her quest, she moseyed into the silver cylinder. She could do a little exploring, then be back in her room by the time Michael brought dinner. No harm done.

But she wasn't going anywhere, she quickly realized. Because as she glanced around, she noticed that there were no buttons to push anywhere.

"All right," she said, touching the smooth walls. "First things first. How do I make this door close?"

Isabella gasped as the door closed instantly.

"I guess that's the way," she muttered. "Now, I

suppose saying the word 'up' would be just too easy.''

The elevator didn't move.

''That's what I thought.''

She tried a few synonyms for the word up, but nothing happened. She tried the words *guest, Michael, Wulf* and *Fielding.* Still the elevator remained immobile.

As she racked her brain for a more clever answer to this riddle, a wrench of pain shot across her lower back. She arched, stretching a little, then settled both hands on her belly and rubbed. ''Are you as frustrated as Mommy, sweetie? Or are you just ready to meet the world and see your new home—''

At that the elevator shot upward. Stunned, Isabella gripped the steel railing to hold her steady and tried to remember the last word she'd uttered.

Home.

An interesting choice.

And one she never would've thought of.

The elevator came to a smooth stop at what she guessed was the top of the house, and the doors slid open. Cautiously she stepped out into a room bathed in bright yellow light. It was an office. And what Michael deemed home.

''Michael,'' she called out tentatively, ''you here?''

There was no answer, and she walked into the room, her gaze riveted on the scenery before her. Constructed primarily of glass and steel, the turret-shaped room boasted hardwood floors covered in tan rugs, two worn brown leather couches, a state-of-the-art workout contraption, a massive television and stereo system, and two arcade-size, freestanding video games.

For just a moment, her gaze rested on the video games. It warmed her heart to see them and to know that her father's influence on Michael had remained.

She walked farther into the circular space toward the massive desk, which held two computers, a fax machine and a printer. She noted the clutter there, as well—stacks of paper, disks, files, pens and pencils.

She would never have guessed it, but stern, rigid Michael Wulf was a messy guy.

She chuckled at the thought just as her gaze caught on a framed drawing just above the desk. It was an etching, very old, but in fine condition. It was a scene from the fairy tale ''Rumplestiltskin.'' And at different points on the wall were more etchings of other fairy tales: ''Sleeping Beauty,'' ''The Princess and the Pea,'' ''The Nightingale,'' ''The Ugly Duckling.''

''What are you doing?''

She whirled around to see Michael emerge from the elevator, looking drop-dead sexy in a dark-gray sweater and black jeans, his jaw tight, his eyes dark as thunderclouds.

''What am I doing in here?'' she asked innocently. ''Or out of bed?''

''Both.''

''I was going a little stir-crazy,'' she said, smiling into his glower. ''You know, locked up in the tower?''

His brow rose. "Obviously you weren't locked in well enough."

She touched her belly. "We're both a little weary of being cooped up."

His eyes softened as he looked at her stomach. "I understand that, but you really should be resting. What happened to doctor's orders?"

"He said I could take a walk if I felt up to it."

Michael didn't move from his spot in front of the elevator. "I don't allow people up here, Bella."

"Not even to clean or—"

"I do that myself."

She glanced at the desk with its overflowing mess and grinned. "So I see."

With something close to a growl, he stepped back into the elevator and motioned for her to follow. "All right. Let's go. Back downstairs and off your feet."

"I could sit," she suggested. The twinge running up her spine heartily agreed.

"You came way too close to having hypothermia yesterday, Bella."

"That's a little overly dramatic, don't you think?"

"What I think is that I'm not taking any chances. I'm going to walk you down—"

"Wait, please. It's nice up here. The view." She laughed. "The clutter."

He glared at her.

"Okay, okay," she muttered dejectedly.

She must've pulled off one great downcast expression, because he breathed an impatient sigh and said,

"How about we go into the kitchen? You can sit down and relax while I make you some dinner."

"How about you make *us* some dinner?" she suggested as she walked toward him.

"We'll see."

"That expression is beginning to annoy me." She stepped into the elevator and tried to ignore the woodsy scent of him.

He mumbled, "Second floor," and they descended.

Shaking her head, she said, "I wouldn't have started with anything that easy."

He turned to look at her, his brow arched. "By the way, how did you manage to get up there?"

She smiled. "I stumbled on the password."

"No more stumbling," he warned.

"But—"

"No buts, either."

She placed her hands on what used to be her hips. "You know, you're not supposed to argue with a pregnant woman."

"Who says?" The look he tossed her was somewhere between irritated and interested.

"It's in the book of pregnancy rules."

"And the author of that book is…"

"Gosh, can't remember."

The elevator stopped and the door opened. "That's convenient."

Laughing, she followed him through the jungle room, past a small dining room and then into a large, open-air kitchen with beamed ceilings.

Much like the other rooms in Michael's house, the

kitchen boasted floor-to-ceiling windows that left you nose to nose with the hillside and snowy landscape, separated only by glass. All the appliances were black and very modern. No buttons or dials. And she couldn't help but wonder just how long it had taken his housekeeper to remember the vocal commands for everything.

But the most interesting thing in the room was happening on top of the center island. Under several glass domes and UV light, herbs grew hydroponically. The setup was incredibly progressive with a small computer attached to each dome. She could actually read the internal temperature and how many hours, minutes and seconds the herbs needed to mature.

It was little wonder that Michael was a millionaire, she thought as she sat down at a green glass table.

She was getting a little tired, and those pricking pains in her back were intensifying. But little twinges were expected in the last month of pregnancy. She just needed a good soak in the tub. Maybe after dinner.

"You know," she began, arching her back a few times, "that book I mentioned also states quite clearly that all pregnant women should receive chocolate-chip ice cream once a day followed by an hour-long foot massage."

He poured her a glass of milk and set it down in front of her. "And husbands actually buy this?"

Her heart tripped awkwardly. "The book or what's in it?"

"Either."

"If they love their wives enough, I guess," she said softly, taking a swallow of the cold milk.

Michael began to assemble a sandwich. "Did your husband own a copy of that book?"

A profound sadness poured through Isabella. Michael probably thought that she and Rick had had a great relationship, typical loving husband and wife. And why wouldn't he? She was pregnant, after all.

She glanced up at Michael. "I don't imagine he did."

"I wasn't thinking, Bella," he said, expelling a breath. "It's none of my business. I'm sorry."

"No, don't be sorry." She took another swallow of milk, trying to think what to say next. For so long, she'd had to pretend that her marriage was a loving union, that her husband was content and satisfied with his life and with her. But she just couldn't lie anymore. "Rick didn't really want to be a husband. I think I was a challenge to him. The last virgin in Minnesota or something. So once he had me, once that wedding night was over…" She shrugged, heat creeping up her neck and dispersing into her cheeks.

Michael's fierce stare was unyielding as he finished her sentence. "He forgot just how lucky he was?"

She smiled. "Something like that. I kept trying, though. You know, I came from a family that stuck together through thick and not-so-thick."

"Yeah, I know."

Beneath his words, Isabella detected a hint of longing, but she wouldn't press him. "Well, Rick wanted a reason to leave, and when I told him I was pregnant he had one.''

''You weren't trying to have a baby?''

She shook her head. ''It just happened.'' She smiled as she rubbed her stomach. ''After he left, I felt so unbelievably angry. I held on to that anger for a while, then I realized that it wasn't healthy for me or the baby, so little by little I let it go. As easy as it would've been, I don't hate him for his weakness of character.''

''Well, you're a better person than me.'' Michael brought her the turkey sandwich he'd made, but he didn't sit down. just stood against the counter. ''I hate him and I never even met him. He left you, Bella.''

''Yes. But look at what he left me with.'' Grinning, she touched her stomach.

He nodded, then looked away.

Isabella took a bite of the sandwich and switched gears. ''Where did you go after you left Fielding? I always wanted to know.''

He paused, and she wondered if he was going to open up to her the way she just had with him. After all, it was a safe subject. But he didn't reply. ''Michael, if you don't—''

''Minneapolis,'' he said, opening a drawer on the outside of the fridge and grabbing a beer. ''I went to Minneapolis.''

''And what did you do there? I mean, you were only sixteen.''

''I was old enough to take care of myself.'' He popped the top of the beer and took a swallow. ''I used the skills your father taught me. You know, even though he worked on video games, the things he showed me opened my mind to what was possible. And opened doors for me in ways I couldn't have imagined.'' He paused to take another swallow of beer. ''That's why I owe him.''

She had to ask. ''And why do you owe me?''

''Let's just say that you were my guardian angel, Bella.''

Lord, she didn't want to be his angel. ''Look, Michael, you don't owe either one of us anything. We both did what we did because we cared about you. Not because we were looking for a payoff later on.''

''Everyone wants a payoff.''

She shook her head. ''You don't believe that.''

''Yes, I do.'' He opened the fridge and started rifling through it. ''Whether the payoff is emotional, physical or monetary, everybody expects one.''

''Maybe that's true of some people, but...'' Her words trailed off as the dull pain in her back suddenly shot down her hips. She sucked in a breath of air and let it out slowly as the pain eased. What she really needed to do was finish her sandwich and go take that bath.

''Well, you've done enough for me,'' she said finally. ''And as soon as this storm clears, we'll call it even, all right?''

''We'll see.''

She rolled her eyes as she scooped up her sandwich. ''Michael, I swear if you say that one more time...''

Something was happening. It wasn't just eight-month pangs or Braxton Hicks contractions. Firecrackers were erupting in her abdomen, shooting what felt like shards of broken cut glass to every corner of her body. Her sandwich fell to the floor as she leaned over, gripping her belly as another spear of pain drove down her spine, through her hips and circled her belly.

Michael was at her side in seconds. "What's wrong? What is it?"

"I need to go—" She gasped.

"Where do you need to go? Back to bed?"

She shook her head. "No. To the hospital. I need to go to the hospital." She glanced up at him, her breath catching in her throat as she felt the pain rising again like a gigantic wave set to crash. "The baby's coming."

Three

The steadfast control that Michael prided himself on threatened to snap. Bella's water had broken and she was in labor. The phone lines had gone down sometime in the afternoon, and his long driveway was knee-deep with snow.

Everything he normally relied on was of no use to him. No cell-phone service—his satellite hookup was worthless in this type of weather—and as he'd designed his home for hibernation, he had no snowmobile.

Which meant there was no way to get her into town.

What they did have, however, were Bella's pregnancy book, Michael's encyclopedias and three backup generators.

For the first time in a long time, he had to rely on instinct, not technology, and it felt completely foreign. But he'd be damned if he was going to let Bella know that.

After several long and very tense minutes, he'd gotten her back in bed, lay several clean towels beneath her, then rounded up some cool water, hot water, scissors, string, washcloths, more clean towels and sheets. He read as much as he could between her contractions. And when the pain gripped her, and she cried out, he tried to comfort her. Never letting her know that the sight and sound of her labor shook him to his very core.

He was lighting a fire when her soft voice broke through his thoughts. "Michael?"

He crossed to the bed and knelt down beside her.

"There's no way to get me to the hospital, right?" she said, her eyes filled with unease.

"No. I'm sorry."

She turned away from him then. Her jaw was set, her eyes glazed as she looked straight ahead, apparently concentrating. On what, he wasn't sure. But he wasn't going to ask any stupid questions.

"Can I get you anything? Ice chips? Juice?"

She shook her head. "Don't go anywhere."

"I'm not going anywhere." Dammit, he had to pull this off, had to keep her safe.

Her eyes suddenly shut, and her hands fisted the sheet. Beads of sweat broke out on her forehead, and she gave a cry of agony that made him want to put his fist through a wall, feel a little of the pain she was feeling.

But instead, he did the practical thing. He rinsed out a washcloth and wiped her face and neck, whispering words of encouragement, assuring her that everything would be all right.

Finally she released an enormous breath and her head dropped to one side.

"How are you feeling?" It was one of those stupid questions he hadn't wanted to utter, but his worry superseded good sense.

She turned to look at him, her eyes large and heavy with fatigue. "Like someone's trying to drive a truck through my abdomen."

He smiled at her and she put on a brave smile of her own.

She was something else.

Back in the boys' home, he'd seen many kids get hurt, sometimes staffers too. Hell, the gardener had practically sliced off his finger cleaning the lawn mower. The man had cried for three hours.

And Bella was actually making jokes, fighting through every bolt of pain with all she had.

"I have to tell you something." She reached for his hand, and he grabbed hold.

"What is it?"

"I'm really scared, Michael."

Without thinking, he brought her hand to his mouth and kissed it lightly. "I know."

"The baby's a month early."

"The baby is going to be perfect." Never in his

life had he felt so humbled—or so helpless. "We're going to do this together. Okay?"

"Okay." Her eyes drifted closed and her breathing slowed. "Distract me. Tell me something."

"Anything."

"Tell me about that day."

"What day, Bella?"

"When…when you first came to town. When you came to Fielding." She squeezed his hand. "The day you left that horrible place."

Michael hesitated. He'd disclosed the practicalities of his past to Bella and her father, but the details had been off-limits to everyone, including himself. The nightmare of the night he'd run away and the salvation he'd run to was something he'd vowed never to revisit. But right now, for Bella, he knew he'd recall both. He'd do anything to ease her mind and her fears.

His throat was dry as dust as he spoke. "I left Youngstown School at two o'clock on a Monday morning with fifty cents in my pocket and only the clothes on my back. I walked for about fifteen miles until I was too tired to go on. So I sat on the side of the road with my thumb out and waited."

Michael glanced down at her, saw that she was a little more relaxed than she'd been a moment ago and continued. "It was summer and hot—I'd sweated right through my T-shirt. And I remember being surprised that someone had actually stopped to pick me up."

Bella smiled and said softly, "With that sweaty T-shirt, I'll bet it was a girl, right?"

He chuckled. "It was a woman in her seventies."

"Seventy or seven—" her face tightened and she sucked in a breath "—teen?"

"Don't talk, Bella," he whispered. "Just breathe."

She whimpered, writhing on the bed, clutching his hand as another contraction clamped her body. The power of it shocked him. "Everything's all right. You're going to be fine. You're going to be a mother soon."

At that, she opened her eyes and looked up at him. He felt his heart squeeze as an expression of pure pleasure radiated from her eyes.

"I *can* do this," she said, biting her lip.

He nodded. "Of course you can."

Within seconds, the storm cloud passed over her face and she let out a sigh. "So…the…woman picked you up, and…and then what?"

He wiped her face with the cool cloth. "I'd bought a bruised banana from the gas station and it was all I'd had for breakfast, so I was starving. The woman had these homemade biscuits in her air-conditioned car, and the smell nearly drove me insane. I remember she told me to take as many as I wanted." He smiled as he began to massage her shoulder with his free hand. "I ate the whole lot and felt guilty as hell. But she said she didn't mind."

"Is that when you knew?" Bella whispered.

"Knew what?"

"That your luck was about to change?"

He thought about that for a moment. Luck wasn't a word in his vocabulary—he'd never really believed in the concept of luck. But then again… "I think I knew that my luck had changed the moment I stepped foot in the Fielding dime store and those kids were calling me—" his throat almost closed "—a cripple and peg leg."

Only the sounds of their breathing and the crackle of the fire could be heard until Bella whispered, "And then I came by with my water gun."

Memories burned in his mind. "You sure did. Shot those boys dead center."

A weary laugh escaped her. "They all looked like they'd just wet their pants."

Michael smiled, remembering the look of horror on those cruel young faces—and the triumph on little Bella's as she'd held her water pistol aloft like a .57 magnum. Maybe she was right. Was it actually possible that luck existed and that it had reached him? "That was a good day."

"Yeah." The look she sent him was soul-searching. "I'm really glad you're here."

It was as if someone had shot an arrow through his chest, jabbing his heart. Bella was counting on him to deliver this baby safely and into her arms. He wasn't going to let her down. His life was built on conquering challenges. Tonight, he was moving from high-tech to human whether he liked it or not.

He watched as her face contorted with pain once again, then listened as she groaned and whimpered. He didn't know much, but he did know they were getting close.

The baby was coming soon.

And he hoped to God he could make both the child and its mother proud tonight.

Night faded into dawn.

The pain was almost unimaginable, and all the control that Isabella had willed herself to possess had faded away. She felt close to collapse. But she refused to give up or give in.

She felt this overwhelming sense of connection with her child. Different and farther-reaching than even the bond she'd felt in the last months of pregnancy. She and her little one were finally ready to meet.

"I need a good solid push, Bella."

Michael glanced up at her, his own brow wet with sweat, his eyes just as determined as she felt. He'd read her pregnancy book and his encyclopedia with diligence, emerging with strength and confidence. She felt no embarrassment with him. His willingness to do whatever it took to bring this baby, whatever it took to make Isabella feel comfortable, made her feel so close to him, so trusting.

"Take a deep breath, Bella," he said, his tone insistent, "and give me everything you got."

Isabella raised herself on her elbows, filled her lungs with air and pushed. A distressed scream escaped her, and she bit her lip, tasted blood. Her knees shook. She felt as if she was being ripped apart.

"That's good," Michael told her. "One more time. Breathe in deep and—"

"Michael, if something happens to me..." she gasped.

His tone was fierce. "Nothing's going to happen to you while I'm around, you understand?"

It was as if time hadn't passed. All Michael's anger had evaporated, and their connection, their reliance on each other, had returned. But this time, it was she who needed his strength.

"Push, Bella," he demanded. "Push hard."

Arching her back, she gulped air and bore down. Through the grunts, the struggle, the sweat, her mind thrashed with worry. Could she do this? The bolts of pain fought with her good sense. Did every woman feel this awful press of panic?

Her breath came out on a sigh just as Michael said, "Oh, God, Bella."

"What?" she cried. "What's wrong?"

"Nothing's wrong," Michael assured her. "I can see the head." Awe, pure reverence filled his voice. "Do you think you can give me one more push?"

All fear left her in that moment. And as the morning wind howled outside and the snow fell by the bucketful, Bella fought for her baby, running on pure adrenaline and anticipation. Gripping the towels in her fists, eyes clamped shut, she inhaled deeply and bore down.

"That's it. That's it, Bella."

Isabella cried out as her child came into the world, their wails intermingled. Collapsing back against the pillows, she smiled weakly, listening to the high-pitched squall of her baby—sweet, miracle-making music.

"Bella?"

She opened her eyes then and saw Michael, his

eyes filled with happiness and amazement, holding her baby. "It's a girl."

A girl, Isabella silently repeated, her eyes filling with tears as she stared at the tiny infant that had come from her body and her soul.

Michael was stunned. Not just because he'd delivered this sweet little girl, but because he'd been here to see what a mother in love with her child looked like.

After he cut the cord and cleaned up the baby, he wrapped her in a towel until she looked like a big burrito. Then he handed the baby to her mother, who cooed and smiled and laughed, and cradled the tiny girl to her breast.

And Michael watched it all.

After a few minutes Bella met his gaze and smiled. "Thank you."

Thank *you* for letting me be a part of it, he wanted to say, but didn't. He was too filled with emotions he didn't recognize.

"You were amazing, Michael Wulf," she said.

"So were you," he said, his gaze fixed on hers. "What are you going to name her?"

She glanced down at the little cherub face. "I was thinking about Emily."

"After your dad?" Emmett would've been so proud of her, he thought as he watched her cuddle her child.

She nodded. "What do you think?

The question startled him. It wasn't something that he had any right to think about.

She touched his hand. "I really want your opinion. You helped bring her into the world."

He shook his head. "This was all you, Bella."

"I don't buy that and neither does Emily," she said with a tired smile.

He looked down at the baby, with her amazing blue eyes. Of course, most babies had blue eyes when they were born, but they didn't all have such an adorable expression or such a beautiful mother.

He couldn't stop the smile that broke across his face. Dammit, he hadn't done this much smiling in his whole life. "I think it's a perfect name for a perfect little girl," he acquiesced gruffly.

Bella glowed with pride. "She is perfect, isn't she?"

Michael just stood there, watching them, wonder coursing through his veins. But when mother and child yawned with fatigue he forced his emotion back and returned to work mode.

After a mild flurry of post-birth cleanup and fresh sheets, Emily's and Bella's eyes drifted closed, long lashes resting against contented faces.

He walked over to the fire, his leg knotted with pain, and fell into his chair. Of all the things he'd accomplished in his life, bringing little Emily into the world and placing her in her mother's arms was his greatest achievement.

And he knew that nothing would ever come close to rivaling it.

Four

The storm raged from morning into the gloomy darkness of afternoon. But Isabella awoke from a much-needed nap feeling only warm and safe and content. Sure, her muscles were slow, and everything below her neck felt stiff and sore, but she'd never felt happier.

And it was all because just a few hours ago, she'd become a mother.

The thought continued to make her smile, not to mention make her forget where she was. She honestly didn't care if the snow ever let up or if she ever left Michael's glass house or if her pastry shop had Christmas buns before Christmas—she just wanted to hang on to this incredible moment in time for as long as it would allow. Although she would've welcomed

Doc Pinta's agreement that her motherly instincts were right—that everything was just as it should be. But she would have to wait a day or two for that.

Emily fussed in her arms, and Isabella rocked her and cooed sweet words—true words. Her blue-eyed bundle responded instantly, blowing a spit bubble as she stared up at her. Then her little round face scrunched up. It didn't take long for Isabella to read the signs and understand what her daughter wanted.

This would be her first time breast-feeding, and Isabella couldn't stop the worrisome tingle in her stomach. During her pregnancy, she'd read everything on the subject and had talked to several nursing mothers. She'd always felt informed and ready. But now, as she opened her robe and guided her child to her breast, she hoped their advice had stuck with her.

But she needn't have been apprehensive. Emily nuzzled as she found her way. At first, there was just a hint of pain, but it slowly subsided. And as her little girl suckled contentedly, finding her own special rhythm, Isabella believed this beautiful process was the most natural thing in the world.

And a moment she wished she could share.

She glanced up. Across the room, sleeping in the velvet chair by the fire, was her knight—minus the shining armor. It seemed that while she and Emily had been resting, Michael had taken off his shirt and hadn't put on a clean one. Not that she minded in the least.

As Emily took her first meal, Isabella let her gaze travel over him. His jet-black hair was mussed from work and sleep, his rugged features were relaxed, and his square jaw was dark with stubble. Her pulse jumped as her gaze moved downward to his chest. He was powerfully built with wide shoulders, a trim waist and a V of dark hair that disappeared beneath the waistband of his jeans.

Her hands itched to touch, her heart longed for him to be closer, but her mind kept those yearnings in check.

He lay there, sound asleep, his breathing as even as her child's. Lord, he certainly deserved the rest. He'd worked hard. He'd kept his promise and brought them both through the night safely. She'd never forget how he'd looked when he'd handed Emily to her.

Proud.

And so handsome.

And in the moment, in that moment when life had felt perfect, she'd wished that he was Emily's father and her husband. But she'd shooed the thought away as quickly as it had come. Michael was just a friend, and she needed to remember that while they endured these forced living conditions. He was a *friend,* and the man who had just paid a debt he'd never truly owed to her in the first place.

On a soft sigh, she forced her gaze away from her sleeping gladiator and put all her focus back on her daughter.

But in that velvet chair, the gladiator was far from asleep.

His eyes closed, Michael listened. It seemed that with every move, every sound Bella and Emily made, a deeper and more profound sense of protectiveness and closeness filled him. The feeling was completely foreign and not necessarily welcome, but he couldn't help acknowledging it.

When he'd first heard the sound of Emily suckling at her mother's breast, he'd been in turmoil. Questions had raced through his mind. Should he leave the room or stay? What right did he have to invade this private world? But his need to be close to them had superceded any sense of inappropriateness.

Just then, the ache in his thigh deepened and he had to move. As quietly as he could, he shifted forward in the chair and stretched out his leg.

"Michael?"

Her call had him cursing softly. The last thing he wanted at that moment was to disturb the peaceful mood that had settled over the room. But he couldn't ignore her.

He turned to look at her. "Yes?"

"I thought you were sleeping."

"My leg's a little cramped."

"Well, as long as you're awake—" she patted the empty space beside her "—I wouldn't mind some company."

His gut twisted. He was safe over here, safe to be part of the scenery and nothing more.

"You can stretch out your leg," she continued.

"Are you sure?" he said, hearing the slight edge in his voice.

"Yes, of course."

All thoughts of impropriety floated up the chimney

like smoke from the fire. Whether it was wise or not, he wanted to be close to them tonight, wanted to share what she was so willing to give. This storm had made it possible for him to forget his past and his anger for a little while. It had thrust all of them into some kind of dreamworld. And who was he to break the spell? After all, it'd break on its own soon enough without any help from him. In a couple of days Bella would leave with Emily, and he'd resume his normal way of life.

His jaw tight at that thought, he walked over to the bed and sat down beside her. Emily was snuggled against Bella's breast, content in her meal.

Isabella smiled up at him. ''You must be exhausted.''

He shook his head. ''I'm fine. What about you?''

''I feel wonderful. Tired, but wonderful.'' Her gaze drifted to the window. ''The storm seems to be lingering.'' She turned back to him. ''Looks like you're stuck with us for a little while longer.''

''And it looks like you're stuck with my cooking for a little while longer.''

She laughed and glanced down at Emily. ''Well, one of us, anyway.''

Without thinking, Michael followed her line of vision. Emily's eyes were closed as she suckled. Bella looked so natural, so beautiful with her breast bared and a soft smile on her lips. It was the sweetest sight he'd ever seen. The sweetest and the—

He stood up and drove a hand through his hair.

Hell, no. He'd be damned before he'd put a name to that feeling.

Was he going crazy? Had this snowstorm brought dementia, as well as ghosts from his past? He needed to get out of this room for a while, away from this intimacy that drew him like a bear to honey.

"Why don't I go make you something?" he offered. "You must be hungry."

"I know I should be starving. I just had a few bites of sandwich last night before Emily came knocking. But I'm really not."

"You need to keep up your strength. The storm and the baby—that's a lot in two days."

Her eyes softened, and she gave him a small smile. "Don't go."

It felt like steel beams were being pressed against his chest. There was nothing he wanted more than to be with her at that moment. And that made him nervous.

Over the years he'd been no monk. Whenever he traveled, women were near. They knew who he was, they were wary of his reputation, but the fact that he was a millionaire several times over usually turned caution into curiosity.

Although he remained aloof, he respected women and was always up front with them, letting them know he didn't have serious relationships. The women who came to his bed had been all right with that arrangement, and after a night or two of pleasure they would part on good terms.

Above all, he avoided needing anyone or being

needed. And he could see that need, that emotional tractor beam, in Bella's eyes right now. Hell, he felt it himself, and it made him even more determined to put some distance between them.

"I'm going to make you another sandwich," he insisted with a trace of a growl.

Regret lit her eyes, but it quickly passed and she nodded. "All right. But after that I want you to get some sleep."

He nodded and left the room. The ache in his thigh traveled like a brushfire down his leg as he walked through the hallway. But his thoughts burned even more.

She wanted him to get some sleep.

He shook his head as he entered the kitchen and uttered the word "lights." If he slept at all, he was going to be doing it in that chair by the fire in her room. Because even though his mind warned him to stay as far away from her as possible, his sense of duty won out. As long as she and Emily were in his house, they were his responsibility.

But how could he explain that to her? he wondered as he put a mug of water into the microwave and muttered, "Boil." And how could he explain to himself the depth of protectiveness that raged inside him?

How was he going to get rid of it before it swallowed him whole?

Later that day Isabella woke from another nap to feed and change Emily's towel-diaper. She was just about to go into the bathroom and wash up when

Michael walked into the room, pushing some kind of cart.

"What in the world is that?" Isabella asked.

He looked at her, his expression serious. "It's a bed for Emily."

Her mouth dropped open, but she quickly recovered. While she inspected the two-level cart, her heart softened. Michael had made this for her daughter. This sexy, bristly man had made a cradle for her baby.

After bringing her a sandwich a couple of hours ago, he'd told her that he had some work to do. With his reclusive ways, she really hadn't expected to see him again until evening. But he'd surprised her.

Something he'd been doing a lot of over the past few days.

"How did you do this?" she asked, switching a fussy Emily to her other arm.

"I unscrewed the top shelf of a computer cart and secured one of my housekeeper's wicker laundry baskets in its place. Then I reworked a feather pillow to make a soft lining and covered the whole thing in a clean sheet." He glanced up at her. "Do you think it'll be all right?"

Isabella couldn't help but smile. Did she think it would be all right? It was amazing. The contraption looked sturdy and safe. A perfect place to change Emily, and a perfect bed for her, too. And with wheels on all four corners, the cart was mobile. "It's just wonderful. Thank you."

He nodded. "I also cut up some more towels for

diapers.'' He gestured to the lower shelf neatly stacked with makeshift diapers.

She shook her head. ''You've thought of everything.''

He shrugged nonchalantly. ''Just trying to take good care of my guests.''

''You've given us the best of care, Michael.''

Michael stared at her, his gaze flickering from her eyes to her mouth, then back again. ''I'm going to make some dinner.'' Her eyes went a soft gray. ''No sandwiches tonight. I think you deserve to have a real dinner.''

His thoughtfulness only made her longing intensify. ''Would it be too much to ask you to take Emily?''

''Take her?'' Wariness filled his tone.

''I'd love to have a hot shower.''

''I don't know anything about babies, Bella. I—''

''You'll be fine.'' She gave him a reassuring smile. ''You're the one who helped bring Emily into the world. I trust you.''

He plunged a hand through his hair and walked over to the bed. ''All right. But if she can't stand me, I'm coming to get you. In the shower or out.''

Her breath caught as a ripple of wonder moved through her. Neither one spoke for a moment, and she wondered if he was going to take his promise back or at least clarify it. But he didn't. ''Dinner should be ready in a half hour.''

Her tongue darted out to moisten her bottom lip. ''Okay.''

Michael's gaze followed the movement, then he exhaled heavily and leaned down. "I'll see you in a half hour," he said as he backed up with Emily in his arms.

She felt heat blast into her cheeks. What was wrong with her? she wondered as she watched Michael gently place Emily in the basket, then wheel her out the door. Acting like a silly schoolgirl, instead of a new mother.

On a dejected sigh, she pulled back the comforter and headed for the bathroom. Her adolescent crush was blossoming into full-fledged hankering, and if she didn't get out of this house soon, she'd be in serious danger of that hankering growing into something stronger.

Something that wouldn't diminish in a few days like the early winter storm that raged outside.

Isabella remained under the hot spray for a good twenty minutes, loosening up her stiff and sore muscles before lathering and shampooing her way to squeaky clean.

After blow-drying her hair and changing into a pair of sweats that Michael had given her, she left the room feeling refreshed, but missing Emily terribly. How strange that in less than a day she couldn't envision her life without Emily, she thought as she walked down the glass hallway.

Opera music played and the scent of baked chicken spilled through the rooms she passed, growing in pungency as she approached the kitchen. Her stomach rumbled as she paused in the doorway, her gaze fixed on the scene in front of her.

On the stove, green beans simmered in a pan and steam rose off what appeared to be a chicken casserole. But the real show was happening on the tile floor. A handsome six-foot-four giant in a red apron stood next to the center island cradling a soft, cooing baby in his arms, arms threaded with muscle beneath the black T-shirt he wore.

As he swayed to the music with Emily blinking up at him and blowing spit bubbles, Isabella's heart dipped. They looked so right together, so content, and she ached to join them. But this was no family moment, and she wouldn't pretend it was. She had more than her own heart to consider now.

''Arthur Murray?'' she asked lightly as she walked toward them. ''Twenty lessons?''

He stopped moving immediately, his expression and manner going from relaxed to tense in two seconds flat. ''She was crying. It seemed to help.'' He raised a brow at her. ''And I didn't want to interrupt your shower.''

Isabella nodded. ''Thanks.'' *I think.*

He placed Emily in Isabella's arms and walked over to the stove, his limp even more obvious than yesterday. His leg was obviously bothering him and yet he'd just been dancing to soothe her child. Isabella fought the longing that surged through her at that realization, along with the urge to ask if he wanted to sit and rest while she did the cooking. But as their relationship was a little tenuous, she didn't want to risk offending him.

Instead, she took a seat at the kitchen table and inhaled deeply. "Smells wonderful."

"Thank God my housekeeper packed a few of these away in the freezer," he said, pointing to the casserole. "This one's called roast chicken surprise."

"My favorite."

He glanced over his shoulder. "I thought chicken soup with stars was your favorite."

She laughed. "It was—when I was thirteen."

"Ah. But now that you're all grown up, you've chosen a far more sophisticated entrée for your favorite?"

"Exactly."

Amusement glimmered in those steely eyes of his.

"You know, you look like one of those cooking show chefs in that apron," she said as she placed Emily in her new cradle.

"And you look…" He paused and she glanced up to see his gaze traveling over her. "Well, you look damn good in my sweats."

Her gaze fell, heat flooding her cheeks. "Thanks, but I know what I must look like."

"And what's that?"

"Tired and…well, like I just had a baby."

"Listen to me, Bella." His tone forced her eyes to meet his. "I don't think I've ever seen a woman more beautiful."

She stared at him for a moment. And then she began to chuckle. She couldn't help it. "That's so not true."

"I can think of a few surefire ways to convince you."

Michael felt all the lightheartedness that had filled him just a moment ago fall away as if he'd been caught laughing at a funeral. Bella stared at him again, heat filling her sexy blue eyes. Was she going to ask him what those ways were? And if she did, would he tell her the truth?

Behind her, Emily started to fuss, breaking the mood. Bella turned to her daughter and Michael went back to fixing dinner.

"What's this she's wearing for a diaper?" Bella asked after a few moments.

Michael didn't turn around. "It's a T-shirt. I changed her. The towels are too bulky."

"What does it say on it?"

"'Computer Programmers Know How to Use Their Hardware,'" he said dryly. "My housekeeper gives me a different one every Christmas. I'm sure she has another one all picked out for this year. She thinks they're very funny. Personally, I think it's funny that she actually believes I'm going to wear them."

"So you've made them into diapers?"

"Yes."

She laughed. "Sounds reasonable."

He set a plate of chicken and green beans in front of her.

"You're not eating with me?" she asked, taking a seat at the table.

"I don't—"

"I know, I remember—you don't eat with any-one." Her eyes grew thoughtful. "Someday I'm go-ing to ask you why."

He sat down across from her and lifted a brow. "And maybe someday I'll tell you."

Bella ate slowly, but she ate all of it and he was glad. She needed food and rest, and he was going to make sure she got plenty of both.

At last she sat back and smiled. "You're a pretty good heater-up-er. I'm impressed. Two great feats in only thirty-one years. Dinner *and* diapering."

"Well, I have to confess that Emily helped me out with the latter. She's one patient girl."

Bella turned to her daughter and whispered, "That's what's called sweet talk, Emily. Watch out for boys who use it."

Michael smiled down at the little girl. "Don't listen to her, princess."

Bella raised a brow. "Princess?"

Where had that come from? And when was that snow going to stop? "She looks like a little princess with all that blond hair and those regal blue eyes, that's all."

And as he said it, he realized he could've been describing Bella. And she must've thought so, too, because she looked up at him with startled eyes.

He sat back in his chair. Endearments were coming from a mouth that rarely uttered anything but words involving business. And talking about nothing in particular, too—just banter? He'd always thought that banter was a waste of time. Get to the point, get the deal done, get out, that was his creed. At least, it had been until Bella had come here.

"So tell me about the pastry shop," he said, diverting his thoughts and the direction of the conversation to something safe. "When did pushing calories on your hometown become business, as well as pleasure?"

"About four and a half years ago. I'd been planning to open it in Fielding, but then I met Rick."

Emily fussed a little and Michael reached over, took the cart's handle and began to rock it back and forth. "And he didn't want you to work?"

She nodded, her gaze shifting from his hand on the cart back to him. "Rick really didn't want a wife who worked," she said. "But whenever I brought dessert to a social event or to a neighbor, they raved and raved."

"I bet they did." He rubbed a hand over his jaw. "I remember you making something pretty special for your dad and me every Sunday morning."

"What was that?"

"You don't remember?" He felt almost as disappointed as he was pretending to be.

She smiled softly. "I must be getting a little tired."

He stood up, concerned. "Of course you are. How about I walk you back to your room?" It was time for her to rest and time for him to say good-night, go upstairs and work, then wait for her to fall asleep and hope that tomorrow the sun would come out.

Emily was sleeping in her cradle on wheels by the time they reached the bedroom door. Bella turned to him and smiled. "I know I'm saying this a lot, but thanks. Thanks for taking such good care of us and being such a good friend."

He nodded even as that razor-sharp word plunged into his gut.

And to make matters worse, Bella stood on tiptoe and kissed him on the cheek. A soft peck, meant for a friend, but it reached him, deep down. And he couldn't be stopped.

His arm snaked around her waist and he pulled her close. Her eyes locked with his and he stared at her mouth like the hungry wolf he was.

"Are you going to kiss me?" she whispered, her breath warm and sweet.

"Would you stop me if I did?"

She shook her head. "No."

A growl escaped his throat as he bent his head and eased her into a series of soft kisses, gentle kisses. But she was no fragile flower. Pressing her tender breasts lightly against his chest, she parted her lips, urging him, welcoming him into her warmth. His pulse smacked against the base of his throat as he tasted, his tongue flicking, moving to a rhythm they created together.

Sweet as honey. He knew she'd taste like that.

"Michael," she breathed as she wrapped her arms around his neck and deepened the kiss.

Her saying his name seemed to drag him back from the brink. Somewhere in the cavern of his mind, he knew this was trouble. He knew he'd better back off before he welcomed that trouble with open arms.

With every ounce of determination he possessed, he dropped his ravenous grip on her waist and stepped back. "I'm sorry, Bella."

Her eyes glowed liquid blue. "I'm not."

Startled at her honesty, it took him a moment to recover. But he did. He had to. "That can't happen again. And I won't let it."

Her jaw quivered with frustration. "Why is that?"

"I don't want you getting involved with me."

"So you're protecting me from you, is that it?"

"In a sense."

Her jaw went tight. "I'm a grown-up, Michael. No longer thirteen and no longer in need of protection." She stared at him, trying to read his eyes. "That's it, isn't it? You don't see me as a woman."

Michael almost laughed at her suggestion. He wanted to tell her that he saw her as every inch a woman. He wanted to tell her he couldn't stop staring at her mouth, pink from his kiss. But what point was there in telling her either? She wasn't for him. She was going to be gone in a day or two and to say anything more or do anything more would be leading her down a pointless path.

"Good night, Bella," he muttered as he turned around and headed down the hall.

But it wasn't really good-night, he thought as he heard the bedroom door shut behind him. Not for him, anyway. As soon as she fell asleep, he'd be back at his seat by the fire, back to watching over his charges—and back to wanting more of what he'd just tasted, more than he would ever allow himself to have.

Five

Five days later the lines were still down and the snow still hadn't let up.

And neither had the impact of that good-night kiss on Isabella's mind and heart.

Even now as she stood at the stove making doughnuts, she wondered what part of her mind had allowed her to start that madness—for she *had* started it. But how could she have known that her simple thank-you kiss would turn so heated?

Maybe because she'd wanted it to.

But look where her want had gotten her. A state of massive confusion.

She walked over to the makeshift cradle that held her sleeping daughter and kissed her softly on the cheek. Emily looked so content, curled up with her blanket in the basket that Michael had made for her.

Michael. She wished she could figure him out. Why had he pulled away from her? Was it Emily? Or was it that he couldn't let down his guard, move away from his past, forget about protecting her and see her as a woman? Had his compliments at dinner been just a ploy to boost her confidence?

The scent of dough turning swiftly into fragrant doughnut wafted through the air. As she plucked the sweet rolls from the hot oil and placed them on a paper towel, she was reminded again of the heat that lay just below the surface of that kiss she and Michael had shared.

He must feel something for her. After all, he still slept in her room every night. He crept in around 1:00 a.m., planted himself in that chair and pretended to be asleep as she fed her child. And every morning when she awoke he was gone.

He had pretty much avoided her during the day, except for the encyclopedia-inspired questions and suggestions about after-care for her and Emily. Concern, but with little emotion.

While time had moved slowly, she'd made use of the kitchen, cooking him meals and sending them up to him on the elevator. True, he'd always come to thank her, but then he'd disappear again. The only variation in that routine was when he offered to take Emily with him to give Isabella a break.

She appreciated his generosity with his time, but

couldn't help wishing that he would open up his heart, as well.

"You're going to draw the whole town up here on snowmobiles with that smell."

She turned at the gruff baritone and her breath caught in her throat. He looked so handsome, freshly shaven, hair wet from the shower, dressed in easy, modern black. So he'd finally emerged, she mused. They always seemed to have an enjoyable time together when he let his guard down. Perhaps that was why he tried to avoid her.

As he paused by Emily's cradle and smiled down at the infant, Isabella wondered if she was given the opportunity, would she be able to help to heal the deep, hidden wounds and complicated past of this man?

"Draw the whole town, huh?" Isabella said, turning around and returning to her task. "Wow, that's the power of a simple doughnut."

She heard him walk toward her, felt him behind her. "They look far from simple, Bella."

As he stood behind her, peering over her shoulder, she couldn't stop herself from breathing him in. Spicy, woodsy and pure male.

She dunked a hot doughnut in the chocolate sauce she'd made. "I'm trying them out as a new recipe for the bakery," she said, even though this was no new recipe at all. In fact, it was that special treat Michael had given her a hard time about not remembering the night they'd...

Well, anyway, she'd never forgotten. She'd made

them so often she knew the recipe backward and forward. And every time she had, she'd thought of him.

"You know," she began, "I'd love an opinion on these."

"Looking for a taste tester?"

She shivered as his warm breath swept over her neck. "Something like that." She glanced over her shoulder. "If you can spare some time."

His gaze darkened. "I think I have a few minutes."

Why did he have to look so sexy? And why couldn't she stop being affected by him?

"Why don't you go sit down at the table?" she said quickly.

He hesitated, his eyes softening. "You've been cooking for me for days. You must be tired. I really should be making breakfast for you."

She shook her head. "Never thought I'd say it, but I don't really like being waited on." Besides, she liked cooking for him, but she wasn't about to reveal that little truth. Doughnuts bubbled in the oil and she went back to work, calling over her shoulder, "Take a seat and I'll bring them to you."

"You made coffee, too." He sounded pleased.

She waved a hand at him. "It was simple. I just said, 'Coffee.' I'm really getting the hang of everything around here." Just in time to leave, she thought as she put a few warm chocolate-dipped doughnuts on a plate and brought them to him.

He glanced up. "You're not having any?"

She cocked her head to the side and grinned. "I don't like to eat with anyone."

Amusement lit his eyes. "That's *my* line."

"Nope. Your line is 'This is one *good* doughnut,'" she said, returning to the stove.

Out of respect, she kept her back to him as he ate. At last he sighed and said, "Nope. Not good."

She whirled around, her heart on the floor. "What do you mean? What's wrong with them?"

"They're not good, Bella." He leaned back in his chair. "They're great. Even better than I remember."

She tossed a dish towel at him. "You jerk."

He caught the towel and grinned. "Gotcha."

This gruff, teasing side of him was new and as potentially addictive as the chocolate that lingered on the side of his mouth. Impulsively she walked over to him and extended a hand toward his face. "You've got—"

"What?"

"A little chocolate…" She touched the side of his mouth just as his hand clamped over her fingers.

They stayed like that for a moment, their eyes locked, heat passing from his fingers to hers. She needed to let go, look anywhere but in those wolf eyes that pinned her where she stood.

She glanced up, then sucked in a breath. "The snow's stopped."

He released her and turned around. "What?"

"The snow. It's stopped."

For the next fifteen minutes, they remained in the kitchen, silent as two sentries, watching the gray bales of cotton in the sky part and allow the early November sun, insistent on being seen, to needle through.

Michael's words broke both the silence and the five-day illusion of domesticity. "By noon tomorrow, the roads will be clear."

Isabella nodded, her throat tight. "And Emily and I will be going home."

He didn't answer. He just watched as a beam of sunlight slowly crawled its way across the kitchen tiles.

"The Wulf" paced, only partly aware of the pain shooting down his thigh as he stalked across the hardwood floors of his den the following day.

The roads had been cleared and Bella had left closer to two in the afternoon, but Michael wasn't going to quibble about being off by a couple of hours. It was enough that she and Emily were gone.

Debt—paid in full.

He shoved a hand through his hair. He should've felt relieved to be rid of them. After all, they'd interrupted his life and his solitude. But relieved wasn't what he felt when, just an hour ago, Thomas Pinta had come to the house. The doctor had examined Bella and Emily thoroughly, deemed them healthy, then took them back into town with him to their new home.

No, not relieved. *Concerned* was more like it.

Michael tossed a sheet of paper onto his desk. He was up to his ears in the remote relay voice-command system that he'd already sold on his recent trip to L.A. That was where his mind should have been. On the groundbreaking software that was going to make him a lot of money. Or on the real reason he'd gotten into this racket in the first place: to help people live easier, safer lives.

It was his biggest project to date. It was due in six weeks and it would be delivered in six weeks.

And he couldn't concentrate worth a damn.

He hadn't gotten that kiss out of his mind or the need to feel and taste her again from his soul. And tonight, when he went to that now empty room and sat in his chair by the fire, he knew he'd miss the closeness and the sweet sound of Bella breast-feeding Emily.

How could he expect to concentrate when he had no idea if Bella and her baby were safe? What if another storm came and she was still cleaning the place? What if the cleaning crew couldn't make it out of St. Cloud for a few more days? He'd never forgive himself if something happened and he wasn't there to help and protect them.

He stalked out of his office and into the elevator. Maybe he'd just run into town and check on them, bring Emily's crib and a set of his long-range communication devices. Then, if she needed him, she could reach him right away no matter what the weather.

That should ease his mind and allow him to get back to business, he thought as he grabbed his coat and headed to the garage.

At least they had heat, Isabella thought as she glanced around the dusty apartment. Getting this place together was going to take at least a week, and there was nowhere else for them to stay in the meantime—the hotel was full.

She hadn't thought her apartment would be this bad. Shoot, she hadn't thought about anything except getting away from the man who made her knees turn to jelly and her heart fill with longing. An impractical reason for bolting, but around Michael… So off she'd gone with Doc Pinta.

The kindly old man had taken her first to the cemetery to see her father, then to the general store to get diapers and other supplies for baby and home. With sympathy in his tone, the doctor had told her that he wished he could offer her and Emily a room at his home, but with no one to help her until the holidays, Mrs. Dalton was staying with him, recuperating from the fall on her hip.

Trying to appear confident, Isabella had thanked him for his thoughtfulness and let him know that she had calls in to a few of her old high-school friends.

But that was a lie. She hadn't called any of her friends. Not Connie the redhead Rickford or meddling Molly or pint-size Wendy. She just couldn't. Not yet. Not with the past so unexplained.

When she'd first moved to Chicago, her friends had tried to call her for months, but Rick had been adamant about cutting off all ties to the past. Back then, she hadn't cared that his behavior was controlling, she'd just wanted the marriage to work, so she'd told herself that he just wanted to start a new life with her. But that dream had quickly faded. After he'd died,

Isabella had wanted to call, wanted to write, but she'd been afraid that her friends wouldn't forgive her. So she'd decided to wait until she'd returned to Fielding to explain things.

Speaking to each of them in person was the right thing to do. But after being estranged for so long, the first round of communication couldn't be asking for a place to stay.

She needed to solve this mess on her own.

"This place looks likes a train wreck."

Isabella whirled around to see Michael standing in the doorway of her apartment, looking like a Wall Street executive in a long black wool coat, expensive leather boots peeking out from beneath the hem of black pants. The frown lines around his mouth deepened as he glanced around the place. Then Emily began to fuss, letting out little bleats of distress that caught his attention.

"Hello, princess," he said, walking into the room and automatically reaching for her.

Isabella's heart lurched. She hadn't expected to see him until the spring thaw—until she'd had time to stop missing him. But no matter what she felt, she couldn't halt the smile that broke out on her face. "So what're you doing down here in the flatlands?" It was strange, but with him around, the mountain of work didn't seem as much like Pike's Peak as it had a moment ago.

"Seeing if you needed any help," he said, expertly cradling a now serene Emily against one strong arm. "And it looks as though you do."

"We're doing just fine. We'll get this place together in no time."

He didn't dispute that, but merely said, "I hear the hotel is full because of the storm."

That piece of news sounded even worse the second time around. "That what you hear?"

He nodded.

Life and the weather had thrown her a curve ball. But over the past eight months she'd grown strong enough to catch it, and without a mitt if she had to. "I have the newspaper. I'm expecting to find a room for rent by the end of the day." She could hope, couldn't she?

His mouth was drawn into a thin line, his brow furrowed. "Didn't anyone ever teach you not to expect anything?"

She chuckled. "Is that dreadful moral support the only kind of help you're offering?"

"No. This is." With his free hand, he took a set of keys out of his coat pocket and tossed them to her.

"What's this?"

"That room you were looking for."

She glanced at the keys, then back up at him.

"You need a place to stay while you're getting this one together, right?" he asked as he looked down at Emily. The little girl's gaze was fixed on him.

"Right," Isabella said slowly, hating where this was going.

"So why don't you and Emily come back and stay with me until then?"

Reaching out, she eased her daughter from his

powerful arms. It was a protective instinct, she knew. Emily was only an infant, but Isabella didn't want her getting even the tiniest bit attached to Michael Wulf. She knew how it felt to lose him. "No, we couldn't."

"Why not? It's a comfortable place."

Too comfortable, she wanted to tell him. Just being near him again had her wishing for things that would never come.

He glanced at her with hooded eyes. "Staying with me a few more nights isn't that big of a deal, Bella."

Yeah, maybe not for a man whose heart is locked up tighter than an oyster shell, she thought. Michael's past had taught him well. Her past had only intensified the yearning for the kind of life, and the kind of love, her parents had enjoyed.

But what was the alternative? She wasn't going to call her friends, and the hotel wasn't going to grow another room.

"I appreciate the offer, Michael. But why would you even want us there? You made it pretty clear that we were in the way."

His jaw bunched. "What are you talking about?"

"You hide away, bury yourself in work and hardly come out, unless it's to thank me for making a meal."

"Work is what I do," he said, his voice distant. "It's the most important thing."

"Is it?"

His eyes narrowed. "What are you trying to say?"

Isabella exhaled heavily. "It just seems to me like lately there's something else that's just as important to you as your work. And that's paying back what you perceive to be a debt.'' She looked up into those familiar dark eyes and said what had been on her mind almost every moment since their brief kiss. ''This debt is paid. You don't have to do anything more for us out of gratitude.''

He shrugged. ''I'm only doing what's right.''

Emily gave a soft little sneeze.

Michael frowned. ''And don't you think you should do what's best for Emily?''

Her chin lifted indignantly as she pulled the blanket more snugly over her little girl. ''I'll always do what's best for Emily.''

''Glad to hear it.'' He nodded as though her ire was exactly what he was aiming for. ''First thing tomorrow, I'll have my housekeeper come and help you get this place—''

''That's not necessary, I'm perfectly capable—''

''Her name is Sara, and she's the best.'' Barely stopping for breath he continued. ''I had your car towed to the shop, and you can borrow one of my SUVs until it's ready. And while you're cleaning and getting the store fixed up, I'll watch Emily. Except when she needs to be fed, of course.''

Her mouth dropped open. ''Michael, you have work to—''

''She's no trouble.''

Isabella was ready to refuse him again, but she stopped. Was the fight really worth it? Michael Wulf was being kind, being a friend. And she and Emily needed both right now. They were in a pickle Isabella hadn't planned for, and she couldn't allow her pride to override practicality.

She sighed. She knew what he was offering was the best thing for her daughter. And she would sacrifice anything to keep her baby safe and healthy. Even her heart.

He lifted a brow. "Deal?"

She nodded slowly. "Deal."

"My car's outside—with a car seat in it."

"Where did you get a car seat?"

"I stopped by Thomas's. He loaned me the one he had in his car. He said we could keep it for as long as we need it. His great-nephew's outgrown it now."

We? We could keep it? As long as *we* need it? The words made her knees as weak as butter, but she wasn't going to allow her body to misinterpret the message. No matter how badly her heart wanted to follow suit. She had to be absolutely clear about his intentions, or lack thereof, going in if she was ever going to survive.

"You were pretty sure I was going to say yes," she said finally.

"I knew your good sense would prevail."

"Well, you're hard to say no to, Michael."

He nodded. "As long as you understand that, then you won't object to my taking the two of you shopping for a few things you need."

Michael ambled up to the counter at Molly's Mother and Child and added three more of what Bella called "onesies" to his already growing pile of clothing, blankets, toys and other baby accessories that looked essential. He could feel Bella watching every move he made. With Emily asleep in her arms, she stood there, aghast, shaking her head first at the pile, then at him.

"I'm taking enough from you, Michael," she scolded for the fourth time in as many minutes as she unbuttoned the top button of her thick navy coat. "Staying at the house, borrowing the car, accepting help from your housekeeper. I won't accept this. *I'm* buying Emily what she needs."

"This—" he pointed to the pile of clothes "—isn't a whim, Bella. This is a birthday present."

Her pretty blue eyes narrowed. "Birthday present?"

He wasn't about to let her win. He had millions and no one to spend it on. And this was the first time he'd ever felt pleasure in buying something for someone.

"She's a week old today," he said simply.

Bella just stared at him, but he saw an ounce of surrender lingering behind that indomitable gaze. So he moved in swiftly. "It's rude to refuse a gift. You don't want to be rude, do you?"

"Of course I don't want to be rude, but—"

"Good, because for a moment there I was starting to feel a little wounded." He touched his chest, where his heart was rumored to be. "Like I wasn't good enough to give Emily a present."

At that she burst out laughing. "You could sell an egg to a chicken, couldn't you."

His brow rose as he plunked down a bunch of baby bottles next to the cash register. "Quite possibly."

"Are you finding everything okay, Isabella?"

Apple-faced Molly Homney scooted around the desk and gave Bella a wide smile, her gaze flicking warily to Michael. He was used to looks like that. He rarely came to town, and when he did he didn't even pretend to be friendly. Hell, half the kids that had teased him way back when had stayed in Fielding as adults—including Molly Homney—and he wasn't interested in making nice with people who only wanted to get to know him now because he could buy the entire town if he had a mind to.

But then again, this woman had been a friend of Bella's. So for her, he would be agreeable.

"I think we've found more than enough," Bella said on a laugh.

Molly sighed. "Did I say how good it is to see you again, Isabella?"

"Yes, you did. But I don't mind hearing it again."

"We missed you so much. The girls are going to be ecstatic when they see you and little Emily." Molly shook her head. "You're just so darn lucky. Since the day I opened this store, Herb and I have been trying and trying, but no baby yet."

"It'll happen," Bella assured her. "When you least expect it."

Molly leaned forward and whispered, "The fun's in the trying, right?"

Bella's gaze flickered toward Michael, then she

looked down at Emily and said softly, and not at all convincingly, "Right."

Michael knew that Molly hadn't missed that glance, and he also knew that the implications of it would be all over town by morning.

Most people already knew that he'd delivered her child. He wasn't looking to ruin her reputation. She'd just returned home, and the rumor of a romantic involvement with the Wulf was only going to hurt her standing in the community.

Michael pulled out a credit card. "Since you left your wallet at the shop, let me get this and you can repay me later."

Bella's eyes widened and her lips parted as though she was about to protest. Just then, Molly reached under the counter, and Michael took the opportunity to lean toward Bella and whisper in her ear, "Repay me in doughnuts. Every morning."

He heard her sharp intake of breath, and something inside him shifted. Damn, she smelled good, he thought, breathing in her delicious scent one more time before he straightened.

After Molly had rung everything up and bagged it, she turned to Bella. "Is your apartment ready yet, or do you need a place to stay?"

"I'm staying with a friend."

Bella answered the question with no reserve and no embarrassment. She'd also had an out, Michael mused, but hadn't taken it.

"Not Connie?" Molly asked.

"Nope."

"Or Wendy?"

"No."

Molly's gaze flickered toward Michael. He raised a brow at her. She quickly returned to her task of bagging up the merchandise.

Bella was smart enough to know that Molly knew exactly who that friend was, yet she'd spoken with pride in her voice. Only one thing had really changed in fifteen years. Bella was still strong and principled, but today when they'd parted, he wasn't willing to let her go. Not yet.

Molly smiled at Bella, then at Emily. "Call me and we'll get the gang together."

Bella thanked her old friend, then gathered up Emily and left. Michael followed them out of the store.

"Staying with a friend, huh?" he said as he opened the car door for her. "I think she knows exactly who you're staying with."

"I didn't lie." Bella placed Emily in the car seat, then stood and met his gaze. "I am staying with a friend. Right?"

Around them the wind picked up, swirling threads of snow into white tumbleweeds. Neither one of them seemed to notice. She was waiting for an answer to a simple question. But then again, nothing was simple between them as of late.

"Let's go home," he muttered, unaccountably irritated.

Her gaze remained on his for a moment, then she let him help her into the passenger side of the SUV.

What was the truth?

He didn't know. Jaw clenched, he put the shopping bags, changing table and crib in the back. He just didn't know.

Six

"**W**here should this go, hon?"

Abandoning her grimy bathtub for a moment, Isabella glanced up. Sara Rogers, Michael's housekeeper, held out a small unmarked box for inspection.

Isabella pulled off her latex gloves and reached for it. After a soft shake, a wave of comfort swept over her.

"Something special?" Sara asked.

"My mother's copper cookie cutters." A smile came to Isabella lips as she handed the box back to the Southern gentlewoman with her short gray bob, thin frame and big violet eyes.

"Oh, my. Well, then, we'll have to be real careful with this." Sara tilted her head and winked. "How about that large drawer off the fridge? I just wiped it down.''

''That'll be perfect,'' Isabella said, reaching for her work gloves. ''By the way, have I thanked you to-day?''

''Yes, you have, hon. Twice in fact.''

''Well, they say that the third time's the charm. So, thank you.''

Sara placed her hands on her hips and studied Isabella for a moment. ''Mr. Wulf's sure right about you.''

At the mention of Michael, Isabella's pulse quickened. ''Right about what? What did…Mr. Wulf say?''

A grin the size of Tennessee, her home state, broke out on Sara's face. ''That you're a good one.''

Isabella's eyes widened. ''What in the world does that mean?''

Sara laughed. ''Don't have a clue, hon, but in all the years I've worked for him, I've never heard him say anything like it.'' She winked again. ''I'm going to put this away and start cleaning that stove.''

After Sara was gone, Isabella went back to scrubbing the tub, but her mind remained on Michael and their living arrangements.

It had been a week since he'd invited her and Emily to stay with him, which she'd thought would be plenty of time to get her place in order. But she'd been wrong. Making the apartment livable and her father's old work space into a pastry shop was taking far more work than just surface cleaning and stocking shelves.

Sara was a godsend, but she was only there for a limited time every day. Old neighbors from town came for a few hours to help out here and there, but most of them wanted to use that time to catch up and find out about Michael's inventions and his intentions toward her. So she'd started politely refusing the offers, extending her guest pass at the ''glass house'' for a while longer.

But the reasons for the slow pace in finishing her apartment were more than her friends wanting to play catch-up or the amount of work to be done. The separation from Emily for more than a few hours at a time had been torture. Isabella had left bottles of breast milk in the refrigerator for Michael to give her, but she'd wanted to be there, too. So she'd started making excuses to come home and check on her, play with her and nurse her.

Michael never seemed surprised to see her turn up several times a day. In fact, he almost seemed pleased to have her there. But at night, he'd always revert back to the lone wolf that he was. Taking his meals alone, staying up in his office, working late. He still slept in that chair by the fire every night, however. She never asked him why. She didn't want her questions to run him out, to drive him back upstairs. He did enough of that. From dusk till dawn, she felt protected and cared for, and Lord help her, she counted on it.

The ring of the Fielding Elementary School bell

several blocks away interrupted her thoughts, and she checked her watch. It was noon. Connie and Molly would probably be arriving anytime now, ready to "help." Somehow the two of them had convinced Isabella that they were geared up to clean her living-room floor.

It felt good to be home now. As soon as Isabella had gotten the chance to explain to her friends what had happened over the past several years, she'd done it. And true to form, they had readily welcomed her back, even welcomed her into their homes if she had a mind to move from Michael's. But she didn't. With a "thanks, but no thanks" to her friends, she'd told them that she and Emily were content where they were and left it at that.

Sighing, Isabella rinsed out the tub, took off her gloves, tossed them into the trash, then left the bathroom to find the pair, mops in hand, standing in the middle of the living-room floor.

Connie gave her a smile. "Sara let us in."

"She's Michael Wulf's housekeeper, isn't she?" Molly asked, fiddling with a bottle of wood soap.

Isabella nodded. "Yes, she is."

Molly had never understood the concept of leaving any juicy subject alone. "We were just talking about the day he moved back here."

Connie rolled her eyes. "Not *we*, Molly. Just you."

Molly snorted. "Don't think I didn't see those ears of yours perk up when I mentioned that Alan Olson said when he delivered that grand piano up there last year, he saw an elevator in Michael Wulf's house."

When she turned to look at Isabella, Connie's brown eyes clearly telegraphed that what Molly said was true. "What *is* his place like, Isabella?"

Molly snorted. "Forget his place, what's *he* like?"

They both stared, waiting for her to give them a confirmation to all those "Wulf" headlines. "He's intelligent and serious and very patient."

Molly grimaced, obviously not hearing what she wanted to hear. "Well, he's certainly gotten handsome over the years. I noticed that right off the day you two came into my shop. But his attitude's the same."

Isabella bristled. "What are you talking about?"

"He didn't want to fit in then and he sure doesn't want to fit in now."

"That's not fair, Molly," Connie argued.

Molly shrugged. "I call 'em like I see 'em."

"He tried to fit in when he first came here," Isabella said, planting her fists on her hips. "And you all shut him out. Why should he be the one to bury a hatchet he never swung?"

Connie looked down at her dustpan. "I was one of those kids that picked on him. And when your aunt couldn't take him in and he had to leave Fielding, I felt so bad about how I'd acted. But honestly, Isabella, I don't think he would even listen to an apology now, much less accept one." Her gaze lifted and so did her brow. "He doesn't need us anyway. He's rich and successful and probably has a ton of fashionable friends in New York and Los Angeles."

"Well, he sure made friends with our little Isabella,'' Molly remarked, her lips curving into a Cheshire-cat grin. "And Emily, too. He watches her during the day, doesn't he?"

Isabella lifted her chin. "Yes, he does."

"That's very generous of him." Connie smiled at her, and Isabella appreciated her for it.

"And who does he watch at night?" Molly asked, her eyes sparkling.

Isabella's stomach clenched. Her friend's teasing was too close to home. "His computer, I imagine."

"Seriously, though, it really doesn't worry you at all?" Molly asked. "That…well, that someone like that is taking care of Emily?"

"Someone like what?" Isabella demanded.

"You know, strange and a little frightening."

Anger shot through Isabella's veins. White-hot anger. As much as she'd wanted to believe that the children of Fielding had grown into mature adults, her friend had just proved otherwise. She wasn't a bad person, just so uninformed. "Michael Wulf is an extraordinary man," she said, her tone ominous. "He has changed the world with his technology. I feel honored that he considers me a friend, and there is no one I trust more with my daughter."

Molly blanched, her gaze shooting to the floor. "I'm sorry, Isabella. I didn't mean to offend you. You know me, I get started yapping and I can't stop."

The fire in Isabella slowly abated. "It's all right."

"I should get back to the store," Molly said, checking her watch before scurrying out the door, a trifle shamefaced. "I'll try and come over tomorrow to finish up the floor. Bye, all."

Isabella shook her head at the floor that hadn't even been touched.

Connie laughed. "She can be a pain in the butt sometimes, but she's relatively harmless. Unless you happen to eat one of her brown-sugar cookies, of course."

Isabella laughed along with her. "Yeah, I remember." She regarded her friend. "You think I overreacted, don't you."

Connie shrugged. "Maybe just a touch. But I have to say, if I ever need someone to defend me, I'm coming to you." Lifting a brow, she added, "So, does Michael have any idea that you're falling in love with him?"

The sound of splashing met Michael at the open bedroom door. He'd come to get the legal pad he'd left by the fireplace last night, but the sound diverted his attention. Bella was in the tub. His groin stirred at the vision of her naked and doused in suds. Driving a hand through his hair, he hoped to force that thought out. For God's sake, she'd just had a child two weeks ago. He shouldn't be having erotic thoughts about her. He shouldn't be having thoughts about her at all.

But when he walked into the room and glanced through the open bathroom door, he was saved from himself. Her hair back in a loose ponytail, Bella was fully clothed and giving Emily a bath. Inside the tub, the baby girl was lying in the soft cradle tub he'd gotten, her tiny hands splashing her mother with the inch or so of water.

He tried to stay quiet as he moved closer and stood in the doorway. But she must've felt him there because she glanced over her shoulder and smiled. "Pull up a towel and grab some shampoo. I was just about to wash her hair."

For Michael, giving a baby a bath was far from a routine task. Ask him to write a zillion lines of code for a complex program and he'd come through with flying colors. But he knew he couldn't say no to either one of the Spencer females.

He knelt beside Bella, rolled up his sleeves and grabbed the no-tears baby shampoo.

She tossed him a sidelong glance. "So, are you looking to add shampooing to your long list of baby tasks?"

He poured some of the yellow liquid into his hands and worked it into a lather. "Am I that transparent?"

"No, actually. You're rather difficult to figure out sometimes."

"Well, that's just force of habit," he said, gently rubbing the shampoo into Emily's pale wisps of hair.

"Interesting. And I thought that prickly-pear demeanor was by choice."

Michael turned to look at her sly grin and playful eyes. For a second he took stock of where he was and what he was doing. Sitting next to the woman that made him feel things he didn't want to feel, bathing another man's child. And yet, there was nowhere he'd rather be. He glanced down at Emily. She blinked up at him, her hand lifted up toward him.

Like a magnet to steel, he reached for her and she wrapped her tiny fingers around his thumb. Something shot up his arm—an electric shock of warmth, a tenderness, an astonishing emotion he'd never felt before and didn't understand. The intensity of it bowled him over and he slowly eased his hand away. "I'm going to let your mother finish up here, princess." He stood. "I need to get back to work."

"Really, Michael?" Isabella's blue eyes searched his now shuttered ones. "Couldn't you just put work aside for a half hour and…well, I don't know, live a little?"

His lips twisted. She saw too much and it annoyed the hell out of him. "I'm living just fine, Bella. Take a look around."

"You know I'm not talking about money or what it can buy."

"I'll see you later," he said as he turned to leave.

"From the safety of your chair by the fire?" she countered.

He stopped at the door, but didn't turn back around.

"I'm going to feed Emily and put her to bed," Isabella said, her tone patient but firm. "Sara made a roast and mashed potatoes, and I made a chocolate torte. I'll be in the kitchen in about a half hour. Have dinner with me."

Another battle broke out inside Michael from a war that had begun the minute he'd opened the door to a car covered in snow and saw its occupant. And that woman was asking him to do something more intimate than she could possibly imagine. She was asking too much. "Enjoy your dinner, Bella."

"Enya, *Watermark,*" Isabella told the CD player as she lit the ten votive candles that decorated the kitchen table.

Although she hadn't intended it, the room looked magical, glistening in the candlelight. The table was set for two with beautiful Prussian-blue place mats, pristine china that had never been used, shining silver and winking crystal. She'd even placed a bowl of fragrant herbs from the hydroponic garden in the center. To anyone who wasn't aware of her true relationship with Michael, the scene appeared set for romance.

Connie's query, the one Isabella had left unanswered, flickered across her mind. Did Michael know that she was falling in love with him? Would he even care to know? She rolled her eyes. Of course he wouldn't. He could barely accept the emotional ramifications when Emily touched him. He seemed incapable of closeness. And Isabella was starting to wonder if that would ever change.

She trudged over to the stove. However uncertain the future, she was determined to have a nice dinner tonight, whether he chose to join her or not.

While she sliced the roast, Isabella listened to Emily's soft, rhythmic breathing on the baby monitor that she kept close to her at all times. Her daughter had gone to sleep with just two songs and a kiss tonight, leaving Isabella with an evening to herself.

A low growl sounded behind her. "You win this battle, Bella."

Or not.

"And the war, too?" Isabella smiled to herself. So he'd actually come. Even after their disagreement earlier, he'd come. She continued to slice the roast, not wanting him to see the look of satisfaction on her face.

"That remains to be seen."

"So where's my peace offering?"

She heard him pull out a chair, sit, then expel a weighty breath. "You wanted to know why I eat alone, right?"

Isabella turned around and faced him.

His voice held little emotion as he spoke. "Up until the age of fifteen, I had absolutely no control over anything. Who I lived with, how I lived or where. Being with a huge group of other pissed-off kids, you can barely breathe. There's no space, nothing to make your own. Then I started taking my food up to my room or out in the yard—no one bothered me. It became my time, the one thing I could claim."

Isabella was amazed. She couldn't believe he was telling her this. All she wanted to do was throw her arms around him and let him know how honored she felt, but she knew he would hate such a gesture. So with a platter of steaming beef in her hands, she walked over to the table and said casually, "And now?"

His gaze fairly burned a hole in her soul. "For some reason, I can breathe when I'm with you."

Her hand paused in the middle of scooping up some potatoes. What did he mean? Was he talking about feeling comfortable with her? Could he breathe around her because of their friendship? Or something altogether different?

With a shaky hand, she filled his plate with potatoes and roast and green beans, then his wineglass with the same sparkling cider that twinkled from her glass.

"Need anything else?" she asked.

He looked up, his gaze moving to her mouth. "What are you offering, Bella?"

The urge to lower herself into his lap, kiss him silly and say, "I'm offering this—take it or leave it," was incredibly tempting. But the fear that he might choose to leave it overpowered the impulse. So she turned away from that searing gaze and sat down across the table from him.

"I'm offering good conversation," she said finally, her breathing uneven. "And a wonderful meal."

His gaze remained on her, and she wondered if he was going to pursue the discussion. But he didn't. He picked at his potatoes and went off on a different direction. "How's the shop coming along?"

She felt thankful for the lighter mood. They both needed it right now. Especially Michael. This being his first meal à la companion and all.

"The shop's not really coming along," she said. "I'm still working on the apartment."

"Taking too many breaks?"

A half smile came to her lips. "Hey, I have to

check up on you and Emily. See if you guys are having too much fun without me.''

"If we were, you'd never catch us.''

"What?''

He adopted a serious visage. "It's like this—while you're away, I have the entire Ringling Brothers circus up here, then after they leave, Emily and I groove to some serious rock and roll.'' He raised a brow. "Rolling Stones.''

She held her grin in check. "And when I come home?''

He shrugged nonchalantly, then took a tentative bite of roast. "We close up shop, and Emily goes straight to sleep.''

Feigning emotional injury, she sucked in a breath. "No circus for me? No dancing to the Stones?''

"I'm sorry.'' His dark gaze moved over her, seeping into her pores like melting chocolate. "You just can't get no satisfaction, sweetheart.''

Her short stint at lightheartedness suddenly dropped away. Heat rushed through her body and her mouth went dry as cotton. How could he disarm her in two seconds flat? It wasn't fair, especially when he was just playing and her heart didn't understand the rules of the game.

And in that instant, his decision about not eating with her seemed like a good one, a safe one, a smart one. Perhaps he could breathe well around her, but the air in her lungs always seemed to get caught when she looked at him.

One thing looked glaringly obvious: if she wanted

to leave this house with her heart intact, she was going to have to pick up the pace on getting her apartment ready.

But the problem was she didn't want to leave this house. Or him.

"I heard you defended me today," he said, dragging her back to the candlelit, Enya-playing present.

She cleared her throat. "I haven't the vaguest idea what you're talking about."

"Oh, you don't, huh?"

Darn that eavesdropping Sara and her Southern charm.

"So there was no discussion about how much I've changed? Or how little?"

Isabella took a sip of her sparkling cider to stall for time.

"How I've gotten stranger and weirder over the years?"

She fairly choked on her cider. "No one said weird. They…"

"What did they say?"

Putting down her knife and fork, she exhaled. "You know what it is, Michael? They don't know you, that's all."

"They don't need to know me." The amusement left his eyes. And just like that, she'd lost him again.

"Maybe they do. And maybe you need to get to know them."

He frowned. "Why the hell would I want to do that?"

"To put the past where it belongs," she argued.

"Or start to, anyway." She leaned forward. "They were stupid, ignorant kids."

"And what are they now?"

"Just townsfolk. Flawed like any others, but not out to get you."

He chuckled bitterly.

"Doesn't it get lonely up here?" Isabella asked.

"Not with you and Emily around."

"We're not going to be around forever." The words were out of her mouth fast, and their meaning settled over the table.

Anguished cries came over the baby monitor, saving them from further discussion. Isabella was on her feet and halfway to the door when she said, "I'm going to check on Emily."

"And I'll clean up in here," he muttered.

As she headed for her bedroom—his bedroom—Isabella pushed away the fierce determination that rose up and claimed her every time he was near. The determination that made her want to heal the man she was falling in love with before he dug himself into an even deeper hole.

But Michael Wulf didn't want to be saved, she thought as she entered the bedroom. Even with the tiny step he'd taken tonight, he was stubborn on every other subject relating to change. And she knew that the more she tried, the harder it would be for her heart to heal when she left.

Emily just needed a clean diaper and a meal. So after changing her, Isabella slipped into her night-gown, lay down on the bed and held her sweet little girl in her arms. Her daughter was happily suckling when Michael knocked on the door.

"Come in," she called softly.

He took one look at her and Emily and turned away. "I'll come back later."

"No." She swallowed hard. Heartache be damned, she wanted him close. She always wanted him close. For as long as it was possible. "Why don't you build a fire and stay?"

Michael stood there for a moment, his jaw tight as he decided what to do and what he wanted. After a few seconds he walked into the room, crossed to the fireplace and set some logs in the grate. It took only a moment for the tinder to catch and a fire to blaze. Then he sat down and stretched out his leg.

"You're early tonight," she said gently. "You usually don't spill in until after midnight."

"I know" was all he said.

The fire crackled, Emily nursed, and after several bouts of *Should I or shouldn't I?* Isabella decided to take a chance and ask for something she'd wanted since the night she'd given birth to Emily.

"Michael?"

"Hmm?"

Her pulse jumped around like a rubber ball. "Why don't you take that rebellion of sharing dinner with me one step further?"

He glanced over at her, so incredibly, rustically handsome in the firelight. "How would I do that?"

She would be gone soon, and so would these

strange and very wonderful moments of time. "Sleep with me."

His eyes went black as coal.

She scurried to clarify. "In the bed. We can share it. You insist on being in the room and…and I insist that you let that leg rest." She bit her lip.

He turned back toward the fire, and she wanted to die of embarrassment. What was she thinking? Why didn't she just get in the car, drive into town and moon the crowd over at Teddie's Pub and Pool? It would've been less humiliating.

After clicking off the bedside lamp, she exhaled and settled back further into the pillows. "Good night, Michael."

No answer came, not any verbal one, that is, but after a moment or two, he stood up and walked over to the bed. She held her breath, her heart pummeling her ribs as he lay down beside her, outside the covers and fully dressed. But she felt his warmth through the barriers.

"Night, Bella," he whispered as he put his arm around her.

As Emily continued to nurse, Michael moved closer, shutting off the small gap between them, and Isabella let her head fall against his shoulder with the understanding that this small glimpse of ecstasy would never be enough.

Seven
_____

The afternoon sun submerged the room in clean yellow light. Michael stared at the computer screen, his fingers poised above the keyboard.

Nothing.

This was unheard of. His mind was normally spilling over with project ideas. But this one in particular had him stumped.

He heard Emily's cry erupt from the baby monitor beside his mouse pad. Because he watched her during the day, he kept it close to him. The little girl now sounded very distressed, he thought, staring at the device. After a moment, Bella's soft soothing voice came over the monitor.

Michael pushed back his chair, wanting to go to them. Then he stopped and shoved himself toward the desk. Dammit, he couldn't react this way every time Emily cried and Bella went to her. Two weeks of sleeping in the same bed, eating dinner together, they were starting to fall into a routine. A very unwise routine.

No matter how right it felt each night stealing into bed with her, no matter how strong the urge to taste her again, pull her closer, feel the softness of her against him, he wasn't a part of their family. Sweet little Emily lay between them as she nursed reminding him, warning him to remember who they were to him. Two individuals he'd sworn to protect.

And that meant protecting them from himself, too.

Bella had told him that her apartment and the bakery were almost ready. Soon they'd be gone. That thought pierced his chest. But even with the frequency in which he had to remind himself of their departure, the blade of pain to come thankfully hadn't reached his heart.

The soft whirr of the elevator rising tore his thoughts away. Bella was always coming upstairs without an invitation. In spite of himself, he looked forward to her impromptu visits, although he could never tell her that.

But when the metal doors parted, it was no curvy blonde with liquid-blue eyes that emerged.

"Hello, Michael."

"What the devil are you doing up here, Thomas?"

"This your office?" Doc Pinta's gaze worked the room like a mother-in-law looking for dust.

"Yes, it is," Michael answered dryly. "How did you get up here?"

"Isabella."

Michael snorted. "Of course. As if I really needed to ask. That woman has invaded my life." And damn if he didn't enjoy it. No one needed to know that sad fact, however.

Thomas fell into a leather chair, crossed one booted foot over his knee and grinned. "You could always tell her to go."

"Their apartment isn't ready yet."

"And are you going to be ready to let them go when it is?"

"Of course I am," he said a little too forcefully. "This, the two of them staying here, well, it's been just a..." He paused.

Thomas's brow shot up. "A what? A good deed?"

"Something like that."

The older man nodded, amusement flashing in his eyes. "So what are you doing for Thanksgiving?"

"The same thing I do every year."

"Hole up in your house?"

"Work."

Thomas chuckled. "Ah, yes, of course."

"Normally I'd stay at the computer from dawn to midnight, but—"

"This year you might stop at dusk?"

"I was going to say that I'll probably stop for an hour or two. Maybe have something with Bella and—"

"Isabella and Emily are coming to my house."

Michael paused. "Are they?" He let that bit of information wash over him like ice water. He felt like three kinds of fool for assuming Bella was staying here with him tomorrow. But what could he do? As his latest mantra warned, they were guests—and soon-to-be-departing guests. Her life and where she chose to spend it and whom she chose to spend it with had nothing to do him.

"And I'm going to put it out there again this year," Thomas was saying. "If you can tear yourself away from the office for an evening, we'd love to have you, too. It won't be anything fancy. Just family."

Even though he and Thomas had always been on friendly terms, Michael had never crossed that line with him. No matter how many times the doctor and his wife invited Michael to their home, he wasn't about to get involved in some warm and fuzzy family thing.

Michael shook his head. "I don't think so. But thanks for the invitation."

"Well, if you change your mind…"

"I won't."

Thomas nodded, then turned and walked into the elevator. "I sure do love Thanksgiving. Reminds a person of all there is to be thankful for in this life, don't you think?"

The door closed on Thomas's query, and for moment Michael stared at the door that had shut him off from everything human until Bella had traipsed back into his life.

A low growl escaped his throat as he turned back

to his work. This, *work*—that's what he was thankful for. He didn't need a holiday to bring on that bit of self-awareness.

"You have to peel them, Michael." Isabella laughed as she dipped into a kitchen drawer and came out with an apple peeler. It was strange, but she knew the workings of Michael's kitchen better than he did. The intimacy of it all still surprised her.

Michael grumbled as he stripped the apple of its protection. "I don't know why I'm helping with a dessert I'm not even going to eat."

"Neither do I," she replied cheerfully. "Why don't you go back upstairs and work?"

"I'm working out an idea in my head." He kept peeling. "I needed some air."

It was how they were. One grumpy and one excessively merry. They seemed to balance each other out, Isabella thought. During the day they each worked, while sharing chores and sharing Emily. At night Michael read Emily a story until she fell asleep and Isabella made dinner. Then, when it was time to go to bed, they lay together while Emily had her late-night snack. They tried not touch, but inevitably each night they'd lose that battle and by morning they would be cuddled together with Emily between them.

Isabella rolled out the pie crust with a fervor that erupted inside her whenever she thought about Michael in her bed. But although she couldn't smother the heated workings inside, she tried to remain cool in demeanor on the outside and opted for idle conversation. "Why aren't you going to Thanksgiving dinner tonight? And don't tell me it's work."

"It *is* work."

"This is a holiday, Michael."

"I don't believe in holidays."

With steady hands, she placed the crust in the glass pie plate. "What do you mean you don't believe in holidays? You had Christmas with me and Dad."

"I have two weeks to deliver my software to Micronics." He started cutting up the apples. "I can't afford any more nights off."

He wasn't fooling anyone with that grouchy declaration. All those nights with Emily and dinners with her hadn't really cut into his work schedule at all.

"Maybe I can help you," she offered.

"Help me what?"

Oh, Lord. That was a loaded question. But one step at a time. "If I can help you solve this problem you're working on, will you go to the Pintas with me?"

His eyebrows rose a fraction.

"C'mon, give me a chance," she said. "I have some great ideas."

The skepticism shadowing his gaze was no surprise, but as she poured the apples into the waiting pie crust, he explained, "The software I've created is for a Web-to-home connection. My original proposal included the ability to turn the thermostat up and down over the Internet, arming or disarming the home-security system, watering the plants and the yard."

"That's sounds wonderful." Fragrant cinnamon

and nutmeg wafted through the air as Isabella sprinkled the spices and sugar over the apples, then dotted the whole thing with butter.

"I don't feel it's enough. I want to add a feature for parents that will allow them to spend more time with their children. Everyone's so busy, especially mothers. I thought that speeding up the small things like having the bathwater already drawn would leave more time for the actual bath."

"It would."

"But I need a few more ideas."

"Okay." Her mind worked as she rolled out the top crust. "I can certainly give you a mother's perspective. How about being able to use a Palm Pilot to start a bottle warming while Mom's still on the drive home? Or an automatic inventory system that keeps track of how many diapers and wipes are used and reorders through an online shopping list?" She turned to face him. "Or you could design a car-pool program where the mom who's driving can send instant messages to the other children's mothers letting them know their kids have safely arrived at their destination."

Michael didn't say anything for a moment, just stared at her, and Isabella wondered if her suggestions sounded ridiculous. But then he moved toward her, backing her against the counter, his hands bracketing her hips, and she couldn't think at all.

His hooded gaze level with hers, he whispered, "Has anyone ever told you how smart you are?"

Caught, pinned, trapped by the sexiest man she'd ever laid eyes on. "I've heard that once or twice."

His eyes moved to her mouth. "How about how beautiful you are?"

She swallowed, but her voice remained caught in her throat. She wanted to kiss him. Just one, then she could go back to town happy. Oh, who was she kidding? A kiss would never be enough. But it was a start.

Her silence seemed to make Michael draw back. "Sorry about that."

Dammit. "About what?" She fought to keep her voice light, playful. "Giving me a compliment?"

But Michael's eyes were shuttered, his mouth drawn into a firm line. "No. It just sounded like a come-on and..." He trailed off.

"And you would never come on to me, right?" she finished for him.

"Bella, listen, you deserve more than—"

She put a hand up. "I have a lot of work to finish, Michael." She had no interest in listening to his excuses for not touching her, no matter how noble and rational they sounded. After such a crummy marriage, she wanted the real thing. She wanted a man who wanted her and wasn't afraid to admit it.

"If you'll excuse me," she said tightly.

"Fine. I'll go." His eyes darkened. "But I'll see you later."

She watched him walk out of the kitchen, all too clear about what he meant. He'd see her in bed later. He'd lie beside her in the spirit of protectiveness, while her hormones raged and her body craved what it couldn't have.

She needed to leave, go to her own home. Because what had started as a fantasy was slowly becoming torture.

Michael stood on the Pintas' doorstep with a poinsettia and a bottle of that sparkling cider Bella liked so much. Sara had thoughtfully made him a small turkey with all the fixings before she'd left for her own family celebration, but he'd packed it up, put it in the fridge and left the house.

He told himself that he was here because he owed Bella. Those ideas she'd spouted off like tennis balls from an automatic feeder were pure genius and would no doubt make Micronics do backflips. But that nagging voice that resided too close to his heart relayed an altogether different story: he couldn't eat alone anymore. Or maybe it was that he couldn't eat without her. Either way, he was in trouble.

The door opened and Thomas presented him with a grand smile. "You came."

"Don't rub it in," Michael grumbled.

Thomas laughed as he escorted Michael inside. The scents of turkey and apples were heavy in the air. First stop was the kitchen where he presented Ruth with the poinsettia and shook the hand of her younger son, Kyle, who was sampling his mother's stuffing and mashed potatoes with a fork. Michael thanked them for inviting him and went into the living room.

Looking extraordinarily beautiful with her long

blond hair loose, a little makeup and that killer smile, Bella sat on the floral couch beside Thomas's oldest son, Derek, talking animatedly. The Pinta sons had been athletes in high school and had had no taste for teasing a young Michael as their schoolmates had. They were pretty decent guys...well, as much as Michael had gotten to know them in the four years he'd been back in Fielding.

Derek had been living in Minneapolis for a few years practicing law, and he looked the part. Casual but expensive suit, slicked-back hair and manicured hands. And, Michael noticed with a trace of annoyance, those hands were holding a crying Emily.

The threesome looked way too comfortable. He knew that someday Bella might have a new husband and Emily would have a father. But that day wasn't today. They still lived with him. And until they moved out, they belonged to him.

"This is a surprise," Bella said as both she and Derek stood up and walked over to greet him.

"We had a deal, right?" Michael said, glancing at her form-fitting blue skirt and blouse. One month and already her figure was all breath-catching curves. Where was the mercy?

She shrugged, her smile tentative. "I wasn't exactly sure."

Emily continued to cry, and Bella took her from Derek, but soon that cry turned into a wail.

"Let me take her," Michael said, easing the little girl into his arms.

Bella smiled at Derek. "He's something of a baby-whisperer."

A very content Emily remained in his arms all through dinner. From time to time, Bella would offer to take her. His excuse was always the same: Emily was fine where she was.

No one made a big deal out of Michael's surprising interest in joining a social event. The awkwardness he'd expected to feel never came. He hated to admit it, but they were a nice group of people, no apparent hidden agendas. Over turkey and dressing and corn pudding, they discussed current events and told jokes. But when dessert time came, so did Michael's waiting cynicism.

"Before anyone takes a bite of either of Bella's delicious pies," Thomas began, "we each have to say what we're thankful for." He glanced at Michael and gave him a one-word explanation, "Tradition."

"My health," Ruth exclaimed.

"I'm incredibly thankful for my daughter," Bella said with a soft smile.

"Mom's sage and onion stuffing," Thomas's younger son offered. "Just the best."

Thomas looked around the table. "For all of you being here."

"Class-action lawsuits," Derek said, deadpan.

Everyone broke out into laughter and Michael hoped to hell that they'd forgotten him. To help that plan along, he picked up his fork and focused on his slice of apple pie. But soon he felt all their eyes on him and he glanced up.

"Come now, son," Thomas said with a hearty chuckle. "Hurry up. I'm dying to take a bite of this pie."

In the past fifteen years, right answers had flowed from his lips more smoothly than Bella's hot caramel sauce. But these people looked at him as though they could spot brightly packaged bull a mile away. "If it's all right, I'd prefer to keep it to myself."

Silence met his answer, and he glanced over at Bella. She smiled and nodded her head. "I think that's fair. But next year we'll expect an answer."

The room settled into approving laughter and enthusiastic pie eating. Michael, however couldn't take his eyes off his beautiful, and highly addictive guardian angel. She'd done it again. Saved him from the torturous crowd. And right now, if she asked him again if that debt he owed her would ever be paid, he knew the only honest answer would be…

No.

After she'd fed Emily and put her to bed, Isabella grabbed the baby monitor and headed down the hallway to the elevator—the same direction Michael had taken when they'd arrived home a few hours ago. It had been plenty surprising to see him at the Pintas', but gratifying to watch him take another step into life.

It made what she had to tell him easier. Almost.

She heard the rock music before the elevator stopped and the doors parted. Garbed in just sweatpants, Michael was stretched out on a workout bench, pressing a metal bar with a tremendous amount of weight on it over his head.

"Need a spotter?" she asked, crossing to stand over him.

"No," he grunted. "That's not what I need."

Her skin warmed at his words and their obvious meaning. Her gaze moved over him as he brought the bar to his chin and back up again. Taut stomach, powerful arms roped with muscle. A fine sheen of sweat glistened on his skin under the lights. Longing surged into her blood. Yes, she understood that hunger, that need.

But she couldn't tell him that. So she did the only thing she could. She plunged headfirst into why she'd actually come up here. "Well, you're missing out, Wulf. It's my last night to spot you."

He brought the bar down and secured it to the rack before he said, "Your last night?"

The smile she gave him was bright. "Emily and I are going to move into town tomorrow."

"Your place is ready?" His voice had an edge.

"It's actually been ready for a few days, but…"

He stood up, wiped his face and chest with a towel. "But what?"

Isabella watched the white cotton with envious eyes as it moved over his chest. Never again would she be able to stare at him so openly. No. She'd have to pine and long in the privacy of her new place. There was no point in telling him that she'd stayed here longer than necessary because being with him was as addictive as chocolate. She had to give herself a chance at a real life, a real love.

"I think I'm going to go downstairs," she said swiftly. "Get ready for bed. I'm pretty tired."

"So am I, Bella. You know that? I'm real tired." His gaze demanded she not look away.

"Well, it's probably all the bench-pressing," she said, gesturing at the weights.

He shook his head. "No, that's not it."

"Tryptophan in the turkey can really mess with—"

"I'm tired of pretending that I don't want you," he said as he caught her arm and gently pulled her to him. "Bella…"

"What?" Her voice shook with want and need and anxiety. This was so unfair. She was weak with him, didn't he know that? Didn't he understand how easily he could hurt her?

His mouth was too close, his eyes were growing too dark. "Would you like to know what I'm thankful for?"

She held her breath as the heat from his sweating body surged into her chest and shot straight downward.

"I'm thankful for that strange October day when the snow turned into a blizzard." He leaned in and kissed her mouth softly. "And I'm thankful that it wouldn't stop." His eyes never left hers, but his fingers moved to her blouse, opening the buttons one at a time.

She shivered, her legs like jelly.

"I'm thankful you let me bring Emily into this world," he whispered, his tone husky.

Isabella's breathing turned into short rhythmic pants as her mind and all good sense fell away.

He eased off her shirt, let it fall to the floor. "I'm thankful that you came back to stay with me a second time."

Cool air warred with the heat blazing on her skin.

"And I'm so thankful," he said, "that you came up here tonight and didn't pull away from me."

Was he serious? "I would never pull away from you, Michael," she said. "Never."

His gaze held hers as he reached behind her. Two little clicks and her bra fell to the floor. "You've driven me insane, Bella."

"Finally." The words came out in a rush as she buried her hands in his hair and drew his mouth to her breast.

It was the sweetest feeling in the world. So far removed from what she'd imagined or dreamed of. His mouth was gentle as he suckled, flicking the hardened bud with his tongue. If he could just let himself go, allow himself to feel for longer than a moment— longer than a kiss—she'd know in her heart that he was taking one more step toward life. And toward her.

"Bella," he whispered, "tell me this is all right."

It was more than all right. It was everything.

Abandoning her aching breast, he looked up at her, eyes dark as the night sky but overflowing with stars of desire. Maybe this was fantasy, maybe she was crazy for falling into the arms of a man who could never love her. But at this moment she didn't care. "It's perfect, Michael."

His eyes flooded with heat as he unzipped her skirt and told the lights to dim.

Eight

Michael knew he'd gone mad with a desire and a yearning he didn't dare stop to examine. If he did, he'd remember how wrong this was. He was Bella's protector and her friend. But right now, friendship was the last thing on his mind. Pleasing her the way she deserved to be pleased was his one and only mission, and he'd suffer the consequences of this foolish decision later.

Bella's mouth called to him and he brushed his lips over hers until she opened. The lower half of him contracted, hard as steel as her hot, urgent tongue slid into his mouth. A moment ago he wouldn't have believed it possible, this level of need. So unfamiliar, so forbidding. But this was Bella. She'd shocked him with more than his staggering desire for her. Everything he'd experienced in the past month had been different with her near.

With an animal growl, he eased down her skirt, then her sheer stockings, grazing her supple hips with his hands, until she stood before him in just a mere wisp of pale-blue lace. A hint of a smile touched her lips, and her eyes were bright and filled with hunger. The look fisted around his heart.

A muscle tensing in his cheek, Michael turned away for a moment. No one had ever ripped a pathway to his soul the way she did.

"I've thought about this too many times." He could hear the frustration in his voice.

He glanced up to see disbelief warring with that killer need in her eyes. "You have?"

"Every night, all night. And then there are the days…"

"Tell me what you imagined," she whispered as she slowly slipped off her panties.

Every ounce of control he possessed snapped like a twig in a tornado. Another growl escaped his throat as he picked her up, walked over to his desk and thrust aside all the papers. In a chaotic wave, they floated in the air a second before fluttering to the floor. But Michael hardly noticed as he sat her down on the smooth surface of his desk.

Bella's mouth fell open in surprise at the bold move, but her eyes burned with a fever his body recognized.

"You wanted to know what I imagined, right?" he

asked as he dropped into the leather chair directly in front of her.

She nodded, and he noticed that her pulse pounded violently at the base of her throat.

His eyes locked on hers, he moved his chair forward until the arms hit the metal desk. ''I thought about filling my hands with you,'' he said as he reached behind her and cupped her buttocks.

Her breath rushed out. ''Then what?''

He slid her toward him. ''I thought about you spreading your legs for me.''

She licked her lips. Slowly, she eased her knees apart. ''And then...?''

A grin split his face. ''Watch.'' He dipped his head and tasted paradise.

Isabella sucked in a breath as she felt Michael's tongue graze the slick heat of her. Windows surrounded them, leaving their actions and reactions open to the world. Out this far, surely no one was going to see them, but the element of erotic risk added to her already heightened sense of need.

Never in her life had she trusted a man so completely. Never in her life had she given herself so fully. But this was Michael, the man she loved, making her breath catch, her nipples tighten and her core flood with aching heat.

The feeling was so foreign it frightened her at first, but when she looked down, watching him move so tenderly, the fear gave way to pleasure. The soft, ragged strokes, the teasing, the pressure. Her mind went blank, totally white.

Then suddenly, through the haze, she felt him ease a gentle finger inside her. She gasped, took him fully. And as he gave her short, little thrusts, something happened. A storm began building inside her, a storm that only Michael could intensify, that only Michael could quell.

Frantic moans erupted from her throat. She felt wild, like a starving lioness with its prey in sight. Her instincts took over and she pressed herself closer to him, letting her head fall back. More than anything, she wanted to give herself to him, all that she was. She wanted him to know that only he could make her feel this way, make her react like this. But she couldn't remember how to speak.

Michael worked his magic as her body quaked. She was a racehorse, frantic, enjoying the journey but desperate for the finish line. She forced her heavy head to lift, her eyes to open. Deep and low, she shuddered at the sight of him, his dark head buried between her thighs.

Lost, she gave in, allowing the ripples of orgasm to take over her body. Squalls of torment crashed into her, and she shuddered. Heat thrashed through her core over and over.

But as the waves lessened in size and power, Michael didn't draw away. As if he knew how sensitive she was, he went on, slowly, building the tension anew with his tongue. Her mind slow, but her body wakening again, she welcomed the building heat inside her—then raging heat that came faster this time. And when lightning hit and climax came once again, she cried out her pleasure, then collapsed back onto his desk.

She felt weightless, replete, as though she were floating down a river of feathers. Gradually she began to mentally paddle to shore, certain that her love for Michael would never wane. She was his.

As her breathing slowed and her body temperature fell, she eased her eyes open. Michael stood above her, tousled hair, his chest once again glistening with sweat and the front of his sweatpants bulging with arousal. Lord, she wanted to touch him, feel his weight on her, feel him inside her. She wanted to make him feel what she was feeling right now. Reaching out, she took his hand and tried to pull him to her.

But his expression stopped her, and she released him. The frown lines around his mouth plainly showed that he wouldn't allow himself the same pleasure he'd just given her. His eyes were like onyx, his body language warning trespassers to beware. Isabella's heart lurched. He'd closed himself off again.

Suddenly she felt very exposed. She looked down to see her clothes mocking her from the floor.

Michael turned to face the window. "I'm not sorry about what just happened. Now you can never say…"

Quickly as she could, she picked up her clothes and dressed, frustration ruling her heart. "Never say what?"

"That I don't want you. Or that I don't see you as a woman. Because, I do." Staring out the window, he exhaled heavily. "When it comes to you, I seem to have no self-control."

For a moment she wanted to believe that his admission was a compliment, but she knew better. She knew he was afraid to care about anyone and anything, and she knew why. She wanted to storm out of the room, let her own anger war with his, but her love wanted to offer him comfort. She walked to the window and put a hand on his shoulder. "Michael, I know that—"

"Maybe it's good that you're leaving tomorrow," he said. "There's nothing for you here."

She dropped her hand from his shoulder. "Maybe you haven't noticed, but I'm not asking for anything."

"You deserve to ask, Bella. You and Emily deserve a man who believes in love, trust and happily-ever-after." His hands were splayed on the glass above his head as he stared out into the night. "You see those pictures on my walls?"

Her gaze swung to the etchings she'd noticed the first time she'd come up to his office. "Yes, I see them."

"They're here to remind me that they're as close as I'm ever going to get to a fairy tale."

Isabella stared at his back, his bitter tone washing over her. She'd had enough. She was growing weary. "If that's what you believe, Michael, then I'm sure it'll come true."

Turning, she left him at the window. She loved him

almost to the point of pain, but she wasn't going to beg him to give up the past that held him hostage.

She stepped into the elevator and said, "Second floor." If he wanted her, wanted the real love she offered, he knew exactly where he could find her.

In the world of the living.

Same road, same car, same driver, same passenger. But no snowstorm.

Michael glanced out the window of the town car as they sped along, half expecting to see Bella's clunker on the side of the road. But this time she wasn't there. More than likely she was happily baking away in her newly opened shop, listening for Emily's cry on her baby monitor, catering to a town that adored cream puffs and apple fritters.

Two weeks had passed with the speed of an ice age. He'd tried to keep his mind off them, but with Thomas calling almost daily to tell him how well Bella and Emily were doing, he hadn't succeeded very well. Sure, he was glad to hear that they were all right, but the calls served as thorny reminders of how empty his house was now. How empty he was.

After a week of that agony, he'd packed up and gone to California early, hoping that work would once again be his saving grace.

But while he was working with Micronics, the CEO had insisted on showing him a few sights. Everywhere Michael had gone, from the ocean to Hollywood and Vine, his mind had remained on his two ladies. How he'd wished that Bella and Emily were

there with him. He'd actually felt jealous of the people in a tiny snow-covered Minnesota town—jealous
because they were now the lucky recipients of Bella's
time and attention the way he had been for almost a
month.

He leaned back against the leather seat and crossed
his arms over his chest. What a fool. He missed her
laugh and the way she battled with him over anything
and everything. He even missed her coming up to his
office and interrupting him ten times a day. And that
image of her on his desk...

He hadn't been able to work there since that night.

But he'd get her off his mind soon enough—he had
to. Just as soon as he stopped by to thank her for her
part in sweetening his deal with Micronics. When he
saw her again, maybe this...spell she'd cast over him
would finally disappear.

He snorted at the absurdity of that thought as the
driver pulled up to her bakery. The first thing Michael
noticed when he stepped out of the car was a shop-
keeper's back-at-such-and-such-a-time sign hanging
in the window. But instead of numbers, different activities related to Emily filled each spot. And right
now both hands pointed to "Quiet. Baby sleeping."

God, he missed...everything about them. With reverence, he eased open the front door. The scents of
chocolate and fruit and spices wafted through the air,
while the most beautiful woman in the world stood
behind the counter, her blond hair up in a loose bun,
her cheeks flushed, her white apron smeared with

goodies, engrossed in helping old Mrs. Boot with her cookie selection.

"So that's two caramel crunchies," Bella whispered. "Four raspberry cobbler bars, seven black diamonds and an éclair, right?"

"I think that'll hold me and Ed till Monday," Mrs. Boot said in hushed tones.

"Four days?" Bella tipped up her chin as though she was thinking about that very hard. "I don't know." With a smile, she grabbed two more éclairs and put them in the bag. "On the house."

"Thank you, my dear." Mrs. Boot's gaze flickered toward the door and Michael. She grinned and said, "Can't tell if she's a devil or an angel."

"I have trouble with that myself," Michael whispered as he walked toward them.

Surprise lit Bella's blue eyes as she watched him approach. No doubt she wondered what he was doing here. And right now, he could hardly remember. All he wanted to do was take her in his arms and plant a kiss on her soft mouth.

Looking from one to the other, Mrs. Boot cackled softly, then made her way to the door, giving Michael an exaggerated wink. "Have a good afternoon."

When the old woman had gone, Bella looked at Michael and said professionally, "Can I help you, sir?"

But her clipped query didn't dissuade him. He'd been an ass the last time they'd been this close. She had a right to be angry with him.

He sidled up to the counter. "Once upon a time,

there was an amazing chocolate doughnut that a magical young lady made for me.'' He raised a dark brow. ''Ever heard of anything like that?''

''I might have,'' she said quietly.

''What'll it cost me to get one?''

She shrugged. ''I don't know. They're pretty special.''

''I'm not going to argue with you there.'' He gave her a half smile. ''How about a night out?''

''Excuse me?'' Guarded tone, guarded eyes.

''Dinner? Tonight? With me.''

Her lips parted, her eyes filled with uneasiness. ''I don't think so. I'm not really comfortable going back to your—''

''Not at the house. Here in town.''

Her brows drew together. ''I don't understand.''

''I thought we should celebrate,'' he continued. ''After all, you're the reason Micronics just doubled their offer for my software.''

''I'm what?'' she said as a hint of warmth lit her eyes.

''Those amazing ideas you gave me. I want to take you out and thank you properly.''

''Oh. Right.'' She looked down. ''Congratulations.''

She didn't sound pleased, and for a moment he wondered if he'd done the wrong thing coming here. But then his gaze found hers again, and he felt the need that had pulled him all the way back here from L.A.

''I miss you, Bella. Please.'' *Don't say no.*

For a long moment she didn't say anything, just stared at him. He was ready to call himself three kinds of idiot for baring his soul when she unexpectedly bent down and took something out of the display case.

When she stood back up again, a tentative smile graced her beautiful face, and a chocolate doughnut lay in her hand. She held it out to him. ''Pick me up at seven?''

Nine

The mouthwatering scents of garlic, onions and grilled meat floated in the air. As Isabella sat across the rough-hewn table from Michael in the Fielding Supper Club—the *Gazette* had called it the best chop house this side of St. Paul—she tried to tell herself that this wasn't a date. That it was just a thank-you for helping him. But she couldn't stop wondering if maybe his tough shell was cracking a little. He'd probably never been ''out on the town'' in Fielding with anyone. Of course, ''out on the town'' in a burg this tiny wasn't saying much, but still, for him it was an unprecedented move.

And then there was the wonderful words he'd uttered, words that made her believe again that anything was possible.

He'd missed her.

Covertly, she abandoned her steak for a moment and stole a glance at him. He looked like a magazine cover in his black turtleneck sweater and jeans, a lock of black hair falling over one eye.

She mentally sighed and went back to her dinner. She'd missed him, too, and the ache had only deepened in the past weeks. It had been impossible to leave him when she had, yet somehow she'd found the strength. But today, when he'd walked into the bakery and looked at her with those mesmerizing eyes, she just hadn't been able to say no.

Maybe this dinner wasn't exactly a date, but Michael was here, in public, and all eyes were on him. And he'd chosen her to accompany him. It was a step in the right direction, a chance, a change. God help her, but she was going to cling to that.

"How's your steak?" he asked, cutting his own superbly grilled porterhouse.

"Wonderful." She glanced around the room at the watchful crowd, then back at him. "Listen, I don't think they'll stop unless you nod and smile at them. They probably don't think you're real."

"And what do you suppose they think I am?"

With a shrug she offered, "Alien, robot. You work with high-tech stuff. You know, rumors start."

"Yes, I do know," he said dryly. "I've had my share of rumors."

"Just give 'em a smile. Make their night."

On a chuckle, he looked up and waved. At first everyone just stared, then each in their turn gave him a return wave or a smile. When he finally brought his gaze back to her, his brow was furrowed.

"What's wrong?" she asked, taking a bite of her baked potato. "Not what you were expecting?"

"I don't know. I'm trying to avoid having expectations."

She smiled at that, took his newly acquired ease as another sign. Maybe if he came to town more often, he'd get to know some people, make some friends.

And see her.

She lifted her mineral water and saluted. "Congratulations again on landing another multimillion-dollar account."

"And to you, for having such amazing insights." His gaze warmed. "I couldn't have done it without you."

That look went straight through her, hitting every sensitive area she possessed. "Sure you could have. But thanks for the compliment."

He drank deeply from his glass of merlot. "Listen, Bella. In all seriousness, without your input, the deal wouldn't have been nearly as lucrative. I wanted to get you a gift, but I know how you feel about paybacks." He paused. "So, since she was the inspiration, anyway, I got Emily a gift." Michael handed Isabella a thick envelope. "I funded a tax-deferred education account for her."

Stunned, Isabella could do nothing but stare at the envelope. A college fund for Emily. It was something a father… She exhaled heavily. Her mind swam. How could she accept such generosity?

But before she could utter a word, he added, "It's for Emily, Bella. I want her to be able to go to the college of her choice. Let me do that for her."

The sincerity of his words tore at her. The wise part of her warned her to say thanks but no thanks. But the part that saw his need to do this couldn't refuse. She didn't know what else to say but, "Thank you, Michael."

He would be tied to them for life now, she thought as he nodded and returned to his meal. Did he understand that? And right now did she care?

If she had the magic eight ball that her father had given her for Christmas when she was ten, she was sure it would read, *Don't count on it.* Because even if this moment, or series of moments, was all there was, she didn't care. She'd take what she could get and let God handle the rest.

After all, He did work in mysterious ways.

When they finished dinner, Michael paid the bill and got their coats. "I forgot to congratulate you on the bakery," he said, holding out her navy wool Peacoat. "I noticed you don't have a sign yet. What are you going to call it?"

"I'm not." She laughed at his perplexed expression. "I'm leaving it up to Fielding. I placed a fishbowl on the counter and asked everyone to write down a name."

He shrugged into his leather jacket and grinned. "A smart businesswoman."

Her smile wide, she shook her head at him. "Letting people decide the name of the store is not just a business decision. I want them to feel like they're a part of the shop.''

''I like that,'' he said thoughtfully as they walked out of the restaurant.

Snowflakes fell from the night sky and the air was scented with holly. Christmas was coming, the time of year for happiness, cheer and goodwill toward men.

To this man, she thought with a smile. ''So how was your first official dinner in Fielding?''

''How do you know it was my first?''

''Just a hunch,'' she said. ''Was it all you imagined it to be?''

''More,'' he said dryly.

She laughed. ''You think you might do it more often now?'' She mentally crossed her fingers.

''That depends.'' He stopped at the door to her shop. ''You going to be there?''

''Maybe.'' There they were, so close. But a gap of uncertainty hung between them. ''Would you like to come up and say good-night to Emily?''

He nodded. ''Yes, I would.''

Michael felt like a world-class fool as he followed Isabella through the bakery and up the stairs. For some stupid reason, he'd hoped that seeing her for a few hours would cool his burning need to be with her. But it hadn't. It had only made him want her more.

Ruth greeted them at the door with a sleeping Emily in her arms. After a quick chat, she handed her off to Michael and left, saying she had to hurry home to watch Jay Leno with Thomas.

For Michael, seeing Emily was like coming home. After a month of caring for her, hearing her different cries, holding her, feeding her, he was due. But the little girl had something else on her mind, so he reluctantly handed her over to her mother.

"I should go and feed her," Bella said hesitantly. "Do you want to—"

"No. I'll stay here." If he was going to save this night from turning intimate, watching Bella nurse was out of the question.

She didn't leave immediately. He knew, because he could feel her eyes on him as he walked around the room, looking at her place. The changes she'd made since he'd last seen it were amazing. Her touch was everywhere. In the dried flowers, comfortable couches, brightly colored rugs, overflowing bookcase, smiling photographs of her and her father and Emily. It all had her signature. Homey, warm and incredibly inviting.

"Your leg bothering you tonight?" she asked, rocking Emily in her arms.

"Some." He turned to face her. "You don't happen to have a whirlpool on the roof or anything, do you?"

She shook her head. "Sorry."

The ache in his leg had turned raw about a half hour ago, but he'd pushed it out of his mind. In the past year, acute pain had started to accompany the ever-present ache. His doctors had said that there was nothing they could do. It came with age and weather. Move to California or Florida, they'd urged. That would probably be the wisest decision. But lately the idea of leaving the sleepy little town of Fielding had sounded more unpalatable than ever.

"Here's a thought," Bella said brightly. "I've got a nice big tub. Why don't I go and nurse Emily and you can soak in it for a while? We get really hot water here." She smiled slyly. "I'll even let you use my Epsom salts."

They were slipping back into comfortable as easily as a summer day on the porch. "I should probably head home."

She nodded, her eyes going lackluster. "All right."

"I should," he clarified, his gaze tightly knit with hers. "But I don't want to."

Her smile lit up the room. "I don't want you to, either. Salts are under the sink. I'll see you in a bit."

Michael refused to curse himself and his actions any more tonight. He wanted to be with her and she wanted to be with him. That had to be enough.

He found the salts, ran a hot bath, stripped, turned off the lights, leaving just the dim runners glowing as he settled down into the steaming tub. Heat surged into his muscles. His mind fell into blessed silence. He'd practically fallen asleep when he heard a knock and the bathroom door opening.

"I thought you might want a—" She stopped when she saw him, her eyes going wide. "I'm sorry, I..."

He slowly sat up, slightly drugged by the hot water.

''Thought I'd be fully clothed and maybe dunking the leg?''

''Something like that,'' she choked out, her nervous gaze moving from the floor back up to him.

He noticed that she'd changed into a set of totally unrevealing sweats. But damn, if she didn't look good enough to eat. ''Emily asleep?''

''She's…out. Like a light.'' Clearing her throat, Bella asked, ''So how's the leg?''

''Still tight.'' Just like the lower half of him.

Concern lit her eyes. ''I could massage it for you.''

He practically groaned. She was killing him here. Beneath the hot water, he was hard as granite. ''No, it's fine.''

''It's not fine,'' she said, walking toward him. ''You just said—''

''I know what I said. Bella, don't—''

''Don't what?'' She knelt beside the tub. ''I just want to help.''

He was done for. And if she touched him… ''Believe me, being massaged by you would be a dangerous way to end our evening.''

''You could think of me as a nurse,'' she offered.

''Not much better.''

''Why don't you just lean back and let me help you?''

He cursed. But it wasn't his arousal that had him frowning as he lay back against the porcelain. It was the shame of her touching his leg, that imperfect, weak leg.

He was ready to call it quits when her gentle hands dipped into the water and found his thigh.

He groaned, his embarrassment forgotten.

"Too hard?" she asked, worry in her voice.

"No, it's good." He knew his eyes had gone to near black as he stared at her, his embarrassment now turning to desire. "Too good."

"I wish I could get a little closer," she said. "I'm in an awkward position—"

His movement was quick. He reached out, grabbed her waist, lifted her up and eased her down on top of him, sweats and all. Water splashed over the sides of the tub, splattered the floor.

"Close enough?" he growled, his mouth inches from hers.

She looked shocked at first, but then her lips parted. "You tell me," she whispered, pressing her hips against the solid length of him, then dragging a hand up the outside of his thigh.

He released a groan of pleasure. "I don't want to go back to my house, Bella."

"Tonight, you mean?"

"Tonight, tomorrow…" He cupped her face and kissed her mouth tenderly. "It's damned lonely up there."

She ran her tongue across his lower lip. "Then stay here."

That nearly undid him, but he managed to utter, "There'll be talk."

"Maybe a few moans, a sigh here and there, and hopefully later—"

''I meant from the town.'' He reached around and cupped her bottom.

''They're already talking.''

''And you don't care?''

''No. I don't care.''

His need to protect her in every way possible reared up. ''Bella, there's one more thing I want to—''

Her fingers touched his lips, stopping him from saying anything more. ''I know what you want and don't want, Michael Wulf. Now shut up and kiss me.''

Ten

The bath grew cool too quickly.

Water splashed onto the already wet bathmat as Isabella pulled Michael out of the tub. Her eyes moved over him. Sleek and sexy and hard, he made her throat ache with want.

"I want to see you," he said as he stripped off her wet sweats. For a moment he simply took in the sight of her body glistening with moisture. She felt absolutely no embarrassment with him. And as her nipples beaded under his steely gaze, she stood taller, as though she needed to be as open as possible for him to be the same.

"You are so beautiful, Bella." Michael dipped his head and took one aching breast into his mouth.

Her fingers threaded through his hair and she pulled

him back up to face her. For fifteen years she'd had a crush on this man. And in a month and a half, that crush had grown into love. She knew what she wanted, and she was ready to take it, consequences be damned.

Impatience flooded her. "Do you want to take this slow?"

His eyes went black. "No."

"Good."

His weighty breath ended on a groaned, "I didn't bring any protection with me."

She grabbed his hand and tugged. "Follow me." She led him into her bedroom, straight to the chest at the foot of her cherry-wood sleigh bed. She opened the trunk, grabbed a small box and tossed it at him.

He caught it, then stared at her, his eyes burning a fever. "What are you doing with these?"

She pulled back her comforter and slid into bed. "They were in my hope chest, Michael." She raised a brow at him. "A girl can hope, right?"

His face broke out in a dangerous smile as he walked toward her. "And what exactly was this girl hoping for?"

Her pulse pounded at the base of her throat. "For Michael Wulf to get into her bed."

He was over her in seconds, his gaze penetrating her very soul, his hands fisted beside her shoulders. But only for a moment, only until she tipped up her chin and nipped his lower lip with her teeth.

Then the dam broke.

His mouth covered hers, took her rough and insistent while his hands ran up her body, feeling the curves of her hips, the fullness of her breasts in his palms.

Sweat broke out on his skin, hers too. He wanted to take his time, but he had none to offer. The scent of dried flowers mingled with the scent they made together, causing his mind to blur.

Under him, she bucked, pressing her core, wet and hot against his arousal, urging him to move with her.

He fought the reckless impulse to rise up and bury himself deep inside her, take her hard and fast. "I don't want to hurt you, Bella," he said, breathing ragged.

With a sensual kiss, she wrapped her legs around his waist and arched, pressed. "You won't."

The brutal heat that burned between them demanded to be set free. Rising up, he slipped on a condom, then pushed slowly into her body.

A branding heat enveloped him.

Bella moaned, whispered against his skin, "You're a perfect fit."

Her words assaulted him, made his need to take and be taken swell. Dominated by something primal, Michael began to move, rise and lower, gentle strokes at first.

But Bella had other ideas.

Beneath him, her thrusts grew wild. Fast, a fevered pitch, that he couldn't help but match. Mind blank, body untamed, he gripped her hips and drove into her frantically, stroke after stroke until it was too much, until he went mad, until her lips parted, until she began to quake.

And when she cried out, when the walls of her womb gripped him tightly, a low, cavernous growl exploded in Michael's throat and he shuddered with her, hissed her name, then followed her into soulshattering climax.

Against the lids of his eyes, insistent sunlight flashed. For a moment he wasn't sure where he was, just that he felt incredibly good. Then the events of the night before rolled across his mind like a lush carpet. He'd never held a woman through the night after making love. That action not only meant something to the woman, it meant something to him. Not exactly a commitment, but a relationship of sorts.

He and Bella had a relationship.

But what sort he wasn't sure.

He pulled her closer, then paused and opened his eyes. Clutched against his chest was one of Bella's pillows. She was gone.

The clock beside the bed blinked eight-fifteen, and he was alone. Cocking his head, he listened for Emily's cry or Bella's soft voice. But there was nothing. He ran a hand through his hair as his mind refocused.

Of course, it was Saturday morning—the bakery.

After dressing quickly, Michael made his way downstairs. He heard the din of hungry customers before he even reached the back door of the bakery. Bella would be swamped. Maybe he could help her out by watching Emily until the shop closed. Upstairs, where no one could see him, where no one would know that he'd spent the night here.

But his plan was quickly foiled when the double doors in front of him flew open, revealing a startled Bella and what appeared to be the entire town of Fielding.

If he'd expected Bella's expression to change into one of embarrassment, he'd probably have to wait all day. She smiled widely at him, said, "Oh, thank God," took his hand and led him behind the counter. "Today is the busiest it's ever been."

People had stopped talking, then resumed, just as they did when John Wayne walked into a saloon in one of those old westerns. And Michael didn't need to guess what the subject had changed to. But if Bella didn't mind, neither did he. It did a man good to know that a woman was proud of him.

And what a woman she was, he mused, taking in her fine, fine figure in a T-shirt, jeans and an apron that only partly obstructed his view. But it didn't matter. He knew firsthand what was under those clothes, how soft and warm her skin felt.

A soft gurgle caught his attention and he turned to see Emily cooing happily, touching her toes and smiling. She was in her playpen, tucked safely between two pillars, out of Bella's way, but still very much in viewing distance.

He turned to look at Bella, who was putting out a plate of doughnut samples on the counter. "Looks like you need a break."

"I'll be right with you," she told a customer at the

counter, then quick as lightning, she slipped something over Michael's head, pulled him down behind the counter and whispered, "What I need is *you*."

"Well, sweetheart, you got—" He glanced down. She'd put an apron on him. "What's this about?"

"Have I ever told you what magical hands you have?" she whispered, her eyes hopeful.

"No," he whispered back. "But I'd say it was probably implied. If we take those cries of pleasure—"

She put a finger to his lips and gave him a patient smile. "As I was saying, you really do have magical hands, Michael."

His brows rose, and so did the level of chatter in the bakery. "And you're sweet-talking me into…?"

"Taking orders, filling bags, making change."

"Anything else?" he asked dryly.

She looked up, probably checking to see if anyone had scaled the counter to hear them. "Be charming."

"I have no experience with that."

"You're a quick learner."

And she was so beautiful she made his hands itch. What was he supposed to do? Say no? He sighed and shook his head. "Damn you."

She laughed softly. "I owe you."

"Yeah, you do." He pulled her to him and kissed her soundly on the mouth. "And I'm collecting tonight."

With bright eyes and a brighter smile, she nodded. "I am your humble servant."

They both stood. Bella immediately started taking

an order, but Michael took a moment, easing a cramp out his leg before finally turning to face his night-mare. A gaggle of people clamoring to get freshly baked everything, trying to pretend they weren't feeling the curiosity written all over their faces.

The hours slipped by, fast and furious, and strangely, Michael actually started to enjoy himself. He'd done little but program computer software for the past fifteen years, and he had to admit it was kind of interesting to help run a small business. But mostly, it was just good to be around Bella. Every time he went into the storeroom to get more supplies, she'd follow him and they'd make out against the door for a few brief seconds.

When they returned, people would smile and chuckle. But she didn't care, so he didn't care. He wasn't afraid to admit she'd cast a spell over him.

When she went upstairs to feed Emily, he continued on with his duties and was surprised to find that the solo interaction with people wasn't so bad. They always offered him a friendly smile and a thank-you. A couple of people even asked what he was doing for Christmas and if he and Bella wanted to come for dinner some night. Not that he was ready to jump right into the fire just because he'd had a pleasant morning at the bakery. But it was surprisingly nice to be asked.

"So that was ten tarts, seven peanut-butter cookies, five double-chocolate-chip cookies, five regular chocolate-chip cookies, one loaf of pumpernickel bread thinly sliced and a Swedish Tea ring." He handed

Mrs. Trotsky her boxes and bags as Bella walked through the double doors holding Emily. "Do you need help out with that?"

The old woman tapped the shoulder of the man standing next to her. "Got my son here with me. But much obliged, Mr. Wulf."

"It's Michael," he said without thinking.

Mrs. Trotsky smiled. "I'm Bev and this is Harold."

Dammit. This socialization crap was all a result of Bella's spell. He clipped a nod at Mrs. Trotsky and her son, muttering, "Come again."

He felt Bella's gaze on him and turned, shooting her a wry glance. "Charming enough for you?"

She winked at him. "You're a natural."

"You're a virgin."

"What?" Michael exclaimed.

Isabella inched closer to him on the sofa as *Romancing the Stone* played on the television. "That's what you are, pal. A Saturday-night-movie-fest-pigout-spooning-on-the-couch-till-you-fall-asleep virgin."

He chuckled. "As much as you may think you just insulted me, Bella, you haven't. Even though I will admit that this—" he hugged the bowl of buttered popcorn to his chest protectively "—pursuit of fun is a first for me."

"Well, I like being your first." She smiled. "I still can't believe you haven't seen *Romancing the Stone*."

"I don't have time for—"

"Anything that's not related to business?" She snatched a piece of popcorn from his bowl and threw it at him.

He caught it and popped it into his mouth. "You trying to humanize me, Bella?"

"Oh, I'm doing my best."

He leaned in, and his mouth found her neck, searing hot kisses all they way to her ear. She shivered and he whispered, "Well, let it be said that I have the best-looking teacher in school. Lucky, lucky me."

Her eyes closed. "And don't you forget it."

"Not possible." His hand sneaked under her sweater. "Human contact is always the best place to start the humanizing process, don't you think?"

"Mmm," was all she could think to say as he nibbled her earlobe while his hand slid up her stomach, then slipped beneath her bra.

"What was that?" he whispered as he palmed her breast. "I didn't understand you."

Heat settled low in her belly and she pressed into his hand, wanting more. "I…said do you want to go into the bedroom?"

"Too far." Popcorn dropped to the floor as he pulled off her sweater in one easy movement, then unhooked her bra.

Gunshots rang out over the TV, but all Isabella heard was the humming of her body, on fire and filled with need. Michael's mouth found her neck, searing slow kisses down, down until he reached her breast.

"Michael," she rasped as he flicked the sensitive bud with his tongue.

"Tell me, Bella." His hand slipped inside her jeans, under the panties. "Tell me how this makes you feel."

His fingers dipped low, stroking her cleft until she couldn't breathe, couldn't think. She spoke through senses only. "Hot and shaky, like fireflies trying to get free…" It could've been gibberish, but it was all she could offer.

She felt his hand leave her, felt him take her with him as he stood up. Her eyes opened to his gaze, so tender.

"Bella…" He wanted to say more—she could see it in his eyes—but he didn't. Instead, he unbuttoned her jeans and slid them down.

With shaky hands, she pulled off his sweater and jeans. When she stood before him once again, she ran her hands up his chest possessively, over the muscle, feeling his heart slamming against his ribs. Her gaze flew to his, his eyes so hot it almost made her step back. Lord, he made her crazy. She wanted this, wanted him forever. But the best she could hope for now was to show him.

She pushed him down on the spacious couch and straddled him.

He growled with surprise. "It looks like you have another assignment planned for tonight, Teacher." His eyes remained on her as his hands once again searched out the wet heat he'd created.

"I've planned a test," she uttered through breaths.

"A test?"

"Of stamina." She moved against his fingers, against the steely length of him. "Mine outlasting yours."

At that challenge, Michael released her and flipped her onto her back. "Oh, sweetheart. You don't stand a chance."

She smiled up at him. "I was hoping you'd say that."

He sat up for a moment, reached down to retrieve a foil packet from his discarded jeans. "I came prepared this time."

"Can I do it?" Isabella heard the shyness in her query, but she reveled in her boldness. It was love, pure and simple, that made her request such an intimacy.

Leaning toward her, he kissed her lips softly. "Yes."

With tentative fingers, she opened the packet. Michael drew in a breath as she slowly moved the latex down his manhood, then groaned as she wrapped her hands around him and guided him to the apex of her thighs.

Deep longing filled his gaze as he hovered at the entrance to her body. In that moment, as their eyes met, Isabella wanted to tell him that she loved him, that she wanted this forever, that with him she felt complete. But when he pushed into her, all she could understand were sensations.

He moved inside her slowly at first, then faster. She wanted to hold on to the sweet heat of the moment, but it was no use. Gasping, she fought for breath and for her sanity as that delicious heat spread through her core. The speed of his thrusts increased to a pitch where nothing existed but the two of them. It was madness, a thirst that needed to be quenched.

She cried out as orgasm hit, but Michael continued to thrust over and over as her walls clenched and tightened. Then he stiffened, a primal groan tearing from his throat.

"Bella..." He thrust into her again and again before their bodies finally cooled and their breathing returned to normal.

Rolling to the side, he took her with him so that they faced each other on the roomy sofa. Michael touched her cheek, kissed her lips softly, then pulled her close.

"You're mine," he whispered, caressing her back in long, easy strokes.

She shivered, but hardly felt it. His words spoke directly to her heart, making her wonder if...

"Tonight you're all mine."

A wave of disappointment poured through her. Michael was talking about right now, not the future. It wasn't the dream she longed for, but she sure wouldn't let that truth kill this time between them. She'd known the rules going in, and she was not about to play the dejected lover now.

"You think you got more in ya, Wulf?" Her tone was teasing.

A smile tugged at the corners of his mouth. "More tasting your sweet nipples until they harden in my mouth? More feeling you grow wet against my fingers?'' As he spoke she felt him begin to grow hard against the apex of her thighs. ''More pushing into your body while you wrap your legs around me?'' With a devilish smile, he pushed inside her. ''Is that what you mean, Ms. Spencer?''

She gasped and draped her leg over his hip, giving him full access. And as all thoughts and questions and wishes drifted from her mind, she whispered, ''You win.''

Eleven

She slept like an angel.

Michael had noticed that once before. Under the same moon on the night she'd first come to his house. He'd sat in his chair beside the fire, watching over her, wondering what dreams filled her mind as he kept his distance.

Just like now, he mused, folding his hands across his chest and leaning back in the desk chair he'd occupied for more than thirty minutes. After he'd made love to Bella a second time on the couch, she'd fallen asleep in his arms. Content just to lie there with her, he'd watched the last few minutes of the movie, then the screen had filled with snow as the VCR shut itself off. Finally he'd carried her to bed and tucked her in.

He'd wanted to go with her, slip beneath the sheets and pull her close. But tonight he knew he didn't dare.

Something had changed. He couldn't put his finger on it, but there was something inside him tonight that begged for release. Perhaps it was a need for more— more of Bella, more connection with this town, more freedom from his solitude. Whatever it was, it had surfaced this weekend in Fielding.

He knifed a hand through his hair. He needed to go back where he belonged before he was sucked into a vortex of certain disappointment. Before he began to believe he belonged to a woman, a child and a community.

But although he could readily leave the town behind when this weekend was over, Bella and Emily were a different story. If Bella was willing, he wanted her and Emily to come home with him. For as long as they wanted to be there. No strings, no promises, just being together.

It was all he could offer, all he was willing to risk. He hoped it was enough.

From the baby monitor beside the bed, he heard Emily begin to fuss. As though she heard her child in her sleep, Bella stirred. She was exhausted, getting up before dawn to bake, serving customers all day and taking care of Emily. Such a rigorous schedule was another solid reason for her to come live with him. He could give her some slack. Thank God she had the good sense to close the bakery on Sundays. Most everyone in town had gotten their provisions today, and Bella could use a full night's sleep.

Emily's fussing strengthened into soft cries. Michael got up, turned down the monitor and threw on his pants, then quietly left the room.

Still decorated with rosebud wallpaper and lace curtains from when a young Bella had occupied it, the only difference in Emily's room was the baby furniture. In the center of the long space a crib was set up atop a plush pink rug, and a mobile of stars and moons hung over it.

"Not tired, either, princess?" he whispered, picking her up and holding her against his chest. "Ah, it's more of a diaper issue, huh?"

Emily mewed softly.

"I'll take that as a yes." He placed her down on the changing table. It was old hat to him now, he realized: talking to her, making faces, giving her those plastic keys she liked to bite on when she was being changed.

After Emily had a clean diaper, Michael rocked her for a few minutes, then tried putting her back in her crib. But the little girl was having none of it. When her back hit the mattress, her round face scrunched up and a wail escaped her lips.

"I'm a little hungry myself," he said, gathering her up in his arms once again. "Let's go see what your mom's got in the fridge."

Several bottles of expressed breast milk lined one shelf of the refrigerator. Michael placed Emily in her baby seat, then heated up one of the bottles. After testing its temperature, he dropped into a chair, cuddled the baby close and gave her the bottle.

She took to it at once, and Michael settled back against the chair and exhaled. Never in his life had he felt so relaxed. Emily stared up at him with wide trusting eyes, making him feel that strange sense of belonging again.

"You're trouble," he told her softly. "Bella's got her work cut out with you."

She blinked up at him.

He chuckled softly. "But I'm guessing there's no sweeter work to be had."

Only the sound of Emily suckling filled the house. He couldn't take his gaze off that cherubic face. And as her eyes drifted closed, he could only whisper, "You're both lucky to have each other."

He knew he must sound like an idiot, talking to a six-week-old baby in a dim kitchen in the middle of the night. But he wanted her to know, to always know, that people loved her and felt fortunate to have her.

And hell, no one was up to hear his foolishness, anyway.

No one but Isabella, that is.

She stood in the living room watching and listening, her breath held, her heart balancing somewhere between wonder and sadness. To anyone who saw what she was seeing, Michael Wulf looked like Emily's father. They were so natural together, the calmness he brought out in her and the softness she brought out in him.

Love surged into her heart. And it seemed quite clear that she wasn't the only one who was taken with

him. Her daughter had fallen in love with
Michael, too.

Feeling as though she was trespassing on sacred
ground, Isabella returned quietly to her bedroom. But
the love in her heart sent questions rocketing through
her mind. Did Michael Wulf have any clue how much
they both needed him? How much they loved him?

And if he didn't, should she tell him?

Anxieties tripped across her heart as she slipped
into bed, then, out of habit, reached over to the monitor and turned up the volume.

"...and he has a long white beard, a red suit and
a whole herd of reindeer that can fly." She heard
Michael's deep chuckle. "I know what you're thinking. It seems scientifically impossible. But with the
power of magic, Emily, anything's possible."

Anything's possible.

Isabella clutched the pillow to her chest and sighed.
She knew exactly what kind of magic she was going
to ask Santa for this year.

At seven a.m., Isabella awoke, content and happy
to feel Michael's warm chest beneath her cheek. He'd
come to bed late last night, but when he had, she'd
snuggled close to him, sighing when he put his arm
around her and gathered her to him possessively.
Only then had she truly been able to sleep.

She'd dreamed of more weekends like this one,
with no Sundays to put an end to her happiness. But
that was just a dream. Sometime today he would put

on his expensive coat, call for an expensive car and leave.

But it was not today yet.

Shamelessly trying to rouse him, Isabella eased her leg across his hips. He stirred, but didn't awake. Lightly she touched his taut stomach, running her hand up the delicious column of hair, threading her fingers in the thick of it. Need coursed through her veins. Every inch of her, inside and out, craved him. It was so unusual for her to want a man so desperately, body and soul, but Michael Wulf wasn't just any man.

She had a few more hours of showing him just how much she loved him. That was all she was guaranteed.

Bypassing subtlety, she pressed her hips against him and moved her hand downward.

Michael's first thought was that he was dreaming—a hell of a delicious dream, too. But then he felt Bella's hand on him, felt her tongue dart out and lave his nipple, and he knew that this was all heaven-sent reality. He was hard as granite in Bella's small hand, and so turned on he could barely remember his name.

Night and day, the woman bewitched him.

And he loved every minute of it.

He let his predatory hands explore everything they could reach—her back, her buttocks, her breasts. His eyes remained closed, but he heard her urgent moans, felt her hips thrusting insistently against his thigh.

"Michael, please..." she uttered, her tone needful and feverish.

Enough playtime. He was awake.

He rolled her to her back, quickly put on protection, then plunged into her. A very satisfied gasp escaped her lips as warm wet heat closed all around him. He couldn't bear to leave her, but knowing the pleasure that would come from it, he rose, hovered at the entrance to paradise, then drove home once again.

"Wrap your legs around me, sweetheart," he instructed, and she instantly did as he asked.

The fevered longing that zipped through his body was so foreign, but so welcome. This connection was a first. The feeling that rushed over him with every stroke made his mind falter, his will weaken.

"I can't hold on," she whispered, dragging her hands down his back, gripping his buttocks.

He groaned. "Take what you want, Bella. Everything you want."

Smiling up at him, she used her hands to pull him deeper. Their eyes remained locked on each other's. It was a lost cause, but as they moved fitfully together, he fought to separate his physical needs from the emotional wants.

She fit him so perfectly, and even though he chose not to give it a name, what he felt for her was undeniable, uncontrollable and totally unstoppable.

Shots of honey-sweet pleasure ripped through him. He dragged in a breath, just as Bella gave a cry and shuddered around him, her muscles gripping him. All thoughts abandoned him.

Out of control and out of his mind, he quickened his strokes, slamming into the center of her where liquid heat resided.

With her soft moans in his ear, he couldn't fight any longer. He didn't *want* to fight any longer. Thunder hit, lightning crashed and he plunged over the edge.

Isabella stood in the center of town, Emily in her arms, Michael by her side, and took in the view. It had been years since she'd seen Fielding dressed up for the holidays, and it was as alive with spirit as it had always been. From the silver bells, handmade ornaments, flocked trees that gave off that wondrous scent of pine, green holly and ivy, and strings of colored lights to the adults and children with that Norman Rockwell look of excitement and anticipation on their faces.

Christmastime was here.

And she wanted to enjoy it for a moment before they started their—

"Christmas shopping, Bella?" Michael raised a brow at her.

She laughed and said wryly, "It's a new concept for you, I know."

He shot her a mock frown. "You're becoming too damn sassy."

With a quick smile, she started down the street. "Thank you. I try." The town truly looked picture-postcard perfect. The sun was shining, the park benches and street lamps had a light dusting of snow, windows were filled with treasures, people waved at one another and children's laughter filled the air.

"Have you given any thought to what you'd like

for Christmas, Michael?'' Isabella asked. *Maybe one more night with me?*

"Peace," he said.

"As in 'peace on earth'?"

"Nope. As in 'peace and quiet.'''

She turned around and gave him a patient smile. "Listen, if you're going to hang out with me and Emily, any and all Scrooge and Grinch references are strictly prohibited."

"Fine." He tipped his chin down. "You're going to make me pick out a tree, too, aren't you?"

"Not until later." She laughed at his beleaguered expression, then the display in the shop window in front of her caught her gaze. "Look at this."

Imitation snow framed the window, setting off the little scene inside perfectly. A handmade train carried angels, nativity figurines, wooden Santas and presents along its little black tracks.

"This is the sweetest, most wonderful time of the year." She glanced over her shoulder at Michael. "Are you really going to tell me that you don't like any of it?"

"All right," he acquiesced with a grumpy huff. "There is one thing."

Isabella regarded him with curious eyes. "Well, don't keep me in such suspense."

He leaned in and kissed her ear. "I happen to be particularly fond of mistletoe. But don't spread that around."

Despite the warmth of her wool coat, a shiver ran down her spine. Since coming home to Fielding, her life had been a series of perfect moments. Standing on the sidewalk, being kissed by the man she loved—in the town she loved—was certainly another.

And God help her, she refused to accept that this perfect time, this perfect weekend, was swiftly coming to a close.

"Your secret's safe with me," she said, forcing a lightness she didn't feel into her tone. "But I can't vouch for Emily."

Michael looked down and brushed the baby's cheek with his thumb. "You won't tell anyone, will you, princess?"

Emily gurgled. Isabella interpreted. "She says no problem. Not until she starts talking, anyway."

"Clever girl." He straightened and put on a game smile. "All right, I'm ready for this shopping expedition. Where are we headed?"

"Let's go in here," she said, nodding at the craft shop. "I want to pick out Emily's first ornament."

He looked up at the sign. "The Crafty Corner? Can't these people come up with something more original?"

She glared at him. "Give 'em a break, okay, Wulf?"

"For you, Bella, I'll give everyone a break." He winked at her. "Today."

"Oh, the generosity," she said on a chuckle as they walked into the store.

Within two minutes Bella was deeply involved in a discussion on how to make a gilded angel for the top of the tree, and Michael was walking around the store wondering what sort of gifts to get Bella and Emily for Christmas. Sure, he'd only celebrated Christmas once, but if the two of them were going to be at his house, he wanted to do the holiday up right, with all the trimmings and loads of presents.

Out of the corner of his eye he spotted a wall of little handmade ornaments. If Bella was going to get Emily one, maybe he'd get one for Bella, he thought, walking to the back of the store where the huge array hung on wooden pegs. He smiled as he spotted the perfect ornament. Hanging from a red-and-white checked ribbon was a miniature pan like the ones Bella used for baking with two miniature gingerbread men on it.

"I'm just telling you, Joan, I don't buy this big change that Michael Wulf has supposedly undergone."

Michael froze, the ornament forgotten. To his left, the stockroom door stood partially open. His jaw tight as a trap, he glanced inside. Molly Homney, hands planted on ample hips, stood above a young woman who was methodically unpacking nativity figures from a box.

"Isabella seems very happy," Joan said.

Molly snorted. "Well, of course she does. She's in love with him."

Michael's chest tightened painfully, his mind rewinding what he'd just heard. Bella? In love with him?

"She can't tell her backside from her elbow right now," Molly continued. "But I can."

Joan sighed. "And what do you see?"

"Trouble. That man is used to living in a cave. And he can survive that way. But can Isabella? Can Emily?"

Cocking her head to one side, Joan said thoughtfully, "Maybe they could get married and live in town."

Molly shook her head. "I've said it before and I'll say it again. It's not the house that Michael Wulf lives in that makes him uncivilized. It's his attitude. He and Isabella could live anywhere and he would still sneer at the world." A look of pure pity crossed her face. "Just think about little Emily growing up that way. No friends." On a sigh, she added, "And Isabella has just come home. Such a shame…"

Michael didn't want to hear any more—didn't need to hear any more. He turned and walked away, pure unadulterated anger roaring through his blood. But it wasn't directed at the town's resident gossip. It was directed at himself. Why the hell hadn't he thought about how his way of life would affect Emily and Bella?

Because he wanted to be with them at all costs, that was why.

Just then, Bella caught his eye and motioned for him to come over to the register. Was Molly right? he wondered as he walked toward her. Did Bella love him? Could a man so incapable of love see such a thing in the eyes of another?

"Doesn't this angel look just like Emily?" Bella said, thrusting the angel-kit package at him and switching her daughter to her other arm. "I thought this would be so cute on top of the tree for her first Christmas."

Struggling for control, Michael looked at it. "It's great."

"I'm not all that crafty." Her voice was filled with enthusiasm. "But I'm willing to suffer through a few mistakes as long as it comes out all right in the end."

Guilt constricted his chest, heavy and imposing, and he forced his gaze to hers. Those magnetic sapphire eyes were filled to the brim with happiness. But love? He wasn't sure what love looked like. Still, there was a certain softness when she looked at him.

What kind of man was he, bringing her into his life, his tortured little world?

He was a selfish bastard, that's what he was.

He raked a hand through his hair. He'd take this last day of holiday cheer, but then he had to give them up. Even if it killed what was left of his heart, he was going to make sure that he protected Bella and Emily from the town's nosy speculation—and from himself.

In front of the bay window in her living room sat the most beautiful tree Isabella had ever seen.

Across the candlelit dinner table, she stared at the blue spruce Michael had picked out, dragged home, then set up while she made dinner. He'd been a bit distant when they'd left the Crafty Corner, but she'd just chalked that up to his being holiday-unfamiliar and coaxed him back into the spirit in time for their tree-buying excursion.

Or, actually, Emily had. She'd been crying when they'd gotten to the tree lot, but as soon as Michael had taken her in his arms, that crying had turned into cooing. Quite proud of himself, Michael had told Isabella to follow him, that he and Emily were going to pick out the biggest and the best tree in the lot, even if they had to cut a hole in the ceiling to make it fit. The enthusiastic gesture had instantly reminded her of her father.

"Remember the Christmas you spent here with me and Dad?" Isabella said, taking the last bite of her roast pork.

He nodded, a forkful of apple stuffing on the way to his mouth. His eyes were hooded. "Yes."

"The scent of pine filling the house, the naked tree just waiting for its dressing."

"You didn't decorate until Christmas Eve, right?"

She smiled. "Dad's tradition." She pointed to the base of the tree. "And there's Mom's tradition. She made that tree skirt the year I was born."

He glanced over his shoulder. "It's beautiful." When he turned back to face her, his eyes had softened. "I know that's really important to you, Bella."

"What?"

"Family. Traditions."

She took a sip of sparkling cider. "It is. And even more so now that I have Emily. I really feel that it's important to give a child a sense of her history, of the memories that made her home what it is, you know?"

Michael chuckled bitterly. "I don't think a child would be interested in *my* history or my memories."

His words stung. Isabella felt as though he'd just taken a giant step backward, and she didn't know why.

"Well, there's always room to make some new ones," she offered quickly. "You could spend Christmas here with Emily and me. Just like old times, but with new memories."

Silence filled the pine-scented air until Michael cleared his throat. "I appreciate the offer, Bella. But I won't be in Fielding for Christmas."

Isabella's heart dipped in her chest. "Where will you be?"

"Los Angeles. I'm going back to work with Micronic's programmers to customize the software."

She just stared at him, trying to read what was behind those steel-gray eyes. But they gave away nothing. In fact, they looked exactly the way they had the day he'd left Fielding as a boy, the way they had the first few days she'd stayed at his house. "You're really going to work over Christmas?"

"No. I'm actually going to stay and check out a few houses in the area."

It was as though the breath had been sucked out of her lungs. For him to go away on business for a few weeks stank, but the possibility of his moving away...

"Something for winter," he continued unemotionally. "The climate should be easier on my leg."

Forcing herself to swallow the Sahara in her throat, Isabella tried not to show the intensity of the pain in her heart. "Well, if you're back for New Year's, Emily and I could come and pick you up at the airport. We could go—''

"I'm not really sure how long I'm staying in California,'' he said quickly, dropping his napkin onto the table beside his plate.

She tried to bite her tongue, to keep the desperation she felt out of her tone, but she couldn't seem to stop the words from coming. "Do you know where you'll be staying when you do come back?"

He leaned forward in his chair and said quietly, "Bella, this isn't the way I live. And nothing's going to change that."

Tears pricked at her eyes. "Living without love is not living, Michael."

"To me, it is."

"I really thought that maybe this weekend you saw something different."

"I did see something."

She shook her head. "But?"

His eyes softened. "Did you really think that after a few dinners in town, a couple of days helping out in the bakery and a little Christmas shopping, I would all of sudden become Joe Citizen?"

"No, Michael." Past tears now, she pressed on. She had words to say, words she'd been sitting on far too long. No doubt, they would fall on deaf ears, but if she had any hope of moving on with her life, Michael Wulf needed to know the truth in her heart. "I hoped that you would want a life with Emily and me." With every ounce of courage she had left, she met his gaze. "I hoped that you would learn to love me the way I love you."

A muscle jumped in his jaw as he stared at her. For a moment she imagined she saw something akin to tenderness in his shadowed gaze, but it was gone in an instant.

"That's not possible for me."

She nodded slowly, her heart breaking silently, the tiny sharp fragments of it scattering like dust. "All right, Michael."

"But as for a friendship—"

She held up her hand. "That's not possible for me." She came to her feet. "I'm going to check on my daughter. Please be gone by the time I get back."

On legs made of water, Isabella turned and left the room. It was like walking in mud. Each step felt heavy, each breath caught as she tried to hold off the wrenching sob that ached to escape her throat.

Nothing had prepared her for this—this mind-numbing moment when she walked away from the love of her life, knowing that her dream of being with him, of having him love her, had just died.

But with a determination she hadn't known she possessed, she did just that.

Twelve

"Ladies and gentlemen, in preparation for our descent, please put away all electronic devices and fasten your seat belts. We will be landing in Minneapolis just before noon. Weather is looking promising for Christmas Eve. Mild windchill and a light snowfall. Happy holidays, everyone, and thank you for flying Northern Airlines."

Michael shut his laptop computer.

What was he supposed to do now? For the past two weeks, work had been the only thing that had kept him from thinking. About Bella, Emily and the damned holidays.

He stared out the tiny window. Tonight was Christmas Eve. The night when Santa zipped down the chimney and gave presents to all the good girls and boys. Well, he'd never been a good boy. And the only presents he wanted were ones he couldn't have.

The plane began its descent into the Minneapolis/ St. Paul airport, and Michael cursed the shot of excitement that rippled through him. He wasn't going to see her. He was going back to that empty glass fortress. The one he'd built to keep the world out.

But Bella's face could haunt him there just as easily as it had in California. He couldn't work every moment, no matter how hard he tried. So whenever he was out, driving or eating, she and Emily would trample into his mind, mess up his sanity again. Whenever he saw a baby with those plastic keys or the book with the fuzzy bunny on the cover, his heart would lurch for Emily. When he fell into bed at night, he wanted Bella beside him. And when he went house-shopping, he couldn't help but wonder what she would think of the place. Especially the kitchen. Would she like it? Could she create in there?

Rubbing a hand over his face, he groaned. He was a fool. He had once again realized that being miles away had only made him want her more. But there was nothing to do except wait it out, let time heal if it could. All he had to do was overcome that feeling of loneliness, that need, that incredible ache. Hell, he'd gotten over it with his parents. He'd do it again.

The plane touched down on the tarmac smoothly, then rolled to a stop. Around him, passengers jolted to their feet, grabbing bags and brightly wrapped packages from the overhead bins before filing out of the plane and rushing down the jetway. They were all, no doubt, anxious to see their loved ones, their families, anxious to start the holiday.

Michael took his time. He had no driver waiting for him this time. He hadn't wanted to steal someone away from their family on Christmas Eve to drive him home. It was easy just to rent a car.

But when he stepped into the terminal, he saw that he didn't have to. "What the hell are you doing here?"

Walking toward him, Thomas chuckled. "Well, that's just fine. I come all the way out here to pick you up, bring you back where you belong, and this is the thanks I get."

Had he told Thomas when he'd be getting in today? Michael wondered, trying to ignore how good it felt to have the man here. "Thanks, Thomas, but you shouldn't have come. Tonight's Christmas Eve and your family—"

"My family is fine. They're expecting me for dinner." Side by side, they walked down the concourse. "Don't tell me you'd rather have some strange limousine driver than a friendly face."

"That depends."

"On what?"

"If that friendly face is going to give me a lecture all the way home."

"Now what in the world would I have to lecture you about?" Thomas asked breezily. "You seem to be doing just fine."

"I am." Michael sounded way too convincing, even to his own ears.

"That's wonderful. Business is good?"

They passed through the double doors and stepped out into a brisk winter afternoon. "Very good, in fact."

"And I must say you look healthy as a jackass."

"Don't you mean 'as a horse'?" Michael asked dryly.

"No. I mean jackass."

Shaking his head, Michael followed him to the car. "This is the beginning of that lecture, right?"

"There's not going to be anything like that." Thomas opened the trunk and waited while Michael dropped his bags in. "No questions, no comments, no offering information on certain people in town. Nothing."

Michael didn't answer right away. They were in the car, heading onto the highway before he couldn't stand it anymore. "All right, I'll bite. How are they?"

"Who?"

"Now which one of us is being the jackass?" Michael chuckled. "Bella and Emily. How are they doing?"

"They're doing beautifully. Emily is sweet and growing bigger every day."

Michael felt a strange little ping in the region of his heart. He'd missed almost two weeks of her life. "And Bella?"

"Isabella's business is booming and she has her friends around her. She seems happy enough. She and Emily are coming to the house tomorrow for Christmas dinner. My wife is making ham *and* turkey this year, and of course her sage and onion stuffing. Kyle and Derek are going to be there, too." He tossed Michael a sly glance. "You know, I think my eldest might have a crush on Isabella."

Michael frowned. "What?"

The doctor shrugged. "Derek *was* the one who called and asked her to come."

Anger seeped through Michael like an oil slick. What was she thinking, accepting Derek's invitation? She just had a baby—she wasn't ready to get involved. And Derek Pinta was...was... Oh, hell he was exactly the kind of man Michael wasn't. Upstanding, sociable, popular and mild-natured, a real citizen of the world.

Dammit, he had no claim on Bella, no right even to want one. But the thought of her with another man made him nuts, and that man being a father to his—

He stopped that thought midstride. He was no husband to Bella, and Emily wasn't his child. It didn't matter if he wanted that status changed. They deserved better than a defeated beast with a wounded leg and a caged heart.

Isabella turned her sign to "Mother and Child Done for the Day."

She'd sold every last one of her silver bells, gingerbread men and red-nosed Rudolphs, and even though her adrenaline was still pumping, it was time to call it quits.

In the past couple of weeks, it hadn't been difficult to move through those mad hours of early rising, baking, filling orders and caring for Emily. The activity had kept her mind occupied—and off Michael Wulf. A little trick she'd learned from him. Work was the answer to all ills, apparently.

At night, she'd be so exhausted that she'd just fall into bed and into a dreamless sleep. And she'd awake before the sun each morning and do it all again. She ran on batteries, it seemed, quite unaware of the world around her at times.

Except for her time with Emily, she thought, picking up her daughter and carrying her upstairs. Those were the magical times. Cuddling, reading to her, playing on the little ducky blanket that Michael had given them.

Then her mind would lose its blessed numbness and fly to him again. What was he doing? Did he ever think of her? When was he coming back? *Was* he coming back?

A strong hand fisted around her heart and squeezed, but she fought it. She had to. If it was just her, she could crawl under the covers and stay there for a week. But it wasn't just her. She had Emily to think of.

Gently, Isabella placed Emily on the changing table and grabbed a clean diaper.

She looked down at her daughter. These thoughts, this aching heart, all were dangerous. She would never get over Michael, she knew that. But for her daughter's sake, she had to find a way to keep trying.

Tonight her friends were coming over for a girls' gab session, and she would put on a brave face, tell

Molly again that she didn't know where Michael was and change the subject.

She sure wasn't about to tell them the truth. How she'd told him to go. Not because she didn't love him, but because she loved him too much to pretend she didn't want more than friendship. And that for a short time, whether he'd wanted to admit it or not, they'd been so much more.

They'd been a family.

"We'll have to hurry," Thomas said as he pulled up alongside the curb and switched off the engine. "It's going to be dark soon."

Michael's hand gripped the car-door handle as his mind rioted over what to do next. This stop at the cemetery had been his idea. But as for the purpose, he wasn't exactly sure.

Thomas put a hand on his shoulder. "Do you want me to go with you?"

"No."

"All right."

"I don't know why I'm here."

"Sure you do," Thomas said gently. "You want to wish Emmett a merry Christmas and ask him if he thinks you're worthy of his daughter."

Michael turned to look at Thomas. "I know I'm not worthy."

"Why do you think that?"

"I don't want to… It's just that…" What? Why couldn't he put a name to this feeling? Why was he so damn afraid?

"You love her."

"Yes." The word came out in a rush. He stilled, letting it seep in, trying to understand how loving anyone was possible for a man like him. But it was true. He loved her. So much he ached with it. And he realized it now. Now, when it was too late. "I love her, Thomas. And that's exactly why I can't have her."

"Excuse my French, but that's crap."

"You know who I am, Thomas. *How* I am. I can't be a part of this town, part of life. I'm no good at it."

"Again, crap."

Frustrated, Michael banged his fist on the side of the door. "Bella and Emily need that good, upstanding citizen type who smiles and shouts hello to his neighbors every morning." He chuckled bitterly. "I know how to shout, but I barely know how to smile."

"Look at me," Thomas demanded, and Michael grudgingly did as he asked. "Do you want Isabella and Emily? Do you want them to be your family?"

"God, yes."

"Then you'll learn how to smile, Michael Wulf." He snorted. "Simple as that?"

"Most everybody in this town has their arms out to you. They want to give you a chance." Thomas's gaze softened. "After what you've been through, I don't blame you for the doubt that's in your heart. But when's it going to end?"

Michael turned back to the window, to his view of the cemetery. "I'm not sure it *can* end."

"Michael," the old man said, reaching out his

gnarled hand and laying it on the smooth wool of Michael's overcoat. "It's time to let go. You have to want them enough to let go of your demons."

Outside, snow fell so softly against the tombstones that Michael almost felt he could hear them whispering.

He had to admit it to himself, let himself feel the truth. There was nothing he wanted more than Isabella and Emily. Nothing. He loved her, loved her child, and he'd squash a thousand demons to have a chance to show them how deep his love ran. If she would still have him.

Ever since his parents had taken off and left him, he'd declined to participate in the game of life and he'd blamed the world. His fear of being discarded again by someone he loved had imprisoned him, had made him take what he'd heard from Molly Homney and use it as a shield.

Bella had opened the door to life and showed him what could be, what he could have. She'd shown him heaven and he'd chosen the comfort of hell.

No more.

Michael opened the car door, got out and walked over to the grave of Emmett Spencer, beloved husband and father, and said the words that would change him forever.

"I love your daughter."

"I need more popcorn," Connie said, holding up her long string of popcorn and cranberry swag for the tree.

"Why did she get the food decoration," Molly moaned, "and I get stuck with construction-paper links?"

April Young rolled her eyes. "Because no one trusts you with a needle."

Wendy snorted. "No one trusts you with the popcorn and cranberries."

Everyone laughed, even Molly. Rid of their husbands, significant others and children for a few hours, the fivesome from high school had fallen easily into their old ways. Sitting around the coffee table, they'd scarfed down all the food they'd brought and talked about old times and old boyfriends.

It was fun and truly lovely, but Isabella's mind was elsewhere. Thank goodness her friends had steered clear of discussions about Michael Wulf. She appreciated them for that and so did her heart.

"I'll make some more popcorn," Isabella announced, coming to her feet.

But before she could get halfway to the kitchen, there was a knock at the door.

"Did you invite some boys, Isabella?" Connie asked with a grin.

Wendy clasped her hands together. "Ooh, I heard Ronnie Mills has a crush on you. And he just got his braces off."

Isabella grinned at the schoolgirl sound of that as she walked to the door.

"Maybe it's a stripper," April offered, and they all laughed.

But it was no stripper.

Looking incredibly handsome in a black sweater, gray pants and his long black coat, Michael Wulf leaned against the door and smiled. "Hi, Bella."

The room behind her fell dead silent, but Isabella could hear her heart battering against her chest. It seemed as though she hadn't seen him in years, not weeks. Her longing for him surged to the surface like a fisherman's bobber.

"You're home," she said inanely, her cheeks growing instantly warm. "I mean, you're back from California."

His gaze roamed over her, drinking her in, unnerving her jumbled nerves. "I couldn't stay away. Not from Fielding or—"

"Your glass house?" The bitter tone was uncontrolled. Why did he have to come here and torture her?

"Can I come in?"

It took every ounce of self-control she had to say, "I have friends over. Maybe some other time—"

Ignoring her protest, he stepped past her into the apartment. "This can't wait." He nodded at her friends. "Hello, ladies."

They all mumbled hellos, then turned their gazes back to what they were doing.

"I'm sorry to interrupt the evening," he said, "but I have something to tell Bella that just can't wait."

Connie stood up. "We should probably go—"

"No. You all—" he looked pointedly at Molly and she blushed. "—need to hear this."

Isabella found her voice. "Michael, what's going on?"

He turned to face her again, his gray eyes softer than she'd ever seen them. "I had a conversation with your father today."

Her heart lurched. "You went to the cemetery?"

He nodded.

"Why?"

"I needed to tell him something." He reached for her hand, lifted it to his mouth and kissed it softly. "I love you, Bella."

Eyes wide, she just stared at him. "You what?"

"He said he loves you," April said. Connie quickly shushed her.

Isabella hardly heard her friends. Her mind was reeling, her heart pounding. "But you told me—"

"I know what I told you. I was a fool. I thought that I was doing you a favor by getting out of your life. I thought that your being involved with the Wulf could only hurt you and Emily." He released her, brought his hands up and cupped her face. "But I changed the day I opened that car door and found you. You changed me from an impenetrable creature who didn't want to leave his cave to a man who wants a life, wants to be known and wants to be loved."

Connie sighed, Molly's eyes filled with tears, and Wendy whispered, "If she doesn't kiss him right now, I will!"

April snorted. "Get in line."

"Goodnight, girls," Isabella said.

After her friends wished them both a Merry Christmas and made a quick exit, Isabella faced the man who made her see stars and spoke what was in her heart. "I love you, too, Michael. I've loved you...Lord, it seems like a lifetime. But I'm afraid to believe this."

"I know what it's like to be afraid, sweetheart," he said gently. "I spent most of my life that way, and I don't recommend it." A grin played about his lips. "You taught me how to love, Bella. And I won't let you go."

"You won't?"

"No. I'm no good without you."

Her heart squeezed painfully. "Are you sure?"

He snaked an arm around her waist and pulled her close. "Positive."

"Oh, Michael." Isabella looked up into his eyes and saw his soul, no mask, no wall—just a man in love—and she knew he was finally hers.

Grinning Michael pulled a sprig of mistletoe out of his pocket and held it between them. "Have I told you how much I love the holidays?" he asked as he lifted the mistletoe above their heads with one hand and pulled her closer with the other. He kissed her softly, then drew back, just far enough so she could feel his warm breath when he said, "You forgive me for being such an idiot?"

Tears welled up in her eyes and she could only nod.

"Then how about marrying me?"

Big fat tears that were directly attached to her heartstrings dropped onto her cheeks. "Say that again."

He grinned. "Marry me, Isabella Spencer?"

She smiled back. "In a heartbeat, Michael Wulf."

Lowering his head, he gave her a series of slow, tender kisses. "Come on. Let's go look in on our daughter."

For a moment she just stared at him, drinking in the man that he had finally allowed himself to liberate. He wanted them. He wanted a life with them. "Our daughter?"

"Oh, sweetheart, that little girl has been mine from the moment I first held her. And I can't wait to make it official, if you'll let me."

All of Isabella's dreams from so many Christmases past were coming true that Christmas Eve night. "Santa sure has come through this year."

Michael brushed his lips over hers, whispering, "Ho, ho, ho," before gently releasing her. "Let's go give our child a good-night kiss. We have a tree to decorate, stockings to hang and presents to wrap." He smiled and eased an arm around her. "My first traditions with the two people I love most in the world. What could be better?"

Smiling contentedly, Isabella let her head fall against his shoulder. "Nothing, Michael. Absolutely nothing."

Epilogue

Four years later...

Cotton-candy snow fell from the darkening sky onto the sidewalks, street lamps and jutting shop signs of Fielding. Anyone just passing through might have a great chuckle over the name on one of those signs, because it looked strangely like ''The Wulf Fam Bakery'' under that random coating of white. But to all who lived there, to all who had named it, they knew better. And every time they passed or entered the Wulf Family Bakery, they remembered the little miracle they'd witnessed all those years ago. When a lonely man had finally found his way home.

Just above the sign, behind a window on the second

floor, was a beautiful blue spruce. It's keepers were tending to it as though it were a member of the family, hanging lights, placing ornaments, flinging wisps of tinsel at its boughs.

And inside that home, under that tree, where so much warmth resided, sat Emily Wulf tearing open a present with the enthusiasm of a defensive lineman. After squealing with delight at the fuzzy-bear ornament she'd eyed at the Crafty Corner the other day, the little girl looked up at her father.

"Where should I put it, Daddy?"

Michael smiled down at his daughter, his heart. "Anywhere you like, princess."

And she truly was that, he thought. Emily was smart and kind and incredibly beautiful. She was her mother and yet…in some ways, she was him, too. Her stubbornness, her capacity for love.

"How 'bout by Annie's ornmant?" Emily said in her toddler speech.

Just at that moment, Bella walked into the room carrying their three-month-old baby girl. "I think putting it beside your sister's ornament is a wonderful idea, Ems."

Michael's heart tumbled at the sight of his wife.

Blue eyes shimmering, long blond hair loose and wispy around her face, Bella smiled first at Emily, then at him. She'd changed from her afternoon party clothes into that old blue robe he'd given her when she'd first come to stay with him. But what really took his breath away was the sight of her holding his child.

Emily tugged at his hand. "Up, Daddy."

With a chuckle Michael lifted her high in the air so she could place her ornament on the bough next to Annie's turtle figurine. This was Christmas Eve at Bella's old apartment—or what they now affectionately called their town house—and it was filled with traditions old and new. It was filled with warmth and love that soothed more than a wounded leg. And it was filled with something Michael Wulf had never expected to deserve: family.

After giving the tree a once-over, Bella deemed it perfection, then settled on the couch with Annie. Michael joined them, tugging Emily onto his lap.

"Can I say it, Daddy?" Emily asked.

Bella laughed and Michael just smiled. His eldest daughter was a *lot* like him. "All right."

Emily took a deep breath and shouted, "Light tree!"

In a blink, the blue spruce sparkled with white twinkling lights, and everyone who could talk oohed and aahed, just as they did every year.

Emily snuggled into the crook of his arm and said softly, "Tell the story."

Bella smiled at him, and he mouthed, "I love you."

This—this night of magic and decorating and dreams and Santa—was beyond wonderful. But the story Emily had asked to hear was a tradition that Michael himself had started.

The room was still and scented with pine. Michael

cuddled Emily close and began. ''The night that Emily Wulf came into the world, it snowed and snowed....''

* * * * * *

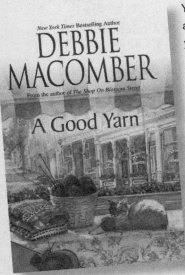

DESIRE!

Available Next Month

Rules Of Attraction
Susan Crosby

Beyond Business
Rochelle Alers

Sleeping With Beauty
Laura Wright

Her Convenient Millionaire
Gail Dayton

Her Texan Temptation
Shirley Rogers

When The Earth Moves
Roxanne St. Claire

AVAILABLE FROM
Target • K-Mart • Big W • Borders • selected supermarkets
• bookstores • newsagents

OR

Call Harlequin Mills & Boon on 1300 659 500 to order
for the cost of a local call. NZ customers call (09) 837 1553.

Shop on-line at www.eHarlequin.com.au

Send in for a FREE BOOK today!

How would you like to escape into a world of romance and excitement? A world in which you can experience all the glamour and allure of romance and seduction?

No purchase necessary - now or ever!

To receive your FREE Harlequin Mills & Boon romance novel, simply fill in the coupon and send it to the address below, together with $1.00 worth of loose postage stamps (80 cents in NZ) to cover postage and handling (please do not send money orders or cheques). There is never any obligation to buy!

Send to: HARLEQUIN MILLS & BOON FREE BOOK OFFER
Aust: PO Box 693, Strawberry Hills, NSW, 2012
NZ: Private Bag 92122, Auckland, 1020

Harlequin Mills & Boon
Direct to you

- -

Please send me my FREE Harlequin Mills & Boon Sexy romance valued at $6.15 (NZ$7.25). I have included $1.00 worth of loose postage stamps (80 cents in NZ). Please do not stick them to anything.

Name: Mrs / Ms / Miss / Mr: _____

Address: _____

_____ P/Code _____

Daytime Tel. No.: (_____) _____

FBBP05/ZFBBP5

This offer is restricted to one free book per household. Only original coupons with $1.00 worth of loose postage stamps (80 cents in NZ) will be accepted. Your book may differ from those shown. Offer expires 31st December, 2005 or while stocks last. Offer only available to Australian and NZ residents over 18 years. You may also receive offers from other reputable companies as a result of this application. If you do not wish to share in this opportunity please tick the box. ☐

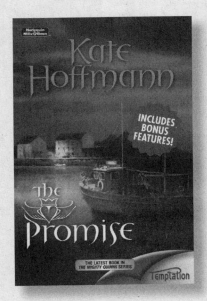